AUTHOR'S WEBSITE: www.storyman.com

DUTTON CHILDREN'S BOOKS

ANTSY DOES TIME

NEAL SHUSTERMAN

DUTTON CHILDREN'S BOOKS | A division of Penguin Young Readers Group

Published by the Penguin Group | Penguin Group (USA) Inc., 375 Hudson Street, New York, New York 10014, U.S.A. | Penguin Group (Canada), 90 Eglinton Avenue East, Suite 700, Toronto, Ontario M4P 2Y3, Canada (a division of Pearson Penguin Canada Inc.) | Penguin Books Ltd, 80 Strand, London WC2R 0RL, England | Penguin Ireland, 25 St Stephen's Green, Dublin 2, Ireland (a division of Penguin Books Ltd) | Penguin Group (Australia), 250 Camberwell Road, Camberwell, Victoria 3124, Australia (a division of Pearson Australia Group Pty Ltd) | Penguin Books India Pvt Ltd, 11 Community Centre, Panchsheel Park, New Delhi - 110 017, India | Penguin Group (NZ), 67 Apollo Drive, Rosedale, North Shore 0632, New Zealand (a division of Pearson New Zealand Ltd.) | Penguin Books (South Africa) (Pty) Ltd, 24 Sturdee Avenue, Rosebank, Johannesburg 2196, South Africa | Penguin Books Ltd, Registered Offices: 80 Strand, London WC2R 0RL, England

Library of Congress Cataloging-in-Publication Data
Shusterman, Neal.
Antsy does time / Neal Shusterman.— 1st ed.
p. cm.
Summary: A Brooklyn eighth-grader nicknamed Antsy befriends the Schwa, an "invisible-ish" boy who is tired of blending into his surroundings and going unnoticed by nearly everyone.
ISBN 0-525-47825-6
[1. Self-perception—Fiction. 2. Friendship—Fiction. 3. Brooklyn (New York, N.Y.)—Fiction.] I. Title.
PZ7.S55987Sbe 2004   [Fic]--dc22   2004045072

Published in the United States by Dutton Children's Books,
a division of Penguin Young Readers Group, 345 Hudson Street, New York, New York 10014
www.penguin.com/youngreaders

DESIGNED BY HEATHER WOOD

Printed in USA | First Edition | 10 9 8 7 6 5 4 3 2 1

For Stephanie,
my editorial muse

"When the parched land yields neither fruit nor flower, grain nor greens, a man will ask himself if the blame lies in the sheer weight of his transgressions, or is it just global warming?"

—JOHN STEINBECK[*]

---

[*]NOT REALLY.

The Real Reason People Sit
Like Idiots Watching Parades

1 It was all my idea. The stupid ones usually are. Once in a while the genius ideas are mine, too. Not on purpose, though. You know what they say: if you put, like, fourteen thousand monkeys in front of computer keyboards for a hundred years, aside from a whole lot of dead monkeys, you'd end up with one masterpiece among the garbage. Then they'd start teaching it in schools to make you feel miserable, because if a monkey can write something brilliant, why can't you put five measly sentences together for a writing prompt?

This idea—I don't know whether it was a brilliant-monkey idea, or a stupid-Antsy idea, but it sure had power to change a whole lot of lives.

I called the idea "time shaving," which probably isn't what you think it is, so before you start whipping up time machines in your head, you need to listen to what it's all about. Nobody's going back in time to nuke Napoléon, or give Jesus a cell phone or anything. There's no time travel at all. People *are* going to die, though—and in strange and mysterious ways, too, if you're into that kind of thing.

Me, I was just trying to help a friend. I never meant for it to blow up like a giant Macy's Thanksgiving Day Parade balloon that gets taken away by the wind.

Which, by the way, is exactly how the whole thing began.

On Thanksgiving morning, my friends Howie and Ira and I were hanging out in my recreational attic. We used to have a recreational basement—you know, full of all our old cruddy furniture, a TV, and a big untouchable space in the corner that was going to be for a pool table when we could afford it in some distant *Star Trek*–like future. Then the basement gets this toxic mold, and we have to seal it off from the rest of the house, on account of the mold might escape and cause cancer, or brain damage, or take over the world. Even after the mold was cleaned out, my parents treated the basement like a radiation zone, uninhabitable for three generations.

So now we have a recreational attic, full of new old furniture, and space maybe for a Monopoly board instead of a pool table.

Anyway, Howie, Ira, and I were watching football that Thanksgiving morning, switching to the parade during commercials to make fun of the marching bands.

"Ooh! Ooh! Look at this one!" said Ira, with an expression that was a weird mix of joy and horror at the same time.

To the band's credit, they were playing an impressive rendition of "(I Can't Get No) Satisfaction," but anything cool about it was ruined by their pink-and-orange uniforms. Howie shakes his head. "As long as they dress like that, they're never getting any satisfaction."

"Antsy, don't you have a shirt like that?" asks Ira. My name's actually Anthony, but people have called me Antsy for so long, I oughta get it legally changed. I like it because there are so many Anthonys in the neighborhood, if some mother calls the name out a window, the stampede stops traffic. I'm the only Antsy, though—except for this one time a kid tried to steal it and call himself Antsy, so I had to start writing my name "Antsy®," and I threatened to punch him out for identity theft.

So anyway, about the shirt, although I hate to admit it, yeah, I do have a shirt in orange and pink, although it was a different shade of pink.

"Just because I have it doesn't mean I wear it," I tell Ira. The shirt was a birthday gift from my aunt Mona, who has no kids or common sense. I'll give you one guess how many times I've worn it since my fourteenth birthday.

"You think anyone's documented seizures from looking at that color combination?" asks Howie. "We should run some tests."

"Great. I'll get my shirt, you can stare at it for six hours, and we'll see if you go into convulsions."

Howie seriously considers this. "Can I break for meals?"

Let me try to explain Howie to you. You know that annoying automated customer-service voice on the phone that wastes your time before making you hold for a real person? Well, Howie's the music on hold. It's not that Howie's dumb—he's got a fertile mind when it comes to analytical stuff like math—but his imagination is a cold winter in Antarctica where the penguins never learned to swim.

On TV, the band had almost passed, and one of the giant parade balloons could be seen in the distance. This one was the classic cartoon *Roadkyll Raccoon*, complete with that infamous tire track down his back, the size of a monster-truck tread. We were about to turn the TV back to football, but then Ira noticed something.

"Is it my imagination, or is Roadkyll on the warpath?"

Sure enough, Roadkyll is kicking and bucking like he's Godzilla trying to take out Tokyo. Then this huge gust of wind rips off the band members' hats, and when the gust reaches Roadkyll, he kind of peels himself off the street, and heads to the skies. Most of the balloon handlers have the good sense to let go, except for three morons who decide to go up with the ship.

Suddenly this is more interesting than the game.

Howie sighs. "I've said it before, I'll say it again. Helium kills."

The cameras were no longer watching the parade—they're all aimed at the airborne raccoon as it rises in an updraft along the side of the Empire State Building, with the three balloon wranglers clinging like circus acrobats. Then, just as it looks like Roadkyll might be headed for the moon, he gets snagged on top of the Empire State Building and punctures. In less than a minute the balloon has totally deflated over the spire, covering the top of the Empire State Building in rubber coonskin and stranding the three danglers, who hang from their ropes for their lives.

I was the first one out of my seat.

"Let's go," I said, because there are some events in life that are better experienced in person than viewed on TV.

We took the subway into Manhattan—usually a crowded ride from our little corner of Brooklyn, but since it was Thanksgiving, the trains were mostly empty, except for others like ourselves who were on their way to the Empire State Building to watch history in the making.

Ira, who has an intense and questionable relationship with his video camera, was lovingly cleaning the lens as he prepared to record today's event for future generations. Howie was reading *Of Mice and Men,* which we all had to read for English. It's a book the teachers use to trick us—because it's really thin, but it's like, deep, so you gotta read it twice.

Across from us in the train was Gunnar Ümlaut—a kid who moved here from Sweden when we were all in elementary school. Gunnar's got long blond hair he makes no excuse for, and a resigned look of Scandinavian despair that melts girls in his path. And if that doesn't work, the slight accent he puts on when he's around girls does the job. Never mind that he's been living in Brooklyn since he was six. Not that I'm jealous or anything—I admire a guy who uses what he's got.

"Hi, Gunnar," I said. "Where you headed?"

"Where else? The Roadkyll debacle."

"Excellent," I said, and filed the word "debacle" in the special place I reserve for words I will never know the meaning of.

So Gunnar's sitting there, all slouched and casual, his arms across seats on either side like maybe there's a couple of invisible girls there. (Don't get me started on invisible. Long story.) Then he takes one look at Howie's book and says, "The dumb guy dies at the end."

Howie looks up at Gunnar, heaves a heavy sigh that can only

come from a lifetime of ruined endings, and closes the book. I snicker, which just irritates Howie even more.

"Thanks, Gunnar." Howie sneers. "Any more spoilers you care to share with us?"

"Yeah," says Gunnar. "Rosebud's a sled, the spider dies after the fair, and the Planet of the Apes is actually Earth in the distant future." He doesn't smile when he says it. Gunnar never smiles. I think girls must like that, too.

By the time we got off at Thirty-fourth Street, the parade crowd had all gravitated to the Empire State Building, hoping to experience the thrill of watching someone they don't know plunge to his death.

"If they don't survive," said Gunnar, "it's our responsibility to witness it. As Winston Churchill once said, *'An untimely end witnessed, gives life deeper meaning.'*"

Gunnar always talks like that—all serious, as if even stupidity has a point.

All around us the police are screaming at the crowds, one hand on their batons, saying things like, "Don't make me use this!"

Up above, the Empire State Building was still wearing a coonskin hat, and the three unfortunate balloon handlers were exactly where they were when we left home—still clinging on to their ropes. Ira handed me the camera, which had a 500X zoom, just in case I wanted to examine one of the guy's nose hairs.

It was hard to hold the camera steady when it was zoomed in, but once I did, I could see firefighters and police inside the Empire State Building, trying to reach the men through the windows. They weren't having much luck. Word in the crowd was that a rescue helicopter was on its way.

One guy had managed to tie the rope around his waist and was swinging toward the windows, but the rescuers couldn't get a grip on him. The second guy clung to the rope and also had it hooked around his feet, probably thanking the New York public school system for forcing him to learn how to do this in gym class. The third guy was the worst off. He was dangling from a stick at the end of his rope, holding on with both hands like a flying trapeze once it stops flying.

"Hey, I wanna look, too!"

Howie grabs the camera from me, and that's just fine, because I was starting to get a bad feeling in the pit of my stomach. Suddenly I started to wonder what had possessed me to come down here at all.

"How much you wanna bet those guys write a book about this?" says Howie. It seems Howie assumes they're all going to survive.

All the while, Gunnar just stood there quietly, his eyes cast heavenward toward the human drama, with a solemn expression on his face. He caught me watching him.

"For the past few months I've been coming to disasters," Gunnar tells me.

"Why?"

Gunnar shrugs as if it's nothing, but I can tell there's more to it. "I find them . . . compelling."

Coming from anyone else, this would be like a serial-killer warning sign, but from Gunnar it didn't seem weird at all, it just seemed like some profound Scandinavian thing—like all those foreign movies where everyone dies, including the director, the cameraman, and half the audience.

Gunnar shakes his head sadly as he watches the souls up above. "So fragile . . ." he says.

"What," says Howie, "balloons?"

"No, human life, you idiot," I tell him. For an instant I caught a hint of what actually might have been a smile on Gunnar's face. Maybe because I said what he was thinking.

There's applause all around us, and when I look up, I can see the swinging man has finally been caught by a cop, and he's hauled through the window. The helicopter has arrived with a guy tethered to a rope like an action hero, to go after the trapeze dangler. The crowd watches in a silence you rarely hear in a city. It takes a few hair-raising minutes, but the guy is rescued and hauled away by the helicopter. Now only one dangler remains. This is the guy who seemed calmest of all; the guy who had it all under control. The guy who suddenly slips, and plunges.

A singular gasp from the audience.

"No way!" says Ira, his eye glued to his camera.

The guy falls. He falls forever. He doesn't even spin his arms—it's like he's already accepted his fate. And suddenly I find I can't watch it. I snap my eyes away, looking anywhere else. My shoes, other people's shoes, the manhole cover beneath me.

I never heard him hit. I'm thankful that I didn't. Yeah, it was my idea to come here, but when it comes right down to it, I know there are some things you just shouldn't watch. That's when I saw Gunnar—for all his talk about witnessing disaster, he was looking away, too. Not just looking away, but grimacing and covering his eyes.

The gasps from the crowd have turned to groans of self-loathing as people suddenly realize this wasn't about entertainment. Even Howie and Ira are looking kind of ill.

"Let's get out of here before the subway gets packed," I tell them, trying to sound less choked up than I really am—but if I'm a little queasy, it's nothing compared to Gunnar. He was so pale I thought he might pass out. He even stumbles a little bit. I grab his arm to keep him steady. "Hey . . . Hey, you okay?"

"Yeah," he says. "I'm fine. It's nothing. Just a part of the illness."

I looked at him, not quite sure I heard him right. "Illness?"

"Yes. Pulmonary Monoxic Systemia." And then he says, "I only have six months to live."

Heaven, Hockey, and
the Ice Water of Despair

2 The idea of dying never appealed to me much. Even when I was a kid, watching the *Adventures of Roadkyll Raccoon and Darren Headlightz*, I always found it suspicious the way Roadkyll got flattened at the end of each cartoon and yet was back for more in the next episode. It didn't mesh with any reality I knew. According to the way I was raised, there are really just a few possibilities of what happens to you in the hereafter.

Option one: It turns out you're less of a miserable person than you thought you were, and you go to heaven.

Option two: You're not quite the wonderful person you thought you were, and you go to the other place that people these days spell with double hockey sticks, which, by the way, doesn't make much sense, because that's the only sport they can't play down there unless they're skating on boiling water instead of ice, but it ain't gonna happen, because all the walk-on-water types'll be up in heaven.

I did a report on heaven for Sunday school once, so I know all about it. In heaven, you're with your dead relatives, it's always sunny, and everyone's got nice views—no one's looking at a disgusting landfill or anything. I gotta tell you, though, if I gotta spend eternity with all my relatives, everybody hugging and walking with God and stuff, I'll go crazy. It sounds like my cousin Gina's wedding before people got drunk. I hope God don't mind me saying so, but it all sounds very hockey-stickish to me.

As for the place down under, the girl who did her report on it got all her information from horror movies, so, aside from really good special effects, her version is highly suspect. Supposedly there are like nine levels, and each one is worse than the last. Imagine a barbecue where *you're* sizzling on the grill—but it's not accidental like my dad last summer. And the thing about it is, you cook like one of them Costco roasts that's somehow thicker than an entire cow, so no matter how long you sit there, you're still rare in the middle for all eternity.

My mother, who I'm sure gives advice to God since she gives it to everyone else, says the fire talk is just to scare people. In reality, it's cold and lonely. Eternal boredom—which sounds right, because that's worse than the roasting version. At least when you're burning, you've got something to occupy your mind.

There is a third option, called Purgatory, which is a kinder, gentler version of the place down under. Purgatory is God's version of a time-out—temporary flames of woe. I find this idea most appealing, although to be honest, it all bugs me a little. I mean, God loves us and is supposed to be the perfect parent, right? So what if a parent came up to their kid and said, "I love you, but I'm going to have to punish you by roasting you over flames of woe, and it's really going to hurt." Social Services would not look kindly upon this, and we could all end up in foster care.

I figure Hell and Purgatory are like those parental threats—you know, like, "Tease your sister one more time, and I swear I'll kill you," or "Commit one more mortal sin, and so help me, I will roast you over eternal flames, young man."

Call me weird, but I find that comforting. It means that God really does love us, He's just ticked off.

Still, none of that was comforting when it came to Gunnar Ümlaut. The thought of someone I know dying, who wasn't old and dying already, really bothered me. It made me wish I knew Gunnar better, but then if I did, I'd be really sad now, so why would I want that, and should I feel guilty for not wanting it? The whole thing reeked of me having to feel guilty for something, and I hate that feeling.

Nobody talked much on the return trip from the Roadkyll Raccoon incident. Between what we witnessed and what Gunnar had told me, there just wasn't much anyone wanted to say. We talked about the football games we were missing, and school stuff, but mostly we looked at subway advertisements and out the windows so we wouldn't have to look at one another. I wondered if Howie and Ira had heard what Gunnar had told me, but didn't want to ask.

"See ya," was all anyone said when we got off the train. Howie, Ira, and Gunnar all went off to their Thanksgiving meals, and I went home to find a note from my parents, with exclamation points and underlines, telling me to be at the restaurant <u>ON TIME!!!</u>

My dad runs a French/Italian fusion restaurant called *Paris, Capisce?* He didn't always do this. He used to have an office job with a plastics company, but he lost it because of me. That's okay, though, because he got the restaurant because of me as well. It's a long story from the weird world of Old Man Crawley. If you've heard of him, and who hasn't, you'll know it's a story best kept at ten-foot-pole distance. Anyway, it all worked out in the end, because running a restaurant is what my dad always dreamed of doing.

We all quickly found out, however, that when you have a restaurant, you don't run it, it runs you. We all got sucked in. Mom fills in when there aren't enough waitresses, I'm constantly on call to bus tables, and my little sister Christina folds napkins into animal shapes. Only my older brother Frankie gets out of it, on account of he's in college, and when he's home, he thinks he's too good to work in a restaurant.

My particular skill is the pouring of water.

Don't laugh—it's a real skill. I can pour from any height and never miss the glass. People applaud.

Thanksgiving, we all knew, was going to be the big test. Not just of the restaurant, but of our family. See, Thanksgiving has always been big with us, on account of we got this massive extended family of aunts, uncles, cousins, and people I barely know who have various body parts resembling mine. That's what family is. But these days more and more people eat out on Thanksgiving, so Dad decided to offer a special

Thanksgiving meal at *Paris, Capisce?* instead of the usual big family meal at our house. That got the relatives all bent out of shape. We told them we're doing Thanksgiving at home one day late, but they flatly refused to postpone the holiday. Now we're family outcasts, at least until Christmas, when everyone will, in theory, kiss and make up. Dad knows better than to keep the restaurant open on Christmas, because Mom told him if he does, he'd better set up a cot in the back room, because that's where he'll be sleeping for a while. Mom says things like this very directly, because my father is not good with subtle hints.

As for Thanksgiving, Mom was very direct with the rest of us as well. "None of youse are allowed to eat any turkey this Thursday, got it? As far as you're concerned, Thanksgiving is on Friday."

"Do turkey hot dogs count?" I asked, because no direct order from my mother was complete unless I found a way around it. Not that I had plans to eat turkey hot dogs, but it's the principle of the thing. Mom's response was a look that probably wilted the lettuce in the refrigerator.

Part of her laying down of the law was that we weren't allowed to have a turkeyless Thanksgiving at friends' houses either—because if we did, our own family Thanksgiving would feel like an afterthought. I didn't think I'd really mind, but right now I didn't want to be alone with my thoughts. I was still feeling funny about the dead raccoon wrangler, and Gunnar's terminal confession, but it was still a while until Mom and Dad wanted me at the restaurant.

I tried to watch some football, and took to petting Ichabod, our cat, who was ninety-one in dog years, although I don't know what that means to a cat. But even Ichabod knew I was distracted, so he went off to watch Christina's hamsters run endlessly on their wheel. I suppose that's the feline equivalent of going to the market and watching the rotisserie chicken, which is how my mom entertained me at the market when I was little.

In the end, I left early, and took a long, wandering path to the restaurant. As I passed our local skate park, I saw one lonely soul sitting outside by the padlocked gate. I knew the kid, but not his name—only his nickname. He used to wear a shirt that said SKATERDUDE, but the E peeled off, and from that moment on he was eternally "Skaterdud." Like my nickname, he had grown into it, and everyone agreed it suited him to a tee. He was lanky with massively matted red hair, pink spots all over his joints from old peeled scabs, and eyes that you'd swear were looking into alternate dimensions, not all of them sane. God help the poor parents who see Skaterdud waiting at the door for their daughter on prom night.

"Hey, Dud," I said as I approached.

"Hey." He gave me his special eight-part handshake, and wouldn't continue the conversation until I got it right.

"So, no turkey?" I asked.

He smirked. "I ain't gonna miss not eatin' no dead bird, am I?"

Skaterdud had his own language all full of double, triple, and sometimes quadruple negatives, so you never really knew if he meant what he said, or the opposite.

"So . . . you're a vegan?" I asked.

"Naah." He patted his stomach. "Ate the dead bird early. What about you?"

I shrugged, not wanting to get into it. "This year we're celebrating Chinese Thanksgiving."

He raised his eyebrows knowingly. "Year of the Goat. Gotta love it."

"So," I asked, "isn't the skate park closed for the winter? What, are you gonna sit here and wait till it reopens in the spring?"

He shook his head. "Unibrow said he'd come down and open it for me today. But I don't see no Unibrow, do you?"

I sat down and leaned against the fence, figuring that chatting with Skaterdud was as good a mental distraction as any. Kind of like playing Minesweeper with a human being. We talked about school, and I was amazed at how the Dud knew more details about his teachers' personal lives than he did about any given subject. We talked about his lipring, and how he got it to stop him from biting his nails. I nodded like I understood how the two things were related. And then we talked about Gunnar. I told him about Gunnar's imminent death, and he looked down, picking at a peeling skull sticker on his helmet.

"That chews the churro, man," said Skaterdud. "But ya can't do nothin' about no bad freakin' luck, right? Everybody's got a song on the fat lady's list." Then he thought for a second. "Of course I ain't got no worries, 'cause I know exactly when I'm doing the dirt dance."

"Whaddaya mean?"

"Oh, yeah," said the Dud. "I know exactly when I'm croaking. A fortune-teller told me. She said I'm dying when I'm forty-nine by falling off the deck of an aircraft carrier."

"No way!"

"Yeah. That's how come I'm joining the navy. Because how screwed would it be to fall off an aircraft carrier when you're not even supposed to be there?"

Then he stood up and hurled his skateboard over the fence. "Enough of this noise." He climbed the fence with the skill of a gecko, then looked back to me from the other side. "You wanna come over? I'll teach you stuff the other kids gotta break bones to learn."

"Maybe another time. Nice talkin'."

"Yeah," he says, and heads off. In a moment he disappears over the concrete lip, and I can hear him zipping in and out of concrete ramps that were slick with patches of ice, not caring how dangerous it might be, because he's so sure he's safe for another thirty-four years.

I got to the restaurant on time, but I felt like I was late because everything was in full swing. Since most of our Thanksgiving reservations were for later in the afternoon, my dad didn't expect it to get crowded until around two, and he didn't want me hanging around with nothing to do, since that was "a recipe for disaster." But they hadn't counted on all the holiday walk-ins. There weren't enough walk-ins to fill the restaurant, but it sure was enough to make my father run around like a maniac, which made my mother do the same. Only my sister Christina was calm as she folded napkins into swans and unicorns, and placed them at each table. Dad had given most of his staff Thanksgiving off, since he's such a pushover, so that meant more work for the family.

Just watching my dad work is enough to exhaust you. He's

like the plate spinner at the circus—he's got to keep everything going, see everything at once. Maybe it's because he's overcompensating. He doesn't have any formal training in running a restaurant, just a head full of great recipes, and a rich, cranky old business partner willing to give him a chance.

"Old Man Crawley is a very hard man to please," my dad had told me. Having worked for Crawley myself last year—as the walker of his many dogs, among other things—I knew more than anyone how hard he was to please. Used to be my dad worked long hours in a job that he hated. Now he works longer hours in a job that he loves, but he seems just as brain-dead at the end of the day.

Anyway, when Dad saw me come in, he took a moment out of the mania to give me a hug, and a mini neck massage.

"Water-pouring muscles all ready?" he asked. It was a bit of an inside joke, on account of my shoulder muscles used to lock into a shrug after my first few days as a busboy. Who knew pouring water could be so strenuous.

"Yeah," I told him.

"Good," he said. "'Cause one of these days they're gonna make 'The Water Pour' an Olympic event, and I expect to see nothing but gold." He handed me an apron, slapped me on the back, then went back to work. I really like being around my dad early in the day, before the stress turns him into what we in our family like to call "Darth Menu."

Pretty soon my mind was occupied pouring water and taking away dirty plates, but thoughts of the doomed raccoon guy and Gunnar never entirely faded into the background.

By 6 P.M., we were already into our second seating, and I

was a bit grumpy, because I kept taking away all these plates of food, but I couldn't eat any of it myself. Both Mom and Dad had come up with great Thanksgiving recipes that fit the French/Italian theme of the restaurant. Pumpkin Parmesan Quiche, and Turkey Rollatini au Vin—stuff like that. I got so hungry I would pick at some of the leftovers I took away from the tables, and that got me a whack on the head from Mom. While the skeleton crew of regular staff had breaks every few hours, family members were slaves today, and I resented it.

So I'm moving plates and pouring water, and I can't help thinking that here are all these people stuffing their fat faces, while some poor slob died simply because he got stuck holding on to a balloon—and then there was Gunnar. How could these people eat when he was suffering from pulmo-whachamacallit?

That's when it happened. The glass of ice water I was pouring overflowed. The moment I realized it, I jerked the pitcher back, but that only succeeded in sloshing ice cubes onto the woman's dinner plate.

"Oops!" Then I reached onto her plate like an idiot and started plucking ice cubes out of her Garlique Yam Puree with my bare fingers.

"ANTSY!"

Like I said, my dad saw everything all at once in the restaurant, and I had been caught red-handed—or orange-handed, as it were.

"What do you think you're doing?!"

"I . . . I spilled. I was just—"

"It's all right," said the woman. "No harm done."

But she was wrong about that. "We'll get you a new plate right away," my father said. "I'm sorry for the trouble. Your meal is on the house."

By now my mom and the other waitress had come over to help clean up the spill. Dad handed me the plate of food and pointed to the kitchen. "Take this away and wait for me."

He apologized to the woman again, and maybe even a third time. I don't know because I was already in the kitchen, cleaning off the plate and awaiting judgment. It wasn't long in coming. In just a few seconds, he was there, all fire and brimstone. I could tell the day had already burned him out, and he had gone over to the Dark Side.

"I can't believe what you did in there! Where is your head?"

"Dad, it was just a spill! I said I was sorry!"

"Just a spill? Your fingers were in her food! Do you have any idea how many health codes you broke?"

I'll admit that I deserved to be reprimanded, but he was out of control.

That's when Mom poked her head in, and said in a whisper that was louder than most people scream, "Will you keep it down? The whole restaurant can hear you!"

But Dad was a runaway train. "How could you be so irresponsible?"

"Well, maybe I have something else on my mind!"

"No! When you're here, you can't have *anything* else on your mind!"

"Why don't you just fire me?" I snapped. "Oh, that's right, you can't fire me—because I don't actually *work* here, do I?"

"You know what, Antsy? Just go home."

"Fine, I will!" And for my parting shot, I dipped my finger in the big pot of Garlique Yam Puree, and licked it off.

It was long after dark now, and the walk home was freezing. I thought my brother Frankie might be at home to keep me company, since he was back from Binghamton for the weekend, but he was off with friends, so I had nothing to do but hang out and stew.

The phone rang at about eight-thirty. On the other end was Old Man Crawley, who owned more of my father's restaurant than my father did. Getting a call from Crawley was worse than getting chewed out by my dad.

"I understand service was sloppy tonight," Crawley said.

"Did my father tell you that?"

"I haven't spoken with your father. I sent an observer to eat at the restaurant."

"You sent a spy to your own restaurant?"

"Espionage is a common business practice."

"Against yourself?"

"Apparently it was warranted."

I sighed. Old Man Crawley had more eyes in more places than anyone I knew. I wouldn't be surprised if right now he told me to stop picking my nose.

In case you've been living under a rock, I oughta tell you a little bit about Old Man Crawley, or "Creepy Crawley," as all the little kids call him. The guy's a legend in Brooklyn—the kind you really don't believe until you actually meet him, but by then it's too late to run. He's very rich, very selfish, and generally mean. He's the kind of guy who'd hand out vomit-inducing candy on Halloween, and then sell Pepto-Bismol across the street at jacked-up prices.

I'm one of the few people who actually knows him, on account of he's mostly a hermit. He used to be entirely a hermit, until he hired me to walk his dogs and to date his granddaughter, Lexie, who's blind, but has managed to make her blindness seem like a mere technicality. Pretty soon dating her stopped being a job, and it became real, much to Old Man Crawley's disgust. There was this one time Lexie and I kidnapped Crawley, and forced him to see the outside world. He liked it so much he now has us kidnap him on a regular basis.

The weird thing is that I kind of like him. Maybe it's because I understand him—or maybe it's because I'm the only person who can call him a nasty old fart to his face and get away with it. I can't quite say that Crawley and I are friends, but he dislikes me less than he dislikes most other people. Still, with Crawley, the line between tolerance and disgust is very thin.

"If you give me the details of tonight's incident, maybe I won't have to ask your father about it," Crawley said.

There was no sense in lying to Old Man Crawley. No sense sugarcoating it either, so I told it to him as plainly, and as simply, as I could. "I spilled some water, and plucked ice cubes off some woman's plate, so my father had to give her a free meal. Then he sent me home."

A long silence on the other end. I could hear dogs barking in the background, and then Crawley said, "I am amazed, Anthony, by your continuing ability to disappoint me." And then he hung up without as much as a good-bye.

Mom came home at about ten that night, with Christina practically asleep in her arms. I knew Dad wouldn't be home until past midnight. It was like that all the time, since he opened the restaurant. On this particular night, though, I didn't mind.

My mom came into my room once she got Christina off to bed. "You gotta understand, Antsy, your father's under a lot of pressure."

"Yeah, well, he doesn't have to take it out on me."

"He doesn't mean to."

"Blah, blah, blah."

She sat on the edge of my bed. "The restaurant's not doing as well as he would like. Mr. Crawley keeps threatening to pull the plug."

I sat up, and before she could launch into the Top Ten Reasons Why I Should Cut My Father Some Slack, I said, "I get it, okay? But just because I get it doesn't mean I gotta like it."

She patted my leg, then left, satisfied.

When Dad got home around midnight, he made a point to stop by my room. Even before he spoke, I could tell that Darth Menu had left the building.

"Things good?" he asked.

Since there was no short answer, I just said, "Things are things."

"So," he asked, with a crooked little smile. "Did you at least like the Garlique Yam Puree?"

This, I knew, was an apology.

"Yeah, it was good," I said. "All your stuff is good."

This, he knew, was me accepting his apology.

"Good night, Antsy."

After he left, I turned off my TV and tried to get to sleep. As I lay there, at the place where your thoughts start to break apart and stop making sense, the day's events began to swim into a soup of raccoon, ice water, and terminal illness. Like Gunnar had said, life is a fragile thing. One moment you could be marching happily in a parade, the next you're hanging from the Empire State Building. Sometimes it's because of the choices you make, or sometimes you're just careless—but most of the time it's just dumb luck—and in my experience few things are dumber than luck, except for maybe Wendell Tiggor, whose brain cells communicate by smoke signal.

Luck was about to take some pretty weird bounces, though. It never occurred to me how something as simple as a pitcher of ice water could change a person's life . . . or how a single piece of paper could change the course of an incurable disease.

Why "NeuroToxin" Is Now My Favorite Word in the English Language

3 Pulmonary Monoxic Systemia. Very rare. Very fatal. Basically the body, which is supposed to turn oxygen into carbon dioxide, turns it into carbon monoxide instead—the stuff in car exhaust that kills you if you breathe it long enough. In other words, when you've got Pulmonary Monoxic Systemia, your own body fails the smog check, and you're eventually poisoned by the very air you breathe. I think I'd rather fall from a giant inflatable raccoon.

There are several different ways to respond when you find out that someone you know has something weird and incurable. Your response all depends on the type of person you are. There are basically three types.

Type One: The "I-didn't-hear-that" people. These are the ones who just go on with life, pretending that nothing is wrong. These are the people who would be sitting in Starbucks during an alien invasion, arguing the virtues of Splenda over Equal. You know this person. We all do.

Type Two: The "not-in-my-airspace" people. These are the ones who believe that everything is somehow contagious and would probably start taking antibiotics if their computer got a virus. These people would do everything within their power to avoid the terminally ill person, and then say, "I wish we had more time with him," once the farm had been bought.

Type Three: The "I-can-fix-this" people. These people, against all logic, believe they can change the course of mighty rivers with their bare hands, even thought they can't swim, and so usually end up drowning.

I come from a family of drowners.

I guess I follow in the family tradition—because even though I couldn't even pronounce the illness that Gunnar had, I was convinced that I could somehow help him live longer. By the time I went back to school on Monday, I had already decided that I wanted to do something Meaningful for him. I wasn't sure what it would be, only that it would be Meaningful. Now keep in mind this was before I met Kjersten, so my intentions weren't selfish yet. I was being what they call "altruistic," which means doing good deeds for no sensible reason—and having no sensible reason for doing things is kind of where I live.

I knew I'd be on my own in figuring this one out—or at least I wasn't going to ask for help from my family. Talking to Dad about it was out of the question, because all of his mental wall space was covered with restaurant reservations. I couldn't tell my mom, because the second I did, she'd get that pained expression on her face and be on my case about praying for Gunnar. Not that I wouldn't pray for Gunnar, but I probably would be strategic about it. I wouldn't do it until he was on his deathbed, because the way I see it, praying is like trying to win an Academy Award; you don't want to come out praying too early, or you get forgotten when it's time for the nominations.

I considered telling Frankie or Christina, but Frankie would just try to top it by telling me all the people *he* knew who died. As for Christina, traumatizing her with this was a bit different from telling her our basement was sealed off because of the zombies. Besides, who goes to their younger sister for advice? She does have a spiritual streak, though, I'll admit that. In fact, lately I've found her sitting in her room, in lotus position, trying to levitate. She read somewhere that monks in the Himalayas have special spiritual mantras they repeat over and over that will make them float in midair. I'm open to all possibilities, but I told Christina that her mantra of "Ama Gonna Levitato" sounded more Harry Potter than Himalaya.

No, this whole thing needed to fly under my family's radar for a while.

Few things got by our school radar, however. It could have been Howie or Ira who overheard Gunnar at the Empire State Building—or maybe Gunnar had been selectively confiding in other kids as well. Whatever the reason, Gunnar's life-span issue was all the whisper around school on Monday.

That was the day we had to sign up for John Steinbeck lit circles in English class. Apparently *Of Mice and Men* was just a prelude to a whole lot of reading. I showed up a few minutes late, and all the short books like *The Red Pony* were gone, leaving monsters like *The Grapes of Wrath* and *East of Eden*.

Gunnar and I were in English together, and I noticed that he was in the *Grapes of Wrath* group. The *Cannery Row* group consisted of Wendell Tiggor and the tiggorhoids—which is what we called all the human moths that fluttered around Tiggor's dim bulb. I make it a habit never to join any group where I'm the smartest member, so I put my name under Gunnar's and prayed that *The Grapes of Wrath* wasn't as deep as it was long. If nothing else, it would give me a chance to get to know Gunnar better, and figure out what Meaningful thing I could do for him.

After class he came up to me. "So I see we're both in the Group of Wrath," he said. "Why don't you come over after school—I've got the movie on DVD."

It was pretty bad timing, because just then Mrs. Casey, our English teacher, was passing by. "That's cheating, Mr. Ümlaut," she said.

"No," I offered, without missing a beat. "It's research."

She raised an eyebrow as she considered this. "In that case, I'm assigning you both to compare and contrast the book with the movie." Then she struts off, very pleased with herself.

Gunnar sighed. "Sorry about that."

I leaned closer to him and whispered, "It's okay—I think my brother's got the Cliff's Notes."

And from the far end of the hall Mrs. Casey yells back, "Don't even think about it!"

Going over to someone's house you barely know is always an adventure of strange smells, strange sights, and strange dogs that will either yap at you or sniff places you'd rather not be sniffed. But there's interesting things at unexplored homes as well, like a giant tank of Chinese water dragons, or a home theater better than the multiplex, or a goddess answering the door.

In the Ümlauts' case, it was choice number three: the goddess. Her name was Kjersten, pronounced "Kirsten" (the *j* is silent—don't ask me how that's possible) and she was the last person I expected to see at Gunnar's house. Kjersten is a junior, and exists on a plane high above us mere mortals—and not just because of her height. She doesn't fit the mold of your typical beautiful girl. She's not a cheerleader, she's not part of the popular crowd—in fact, the popular crowd hates her, because Kjersten's very presence points out to them how pitiful they really are. She is a straight-A student, rules the debate team, is on the tennis team, is practically six feet tall, and as for other parts of her, well, let's just say that the lettering on her T-shirt is like one of those movies in 3-D.

"Hi, Antsy."

My response was a perfect imitation of Porky Pig. "Ibbidi-bibbiby-dibbity . . ." The fact that Kjersten even knew I existed was too much information for me to process.

She gave a little laugh. "NeuroToxin," she said.

"Huh?"

"You were looking at my shirt." She pointed to the logo on her chest. "It's the band NeuroToxin—I got it at their concert last month."

"Yeah, yeah, right." To be honest, in spite of where my eyes were staring, my brain had turned everything between her neck and her navel into that digital blur they put up on TV when they don't want you to see something. Her shirt could have had the answers to tomorrow's math test on it and I wouldn't have known.

"What are you doing here?" I said, like a perfect imbecile.

She gave me a funny look. "Where else would I be? I live here."

"Why do you live with the Ümlauts?"

She laughed again. "Uh . . . maybe because I *am* an Ümlaut?"

With my brain somewhere between here and Jupiter, I was only now catching on. "So you're Gunnar's sister?"

"Last I checked."

The concept that Kjersten could be the sister of someone I actually knew had never occurred to me. I suppressed the urge to do another Porky Pig, swallowed, and said, "Can I come in, please?"

"Sure thing." Then she called to Gunnar, letting him know that I was here. I shivered when she said my name again, and hoped she hadn't seen.

There was no response from Gunnar—the only thing I heard was a faint, high-pitched banging sound.

"He's out back working on that *thing*," Kjersten said. "Just go on through the kitchen and out the back door."

I thanked her, tried not to stare at any part of her whatsoever, and went into the house. As I passed through the kitchen I saw their mother—a woman who looked like an older, plumper version of Kjersten.

"Hello!" she said when she saw me, looking up from some vegetables she was cleaning in the sink. "You must be a friend of Gunnar's. Will you stay for dinner?" Her accent was much heavier than I expected it to be, considering Gunnar and Kjersten barely had any accent at all.

Dinner? I thought. That would mean I'd be at the same dinner table with Kjersten, and the moment I thought that, my own mother's voice intruded into my head, telling me that I used utensils like an orangutang. Whenever Mom said that, I would respond by telling her that orangutan had no *g* at the end and then go on shoveling food into my mouth like a lower primate. My eating habits didn't matter with my last girlfriend, Lexie, on account of she's blind. She would just get mad when I scraped the fork against my teeth, so as long as I ate quietly, I could be as apelike as I pleased.

Now, thanks to my own stubbornness, I had no practice in fine dining skills. Kjersten would take one look at the way I held my knife and fork, would burst out laughing, and share the information with whatever higher life-forms she communed with.

I knew if I dwelt on this much longer, I would either talk myself out of it or my head would explode, so I said, "Sure, I'll stay for dinner." I'd deal with the consequences later.

"Antsy, is that you?" Gunnar called from the backyard, where the loud tapping sound was coming from.

"Maybe," Mrs. Ümlaut said quietly, "you shall get him away from that *thing* he works on."

Gunnar was, indeed, working on a thing. I wondered at first if it was something for our *Grapes of Wrath* project. It was a stone sculpture. Granite or marble, I guessed. He was tapping away at it with a hammer and chisel. He hadn't gotten too far, because the block of stone was still pretty square. "Hi, Gunnar," I said. "I didn't know you were an artist."

"Neither did I."

He continued his tapping. There were uneven letters toward the edge of the block. *G-U-N*. He was already working on the second *N*. I laughed. "You gotta make the sculpture before you sign it, Gunnar."

"It's not that kind of sculpture."

It took me a moment more until I got the big picture, and the moment I realized just what Gunnar was doing, I blurted out one of those words my mother smacks me for.

Gunnar was carving his own tombstone.

"Gunnar . . . that's just . . . *wrong*."

He stood back to admire his work. "Well, the letters aren't exactly even, but that will add to the overall effect."

"That's not what I mean."

He looked at me, read what must have been a pretty unpleasant expression on my face, and said, "You're just like my parents. You have an unhealthy attitude. Did you know that in ancient Egypt the Pharaohs began planning their own tombs when they were still young?"

"Yeah, but you're Swedish," I reminded him. "There aren't any pyramids in Sweden."

He finished off the second *N*. "That's only because Vikings weren't good with stone."

I found myself involuntarily looking around for an escape route, and wondered if maybe I was a "not-in-my-airspace" type after all.

Then Gunnar starts launching into all this talk about death throughout history, and how people in Borneo put their departed loved ones in big ceramic pots and keep them in the living room, which is worse than anything I've told my sister about our basement. So I'm getting all nauseous and stuff, and his mother calls out, "Dinner's ready," and I pray to God she's not serving out of a Crock-Pot.

"Borrowed time, Antsy," he said. "I'm living on borrowed time."

It annoyed me, because he wasn't living on borrowed time—he was living on his own time, at least for six months, and I could think of better things to do with that time than carving a tombstone.

"Will you just shut up!" I told him.

He looked at me, hurt. "I thought you of all people would understand."

"Whaddaya mean 'me of all people'? Do you know something I don't?"

We both looked away. He said, "When that guy . . . the other day . . . you know . . . when he fell from Roadkyll Raccoon . . . everyone else was staring like it was some show, but you and I . . . we had respect enough to look away. So I thought you'd have respect for me, too." He glanced at the unfinished gravestone before him. "And respect for this."

I hadn't meant to hurt his feelings, but it was hard to respect a homemade gravestone. "I don't know, Gunnar," I said. "It's like you're getting all Hamlet on me and stuff. I swear, if you start walking around with a skull, and saying 'to-be-or-not-to-be,' I'm outta here."

He looked at me coldly, and said, insulted, "Hamlet was from Denmark, not Sweden."

I shrugged. "What's the difference?"

And to that he said, "Get out of my house."

But since we were in his backyard, and not in his house, I stayed put. He made no move to physically remove me from his presence, so I figured he was bluffing. I looked at that stupid rock that said GUNN in crooked letters. He had already returned to carving. I could hear that his breathing sounded a little bit strained, and wondered whether that was normal, or if the illness was already making it difficult for him to breathe. I had looked up the disease online—Pulmonary Monoxic Systemia had symptoms that could go mostly unnoticed, until the end, when your lips got cyanotic—which means they turn blue, like they do when you're swimming in a pool someone's too stinking cheap to heat. Gunnar's lips weren't blue, but he was pale, and he did get dizzy and light-headed from time to time. Those were symptoms, too. The more I thought I about it, the worse I felt about being so harsh over the tombstone.

Then, on a whim, I reached into my backpack, pulled out a notebook and pen, and began writing something.

"What are you doing?"

"You'll see."

When I was done, I tore the page out of the notebook, held it up, and read it aloud. "'I hereby give one month of my life to Gunnar Ümlaut. Signed, Anthony Bonano.'" I handed it to him. "There. Now you've got borrowed time. Seven months instead of six months—so you don't gotta start digging your own grave for a while."

Gunnar took it from me, looked it over, and said, "This doesn't mean anything."

I expected him to launch into some Shakespearean speech

about the woes of mortality, but instead he showed me the paper, pointing to my signature, and said, "It's not signed by a witness. A legal document must be signed by a witness."

I waited for him to start laughing, but he didn't.

"A witness?"

"Yes. It should also be typed, and then signed in blue ink. My father's a lawyer, so I know about these things."

I still couldn't tell whether or not he was kidding. Usually I can read people—but Gunnar, being Swedish and all, is as hard to figure out as IKEA assembly instructions; even if I think I'm reading him right, it's guaranteed I've done something wrong and I'll have to start over.

Since his expression stayed serious, I thought of something to say that sounded seriously legal. "I'll take it under advisement."

He grinned and slapped me hard on the back. "Excellent. So let's have dinner and watch *The Grapes of Wrath*."

Five places were set for dinner—including one for Mr. Ümlaut, who was presumably working late, but would be home "eventually." Mrs. Ümlaut made hamburgers, although I was expecting something more Scandinavian. I knew about Scandinavian food on account of this Norwegian smorgasbord place my family once accidentally ate at, because it was called DØNNY'S and my parents thought the ø was an *e*. Anyway, there was a lot of food at the buffet, including like fourteen thousand kinds of herring—which I wouldn't touch, but it was satisfying to know there were so many different things I could refuse to eat. I was oddly disappointed that not a single form of herring was on the Ümlauts' menu.

Sitting at the Ümlauts' dinner table that night was not the nerve-racking ordeal I had thought it would be. No one talked about Gunnar's illness, and I didn't say anything too terribly stupid. I talked about the proper placing of silverware, and the cultural reasons for it—something my father made sure to teach me, since I had to put out place settings at the restaurant. It made me look sophisticated, and balanced out anything subhuman I might have done at the table. I even demonstrated my water-pouring skill, pouring from high above the table, and not spilling a drop. It made Kjersten laugh—and I was pretty certain she was laughing *with* me instead of *at* me—although by the time I got home, I wasn't so sure.

Mr. Ümlaut didn't make it in time for dinner. Considering how much my own father worked lately, I didn't think much of it.

Dad came home early from work that night with a massive headache. Nine-thirty—that's early by restaurant standards. He sat at the dining table with a laptop, crunching numbers, all of which were coming up red.

"You could change your preferences in the program," I suggested. "You could make all those negative numbers from the restaurant come up green, or at least blue."

He chuckled at that. "You think we could program my laptop to charm the bank so we don't have to pay our mortgage?"

"You'd need a sexier laptop," I told him.

"Story of my life," he answered.

I thought about talking to him about Gunnar, but his worries tonight outweighed mine. "Don't work too hard," I told him—which is what he always said to me. Of course he usually said it when I was lying on the sofa like a slowly rotting vegetable.

Before I went to bed that night, I took a moment to think about the various weirdnesses that had gone on in Gunnar's backyard that afternoon—particularly the way he acted when I gave him that silly piece of paper. I had written it just to give him a laugh, and maybe get him to shift gears away from dying and stuff. Had he actually taken me seriously?

I opened a blank document on my computer, and typed out a single sentence. Then I pulled up the thesaurus, changed a few key words, found a really official-looking font, put the whole thing in a hairline box, and printed it out:

I, Anthony Paul Bonano, being of sound mind and body, do hereby bequeath one month of my natural life to Gunnar Ümlaut.

_____

Signature

_____

Signature of Witness

I have to confess, I almost didn't sign it. I almost crumpled the thing and tossed it into the trash, because it was giving me the creeps. I'm not a particularly superstitious guy . . . but I do have moments. We all do. Like, when you're walking on the street, and you start thinking about that old step-on-a-crack rhyme. Don't you—at least for a few steps—avoid the cracks? It's not like you really think you're gonna break your mother's back, right? But you avoid the cracks anyway. And when somebody sneezes, and you say "God bless you," you're not saying it to chase away evil spirits—which is why people used to say it in the old days—but you don't feel right if you don't say it.

So here I am, looking at this very legal-looking piece of paper, and wondering what it means to sign away one month of my life. And then I think, if this was an actual contract—if it was true and somewhere in the Great Beyond a tally of days *was* being kept—would I still do it, and give Gunnar an extra month?

Sure I would.

I knew that without even having to think about it.

So I bit back the creepy step-on-a-crack feeling, got a blue pen, and signed my name. Then, during my first class the next morning, I got Ira to sign as witness.

And that's when things began to get weird.

Photo Ops, Flulike Symptoms, and Trident Exchange in the Hallway of Life

4 There are very few things I've done in my life that I would consider truly inspired. Like the time I e-mailed everyone at school to tell Howie his pants were on backward. After dozens of people pulled him aside to tell him, he finally gave in to peer pressure, went into the bathroom, and turned his pants around, so they really *were* on backward.

That was inspired.

Giving Gunnar a month of my life—that was inspired, too. The problem with inspiration, though, is that it's kind of like the flu—once one person gets it, it spreads and spreads until pretty soon everyone's all congested and hawking up big wads of inspiration. It happens whether you want it to or not, and there's no vaccination.

I tracked Gunnar down in the hallway between third and fourth periods that day, and presented him with his extra month, officially signed and witnessed.

He read it over, and looked at me with the kind of gaze you don't want a guy giving you in a public hallway.

"Antsy," Gunnar said, "there are no words to express how this makes me feel."

Which was good, because words might have made me awkwardly emotional, and that would attract Dewey Lopez, the school photographer—who was famous for exposing emotions whenever possible. Such as the time he caught star football jock Woody Wilson bawling his eyes out in the locker room after losing the first game that season. In reality, Woody was crying because had just punched his locker and broken three knuckles, but nobody remembers that part—they just remember the picture—so he got stuck with the nickname "Wailing Woody," which will probably stick to him like a kick-me sign for the rest of his life.

So here we are, Gunnar and me, standing there all ripe for a humiliating Kodak moment, and Gunnar finds the words I had wished he wouldn't: "As Lewis once said to Clark, *'He who would give his life for a friend is more valuable than the Louisiana Purchase, entire.'*" And now all I can think about is what if he hugs me—and what if Dewey gets a picture, and I'm known as "Embraceable Antsy" for all eternity?

But instead Gunnar looks at the paper again and says, "Of course you didn't specify which month you're giving me."

"Huh?"

"Well, each month has a different value, doesn't it? September has thirty days, October has thirty-one, and let's not even mention February!"

I have to admit, I was a little stunned by this, but that's

okay, since stunned is an emotion I can handle. It is, in fact, an acceptable state for me. I was willing to go with Gunnar's practical approach—after all, he was the one who was dying, and I wasn't going to question how he dealt with it. I did some quick counting on my fingers. "You got six months left, right? A seventh month would put you into May. So I'm giving you May."

"Excellent!" Gunnar slaps me on the back. "My birthday's in May!"

That's when Mary Ellen McCaw descends out of nowhere, grabs the paper away from Gunnar, and says, "What's this?"

Just so you know, Mary Ellen McCaw is the under-eighteen gossip queen of Brooklyn. She's constantly sniffing out juicy dirt, and since her nose is roughly the size of Rhode Island, she's better than a bloodhound when it comes to sniffing. I'm sure she knew about Gunnar's illness; in fact, she was probably responsible for broadcasting the information across New York, and maybe parts of New Jersey.

"Give it back!" I demanded, but she just holds the thing out of reach, and reads it. Then she looks at me like I've just arrived from a previously unknown planet.

"You're giving him a month of your life?"

"Yeah. So what?"

"Giving Gunnar a new lease on life? Antsy, that's so sweet!"

This leaves me furtherly stunned, because no one has ever called me sweet—especially not Mary Ellen McCaw, who never had a nice word to say about anybody. I figure at first that maybe she means it as an insult, but the look on her face is sincere.

"What a nice thought!" she says.

I shrug. "It's just a piece of paper."

But who was I kidding? This thing was already much more than a stupid piece of paper. Mary Ellen turns from me to Gunnar, and bats her eyes at him. "Can I donate a month of my life, too?"

I look at her, wondering if she's kidding, but clearly she's not.

Gunnar, all flattered, gives her an aw-shucks look and says, "Sure, if you really want to."

"Good, then it's settled," says Mary Ellen. "Antsy, you write up the contract, okay?"

I don't say anything just yet, as I'm still set on stun.

"Remember to specify the month," says Gunnar.

"And," adds Mary Ellen, "make sure it says that the month comes from the end of my life, not the middle somewhere."

"How could it come from the middle?" I dare to ask.

"I don't know—temporary coma, maybe? The point is, even a symbolic gesture should be clear of loopholes, right?"

Who was I to argue with logic like that?

"So what's it like at the Ümlauts'?"

Howie and Ira were all over me in the lunchroom that day, as if going over to the Ümlauts' was like setting foot in a haunted house.

"Was there medical stuff everywhere?" Howie asked. "My uncle had to build a room addition just for his iron lung—the thing's as big as a car."

"I didn't see anything like that," I told them. "It's not that kind of illness."

"It must have been weird, though," Ira said. I considered telling them about Gunnar's do-it-yourself tombstone, but decided not to turn something so personal into gossip.

"It was fine," I told them. "They're just a normal family. The dad's always off working. Their mom's pretty cool, and Kjersten and Gunnar are just like any other brother and sister."

"Kjersten . . ." Ira said, and he and Howie gave each other a knowing grin. "Did you get some quality time with *her*?"

"Actually, I did. We all had dinner together." Ira and Howie were disappointed at how normal the whole thing was, considering. Still, it didn't stop them from being envious that I actually got to eat a whole meal with Kjersten. I didn't even have to exaggerate. The more I downplayed it, the more jealous they became.

There's something to be said about being the envy of your friends. They made some of the standard rude jokes friends will make about beautiful girls out of their reach—the same ones I was tempted to make myself, but didn't. Then the conversation came back to the subject of death, which is just as compelling and almost as distant as sex.

"Were they all religious and stuff?" Ira asked. "People always get that way when someone gets sick—remember Howie's parents when they thought he had mad cow?"

"Don't remind me," says Howie.

I thought about it, but didn't remember anything like that at the Ümlauts'. They didn't say grace like we do at my house when someone remembers to. Ira was right—if Gunnar was my kid, I'd be saying grace all the time.

"His mom doesn't talk about his illness at all," I told them.

"I guess that's how they deal with it. It's creepy, because there's always, like, an elephant in the room."

Then Howie looks at me with those drowning-penguin eyes, and I know where this is going.

"You're joking right? Is that even legal?"

"Yeah," I tell him, without missing a beat. "It's housebroken, too, and can paint modern art with its trunk."

"Okay," Howie says, getting mad, "now you're just making stuff up."

I could keep this going for hours, but Ira chimes in. "It's an expression, Howie. When something's completely obvious but everyone's ignoring it, you say 'there's an elephant in the room'—because, just like an elephant, it's big and fat, and hard to ignore."

Howie thinks about it and nods. "I get it," he says. "Although that kind of weight gain could be glandular. Is it his mother?"

This time Ira doesn't even throw him a life preserver.

That afternoon I had a second hallway encounter. It was one of those moments that gets burned into your brain like a cigarette on a leather couch. I'm convinced it left me with brain damage.

It was just before last period. I was scrambling to get my math book out of my locker before the tardy bell when I heard a familiar voice behind me saying my name for the third time in as many days.

"Antsy?"

I turned to see none other than Kjersten Ümlaut behind me.

Her eyes were all moist and shiny, and the first thing that struck my brain was that Kjersten was even more beautiful in tears.

"I heard about what you did for Gunnar," she said.

I'm figuring maybe she's gonna slap me for it, so I say, "Yeah, sorry about that. It was a dumb idea."

"I just wanted you to know how thoughtful it was."

"Really?"

"Really. And I wanted to thank you."

And that's when it happened. She kissed me. I think maybe she meant to give me a little peck on the cheek, but I had just closed my locker and was turning, so the kiss landed a bull's-eye on the mouth.

Okay—now you'd think this would be the stuff of dreams and fireworks and time-stopping, *Matrix*-like special effects, right? The thing is, that only happens when you're expecting it and have time to set the moment up. But this was sudden. It was kind of like overcranking a cold car engine. It just grinds instead of starting. And so, what should have been the kiss from heaven was instead the lip-lock from hell.

See, I had just come back from phys ed, where we were running outside in the cold, so my nose was kinda stuffy and I was doing a whole lot of mouth breathing. In other words, my mouth is open like a fish when she comes at me.

The second it happens, a million volts go shooting through my head, and it's too much to handle, so my brain decides to take a Hawaiian vacation—I can almost hear the jet engines as it takes off from LaGuardia—and now the only thing in my head is gratitude that I got my braces off last month, followed immediately by horror, because now she's getting nothing but retainer, and why did I pick today of all days to have salami for lunch, and would the brownie I ate afterward provide enough cover, and where's that mint flavor coming from?

Then in a second I'm hearing bells, and I think it's some sort of mental shell shock, until I realize it's the tardy bell, which means I'll get detention, but none of that matters, because there's Dewey Lopez with his camera, preserving the moment for eternity and saying, "Thanks, guys, that one's a keeper!" and he's gone, maybe to look for my brain on that beach in Maui.

Kjersten finally pulls away, and I say—I swear I actually say this: "Do you want your gum back, or should I keep it?"

She's a little red in the face, or maybe it's green, because I think my brain-burn left me temporarily color-blind.

"Sorry," she says, and I'm thinking it's me who should be saying sorry, but I'm still figuring out what the hell I should do with the gum, and then she says, "Well, I just wanted to thank you. It's just what Gunnar needs."

"Thanks for thanking," I say. "Thank me anytime!" And then she's gone faster than Dewey Lopez.

As for me, I went off to sit in a math class that I have absolutely no memory of.

My experience with girls is limited, and usually ends in pain. The one exception is Lexie Crawley. The crash site of *that* relationship eventually grew flowers, instead of poison ivy and fly-traps. In other words, after breaking up, Lexie and I became friends—and it's not like the friendship I've got with Howie and Ira. See, Howie and Ira, they're more like family. You can't get rid of them, so you don't even try, and learn to live with them. It's okay having friends like that, because no matter what direction your life takes, you'll always have the Howies and Iras of the world to raise your self-esteem, because they make you look good by comparison.

But Lexie was different. First of all, she's got insight instead of sight. Being blind doesn't necessarily make a person remarkable, but Lexie has managed to build something wonderful around what others would call a disability. Secondly, Lexie's got more class than anyone I know, and I'm not talking snooty I'm-better-than-you kind of class. I mean real class. I admire her for who she is.

Here's what it's like between Lexie and me: she can tell me that I'm a much better friend than boyfriend, and I can actually take it as a compliment. That's a big deal, because most girls use that "I like you as a friend" line as secret code for "Keep your paws away from me, you slimeball," but not Lexie. I knew if there was anyone I could ask for advice on what Kjersten's kiss really meant, it was her.

I went to Crawley's restaurant straight from school that day, looking for Lexie. Although Crawley also owned most of *Paris, Capisce?*, the original Crawley's is his main restaurant. He and Lexie actually live in it. Sort of. See, it's a huge mansion, but only the first floor is restaurant. The two of them live on the second floor, with fifteen dogs: one for each of the seven deadly sins, and seven virtues, plus one Seeing Eye dog that must have identity issues, because it's the only yellow Lab in a sea of fourteen Afghan hounds.

"What do *you* want?" Old Man Crawley growled when he

answered the door. He always said that to me. Except when he was expecting me. Then he'd say, "You're late!" even if I was early. It wasn't just me he treated this way, though. The whole world was an enemy waiting to happen. According to my father, Crawley's greatest joy came from watching him squirm. In this I could teach my dad a thing or two, because Crawley never made me squirm. I just laughed at him. It annoyed him, but I think he respected me for it.

The dogs barked and pawed me with their usual greeting. Crawley pulled Gluttony back by the collar, and sent him off. Since Gluttony was the alpha male of the pack, the other dogs followed.

"Is it that time already?" Crawley asked as I stepped in.

"You'll never know," I told him with a grin.

"I always know," he said. He was, of course, referring to our monthly kidnapping—the planning of which was usually why I came over to chat with Lexie. Like I said, Crawley had us kidnap him once a month, and force him to do something exhilarating. He even paid me for it. The fact that he's rich and we get to use his money to plan our adventure outings allows us some really unique opportunities. Last month was a dolphin encounter at the Brooklyn Aquarium, with a shark thrown in for added excitement.

"What are you planning for this month?" he asked.

"Space shuttle," I told him. "We're sending you to blow up a comet before it can destroy the earth. You'll be strapped to the tip of the warhead."

"Smart-ass." He poked me with his cane. Although he broke his hip last year, I don't think he needed the cane to walk anymore. I believe he kept it as a weapon.

"So tell me," he asked, "what new things have you botched up at *Paris, Capisce?* lately?"

"You mean besides Thanksgiving? Sorry, but I have no other screwups to entertain you with."

He shook his head and scowled at me, annoyed that I had no humiliating food-service moments to share. "Incredible," he said. "You're disappointing even when you're *not* disappointing." Then he went off into the kitchen, where he was quickly surrounded by amber waves of dog.

Lexie got home ten minutes later and was surprised, but pleased, to find me there. She let Moxie, her Seeing Eye dog, out of his halter, and he came bounding to me, expressing all the emotion that Lexie was too proper to display. She did give me a hug, though.

"I'm glad you came by," she said. "I've been thinking about you."

"You have?" I instantly wondered what she was thinking, and why, and whether I should feel embarrassed, flattered, or awkward.

"There's this new boy at school who sounds like you. I keep hearing him in the lunchroom. It's very distracting."

"Yeah," I said. "If he sounds like me, he must be distracting."

She laughed at that. "It's only distracting because I keep expecting it to be you."

I sat across from her in the living room and got right to business, telling her the reason for my visit. I expected her to be full of wisdom, and maybe give me a road map into the mind of Kjersten Ümlaut. Instead she just folded her arms.

"So let me get this straight," she said. "You're telling me

you've been kissed by a beautiful girl, and you want *me* to give *you* advice about it."

"Yeah, that's the general idea."

I could already tell this was going south. I'm not the most observant guy in the world, but I've learned that reading Lexie's body language is very important. See, lots of people put on fake body language, making you see what they want you to see—but since Lexie doesn't think in terms of sight, her body language is always genuine. And right now she was genuinely peeved.

"So, a girl kissed you. Why does that have to involve me?"

"She's not a girl, she's a JUNIOR, and every guy in school would give their left arm to go out with her—but she kissed *me*."

Still, Lexie's all cross-armed and huffy. Even the dogs are looking at her like there's something wrong.

And then I finally get it.

"Are you jealous?"

"Of course not," she says, but her body language says different.

"How can you be jealous?" I ask. "You're dating that guy who clicks, right?" The guy I'm talking about is this blind dude with the very rare gift of echolocation. By making clicking noises, he can tell you exactly what's around him. It's kind of like human sonar—he's been on the news and everything.

"His name is Raoul," says Lexie, all insulted.

"Yeah, well, if *my* name was Raoul, I'd rather be called 'that guy who clicks.'"

The scowl on her face scares away at least four of the dogs. I figure it's time to backtrack a little bit, so I give her the whole story—about Gunnar, and his weird incurable illness, and the extra month, figuring if she has the background, she might not be so annoyed by the whole thing. The second I mention the free month, she unfolds her arms.

"You gave him a month of your life?"

"Yeah, and that's why his sister kissed me—so she says."

"Antsy, that was a really nice gesture!"

"Yeah, sure, but we're not talking about that right now, we're talking about the kiss."

"Fine, fine—but tell me, what did that boy say when you gave him the month?"

By now I'm getting all exasperated myself. "He said 'thank you,' what do you think he said? Can we get back to the other thing now?"

But if there was any hope of getting advice on the subject, it flew out the window when Old Man Crawley came traipsing in, having eavesdropped on the whole conversation.

"What did he give you in return for signing away a month of your life?" Crawley asked.

I sighed. "Nothing. It was a gift. Kind of a symbolic gesture."

"Symbolism's overrated," said Crawley. "And as a gift, it's just plain stupid. It's not even tax-deductible. You should have gotten something in return."

So out of curiosity I asked, "What do you think a month of someone's life is worth?"

He looked me over, curling his lip like I was a bad piece of fish at the market. "A month of *your* life?" he said. "About a buck ninety-eight," and he left, cackling to himself, profoundly amused at how I had walked right into that one.

"Well," said Lexie, no longer peeved at me. "I think a month of your life is worth a lot more than 'a buck ninety-eight.'" She reached out for my hand, and I moved it right into her path so she didn't have to go searching for it. She clasped it, smiling. Then she sighed and reluctantly said, "As for the kiss, my opinion, as your friend, is that it *does* mean something. There's no such thing as a 'thank-you kiss'. At least not in high school."

People Sign Their Lives Away for
the Dumbest Reasons, but Don't Blame Me,
I Just Wrote the Contract

5 I don't think it's possible not to be selfish. Of course that doesn't mean everyone's gotta be like Old Man Crawley either, but there's a little bit of selfishness in everything. Even when you give something from the bottom of your heart, you're always getting something back, aren't you? It could just be the satisfaction of making someone happy—which makes you feel better about yourself, so you can balance out whatever awful thing you did earlier in the day.

Even Howie, who gets screamed at for always buying the wrong gift for his mother, is getting something out of that; each time he gets smacked for getting flowers his mother is allergic to or something, he's left with the warm-fuzzy feeling of knowing some things never change, and his universe is all solid and stable.

My motivations were getting very muddy when it came to my so-called good deeds for Gunnar, and it was starting to feel more and more like disguised selfishness, because of the Kjersten complication.

Lexie believed that Kjersten's kiss meant something. I put a lot of stock in what she said, not just because I trusted Lexie's judgment, but because deep down, I was pretty sure it meant something, too. At the very least it was an invitation to *make* it mean something. Was it wrong to perpetrate good deeds when attention from Kjersten was one of the perks?

I, Mary Ellen McCaw, being of sound mind and body, do hereby bequeath one month of my natural life to Gunnar Ümlaut, that month being the month of June, which shall be taken from the end of my natural life, and not the middle.

Mary Ellen McCaw
Signature

ANTHONY BONANO
Signature of Witness

Thanks to Mary Ellen, the word about "time shaving" had spread quickly. She bragged to the known world about how she donated a month of her life to poor, poor Gunnar Ümlaut, and how the idea was all hers, although I may have contributed a piece of paper.

As people were not entirely stupid, they saw right through Mary Ellen and realized she was leeching off of my idea—so the next day about half a dozen people came out of the woodwork wanting to donate some of their time. Gunnar was more than happy to accept whatever months came his way, and Kjersten was sufficiently impressed.

"This is just what Gunnar needs," she said when I showed her Mary Ellen's contract. "I don't know how to thank you."

I could have given her some suggestions.

There was this one girl—Ashley Morales—who was clearly in love with Gunnar—even more so than most of the female student body. She wanted her month to be special. "I want my month to be his last," she told me. "Can you make sure that he knows my month is his last?"

Since no one else had claimed the honor, I was happy to oblige.

I, Ashley Morales, being of sound mind and body, do hereby bequeath one month of my natural life to Gunnar Ümlaut. The month shall <u>not</u> be this coming May or June, which are months already reserved by others. The month shall be taken from the end of my natural life, and not the middle. The month shall be the absolute <u>last additional month</u> of Gunnar Ümlaut's life, beyond which there shall only be afterlife, if applicable.

Ashley Morales
Signature

Neena Wexler
Signature of Witness

Then there was this other guy who had come from confession, and his priest wanted him to say like fourteen thousand Hail Marys for writing obscene graffiti on the Gowanus Expressway. He negotiated it down to one month of community service. I guess the kid figured a month donated to Gunnar was just as good.

The kid was all worried about it, though, and took it even more seriously than Ashley.

"I don't want to give up a month if I'm gonna croak tomorrow or anything," he told me, "because it means I'll owe days from last month, and I don't need that kind of grief."

"C'mon, it's not like it's real or anything," I remind him. "It's just to make Gunnar feel better."

"Yeah," he says, "but what if turns out to be real after all—like those chain e-mails you gotta forward to ten people, or you die?"

"Those aren't real!" I tell him.

"Yeah," he says. "But how can you be sure . . . ?"

I think about that and get all uncomfortable, because I have been guilty of forwarding those stupid e-mails, too. But I usually just send them to people I don't like.

I sigh. "Okay. What if I make your contract void if you're scheduled to croak before next month? That way you won't owe any days, and you can enter the pearly gates totally free of debt."

He thought about that some more, finally agreed, and happily went back to his priest, mission accomplished.

I, Jasper Horace Januski, being of sound mind and body, do hereby bequeath one month of my natural life to Gunnar Ümlaut, subject to the stuff listed below:

    1. The month shall not be this coming May or June, or the last month of Gunnar Ümlaut's life, which are all already reserved by others.

    2. The month shall be taken from the end of my natural life and not the middle.

    3. The donated month shall be null and void if my own expiration date is less than 31 days from the date of this contract.

Jasper Januski
Signature

Dewey Lopez
Signature of Witness

I have to admit, it felt good to be doing something positive for Gunnar, in spite of the fact that it hadn't brought forth a second kiss from Kjersten, regardless of how little salami I ate, or how much mouthwash I used. I think maybe her reluctance came from the picture Dewey Lopez published in the school paper of our first kiss. Luckily it wasn't on the front cover, since he also snapped a picture of Principal Sinclair coming out of the bathroom with his fly open and a piece of shirttail hanging out. Definitely front-page material. Still, the page-four article was seen by the whole school, with the unpleasant headline LOVE SKIPS A GRADE.

I don't know how it affected Kjersten's social standing, but it sure did elevate mine. Everybody wanted to know about it, but I kept quiet, because I figured Kjersten might respect a guy who didn't kiss and tell—even if that guy was one year and seven months younger than her. (Yes, I snuck into the office and checked her school record to find out exactly how much older than me she was.)

Kjersten never mentioned the article or the picture or, for that matter, the kiss. But she did continue to tell me what an entirely great guy I was, which meant another piece of Trident might only be a few days away.

"It's so, so special that you're sensitive to Gunnar's little problem," Kjersten told me when I handed her the month Howie gave me—which was month number seven and counting.

At the time I had laughed, and wondered how she could call it "a little problem." I'm not wondering anymore. And I'm not laughing either.

I, Howard Bernard Bogerton, being of somewhat sound mind and body, do hereby bequeath one month of my natural life to Gunnar Ümlaut, subject to the stuff listed below:

1. The month shall not be this coming May or June, or the last month of Gunnar Ümlaut's life, which are all already reserved by others.

2. The month shall be taken from the end of my natural life, and not the middle.

3. The donated month shall be null and void if my own

expiration date is less than 31 days from the date of this contract.

4. Should Gunnar Ümlaut use my month for criminal acts such as shoplifting or serial killing, I shall not be held responsible.

HOWIE BOGERTON

Signature

Ira Goldfarb

Signature of Witness

By Friday, I had gotten Gunnar a full year.

A Nasty Herd of Elephants
That Are Nowhere Near as
Embarrassingly Adorable as Me.
Don't Ask.

6 Nobody gets up early on Saturday morning in our house anymore. Friday night's a late night for the restaurant. Mom and Dad are usually up even later than me—and that's saying something. I slunk into the kitchen at around eleven that morning to see Mom, clearly still on her first cup of coffee, trying to comfort an inconsolable Christina.

"But I don't want to put Ichabod to sleep," Christina said through her tears. "It's inhumane."

"It's inhumane to let him suffer." She looked at our cat, who was now lying on the windowsill in the sun. If he was suffering, he wasn't showing it. It was actually the rest of us who were suffering, because poor Ichabod was so old he had forgotten the form and function of a litter box, and had begun to improvise, leaving little icha-bits in unlikely places.

"It's the way of all things, honey," Mom said sympathetically. "You remember Mr. Moby—and what about your hamsters?"

"It's not the same!" Christina yelled.

Mr. Moby was Christina's goldfish. Actually a whole series of goldfish. She named them all Mr. Moby, the same way Sea World named all their star whales "Shamu." Then she graduated to hamsters, which were cute, cuddly, vicious little things that would devour one another with such regularity you'd think cannibalism was in their job description. But Christina was right—this was different. A cat was more like family. Besides, in my current state of mind, mortality was kind of a sore spot.

"Mom," I said, "couldn't we just let nature take its course, and let Ichabod go when he's ready?"

"I'll clean up if he misses the litter box," Christina said. "Promise."

"Yeah," I said. "Maybe she can levitate it out the window."

Christina scowled at me. "Maybe you could give Ichabod one of your friend's extra months."

This surprised me—I didn't even know she knew about that, but I guess word gets around. Fortunately it flew miles over Mom's head.

"You know what?" Mom said. "I'm not gonna worry about this anymore. It's on your head." Then she poured herself a fresh cup of coffee.

I went over to Gunnar's house that afternoon, using our *Grapes of Wrath* project as a cover story, but what I was really hoping for—and dreading at the same time—was seeing Kjersten. It turns out she had left early for a tennis tournament. I was deeply disappointed, and yet profoundly relieved.

We were halfway through *The Grapes of Wrath* and had decided that, for our project, we were going to re-create the dust bowl in Gunnar's backyard, then arrange for our class to come see it. The dust bowl is what they called the Midwest back in the thirties, when Oklahoma, Kansas, and I think maybe Nebraska dried up and blew away—which has nothing to do with *Gone with the Wind*, although that movie was made during the same basic time period.

Mrs. Ümlaut fretted a lot when we told her about our plan. *Fretted:* that's a word they used during the dust bowl. ("Fretted," "reckon," and "y'all" were very popular in those days.) But since the backyard was mostly crabgrass already going dormant for the winter, she reluctantly agreed to let us kill the whole yard as long as we promised to redo everything in the spring. I couldn't help but glance at Gunnar when she said that, because what if he wasn't around in the spring? Then again, maybe this was her way of implying to him that he would be.

I figured the biggest problem with the dust bowl was Gunnar's unfinished gravestone smack in the middle of the yard. By now Gunnar had finished his first name and begun working on his middle name, Kolbjörn, which he was worried wouldn't fit on one line. "I may have to start over on a fresh piece of granite," he told me. I just nodded. I decided it was best if I didn't involve myself in tombstone-related issues.

Before we began murdering helpless vegetation, Gunnar took me up to his room to show me what he had done with the twelve months I had gotten for him. He had three-hole-punched them, and put them in a binder labeled *Life*. He displayed it proudly, like someone else might display a photo album.

"I consulted with Dr. G yesterday," Gunnar said. "He says I might make nine months—maybe more, because my symptoms haven't been getting worse." Then he patted his Binder of Life. "But maybe the real reason's right here."

I let out a nervous chuckle. "Whatever it takes, right?"

I still didn't know if he was serious, or just playing along. The kids who donated their months were, for the most part, treating it like a game. I mean, sure, they were hung up on the rules, but it was more like how you argue over a Monopoly board, and whether or not you're supposed to get five hundred bucks if you land on "Free Parking." The rules say no, but people still insist it's the cash-bonus space. In fact, my cousin Al once busted a guy's nose over it—which sent him directly to jail, do not pass "Go."

The point is, even when a game gets serious, there's still a line between game-serious and *serious*-serious. If I was sure which side of that line Gunnar was on, I'd have felt a whole lot better. Apparently I wasn't the only one who felt a little unsettled around Gunnar. Sure, girls flocked to him, but when it came to our literature circles, they divided right along gender lines, with all the girls going for things that sounded romantic, like *East of Eden*. We had four guys in our group to start with, but they had all migrated to other novels. I suspected their migration was, much like the farmworkers in our book, driven by empty plains of death. In other words, they couldn't handle Gunnar's constant coming attractions about the end of his life.

"I'll never forget," he said to Devin Gilooly, "that you were my first friend when I moved here. Would you like to be a pall-bearer?"

Devin went bug-eyed and vampire-pale. "Yeah, sure," he said. The next day, he not only switched to a different novel, he switched to a different English class. If it were possible, I think he would have switched to another school altogether.

"Doesn't your culture ululate for the dead?" Gunnar asked Hakeem Habibi-Jones.

"What's 'ululate'?" Hakeem asked, making it clear that any cultural traditions had been lost in hyphenation. Gunnar demonstrated ululation, which was apparently a high-pitched warbling wail that was maybe meant to wake the dead person in question. All it succeeded in doing was chasing Hakeem away.

After that, it was just Gunnar and me. Even now, as we started pumping out poison in his yard, I was afraid Gunnar would talk about the death of weeds and find a way to relate it to himself, like maybe he was some unwanted plant targeted by the Weedwhacker in the sky.

He didn't talk about himself, though. Instead he talked about me. And his sister.

I was all set to put a painfully ugly shrub out of its misery when Gunnar said, "You know, Kjersten really likes you."

I turned to him, and ended up spraying herbicide on his shoes. "Sorry."

He took it in stride, just wiping the stuff off with a rag. "You shouldn't be surprised," he said. "Not with that kiss all over the school paper."

I shrugged uncomfortably. "It wasn't all over the paper. It was on page four. And anyway, it wasn't really a kiss—it was just a peck. Or at least I think it was supposed to be." But I couldn't help but think about what Lexie had said. "Has Kjersten . . . said anything about it to you?"

"She doesn't have to *say* anything—I know my sister. She doesn't kiss just anybody."

There it was—confirmation from a sibling! "So, are you saying she Likes me, as in 'Like' with a capital *L*?"

Gunnar considered this. "More like italics," he said. Which was fine, because the capital *L* was more than I could handle.

"So . . . are you okay with her *liking* me?"

Gunnar continued to kill the plants. "Why shouldn't I be? Better you than some other creep, right?"

I wasn't sure whether he was REALLY okay with it, or just pretending to be okay with it. The only similar situation in recent memory had to do with Ira's ten-year-old sister, who was kissed in the playground by some twelve-year-old last Valentine's Day. The second Ira heard about it, he assembled a posse to terrorize the kid, and now she might never be kissed again.

This situation was different, though. First of all, *she* kissed *me,* not the other way around. Secondly, she's Gunnar's *older* sister, so it's not like he's got to be protective, right?

"She likes you because you're genuine," Gunnar said. "You're the real thing."

This was news to me. I don't even know what "thing" he meant, so how could I be the real one? But if it's a thing Kjersten liked, that was fine with me. And as for being "genuine," the more I thought about it, the more I realized what a big deal that was. See, there's basically three types of guys at our school: poseurs, droolers, and losers. The poseurs are always pretending to be somebody they're not, until they forget who they actually are and end up being nobody. The droolers have brains that have shriveled to the size of a walnut, which could either be genetic or media-induced. And the losers, well, they eventually find one another in all that muck at the bottom of the gene pool, but trust me, it's not pretty.

Those of us who don't fit into those three categories have a harder time in life, because we gotta figure things out for ourselves—which leaves more opportunity for personal advancement, and mental illness—but hey, no pain, no gain.

So Kjersten liked "genuine" guys. The problem with genuine is that it's not something you can try to be, because the second you try, you're not genuine anymore. Mostly it's about being clueless, I think. Being decent, but clueless about your own decency.

I don't know if I'm genuine, but since I'm fairly clueless most of the time, I figured I was halfway there.

"So . . . what do you think I should do?" I asked, parading my cluelessness like suddenly it's a virtue.

"You should ask her for a date," Gunnar said.

This time I sprayed the herbicide in my eyes.

My advice to you: avoid spraying herbicide in your eyes if at all you can help it. Use a face mask, like the bottle says in bright red, but did I listen? No. The pain temporarily knocked Gunnar's suggestion to the back of my brain, and the world became a faraway place for a while.

I spent half an hour in the bathroom washing out my eyes while Gunnar threw me a few famous quotes about the therapeutic nature of pain. By the time my optical agony faded to a dull throbbing behind my eyelids, I felt like I had just woken up from surgery. Then I step out of the bathroom, and who's coming in the front door? Kjersten.

"Antsy! Hi!" She sounded maybe a little more enthusiastic

than she had intended to. I think that was a good thing. Then she looked at me funny. "Have you been crying?"

"What? Oh! No, it's just the herbicide."

She looked at me even more funny, so I told her, "Gunnar and I were killing plants."

Kjersten apparently had a whole range of looking-at-you-funny expressions. "Is this . . . a hobby of yours?"

I took a deep breath, slowed my brain down—if that's even possible—and tried to explain our whole dust-bowl project in such a way that I didn't sound either moronic or certifiably insane. It must have worked, because the funny expressions stopped.

Then Mrs. Ümlaut called from the kitchen. "Are you staying for dinner, Antsy?"

"Sure he is," Kjersten said with a grin. "He can't drive home with his eyes like that."

"I . . . uh . . . don't drive yet."

She nudged me playfully. "I know that. I was just kidding."

"Oh. Right." The fact that she was old enough to drive and I wasn't was a humiliating fact I had not considered. Until now. As I thought about this, I could tell I was going red in the face, because my ears felt hot. Kjersten looked at me and laughed, then she leaned in close and whispered:

"You're cute when you're embarrassed."

That embarrassed me even more.

"Well," I said, "since I'm mostly embarrassed around you, I must be adorable."

She laughed, and I realized that I had actually been clever. I never knew there could be such a thing as charming humiliation. Gold star for me!

Tonight Mrs. Ümlaut made fried chicken—which was as un-Scandinavian as hamburgers, but at least tonight there was pickled red cabbage, which I suspected had Norse origins but was less offensive than herring fermented in goat's milk, or something like that.

It was just the four of us at first—once more with a plate left for Mr. Ümlaut, like he was the Holy Spirit.

Sitting at the Ümlaut dinner table that night was much more torturous than the first time. See, the first time I was desperately trying not to make an ass of myself, just in case Kjersten might notice. But now that she was certain to notice, it was worse than my third-grade play, where I had to dress in black, climb out of a papier-mâché tooth, and be a singing, dancing cavity. I forgot the words to the song, and since Howie had spent half that morning whistling "It's a Small World" in my ear, that was the only song left in my brain. So when I jumped out of the papier-mâché tooth, rather than standing there in silent stage fright, I started singing all about how it's a world of laughter and a world of tears. Eventually, the piano player just gave up and played the song along with me. When I was done, I got applause from the audience, which just made me feel physically ill, so I leaned over, puked into the piano, and ran offstage. After that, the piano never sounded quite right, and I was never asked to sing in a school play again.

That's kind of how I felt at dinner with the Ümlauts that night—and no matter how attractive Kjersten might have found my embarrassment, it would all be over if the combination of fried chicken, pickled cabbage, and stress made me hurl into the serving bowl.

"I had a consultation with Dr. G today," Gunnar announced just a few minutes into the meal. His mother sighed, and Kjersten looked at me, shaking her head.

"I don't want to hear about Dr. G," Mrs. Ümlaut said.

Gunnar took a bite of his chicken. "How do you know it's not good news?"

"Dr. G *never* gives good news," she said. It surprised me that she didn't want to hear about her son's condition—and that she hadn't even accompanied him to the doctor—but then everybody deals with hardship in different ways.

"I may have more time than originally predicted," Gunnar said. "But only with treatment from experts in the field."

That wasn't quite what he had told me, but I could see there were more layers of communication going on here than infomercials on a satellite dish—which, by the way, I am forbidden to watch since the time I ordered the Ninja-matic food processor. But I suspected that whatever treatments Gunnar was talking about were going to cost more than twelve easy payments of $19.99. Maybe that was it—maybe the cost of medical treatment was the elephant in the room here—although I'm sure that wasn't the only one; the Ümlauts seemed to breed elephants like my sister breeds hamsters.

Then, as if that wasn't enough, an entire new herd arrived. Mr. Ümlaut came home.

I always hear people talk about "dysfunctional families." It annoys me, because it makes you think that somewhere there's this magical family where everyone gets along, and no one ever screams things they don't mean, and there's never a time when sharp objects should be hidden. Well, I'm sorry, but that family doesn't exist. And if you find some neighbors that seem to be the grinning model of "function," trust me—that's the family that will get arrested for smuggling arms in their SUV between soccer games.

The best you can really hope for is a family where everyone's problems, big and small, work together. Kind of like an orchestra where every instrument is out of tune, in exactly the same way, so you don't really notice. But when it came to the Ümlaut orchestra, nothing meshed—and the moment Mr. Ümlaut walked through the front door everything in that house clashed like cymbals.

It started with the dinner conversation. From the moment I heard the key turning in the lock, all conversation stopped. I glanced at Gunnar, who stared into his food. I turned my eyes to Kjersten, who turned her eyes to the clock. And when I looked to Mrs. Ümlaut, she didn't seem to be looking at anything at all.

Mr. Ümlaut came into the kitchen without a word, noticed there was a guest at the table, but didn't comment on it. He took out a glass and dispensed himself some water from the refrigerator door.

"You're home," Mrs. Ümlaut finally said, bizarrely stating the obvious.

He took a gulp of his water, and looked at the table. "Chicken?"

Without standing up, Mrs. Ümlaut reached over and pulled out his chair. He sat down.

I took a moment to size the man up. He was tall, with thinning blond hair, small glasses, and a wide jaw that Gunnar was starting to develop. There was a weariness about him that had nothing to do with sleep, and he had a poker face that was completely unreadable, just like Gunnar. To me that was the most uncomfortable thing of all. See, I come from a family where we wear our hearts on our sleeves. If you're feeling something, chances are someone else knows about it even before you do. But this man's heart was somewhere in a safe behind the family portrait.

"I don't believe we've met," he said to me.

His cool gray eyes made me feel like I was on a game show and didn't know the answer.

"Antsy, this is my dad," Gunnar said.

"Pleased to meet you," I said, then silence fell again as everyone ate.

I don't do well with silence, so I usually take it upon myself to end it. My brother says I'm like the oxygen mask that drops when a plane loses air pressure. "People stop talking and Antsy falls from the ceiling to fill the room with hot air until normality returns."

But what if normality is never going to return, and you know it?

I opened my mouth, and words began to spill out like I was channeling the village idiot. "Working today? Yeah, my dad works on Saturdays, too. We got a restaurant, so he's always working when people are eating, and people are always eating—of course that's different from being a lawyer, though—isn't that what Gunnar said you do? Wow, it must have been hard work becoming a lawyer—a lot of school, just like becoming a doctor, right? Except, of course, you don't gotta practice on dead bodies."

I was feeling light-headed, and then realized I had said all that without breathing. I figured maybe I should have put my own oxygen mask on first before helping others, like you're supposed to.

Gunnar didn't say anything—he just stared at me like you might stare at a car wreck you pass on the side of the road. It was Kjersten who spoke.

"He wasn't at work," she said, almost under her breath.

"More chicken?" Mrs. Ümlaut asked me.

"Yes, please, thank you." But even as I tried to plug up my mouth up with food, I couldn't stop myself from talking. "My dad had one of his recipes stolen by a restaurant down the block and he says he should sue—maybe you can be his lawyer, or at least tell him if it makes sense to sue, because I hear it costs more money than it's worth, and then there are like fourteen thousand appeals and no one ever sees a penny—of course I could be wrong, you'd know better than me, right?"

He seemed neither amused nor irritated. I would have felt much more comfortable if he were one or the other. "I'm not that kind of lawyer," he said flatly, between bites of food. Gunnar continued his car-wreck gaze, although I think by now it was a multicar pileup.

"Something to drink, Antsy?" Mrs. Ümlaut asked.

"Yes, please, thank you." She poured me a tall glass of milk, and I quickly began to drink—not because I wanted it, but because I knew that unless I was a ventriloquist and could make words come out of somebody else's mouth, drinking would shut me up for a good twenty seconds, and maybe the urge to blather would go away like hiccups.

It worked. Once the glass was drained, my words were drowned. The rest of the meal was filled with an unnatural silence, in which no one made eye contact with anyone else, least of all with Mr. Ümlaut. I made it through the meal listening to clinking silverware, and the ticking of the clock, until Gunnar finally rapped me on the arm and said, "The dust bowl awaits."

I had never been happier to get away from a dinner table, and it occurred to me that this was the first time in the Ümlaut home that it felt as if someone was dying.

It was dark now, with nothing but the back-porch bulb to light up the backyard. We sprayed until both drums of herbicide were empty. Gunnar had brought with him the silence of the dinner table. It drove me nuts, because, just like with his father, I had no idea what he was feeling or thinking—and although I swore to myself I wouldn't bring it up, I couldn't leave without asking Gunnar the big question.

"So what's the deal with your dad?"

Gunnar laughed at that. "The deal," he said. "That's funny." And that's all he said. He didn't tell me that it was none of my business, he didn't tell me to go take a flying leap. He just brushed it off like the question had never been asked.

He took a quick glance at the instructions on his herbicide canister. "Says here that the plants will all be dead in five days, and then it should be easy to pull them out."

"We could sign over two extra days of life to the plants if

you want to wait until next weekend," I said, and laughed at my own joke.

"That's not funny."

"Sorry."

To be honest, I had no clue what I was and wasn't allowed to laugh at anymore.

The moment was far too uncomfortable, so I tried to salvage it. "Hey, by the way, I think there are still a few people at school willing to donate months, if you still want them."

"Why wouldn't I want them?" he asked. "As Nathaniel Hawthorne said, *'Scrounging for precious moments is the most primary human endeavor.'*"

He was always so matter-of-fact about it, you could almost forget what was happening to him. Like the end of his life was just an inconvenience.

"Does it ever . . . scare you?" I dared to ask him.

He took a while before he answered. "A lot of things scare me," he said. Then he looked at his unfinished gravestone in the middle of the dying yard. "No doubt about it—I'm going to have to start over."

Before I left, I stopped by Kjersten's room. She was sitting at her desk, doing homework. I suppose she was the type of student who would do homework on a Saturday. I knocked even though the door was open, because there's this instinct we're born with that says you don't walk into a girl's room uninvited, and even when you're invited, you don't walk in too far unless, of course, you're related to each other, or her parents aren't home.

"Hi," I said. "Whatcha doin'?"

"Chemistry," she said.

"Are you studying whether *we* got chemistry?"

She laughed. I have to say, this whole you're-attractive-when-you're-embarrassed thing was great. It was like a free license to say all the things I'd never actually have the guts to say to a girl, because the more embarrassed it made me to say it, the more it worked in my favor.

She turned her chair slightly toward me as I stepped in. Still riding on the fumes of my chemistry line, I thought I might actually dredge up the guts to sit on the edge of her bed . . . Then I realized if I did, I wouldn't be much for conversation, because the phrase *My God, I'm sitting on Kjersten's bed* would keep repeating over and over in my mind like one of Christina's Himalayan mantras, and I might start to levitate, which would probably freak Kjersten out.

So instead of sitting down, I kind of just stood there, looking around.

"Nice room," I told her. And it was: it said a lot about her. There was a NeuroToxin concert poster on the wall, next to a piece of art that even I could recognize as Van Gogh. There was a mural on her sliding closet doors that she clearly had painted herself. Angels playing tennis. At least I think they were angels. They could have been seagulls—she wasn't that great of an artist.

"I like your mural," I said.

She grinned slightly. "No you don't, but thanks for saying so." Like I said, people can pick up my emotions like a podcast. "I like painting, but it's not what I'm good at," she told me. "That's okay, though, because if I was good, then I'd always worry if I was good *enough*. This way I can enjoy doing it, and I never have to care about being judged."

"In that case," I said, "I really DO like your mural. I wish I had the guts to do things I stink at."

She took a measured look at me. "Like what?" she asked.

Now I was put on the spot, because there were so many things to chose from. I thought of her on the debate team, and finally settled on, "I'm not very good speaking in front of an audience."

"It just takes practice. I could teach you."

"Sure, why not?" I was thrilled by the prospect of her coaching me in verbal expression, even though me being a public speaker was about as likely as angels playing tennis. Or seagulls. "I promise to give speeches even worse than you paint," I told her.

She laughed, I laughed, and then the moment became awkward.

"So . . ." I said.

"So . . ." she said.

What happened next was kind of like jumping off the ten-meter platform at the Olympic pool they built when someone in public planning got high and actually believed the Summer Olympics might come to Brooklyn. A couple of years ago, I stood on that platform for five minutes that seemed like an hour, while my friends watched. In the end the only way I was able to jump was to imagine that I was a nonexistent ultracool version of myself. That way I could trick my self-preservation instinct into believing it wasn't actually me jumping.

Standing there in front of Kjersten, I dug down, found ultracool Antsy sipping on a latte somewhere in my head, and pulled him forth.

"So I was wondering if maybe you'd like go out sometime," I heard myself say. "A movie, or dinner, or trip to Paris, that kinda thing."

"Paris sounds nice," Kjersten said. "Will we fly first class?"

"No way!" I told her. "It's by private jet, or nothing." I was dazzling myself with my own unexpected wit, but then ultracool Antsy left for Starbucks, and I was alone to deal with the fallout of his cleverness.

"A movie would be nice," she said.

"Great . . . uh . . . yeah . . . uh . . . right." This is like the guy who lifts a five-hundred-pound barbell, then realizes he has no idea how to put it down without dying in the process. "A movie's a good choice," I told her. "It's dark, so people you know won't see us together."

"Why would that matter?"

"Well, you know—you being older and all."

"Antsy," she said, in a lecturing tone that really made her sound older, "that doesn't matter to me."

"Well, good," I said, enjoying the prospect of walking into the multiplex with Kjersten. "And anyway, a movie-theater date will give me lots of great opportunities to be embarrassed."

"I certainly hope so," she said, smirking. Which of course made me go red, which of course made her smirk even more.

This was all going so well! It would have been perfect, except for the fact that her father was weird, and her brother was dying. She must have read what I was thinking, because her smile faded and she looked away.

"I'm sorry about my father," she said.

I shrugged, playing dumb. "He didn't do anything."

"He came home," she said. "These days, that's enough."

Even though I was curious, I didn't want to ask what she meant, just in case she didn't want to tell. I looked at the mural, giving her time to gather her thoughts. Then she said, "He was a partner in a law firm, but a few months ago the firm fell apart. He hasn't worked since."

"But he's gone all the time—what does he do all day, look for work?"

And Kjersten said, "We don't know."

Recipes for Disaster from
the Undisputed Master of Time,
Live on Your TV Screen

7 After my Kjersten encounter, I walked home, nearly getting run over twice on the way, because my head was stuck in an alternate universe. Everything Ümlaut was one step removed from reality; the way they dealt with Gunnar's illness; the Mystery of the Disappearing Dad—even the fact that Kjersten was going to date me was weird, although it was the kind of weirdness I needed more of in my life.

My own father's arrival at home later that same night didn't raise the homeland security index, as it did in the Ümlaut household. That was mainly because everyone but me was already in bed.

"Hi, Antsy," he said as he shuffled into the kitchen. "You're up late."

"Just came down for a drink," I told him, even though I'd been stalking around the house all night with thoughts of Kjersten and Gunnar clogging up my brain. We sat down at the table. He grabbed himself some leftovers from the fridge, and I ate a little, even though I wasn't hungry. I thought it was strange how he can be at a restaurant all night, then come home and have to eat leftovers.

"I heard your friend is real sick," he said. "I'm sorry."

That surprised me. "I didn't know you knew about it."

"Your sister keeps me informed on things."

I could tell he wanted to say something meaningful. Thoughtful. But whenever he opened his mouth, all that came out was a yawn, which made me yawn, and pretty soon whatever he wanted to say got KO'd by the sandman. We left the dirty dishes in the sink, too tired to put them in the dishwasher, and said our good nights.

It was like this more and more between us—more yawning, and less talking. For my father, the restaurant was like the crabgrass in Gunnar's backyard. It had taken over everything. Even on Monday, which was supposed to be his day off, he would do taxes, or go to the fish market to get a jump on the fancy Manhattan restaurants. I think I liked it better when he had a mindless corporate job. His work was miserable, but when he wasn't working, he did stuff. Now, instead of a job and a paycheck, he had a business and a "calling"—as if feeding Brooklyn was a holy mission.

As I went to bed that night, I thought about Mr. Ümlaut, and the weirdness that filled that house like a gas leak. If nothing else, I could be thankful that my own family weirdness was not lethal.

I got a call from Lexie on the way to school the next morning.

"I want to make sure you're free on Saturday the nineteenth," she said.

"Let me check with my social secretary." I glanced over at some fat guy sitting next to me on the bus. "Yeah, I'm free." And then I realized with a little private glee that I might actually need to keep a social calendar now, if things worked out with Kjersten.

The nineteenth was the first day of Christmas vacation, when rich people went off to exotic places where they hate Americans. Sure enough, Lexie said, "My parents are flying me to the Seychelles, to spend the holidays with them," and she added "again," as if it would make me feel better to know she was legitimately embarrassed by her lap of luxury. "They haven't bothered to visit since the summer, so I have to go—but before I do, I've planned a special adventure for Grandpa."

The phone signal kept going in and out—all I heard was something about a team of engineers and lots of steel cable.

"Sounds like fun," I told her. Sure, I could do it. It's not like "vacation" was in my family's vocabulary since the restaurant opened. Then she got to the real reason for her call.

"Oh, and by the way, I'm having dinner at the restaurant with Raoul, and you're invited."

By "the restaurant," I knew she meant Crawley's, her grandfather's first restaurant. By "you're invited," she could have meant a whole lot of things.

"Just me?" I asked.

"No. You . . . and a date . . . if you like."

Now I knew what "you're invited" actually meant. "Wow—an invitation to a five-star restaurant for me and a date. Wouldn't it be easier to put one of those electronic tags on my ear before you release me into the wild?"

She huffed into the phone.

"Admit it—you just want to keep track of me."

She didn't deny it, she just continued the hard sell. "Don't you think whatserface will be impressed if you take her out for a fancy lobster dinner on your first date?"

"How do you know it's our first date?"

"Is it?"

"Maybe it is, maybe it isn't."

She huffed again. I was really enjoying this.

"C'mon," she said, "are you going to turn down a free meal at one of Brooklyn's most expensive restaurants?"

"Ooh! Manipulating me with money," I teased. "You're sounding more and more like your grandfather every day."

"Oh, shut up!"

"Admit it—you're curious to know what kind of girl would kiss me in a school hallway."

At last she caved. "Well, do you blame me? And besides, I really want you to meet Raoul. It's important to me."

"Why? It's not like you need my approval to be dating him."

"Well," she said after a moment's thought, "I'll give you mine, if you give me yours."

Lexie was right about me not being able to turn down the invitation. She had pushed my buttons, and we both knew it. It wasn't the money thing—it was the fact that I desperately wanted to impress Kjersten.

I arrived at school in full grapple with the concept of going on a date with an ex-girlfriend, a prospective girlfriend, and a guy who clicks. I was so distracted, I had to go back to my locker twice for things I forgot, making me late for my first period. Even before I sat in my seat, the teacher handed me a yellow slip summoning me to the principal's office for crimes unknown. People saw the yellow slip and reflexively leaned away.

This was my first experience in a high school principal's office. I don't know what I was expecting that would be different from middle school. Fancier chairs? A minibar? I wasn't scared, like I used to be when I was younger—I was more annoyed by the inconvenience of whatever punishment was forthcoming.

Our principal, Mr. Sinclair, tried to be an intimidating administrator, but he just couldn't sell it. It was his hair that undermined him every step of the way. Everyone called it "The Magic Comb-over." Because if you were looking at him straight-on—the way he might see himself in a mirror—he actually appeared to have hair. But when viewed from any other angle, it became clear that he had only twelve extremely long strands woven strategically back and forth over a scalp that had suffered its own human dust bowl.

It was even harder to take him seriously today, because as I stepped into his office I could see his tie was flipped over his shoulder. There's only one reason a guy has his tie flipped over his shoulder. If you haven't figured it out, you don't deserve to be told.

So I'm sitting there, trying to decide which is worse: pointing out that his tie is over his shoulder and embarrassing him, or not saying anything, which would make it even more embarrassing once he realized it for himself. Either way he'd take it out on me, so this was a lose-lose situation. What made it worse is that I couldn't stop smirking about it.

He poured himself a glass of sparkling water, offering me some, but I just shook my head.

"Mr. Bonano," he said in his serious administrative voice, "do you know why I've called you in?"

I couldn't take my eyes off his tie. I snickered and tried to disguise it as a cough. I sensed myself about to launch into a full-on giggle fit, and I prayed for a light fixture to fall from the ceiling and knock me unconscious before I could—because then I'd become sympathetic.

"I said, do you know why I called you in?"

I nodded.

"Good. Now let's talk about this situation with Gunnar Ümlaut."

"Your tie's over your shoulder," I said.

There was a brief moment where I could tell he was thinking, *Should I just leave it there, and insist it's there for a reason?* But in the end, he sighed, and flipped the tie down . . . right into the glass of sparkling water.

By now, my eyes are tearing from holding back the laughter—and then he says, "I never liked this tie anyway," so he takes it off, and drops it in the trash.

That's when I lost it. Not a giggle fit. No—this was an all-out raging guffaw fest; the kind that leaves your insides hurting and your limbs quivering when you're done.

"HahahahahahahahaI'msorry," I squealed. "Hahahahahahaha can'thelpithahahahahaha."

"I'll wait," said the man who had the power to expel me.

I tried to stop by tensing all my muscles, but that didn't work. Finally I made myself imagine the look on my mother's face when she found out I was expelled from the New York City Public School System for laughing at my principal, and that image drowned my laughter just as effectively as the sparkling water had drowned his tie.

"Are you done?"

I took a deep breath. "Yes, I think so."

He waited until the last of my convulsions faded, pouring the glass of sparkling water into a bonsai at the edge of his desk. "What's life if we can't laugh at ourselves?" he said. Oddly, I found myself respecting him all of a sudden, for the way he kept his cool.

"How many hours?" I asked, not wanting to draw this out any longer than necessary.

"I'm not sure I understand the question?"

"I got detention, right? Because of the stuff with Gunnar. I just want to know how many hours? Does it include Saturday school? Do my parents have to know, or can we keep this between you and me?"

"I don't think you understand, Anthony." And then he smiled. It's not a good thing when principals smile.

"So . . . I'm suspended? C'mon, it's not like I hurt anybody— it's only pieces of paper—I was trying to make the guy feel better about dying and all. How many days?"

"You're not in trouble," said Principal Sinclair. "I called you in because I wanted to donate a month of my own."

I just stared at him. Now it was his turn to laugh at me, but he didn't bust up laughing like I did, he just chuckled. "Actually," he said, "I'm impressed by what you've started. It shows a level of compassion I rarely see around here."

"So . . . you want me to write you up a contract?"

"For me, and for the secretaries in the front office—and for Mr. Bale."

"The security guard wants to give a month, too?"

"You've started a schoolwide phenomenon, Anthony. That poor boy is lucky to have a friend like you."

He gave me a list of names to write contracts up for, and I was a little too shell-shocked to say much more. Then, just before I left, I looked into the trash can. "Keep that tie," I told him. "Throw away the yellow paisley one. *That's* the one everyone makes fun of."

He looked at me like I had just given him an early Christmas gift. "Thank you, Anthony! Thank you for letting me know."

I left with a list of five names, and the strange, unearthly feeling that comes from knowing your principal doesn't hate your guts.

Following up on his schoolwide-phenomenon speech to me, Principal Sinclair insisted that I go on Morning Announcements, to make the whole donated-month thing legitimate school business.

Morning Announcements are kind of a joke at our school. I mean, we got all this video equipment, right, but no one knows how to use it. There's an anchor girl who reads cue cards like she's still stuck in the second level of Hooked on Phonics. And let's not forget the kid who has the nervous habit of adjusting himself on-air whenever he's nervous—which is whenever he's on-air. Occasionally Ira would submit a funny video, but lately there hasn't been much worth watching.

"Just read your lines off the cue cards," the video techie told me, but like I said, public speaking ranks right up there with being eaten alive by ants on my list of unpleasant activities.

After doing my own morning announcement, I now know firsthand why those other kids look like idiots on TV, and I have new respect for Crotch Boy and Phonics Girl.

"Hello, I'm Anthony Bonano with news for you. As many of you know, our friend Gunnar Ümlaut has been diagnosed with PMS, which is a rare life-threatening disease, pause, so I'm asking you, point at camera, to open up your hearts and donate a month of your life as a symbolic gesture, to show Gunnar that we really care. And in return, you'll get a T-shirt that says 'Gunnar's Time Warriors.' Really? There's a T-shirt? Cool! Our goal is to collect as much time as possible. Remember, 'Don't be a dunth. Donate a month.' Now excuse me while I go beat the crap out of whoever wrote that. Did I just say crap on live TV?"

Crotch Boy, Phonics Girl, and now the Blithering Wonder.

It began even before I went to my next class. I was grabbed in the hallway by people who didn't seem to care how moronic I looked on TV. They all wanted to make time donations. Everyone had their own reason for it. One guy did it to impress his girlfriend. One girl hoped it would get her into the popular crowd. Although I didn't want to spend all my free time at my computer printing out time contracts, I couldn't just walk away from what I had started, could I? Besides—there was a kind of power to being the go-to guy. The Master of Time. I even felt like I should start dressing for the part, you know? Like wearing a shirt and tie, the way the basketball team does on the day of a big game. So I found this tie covered with weird melting clocks designed by some dead artist named Dolly. Okay, I admit it, this was really starting to go to my head—like when Wendell Tiggor said he wanted to donate some time.

"You can't," I told him, "on account of Gunnar needs *life,* not wastes-of-life."

The thing is, Tiggor's famous for having really lame comeback lines, like, "Oh yeah? If I'm a waste of life, then you're a stupid stupidhead." (Sometimes the person he was insulting would have to feed him a decent comeback line out of pity.)

This time, however, Tiggor didn't even try. He just pouted and slumped away. Why? Because the Master of Time had spoken, and he was deemed unworthy.

What happened next, well, I guess I could blame it on Skaterdud, but it's not his fault—not really. I blame it on Restless Recipe syndrome. That's something my father once taught me.

It was a month or so before the restaurant first opened, and he was trying to figure out what the official menu would be. It was the first time in his life he'd been forced to write down recipes he had always just kept in his head.

He and Mom were in the kitchen together, cooking one meal after another, which we were giving away to neighbors, because not even Frankie could eat an entire menu. Mom had taken courses in French cooking last year, after finally admitting that Dad was the better Italian chef. It was her way of staking out new taste-bud territory. They had created these fusion French-Italian dishes, but that particular night as they cooked, Dad kept having to stop Mom from adding new ingredients.

"You know what your mother's problem is?" he said to me as they cooked. He knew better than to ever criticize Mom directly. It always had to be bounced off a third person, the way live TV from China has to bounce off a satellite. "She suffers from 'Restless Recipe syndrome.'"

Mom's response was to throw me a sarcastic "Oh, please" gaze, that I would theoretically relay back to my father at our stove somewhere in Beijing.

"It's true! No matter what recipe she's cooking, she can't leave it alone—she has to change it."

"Listen to him! As if he doesn't do the exact same thing!"

"Yes—but at a certain point I stop. I let the recipe be. But your mother will get a recipe absolutely perfect—and then the next time she cooks it, she's gotta add something new. Like the time she put whiskey in the marinara sauce."

It made me laugh when he mentioned it. Mom had added so much whiskey, we all got drunk. It's a cherished family memory that I'll one day share with my children, and/or therapist.

Finally she turned to talk to him directly. "So—I didn't cook out the alcohol enough—big deal. I'll have you know I saw that on the Food Channel."

"So go marry the Food Channel."

"Maybe I will."

They looked at each other, pretending to be annoyed, then Dad reached around and squeezed her left butt cheek, she grinned and grabbed his, then the whole thing became so full of inappropriate parental affection, I had to leave the room.

I'm like my father in lots of ways, I guess, but in this respect I'm like my mother. Even when the recipe's working perfectly, I can never leave well enough alone.

With about a dozen time contracts to fill out—each one a little bit different—I tried to hurry home from school that day, hoping to avoid anyone else who wanted to shave some time off their miserable existence. That's when I ran into Skaterdud. At first he rolled past me on his board like it was just coincidence, but a second later he looped back around. He flustered me with his eight-part handshake before he started talking.

"Cultural Geography, man," he said, shaking his head—it was a class we were both in together. "I just don't get it. I mean—is it culture? Is it geography? You know where I'm going, right?"

"The skate park?" I answered. Sure, it was closed for the winter, but that never stopped Skaterdud before.

"I'm talking conceptually," he said. "Gotta follow close or you're not never gettin' nowhere."

I've learned that silence is the best response when you have no idea what someone is talking about. Silence, and a knowing nod.

"I'm thinking maybe one favor begets another, *comprende*?"

I nodded again, hoping he hadn't suddenly become bilingual. It was hard enough to understand him in one language.

"So you'll do it?" he asked.

"Do what?" I had to finally ask.

He looked at me like I was an imbecile. "Write my Cultural Geography paper for me."

"Why would I do that?"

"Because," he said, "I'm gonna give up six whole months of my life to your boy Gunnar."

That got my interest. No one had offered that much. The Master of Time was intrigued.

Skaterdud laughed at the expression on my face. "Ain't no biggie," he said. "It's not like it's never gonna matter—'cause don't I already know when I'm gonna be pushin' up posies? Or seaweed, in my case? *That* date with destiny ain't never gonna change, because the fortune-teller's prediction would have already taken into account whatever life I'd give away to Gunnar. Smart, right? Yeah, I got this wired!"

I was actually following his logic, and it scared me. "So . . . why just six months?" I said, playing along. "If your future's all set in stone no matter what you do, why not give a year?"

"Done," said Skaterdud, slapping me on the back. "Don't forget—that Cultural Geography paper's due Friday."

"Whoa! Wait a second! I didn't say it was a deal." I was getting all mad now, because I felt like I was a sucker at a carnival, and had gotten tricked into this—so I said the first thing that came to mind, which, sadly, was: "What's in it for me?"

Skaterdud shrugged. "What do you want?"

I thought about how stockbrokers get commissions when they make a deal, so I thought, *Why not me?* "One extra month commission for me. Yeah, that's it. An extra month to do with as I please."

"Done," he said again. "Let me read the paper before you turn it in so I know what I wrote."

I, Reginald Michaelangelo Smoot, aka Skaterdud, in addition to the twelve months donated to Gunnar Ümlaut in the attached contract, do hereby bequeath one month to Anthony Paul Bonano for his own personal use in any way he sees fit, including, but not limited to:

A.) Extending his own natural life.

B.) Extending the life of a family member or beloved pet.

C.) Anything else, really.

R.M. Smoot
Signature

Ralphy Sherman
Signature of Witness

Who Needs Cash When You've Got Time Coming Out of Your Ears?

8 I have never been in the habit of cheating at school. I mean, sure, the occasional glance at my neighbor's paper on a multiple-choice test or a list of dates written on my forearm, but nothing like what Skaterdud wanted me to do. Now not only did I have to write two passing papers, but I had to make one of them sound like he wrote it—which meant sounding all confusing but making enough sense to get a passing grade.

The Dud's paper got a B with an exclamation point from the teacher, and since I used all the good stuff in his paper, I got a C-minus on mine. Serves me right. The Dud gave me my month commission the morning we got our grades back, slapped me on the back when he saw my grade, and said, "You'll do better next time."

That day I went off campus to get pizza for lunch, because the lunch ladies were secretly spreading the word that this was a good day to do a religious fast.

Problem was, I didn't have any money. Rishi, who ran the

pizza place down the street, was Indian. Not Native American, but Indian Indian—like from India—and, as such, made pizza that was nothing like the Founding Fathers ever envisioned. Not that it was bad—actually each type he made was amazing, which is maybe why the place was always crowded, and he could keep raising his prices.

I stood there, drooling over a Tandoori Chicken and Pepperoni that had just come out of the oven, and began rummaging through my backpack for spare change—but all I came up with were two nickels, and a Chuck E. Cheese game token that came out as change from one of those high-tech vending machines that was either defective or knew exactly what it was doing.

Rishi looked at me, and just shook his head. Meanwhile the people in line behind me were getting impatient. "C'mon," said Wailing Woody, his beefy arm around his girlfriend's shoulder. "Either order or get out of the way."

What I did next was probably the result of low blood sugar. I opened my binder to see if maybe some coins got stuck under the clasp, and saw the page I had gotten from Skaterdud. My commission. I pulled it out, looked once more at the pizza, and desperately held it up to Rishi.

"I don't have cash, but what about this?" I said. "One month of some guy's life."

A couple of people in line snorted, but not everyone. After all, I had been on Morning Announcements. I was legit. People actually got quieter, waiting to see what Rishi would do. He took it from me, laughed once, laughed twice, and I figured my religious fast was about to begin . . . until he said, "What kind of pizza would you like?"

I was still staring at him, waiting for the punch line, when Woody nudged me and said, "Order already!"

"Uh . . . how many slices is it worth?"

"Two," Rishi said, without hesitation, like it was written on the menu.

I ordered my two slices of Tandoori Chicken-and-Pepperoni, and as he served them he said to me, "I shall frame this and hang it on the wall, there." He pointed to a wall that held a bunch of photos of minor celebrities like the Channel Five weatherman, and Cher. "It will be the cause of much conversation! Next!"

At this point, I'm just figuring I'm lucky—that this is a freak thing. But like I said, other people saw this—people who hadn't eaten, and maybe their brains were working like that high-tech vending machine, which, when I got back to school, gave me a can of Coke for a Chuck E. Cheese token, thinking it was a Sacagawea dollar coin.

The second I popped that soda open, Howie appeared out of nowhere, in a very Schwa-like way, complaining of the kind of thirst that ended empires. "Please, Antsy, just one sip. I swear on my mother's life I won't backwash."

I took a long, slow guzzle from the can, considering it. Then I said, "What's it worth to you?"

I walked away with two weeks of his life.

There's this thing called "supply and demand." You can learn about this in economics class, or in certain computer games that simulate civilizations. You also can blow up those civilizations with nuclear weapons—which is only fun the first couple of times, and then it's like enough already—why spend three hours building a civilization if you're just gonna blow it up? That's three hours of your life you're never gonna get back—and ever since time shaving became a part of my daily activities, I've become very aware of wasted time—whether it be time wasted on the couch watching reruns, or time spent destroying simulated nations. When I first got that game, by the way, it cost fifty bucks, but now you can get it in the sale bin for $9.99. *That's* supply and demand. When everybody wants something and there's not enough to go around, it costs more. But if nobody wants it, it costs next to nothing. In the end, it's people who really decide how much something is worth.

As the undisputed Master of Time, I was the one in complete control of the time-shaving industry. That meant I controlled the supply, and now that I knew I could trade time for other stuff, I began to wonder how big the demand could be.

Turns out I didn't have to wait long to find out. The next morning, Wailing Woody Wilson came to me with his girlfriend to settle a dispute.

"I forgot we had a date last night, and Tanya was all mad at me."

"I'm still mad at you," Tanya reminded him. She crossed her arms impatiently and chewed gum in my general direction.

"Yeah," said Woody. "So I said I'd give her a month of my life." Then he looked at me pleadingly, like I had the power to make it all better.

Well, maybe I'm psychic, or maybe I'm smart, or maybe my stupidity quotient was equal to theirs, because I had anticipated just this sort of thing. In fact, the night before, I had printed out a dozen blank contracts—all they needed to do was fill in the names. I reached into my backpack and pulled a contract out of my binder . . . along with a certificate that would give me my own bonus week as payment for the transaction.

"Oh, and while we're at it," said Woody, "I'll throw in a month for Gunnar, too."

Tanya stenciled hearts all over her certificate, had it laminated, and posted it on the student bulletin board for the whole world to see. From that moment on, any guy who was not willing to give a month of his life to his girlfriend didn't have a girlfriend for long. I was swamped with requests. And on top of romantic commerce, there were other kids who came to me with same-as-cash transactions.

"My brother says he'll give me the bigger bedroom for a month of my life."

"I broke a neighbor's window, and I can't afford to pay for it."

"Could this be used as a Bar Mitzvah gift?"

Between all this new business, and the months that were still pouring in for Gunnar, I was collecting commissions left and right. In a few days I had thirty weeks of my own—which I was able to trade for everything from a bag of chips to a ride home on the back of a senior's motorcycle. I even got a used iPod; trading value: three weeks.

I could not deny the fact that I was getting amazing mileage out of Gunnar's imminent death. I felt guilty about it, since I never got permission from Gunnar to shamelessly use his terminality but as it turns out, Gunnar was actually pleased about it. *"Misery loves company, but it loves power to a greater degree,'"* he said, quoting Ayn Rand. "If my misery has the power to change your life, I'm happy."

Which I guess was okay—if he could be happily miserable, it was better than being miserably miserable—and Gunnar was definitely the most "up" down person I knew.

Even so, I couldn't tell him about the daydreams. Some things are best kept to oneself. See, you can't help the things you daydream about—and they're not always nice. In fact, sometimes they're more nightmares than dreams. Daymares, I'd guess you'd call them. Like the times you get all caught up imagining irritating arguments you never had but might have someday—or the daymares where you put yourself through worst-case scenarios. The sinkhole daymare, for example. See, a while back there was this news report about a sinkhole that opened up beneath a house in Bolivia or Bulgaria, or something. One morning in this quiet neighborhood, there's all this moaning and groaning in the walls, and then the ground opens up, a house plunges a hundred feet into the earth, and everyone inside is swept away in an underground river that nobody knew about except for some braniac in a nearby university who's been writing papers about it for thirty years, but does anybody read them? No.

So you get a daymare about this sinkhole, and what if it happened right beneath your house. Imagine that. You wake up one morning, hit the shower, and as you're drying off, suddenly the ground swallows your entire house, and there you are wrapped in a towel, trying to figure out which is more important at the moment—keeping the towel on, or keeping from being washed away in the underground river?

In these daymares you always survive—although occasionally you're the only one, and it ends with you telling the news reporters how you tried so desperately to save your family, if only they could have held on and been strong like you.

My current recurring daymare involved me at Gunnar's funeral. I'm there and it's raining, because it's always raining at funerals, and all the umbrellas are always black. Why is that? What happens to all those bright flowery umbrellas, or the Winnie-the-Pooh ones? So anyway, there I am holding a depressingly black umbrella with one hand, and my other hand is holding Kjersten, comforting her in her grief. I'm strong for her, and that makes us even closer—and yeah, I'm all broken up, but I don't show it except for maybe a single tear down one cheek. Then someone asks me to say something. I step forward, and unlike in real life, I say the perfect thing that makes everyone smile and nod in spite of their tears, and makes Kjersten respect me even more. And then I snap myself out of it, seriously disgusted that in my head, Gunnar's funeral is all about me.

In a couple of days I had gone through my entire paper supply printing out time-contract forms, and donations were still pouring in. The student council, refusing to be outdone by a lowly commoner like me, put up a big cardboard thermometer outside the main office. I was instructed to notify them daily how much time had been collected for Gunnar so they could mark it off on the thermometer. The goal they set was fifty years, because fifty additional years would make Gunnar sixty-five, and they felt that giving him time beyond retirement age would just be silly.

"It's amazing how generous people can be when you're dying," Gunnar said when I handed him the next stack of months.

"So what's the word from Doctor G?" I asked him. "Any good news?"

"Dr. G is noncommittal," Gunnar told me. "He says I'll be fine, until I'm not."

"That's helpful." I wondered which was worse, having a disease with few symptoms, or one with enough symptoms to let you know where you stood. "Well," I offered lamely, "at least your lips haven't gone blue."

Gunnar shrugged, and swayed a little, like maybe he was having one of his dizzy spells.

"So . . . you think you might make it all the way through next year?" I asked.

Gunnar looked at the stack of time in his hands. "It's possible that I could linger."

Which was more than I could say for his backyard. I went over to his house that Wednesday to continue work on the dust bowl. It was hard spending time in the Universe of Ümlaut now. There were just too many things hanging in the air. Gunnar's imminent death, for example. And the weirdness with their father, and then there was the looming date with Kjersten.

I know that a date with the girl of your dreams shouldn't "loom," but it does. It's worse when you gotta see each other *after* you've asked her out but *before* the actual date. It's kind of like saying good-bye to somebody and then realizing you both gotta get in the same elevator. You can't talk because you already said good-bye, so usually you both stand there feeling like idiots.

So now I'd asked Kjersten out, she said yes, and here I was at her house two days before the actual date. I knew as soon as she got home from tennis practice, it would be elevator time.

As for the Ümlaut backyard, it was officially dead—nothing had survived our herbicidal assault. Even a few of the neighbors' plants had suffered, because the herbicide had seeped into their soil a bit.

"That's what you call 'collateral damage,'" Gunnar said. He looked at the growing desolation around us. "Maybe we can hire some bums and urchins to populate the scene."

Right about then Mrs. Ümlaut called from the house, asking if we wanted hot chocolate since it was getting cold. Instead we asked for "a cuppa joe straight from the pot," which was satisfyingly Steinbeck-like. Of course it would have worked better if she hadn't brought out an automatic-drip glass pot with a floral design.

That's when Kjersten got home, and came out to say hello. I was happy to see her, in spite of it feeling awkward.

"I hear you're the school's official Cupid," she said with a smirk, obviously referring to the new currency of love in our school, for which I was supplying the paperwork.

"I don't shoot the arrows, I just load the bow."

Gunnar groaned and rolled his eyes at that. The smile Kjersten had for me faded when she looked at the big hunk of granite in the middle of our dust bowl. I had gotten so used to seeing the unfinished tombstone there, I had forgotten about it.

"You should move that thing," Kjersten told him. "It's an eyesore."

"Naa," Gunnar said. "People died in the dust bowl, so having a gravestone makes it more authentic."

Kjersten threw me a look, but I turned away. I knew better than to put myself in the middle of this. Instead I just busied myself brushing dirt clods off my jeans.

"Are you staying for dinner?" Kjersten asked.

"No," I told her, way too quickly. "I'm working at my dad's restaurant tonight." After the last Ümlaut meal, I'd rather be pushing menus and pouring water than having to sit at that table again. I think I'd rather be ON the menu than have to eat with their father, if he came home.

Kjersten must have read my mind, because she said, "It's not always that bad."

"Yes it is," said Gunnar, chugging some of the hot coffee.

"Do you always have to be so negative?" Kjersten asked. I wanted to tell her that maybe she should cut her dying brother a little slack, but siding against a prospective girlfriend in any situation is unwise.

Gunnar shrugged. "I'm not being negative, I'm just telling the truth." Then he glanced at the coffeepot. "Just like Benjamin Franklin said, 'Truth can only be served from a scalding kettle; whether you blister or make tea is up to you.'"

Kjersten gave him a disgusted look that actually made her appear slightly less beautiful, which I hadn't thought was possible. "My brother's nowhere near as smart as he thinks he is."

Then she turned to storm off.

"I'm smart enough to know where Dad goes," said Gunnar.

It stopped Kjersten in midstorm, but only for an instant. Then she picked up her stride and continued inside, without even turning back to give Gunnar an ounce of satisfaction.

Once she was gone, Gunnar and I continued to hurl plants into Hefty bags in silence. Now that Kjersten had reminded me of the gravestone, I couldn't stop looking at it. The elephant in the dust bowl. But for once Gunnar wasn't obsessing over his own eventual doom. His thoughts were somewhere else entirely.

"Three times," Gunnar said, finally breaking the silence. "Three times I checked the odometer in my dad's car before he left and after he got back, then did the math. All three times, he traveled somewhere that was between a hundred and thirty and a hundred and forty miles away."

It was good detective work, I guess, but was only half the job. "It doesn't mean much if you don't know which direction he's going."

"Try northwest." Then Gunnar reached into his pocket and flipped me a red disk. "I found this in his car." Even before I caught it, I knew what it was.

"A poker chip? He's playing poker?"

"Probably blackjack or craps," Gunnar said "Take a closer look."

The chip was red with black stripes around the edge. There was an *A* printed in the center.

"The Anawana Tribal Casino," Gunnar said. "And, according to MapQuest, it's one hundred and thirty-seven miles from our front door."

Echolocate *This*

9 Everybody gambles. You don't have to go to a tribal casino to do it either. You do it every day without even realizing it. It could be as simple as skipping your math homework on Tuesday night because you know that your math teacher has cafeteria duty before class on Wednesday, so chances are homework won't be checked, because cafeteria duty will crush the spirit of any teacher.

You gamble when you put off applying for a summer job until July 1—betting that your desire to earn money is outweighed by the fact that you probably won't get the job anyway, so why bother wasting valuable time that could be spent not cleaning your room, or not doing the dishes, or not doing math homework on Tuesday?

The point is, every decision we make is a gamble. My parents are in the middle of a major gamble themselves. They're risking everything on the restaurant. I admire them for it, because they're betting on themselves, which is kind of a noble thing to do. Then, on the other hand, there are the ten lottery tickets my mom buys each week, which are just plain embarrassing.

"What's the point?" my brother Frankie says whenever he sees one lying around. "Do you know scientists have determined that you're more likely to get struck by lightning five times than win?" Which makes me wonder if some poor slob gets his fifth lightning strike every time someone wins the lottery, and how badly do you have to piss off God to be that guy?

"I know the odds are terrible," Mom always says. "But I still get excited. The excitement is worth ten dollars a week."

I guess that's okay—but what happens when ten dollars becomes a hundred? Or a thousand? When does it become a problem? It must happen so slowly, so secretly, that nobody notices until it becomes a terminal illness of its own.

See, my parents can gamble with their restaurant and it's okay, because hard work and talent can change the odds in your favor.

But nothing changes the odds in a casino; they got all these big fancy hotels in Vegas to prove it. The house takes back around 15 percent of all the money gambled, guaranteed. You might win a thousand bucks today and you'll be all excited, totally forgetting that over the past year you lost a lot more than you just won.

Life is kind of like that—I guess Gunnar knew that more than anyone. All our little daily thrills don't change the fact that our chips eventually run out. It's the scalding pot of truth we gotta make tea out of. The tea's pretty good most of the time, unless you're that poor slob who got struck by lightning five times. If you're him, I can't help you, except to point out that your life has the noble purpose of making the rest of us feel lucky.

I didn't know where Mr. Ümlaut was on the lightning-lottery scale, but I had a feeling he was standing in a stormy field, wearing lots of metal.

On Saturday night I was determined to put all the struggles of the Ümlaut family out of my mind entirely. This was to be a night of fun. This was my first date with Kjersten.

Of course we wouldn't be alone—it was a double date with Lexie and Clicking Raoul. Like I said, I couldn't turn down the chance to take Kjersten to a fancy restaurant, and Crawley's was among the fanciest. I was quick to discover that the responsibility of dating an older woman is enough to fry all your brain cells. The logistics alone . . . How are you going to travel? Does she drive you? Is that humiliating if she does? Do you take a bus, and if you do, does that make you seem cheap? Do you call a taxi and go broke from cab fare even before you get where you're going? Or do you walk there together and have everyone snicker at you because she's taller than you?

In the end, I settled for simply meeting her at the restaurant.

My mother raised an eyebrow when I let it slip before I left that Kjersten had a car.

"This girl you're seeing drives?"

"No," I answered. "It's one of those self-driving cars—she just sits there."

My mother is usually pretty quick, but I suppose she didn't

trust her own grasp of changing technology, because she said, "You're kidding, right?" It was very Howie-like. I found that disturbing.

"I'll be home by eleven," I told her as I headed out the front door. "And just in case I'm not, I put the morgue on your speed dial."

"Cut my heart out while you're at it."

"I'll put it on my to-do list."

I made a mental note to actually put the morgue on her speed dial. She'd be mad, but I also knew she'd laugh. Mom and I have a similar sense of humor. I find that disturbing, too.

I arrived ten minutes early, dressed in my best shirt and slacks. Kjersten arrived three minutes late, and was dressed for an evening on the Riviera.

"Is this too much?" she asked, looking at her gown that reflected light like a disco ball. "I heard that Crawley's has a dress code." Don't get me wrong, it wasn't tacky or anything—in fact, it was the opposite. Heads turned when she walked in. I kept expecting flashes from the paparazzi.

"It's perfect," I told her with a big grin. The gown and the way she had put up her hair made her look even older, and I started to imagine us like one of those tests they give little kids. The one that goes: *What's wrong with this picture?* A girl in a gown, crystal chandeliers, a waiter carrying lobsters, and Antsy Bonano. A first grader would pass this test easy.

I greeted her with a kiss on the cheek in clear view of the entire restaurant, in case there was any doubt who she was with.

"You look great," I told her. "But you already know that, right?"

We were seated at a table for four, and I wasn't quite sure whether I was supposed to sit next to her, or across from her, so I sat down first, and let her choose. This was probably the wrong thing to do, because the waiter gave me a look like my mother gives when I do something inexcusable. Then he went to pull out Kjersten's chair for her—clearly what I was supposed to have done.

"I hope you don't mind this double-date thing," I said.

"Just as long as they're not all double dates," she said with a little smile. She reached across the table and took my hand. "I've never been taken on a date to a place this fancy before. You score a ten."

Which meant there was nowhere to go but down.

"Of course," she said . . . a little bit awkwardly, "I've never been on a double date with a blind couple before."

"Don't worry—they're just like people who can see," I told her. "Except that they can't."

"I don't want to say or do anything wrong . . ."

"Don't worry," I told her, "that's *my* department."

Lexie and Raoul arrived a minute or so later, and I wondered where they'd been, since Lexie lives right upstairs, and then I wondered why I'd wondered. I went up to Lexie and took her hand. Kjersten was confused by this, until I guided Lexie's hand into hers. It was something I was just used to doing; it spared Lexie the awkwardness of an inexact docking procedure when it came to shaking hands.

We sat at a table that used to be reserved for famous people from Brooklyn, until they realized that people from Brooklyn who got famous never came back.

Lexie released Moxie, her Seeing Eye dog, from his harness as soon as we sat down, and he obediently took his place beside her chair.

We made awkward small talk for a while about the differences between public high school and their ultra-high-end school for the wealthy blind. For a brief but unpleasant few moments, the girls had this little tennislike discussion about me, like I wasn't there—all I could do was follow the ball back and forth.

"I like Antsy because he's not afraid to say what's on his mind," serves Kjersten.

"Believe me, I know," returns Lexie. "Even when he shouldn't say anything at all."

"Oh, but that's the fun part," Kjersten smashes for the point.

I decided a change in subject matter was called for.

"So," I said to Raoul as the busboy poured water not quite as expertly as I did, "you don't have a guide dog—is that because clicking does it all?"

"Pretty much," said Raoul proudly. "Echolocation makes canes and canine companions seem positively medieval." He'd been pretty quiet until now, but once the conversation became about him, he perked up. "Personally, I think it could be an adaptive trait. Evolutionary, you know?"

"Raoul doesn't have a guide dog because most people don't get them until they're older," Lexie explained curtly. "Technically I'm not supposed to have one either, but you know my grandfather—he pulled some strings."

"I don't need one, anyway," Raoul said. Then he clicked a few times and determined the relative location of our four water glasses, and the fact that mine was only half full, on account of the busboy had run out of water since he didn't check his pitcher the way you're supposed to before you start pouring. And he calls himself a busboy!

"That's amazing!" Kjersten said.

But I wasn't so convinced. "He could have heard the water being poured."

"Could have," Raoul said, "but I wasn't paying attention."

"Okay, then," I said, crossing my arms. "How many fingers am I holding up?"

"He can't be that specific," said Lexie, jumping to his aid, but Raoul clicked, and said: "None. You didn't even put up your hand."

Kjersten looked at me, and grinned.

"All right, Raoul wins," I admitted. "He's amazing."

"And the crowd goes wild!" said Raoul.

"Can we just order?" said Lexie, running her finger across the Braille menu. Maybe it was my imagination, but she was moving her finger a little too fast for her to actually read it. I've seen Lexie read before. I knew the pace of Braille—or at least *her* Braille. Kjersten was watching me watching her, so I looked away. Maybe a double date with Lexie wasn't a good idea after all.

"They're flying me out to Chicago next week," Raoul said. "To do a national talk show."

At that, Lexie closed her menu a little too hard. The sudden clap made Moxie rise to his feet, then sit back down again.

Raoul reached out, gently rubbed his hand along her sleeve, and then took her hand. "What's wrong, baby?"

I grimaced at that. I couldn't help myself. If you knew Lexie Crawley at all, you knew never to call her "baby." That, and the fact that he was holding her hand, just kind of gave me mental dry heaves. I mean, sure, I was dating Kjersten, but I think the human brain isn't designed to deal with situations like this.

I looked over at Kjersten, who noticed my reaction, and again I looked away.

"You don't have to accept all those TV invitations," Lexie told Raoul. "And you don't have to echolocate for people all the time. You're not a sideshow act."

"I don't mind."

"Well, you should."

Suddenly I found my menu to be a place of safety. "I'm thinking maybe the ribs," I said. "How about you, Kjersten?"

"Isn't this a seafood place?"

"Yeah, well, I don't like seafood."

That's when Kjersten's phone rang. Even her ring tone was cool. NeuroToxin's new hit. She pulled the phone out of her purse, looked at the number, then dropped it back in. "Not important," she said, although the look on her face said otherwise.

The waiter took our orders, and once he was gone, small talk became big silence, until Raoul said, "I can echolocate the number of people in the room—wanna see?"

Lexie stood up suddenly. "I need to freshen up." Moxie rose when she did, but she went off without him.

Even though Lexie knew this restaurant inside and out, there were enough people moving around to make navigating to the bathroom like flying through an asteroid field. I got up to escort her.

"I'll be right back," I said to Kjersten, who smiled at me politely. "I gotta go to the bathroom anyway."

As Lexie and I neared the restroom, I heard Kjersten's phone ring again. I glanced back just long enough to see her answer it.

"I like Raoul," I told Lexie. "He's kinda cool."

"If he ever stops talking about himself." We were at the restroom doors, but Lexie didn't make a move to go in. "Having a special ability is all fine and good. But there's got to be more to a person than sonar."

"Yeah . . . I guess if he didn't have that, he'd be pretty boring, huh." I thought about how the conversation was all about him and his uniqueness back at the table, and I realized it wasn't because he was conceited; it was because he had nothing else to talk about.

"Kjersten seems very nice," Lexie said. "I'm happy for you . . ." I knew Lexie well enough to know there was an implied "but" at the end of that sentence. I waited for the but to present itself.

"But . . . there's something about her," Lexie finally said. "I don't know, it's not quite right."

"You barely said a word to each other—how can you tell anything?"

"I have a sense about these things."

"Being blind doesn't make you psychic," I said, sounding more annoyed than I intended to. No—actually I intended to sound exactly like that.

"There's something in her tone of voice," Lexie said, "something in the silences. It's . . . *off*."

"So what? She's got family stuff going on, that's all," I said. "Her brother's illness."

"That may be part of the reason."

"The reason for what?"

"For why she's going out with you."

I didn't like the way this conversation was heading. "Maybe she just likes me—did you ever think of that?"

"Yes, but *why* does she like you?"

"Why does she need a reason? She just does! What—you think it's strange that a girl who's two years older than me, really smart, and looks like a supermodel would want to date me?" There are some things you just shouldn't say out loud. "Okay, maybe it *is* strange. But what's wrong with that? So she's strange. So am I—so are you—since when was there a law against that?"

"Maybe it's not you she likes. Maybe it's the *idea* of you."

"Yeah?" I said. "Well, maybe you should take the *idea* of yourself into that bathroom, because I don't want to talk to you anymore."

She stormed into the bathroom without anyone's help, and with the grace of someone who knew exactly where they were going. Any human asteroid in her way had better watch out. Well, I wasn't going to walk her back. I pulled aside the busboy who couldn't pour water right and told him to escort Miss Crawley back to the table when she was done.

She was jealous. That was it. Had to be. Just like I was jealous of her and her clicking celebrity boyfriend. But that would pass. Things were just getting started between Kjersten and me, and I wasn't going to let Lexie ruin it.

When I got back to the table, Kjersten was putting on her coat.

"What's the matter? You cold?"

"I'm sorry, Anthony. I've got to go."

My first response was to look at Raoul. "What did you do?" I asked, figuring maybe he clicked her cleavage, and told her the size of her bra.

"Nothing," said Raoul. "She had a phone call."

"It was my father. I'm grounded."

I just looked at her for a while in stunned denial, like the time I was a kid and my mother told me we're not going to Disney World, on account of the airline suddenly decided to go out of business.

"What? You can't get grounded in the middle of a date. That's like . . . that's like against the law."

"I was grounded *before* the date," she admitted. "I'm not supposed to be out, but my mom doesn't care, and my dad wasn't home."

"Exactly—he's never home, so that voids the grounding, right?"

"He's home now." She zipped up her jacket, sealing away the view of her amazing dress from me and the paparazzi.

"Can't you be like . . . rebellious or something?"

"I *was* rebellious—that's why I'm grounded."

I found myself wondering what she had done, and coming up with things that were probably much more exotic than what really happened. Then I said in a voice far more whiny than I meant it to be, "Can't you be rebellious with *me*?"

She looked at me, and I could tell that she really did want

to stay. But I could also tell from that look that she wouldn't. Then she kissed me, and by the time I recovered from the kiss, she was gone. The waiter, totally clueless, brought the meals and set them down, but right now it was just me and Raoul—and it was anyone's guess if Lexie would come out of the bathroom after what I said to her.

I sat down, dazed by the crash-and-burn of it all, and Raoul says, "So do you want me to echolocate the number of people in the room, or not?"

Collateral Damage, Relative Humidity, and Lemon Pledge in the Dust Bowl of My Life

10 I want to make it absolutely clear that what happened to Gunnar's neighbors was an accident—and for once, I get to share the blame with someone else.

With our dust-bowl due date just a few days away, Gunnar and I were under a time constraint, and we were working too hard on this Steinbeck project to get marked down for being late. I have experience in that department, and know for a fact that there are teachers who measure lateness in microseconds on that world clock they got in England. And there's no bottom to this pit. I actually once got a Z-minus on a late paper. I pointed out to the teacher that she coulda marked me even lower if she used the Russian alphabet, on account of it has something like thirty-three letters instead of twenty-six. She was impressed enough by the suggestion that she raised my grade to a Z-plus.

To avoid letter grades in the lower half of the alphabet, Gunnar and I needed to kill off the plants quickly to get our dust bowl rolling, so we used a lot of herbicide. Now Gunnar's next-door neighbors were all ticked off because their yards were smelling like toxic waste. It was Sunday morning. The day after my not-quite-a-date with Kjersten. I really didn't want to be there and have to face Mr. Ümlaut, who I held personally responsible for ruining my evening. And I didn't want to face Kjersten just yet, because it was too soon after the walkout. But I had to go through the house to get to the backyard. I was hoping Gunnar would answer the door, but he was already working out back.

Kjersten answered the door.

"Hi."

"Hi."

"Nice day."

"Sunny."

"Sun's good."

"Yeah."

"Anyway . . ."

"Right."

I tried to put an end to the misery by moving toward the back door, but she wasn't letting me. Not yet.

"Sorry about last night," she said. "We'll do it again, okay?"

"Yeah, sure, no problem."

"No," she said. "I mean it."

And I could tell that she really did mean it. Deep down, I had kind of felt that a ruined evening meant ruined hopes. It was good to know that another, better date was still on the horizon.

"When's your grounding over?" I asked.

"As soon as I get the grade back on my chemistry test tomorrow—and my father can see I didn't need to skip my tennis tournament to study."

I smiled. "And here I thought you cut school for a wild ski trip." Which was one of my tamer scenarios. I took her hand and stood there for a long moment that, believe it or not, didn't feel awkward at all, then I went out to the backyard.

There was all this cardboard in the yard, because today's project was a cardboard shack for Steinbeck's starving farmers. At the moment I arrived in our little dust bowl, Gunnar was being scolded by his next-door neighbor over the fence. "Look what you've done to my yard! It's all dead!"

"It's that time of year," I offered, pointing out the dead leaves around her yard. "That's why they call it 'fall.'"

"Oh yeah?" she said. "What about the evergreens?"

She indicated some bushes way across the yard that had gone a sickly shade of brown. Then she looked bitterly down at some thorny, leafless bushes in front of her that could have just been dormant if we didn't already know better—because if the herbicide had made it all the way across the yard, these nearby bushes were history.

"Do you have any idea how long I've cultivated this rose garden?"

My next response would have been a short and sweet "Oops," but Gunnar has last week's vocabulary word, which I lack: eloquence.

"'Only when the Rose withers can the beauty of the bush be seen,'" he told her. It shut her up and she stormed away.

"What does that even mean?" I asked after she was gone.

"I don't know, but Emily Dickinson said it."

I told him that quoting Emily Dickinson was just a little too weird, and he agreed to be more testosterone-conscious with his quotations. He looked over at the neighbors' yard, surveying the ruins of the garden. "A little death never hurt anyone," he said. "It gives us perspective. Makes us remember what's important."

I hadn't been too worried about the about the neighbors' plants dying until now. Collateral damage, right? Only this was more than just collateral damage—and only later did we realize why. See, guys all have this problem. It's called the we-don't-need-no-stinkin'-directions problem. Gunnar and I had bought half a dozen jugs of herbicide, coated the plants with the stuff like we were flocking Christmas trees, and we were satisfied with the results. We could have done a commercial for the stuff . . . However, if we had read the directions, we would have seen that the stuff was concentrated—you know, like frozen orange juice: we were supposed to use one part herbicide to ten parts water. So basically we sprayed enough of the stuff to kill the rain forests.

Now all the lawns around Gunnar's house, front and back, were going a strange shade of brown that was almost purple. Our dust bowl was spreading outward like something satanic.

When I got home, my mom wasn't with my dad at the restaurant, like she usually is on Sunday afternoons. She was home, cleaning. This was nothing unusual—but the sheer intensity of the scouring had me worried—like maybe the toxic mold was back, and this time it was personal.

Turns out, it was worse.

"Aunt Mona is coming to visit," Mom told me.

I turned to my sister Christina, who sat cross-legged on the couch, either doing homework or trying to levitate her math book. "No—tell me it's not true!" I begged.

Christina just lowered her eyes and shook her head in the universal this-patient-can't-be-saved gesture.

"How long?"

"How long till she comes, or how long will she stay?" Christina asked.

"Both."

To which Christina responded, "Next week, and only God knows."

It's always that way with Aunt Mona. Her visits are more like wartime occupations. She's the most demanding of our relatives—in fact, we sometimes call her "relative humidity," on account of when Mona's around, everybody sweats. See, Aunt Mona likes to be catered to—but lately the only catering Mom and Dad have been able to do is of the restaurant variety. Plus, when Aunt Mona arrives, all other things manage to get put on hold, and we're all expected to "visit" with her while she's here—especially those first couple of days. With the dust bowl due, tests in every class before Christmas vacation, another date to schedule with Kjersten, and Gunnar's illness hovering like a storm, Aunt Mona was the last thing I needed.

Just so you know, Aunt Mona's my father's older sister. She has a popular business selling perfume imported from places

I've never heard of, and might actually be made up—and she always wears her own perfume. I think she wears them all at one once, because whenever she visits, I break out in hives from the fumes, and the neighborhood clears of wildlife.

She's very successful and business-minded. Nothing wrong with that—I mean, my friend Ira's mom is all hard-core business, and she's a nice, normal, decent human being. But Aunt Mona is not. Aunt Mona uses her success in cruel and unusual ways. You see, Aunt Mona isn't just successful, she's *More Successful Than You,* whoever you happen to be. And even if she's not, she will find a way to make you feel like the pathetic loser you always feared you were, deep down where the intestines gurgle.

Aunt Mona works like 140-hour weeks, and frowns on anyone who doesn't. She has a spotless high-rise condo in Chicago, and frowns on anyone who doesn't. In fact, she spends so much time frowning and looking down her nose at people, she had a plastic surgeon change her nose and Botox her frown wrinkles.

It goes without saying, then, that Aunt Mona is the undisputed judge of all things Bonano—even though she changed her name to Bonneville because it sounded fancier, and because Mona Bonano sounded too much like that "Name Game" song. I'm sure as a kid she was constantly teased with "Mona-Mona-bo-bona, Bonano-fano-fo-fona." And as if Bonneville wasn't snooty enough, she added an accent to her first name, so now it's not Mona, it's Moná. I refuse on principle to ever pronounce it "Moná," and I know she resents it.

It turns out that Aunt Mona was considering moving her

entire company to New York, so she was going to be here for a while. She could, of course, afford one of those fancy New York hotels, where the maids clean between your toes and stuff, but there's this rule about family. It's kind of like the Ten Commandments, and the Miranda rights they read you when you get arrested: Thou shalt stay with thy relatives upon every visit, and anything you say can and will be used against you for the rest of your life.

So Mom's Lemon Pledging all the dining-room furniture until the wood shines like new, and she says to me, "You gotta be on your best behavior when Aunt Mona comes."

"Yeah, yeah," I tell her, having heard it all before.

"You gotta treat her with respect, whether you like it or not."

"Yeah, yeah."

"And you gotta wear that shirt she gave you."

"In your dreams."

Mom laughed. "If that shirt's in my dreams, they'd be nightmares."

I had to laugh, too. The fact that Mom agreed with me that the pink-and-orange "designer" shirt was the worst piece of clothing yet devised by man somehow made it okay to wear it. Like now it was an inside joke, instead of just an ugly shirt.

I picked up one of her rags and polished the high part of the china cabinet that she had trouble reaching. She smiled at me, kinda glad, I guess, that I did it before she asked.

"So, do I gotta wear the shirt in public?"

"No," she says. "Maybe," she adds. "Probably," she concludes.

I don't argue, because what's the use? When it comes to Aunt Mona, the odds of walking away a winner are worse than at the Anawana Tribal Casino. Anyway, I suppose wearing the shirt was better than Mom and Christina's fate. They'd have to wear one of Aunt Mona's perfumes.

Right around then the doorbell rang, and Mom looked up at me with wide eyes and froze. I know what she was thinking. Aunt Mona never showed up when scheduled. She would come early, she would come late, she would come on a different day altogether. But a whole week early?

"Naa," I said to Mom. "It couldn't be."

I went to answer it, fully prepared for a blast of flesh-searing fragrance. But it wasn't Aunt Mona—instead it was two kids—fourth or fifth graders by the look of them, holding out pieces of paper to me.

"Hi, we're collecting spare time for a kid who's dying or something—would you like to donate?"

"Let me see that!" I snatched one of the papers from them. It was my own blank contract—second- or third-generation Xerox, by the look of it. Someone had taken one of my official contracts and was turning out counterfeits!

"Where'd you get this? Who said you could do this?"

"Our teacher," said one kid.

"Our whole class is doing it," said the other.

"So are you going to donate, or what?"

"Get lost." I slammed the door in their faces.

So now collecting for Gunnar had become a school fund-raiser. I felt violated. Cheated. Betrayed by the educational system.

I didn't bother my parents with this—they had enough on their minds, and they'd probably just say "So what?" and they'd be right. It was petty and dumb to think that I owned the whole idea . . . but the thing is, I liked being the Master of Time. Now there were people running around, doing it on their own, without official leadership. They call that anarchy, and it always leads to things like peasants with pitchforks and torches burning things down.

"Think of those little kids as disciples," Howie said, when I mentioned it to him the next day. "Jesus' disciples did all the work for him after he wasn't around no more."

"Yeah, well, I'm still here—and besides, Jesus *knew* his disciples."

"That's only because the lack of technology in those days forced people to have to know each other. Now, because of computers, we really don't gotta know anybody, really."

Then he went on about how today the Sermon on the Mount would be a blog, and the ten plagues on Egypt would be reality TV. None of this addressed the issue, so I told Howie I was leaving, but by all means he should continue the conversation without me.

I think this whole prickly, offended feeling was the first warning. I was sensing things getting out of control—not just out of MY control, but out of control in general. My little idea of giving Gunnar a month to make him feel better was now turning into a monster. And everyone knows what they do to monsters. It's pitchforks and torches again. That happens, see, because people think the monster's got no soul.

As it turns out, they'd be right this time. My monster didn't have a soul . . . and I was about to find that out.

It's Amazing What You Can Get for $49.95

11 There's this junkyard off of Flatlands Avenue where they salvage anything they can from junked cars and dump the cars into massive piles before crushing them into metal squares about the size of coffee tables. It's the kind of place you might invent in a dream, although in a dream, the metal squares would talk to you, on account of they'd be haunted by the people who got murdered and thrown into the trunk before the car got crushed.

Gunnar and I went there looking for rusty engine parts to put in a corner of our dust bowl, to add to the atmosphere of despair.

I did most of the looking, because Gunnar was absorbed in the catalog he was reading. "What do you think of this one?" he said to me while I was looking at a pile of bumpers too modern for our purposes. I didn't look at the catalog because I didn't want any part of it.

"Tell you what. Why don't you make it a surprise?"

"Come on, Antsy, I need your opinion. I like this white one, but it's a little too girlie. And then this one—I don't know, the wood looks like my kitchen cabinets. That just feels weird."

"It *all* feels weird," I told him.

"It must be done."

"So let someone else do it. Why should you care? You're gonna be inside it, you're not gonna be looking at it."

Now he was getting all miffed. "It's about the image I want people to be left with, why can't you understand that? It needs to express who I was, and how I want to be remembered. It's about image—like buying your first car."

I glanced at the catalog and pointed. "Fine—then go with the gunmetal-gray one," I said, fairly disgusted. "It looks like a Mercedes."

He looked at it and nodded. "Maybe I could even put a Mercedes emblem on it. That would be cool."

The fact that Gunnar could discuss coffins like it was nothing didn't just freak me out, it made me angry. "Can't you just pretend like everything's okay and go about your life, like normal dying people?"

He looked at me like there was something wrong with me instead of him. "Why would I want to do that?"

"You're not supposed to be enjoying it. That's all I'm trying to say. Enjoy *other* stuff . . . but don't enjoy . . . that."

"Is it wrong to have a healthy attitude about mortality?"

Before I can even deal with the question, I hear from behind me—

"Yo! Dudes!"

I turn to see a familiar face coming out from behind a pile of taillights. It's Skaterdud. He gives me his official Skaterdud handshake, which I've done enough to actually remember this time. He does it with Gunnar, who fakes his way through it convincingly.

"D'ya get my kick-butt donation?" Skaterdud asks.

"Huh?" says Gunnar, "Oh, right—a whole year. That was very cool."

"Liquid nitrogen, man. We're talking freeze-your-head-till-they-can-cure-you kind of cool, am I not right?"

"No . . . I mean yes. Thank you."

"Hey, ever consider that, man—the deep freeze? Cryonics? I hear they got Walt Disney all frozen underneath the Dumbo ride. The chilliest place on earth, right? Gotta love it!"

"Actually," I said, "that's made up."

"Yeah," admitted Skaterdud, "but don't you wish it wasn't?"

It's then that I realize that I am the gum-band of sanity between these two jaws of death. On the one hand there's Gunnar, who has made dying the focus of his life, and on the other hand, there's Skaterdud, who sees his fatal fortune as a ticket to three carefree decades of living dangerously.

Suddenly I wanted to be anywhere else but in the mouth of madness.

"Listen, Skaterdud, I got somewhere I gotta be," which was true—and for once I was grateful I was needed to pour water at my dad's restaurant. "Do you know where we could find car parts so old and cruddy nobody actually wants them?"

Turns out Skaterdud knew the salvage yard well—his dad was the guy who crushed cars.

"Go straight, and turn left at the mufflers," he told us. "Best be careful. Ain't no rats don't got steroid issues around here. We're talking poodle-sized, *comprende*?"

"Rats don't bother me," Gunnar said.

I, on the other hand, have no love of furry things with non-furry tails. As I rummaged through the appropriate junk pile, afraid to put my hand in any dark hole, I began to wonder if I'd be more like Gunnar or Skaterdud if I knew the time of my final dismissal. Would all of life's dark holes seem insignificant?

"You're right," Gunnar said out of nowhere. He put down his catalog and reached deep into the pile of junk to dislodge a truck piston. "I'll go for the gunmetal-gray coffin. It's classier."

Maybe it's just me, but I'd rather be scared of rat holes than not care.

As Gunnar went off in search of boxes we could carry the stuff in, Skaterdud called me aside and waited until Gunnar was too far away to hear.

"Something ain't wrong about that friend of yours," said the Dud.

I was a little too tired to decipher dud-ese right now, so I just shrugged.

"No, you gotta listen to me, because I see things."

That didn't surprise me entirely. "What kinds of things?"

"Just things. But it's more the things I *don't* see that's got my neck hairs going porcupine on me." Then he looked off after Gunnar again, shaking his head. "Something ain't wrong about him at all—and if you ask me, he's got iceberg written all over him."

———

We rode home from the junkyard in a public bus, carrying heavy boxes of car parts that greased up the clothes of anyone who passed. We didn't say much, mostly because I was thinking about what Skaterdud had said. Talking to the Dud was enough to challenge anyone's sanity, but if you take the time to decode him, there's something there. The more I thought about it, the more I got the porcupine feeling he was talking about—because I realized he was right. It had to do with Gunnar's emotional state. It had to do with grief. All this time I was explaining away Gunnar's behavior, as if it was all somehow normal under the circumstances, because, face it, I've never been around someone who's got an expiration date before. There was no way for me to really gauge what was standard strangeness, and what was not.

But even I had heard about the five stages of grief.

They're kind of obvious when you think about them. The first stage is denial. It's that moment you look into the goldfish bowl that you haven't cleaned for months and notice that Mr. Moby has officially left the building. You say to yourself, *No, it's not true! Mr. Moby isn't floating belly-up—he's just doing a trick.*

Denial is kinda stupid, but it's understandable. The way I see it, human brains are just slow when it comes to digesting really big, really bad hunks of news. Then, once the brain realizes there's no hurling up this double whopper, it goes to stage two. Anger.

Anger I can understand.

How DARE the universe be so cruel, and take the life of a helpless goldfish!

Then you go kick the wall, or beat up your brother, or do whatever you do when you get mad and you got no one in particular to blame.

Once you calm down, you reach stage three. Bargaining.

Maybe if I act real good, put some ice on my brother's eye, clean the fishbowl and fill it with Evian water, heaven will smile on me, and Mr. Moby will revive.

Ain't gonna happen.

When you realize that nothing's going to bring your goldfish back, you're in stage four: sadness. You eat some ice cream, put on your comfort movie. Everybody's got a comfort movie. It's the one you always play when you feel like the world is about to end. Mine is *Buffet of the Living Dead*. Not the remake, the original. It reminds me of a kinder, simpler time, when you could tell the humans from the zombies, and only the *really* stupid teenagers got their brains eaten.

Once the credits roll, and you've completed stage four, you're ready for stage five. Acceptance. It begins with a flush, sending Mr. Moby the way of all goldfish, and ends with you asking your parents for a hamster.

So I'm sitting there on the bus holding car parts while Gunnar's browsing through his catalog again, and I suddenly realize exactly what Skaterdud meant.

Gunnar never faced stages one through four.

He went straight to acceptance. This crisis, which would have thrown most people's worlds into a tailspin, instead left Gunnar in a perfect glide. There was something fundamentally wrong about things being so "right" with Gunnar. So maybe, as Skaterdud suggested, Pulmonary Monoxic Systemia was just the tip of this iceberg.

Gunnar and I invited our whole English class to our dust bowl for dinner a few nights later, promising "authentic dust-bowl cuisine." Since everyone knew my dad had a restaurant, more than a dozen people actually showed—including our teacher, so we were able to present our report right there. We served everyone a single pea on dusty china, to emphasize what it meant to be hungry in 1939. Our classmates thought we were jerks, but Mrs. Casey appreciated the irony. People kept asking what the faint chemical smell was, and I kept looking to the sky, praying for rain, probably looking like one of Steinbeck's characters—although I wasn't interested in making the corn grow, I just wanted the herbicide to wash away. Gunnar gave the verbal presentation, and I handed Mrs. Casey the written contrast between the book and the movie. She said we did a credible job, which, I guess is better than incredible, because we got an A. I wonder what she would have said if she saw Gunnar's unfinished gravestone, which I forced him to cover with a potato sack before anyone showed up. When she gave back the written report, it came with a contract for two months, signed, witnessed, and stapled to the back of the report.

I went to my computer that night to escape thinking too much, or at least to force myself to think about things that didn't matter. See, when you're on the computer, you get really good at what they call multitasking, and usually the tasks you have to multi are so pointless you can have endless hours without a single useful thought. It's great.

So I'm chatting online with half a dozen people, trying to maintain all these conversations while simultaneously trying to read all these e-mails filled with OMGs and LOLs that aren't even F, while attempting to delete the obvious spam, like all those people in Zimbabwe who have like fourteen million dollars to give me, and the e-mails offering pills "guaranteed" to enlarge your muscles and other things.

Anyway, there I am, sorting online crud, when I notice something I rarely give any attention to: the ad banner at the bottom of the screen. Usually those ad banners are bad animations that say things like SHOOT THE PIG AND QUALIFY FOR OUR MORTGAGE. I've never lowered myself to shooting the pig. But right now the only thing on that banner was a single question, in bright red.

WHAT'S WRONG WITH YOU?

I think I must have seen this one before but it was all subliminal and stuff, because there are many times I'm sitting at this computer asking myself that same question. Meanwhile, all the chats are demanding responses. Ira's is on top. At first he was trying to convince me about how old movies are better than new ones. He's gotten snooty all of a sudden that way, and anytime you're over his house, he forces you to watch classic movies like *Casablanca* and *Alien*. After chatting for like half an hour, he's gotten tired of movie talk, and now he's just telling dead-puppy jokes. This is where things go with Ira, no matter how snooty he pretends to be. I ignore it, and keep my eyes on the ad. Now the answer dances across the banner to join the question.

WHAT'S WRONG WITH YOU?
ASK DR. GIGABYTE!

At first I just chuckled. Everything's a website now. It was the next line that really got me.

WITH DR. G, DIAGNOSIS IS FREE!

I sat there staring and blinking, and shaking my head. Gunnar's doctor was also a "Dr. G." I figured it was just a coincidence. It had to be. I mean, one out of every twenty-six doctors would be Dr. G, right? Well, not exactly, but you know what I mean.

A scoop of ice cream, some root beer, and a dead puppy, Ira's instant message says. He's waiting for my LOL, but right now I've got bigger puppies to fry.

RU still there?

BRB, I type.

I keep wanting to ignore the Dr. G thing, but I can't. It's stuck in my head now.

Maybe it's legitimate, I tried to tell myself. Maybe it's just a real, live doctor who does online consultations.

What did one dead puppy say to the other dead puppy?

I don't care, I answered. *GTG. TTYL,* I told him, and then I added, *IGSINTDRN.* I closed the IM window, taking a little pleasure in the fact that Ira would spend hours trying to figure out what that meant.

I watched a string of other ad banners. Singing chickens, man-eating french fries, aliens in drag. I have no idea what they were all advertising, and I really don't want to know. Then the ad for Dr. G came back. *WHAT'S WRONG WITH YOU?* I clicked on the ad.

It took me to a very professional-looking page that asked me to enter my symptoms. Did I have symptoms? Well, I was overdue for new shoes, and the ones I had were too small, so my toes have been hurting. I entered *Toes hurt.* Then it asked me about twenty other questions, all of which I answered as honestly as I could.

> **Are your toes discolored?**
> No.
> **Do you live in a cold climate?**
> Yes.
> **Are your ankles swollen?**
> No.
> **Have you been bitten by a rodent?**
> Not to my knowledge.

When all the questions had been answered, the website made me wait for about a minute, my anticipation building in spite of myself, and then it gave me a bright blinking diagnosis.

> **You may be suffering from rheumatic gout complicated by lead poisoning.**
> **To avoid amputation or death, seek a full diagnosis, available here for $49.95.**
> **All major credit cards accepted.**

When I clicked *no thanks* it took me to a screen that offered pills to relieve my symptoms, which also had the favorable side effect of enlarging muscles and other things.

I tried it three more times. My growling stomach was intestinal gangrene. The crick in my neck was spinal meningitis. The tan line from my watch was acquired melanin deficiency. All could be further diagnosed for $49.95, and all could be treated with the same pills.

I did a lot of pacing that evening. So much that Christina, buried in her homework, actually noticed.

"What's up with you?" she asked as I paced past her room.

I considered telling her, but instead I just asked, "Have you ever heard of Dr. Gigabyte?"

"Yeah," she said. "It told me my zit was late-stage leprosy."

And, grasping at my last straw of reason, I asked, "What if it is?"

"Please, God, let it be true," Christina said. "Because a leper colony would be better than this." Then she turned her attention back to her math book.

There are no words to describe the muddy mix of things you feel the moment you realize your friend probably isn't dying, but instead is conning you. It means that no matter how much you thought you knew him, you don't know him at all.

I still had no proof, only suspicion—after all, Gunnar really could have a different Dr. G—but I had a gut feeling that was impossible to ignore. The more I thought about it, the more certain I was. If Gunnar wasn't dying, it would go a long way to explaining his family's behavior. The way they never talked about it, as if . . . well, as if it wasn't actually happening. And what about Kjersten? Was Kjersten in on this? Could she be? I suppose I could wrap my mind around Gunnar pretending to be sick—but I couldn't believe Kjersten would be in on it, too. It made me realize I didn't know, or understand, her all that well either.

I truly hoped his illness was fake. I'd be relieved if it was—and yet at the same time, the thought was already making me mad. See, I had wasted all that time collecting months for him, thinking I was doing something noble—something that might make his limited time a little brighter—and he accepted those months without the slightest hint of the lie. If this was a con, then everyone had been taken in—there was even that stupid time thermometer by the main office. Sure, I'd be thrilled to know he wasn't dying—but I couldn't deny the dark river of anger running beneath it. Just the right conditions for a sinkhole.

Repossession Is Nine-tenths of the Law,
The Other Tenth Is Not My Problem

12 Mr. Ümlaut was home that night. I had hoped he wouldn't be, because his presence added an even greater air of tension. His Lexus was in the driveway, but not for much longer, because it was being hooked up to a tow truck.

Good, I thought. *If his car is in the shop, maybe he won't go running off to that casino as much.*

He stood there in an undershirt, in spite of the cold, watching his car as it was raised. His hands were in his pockets, and his shoulders slumped.

"Hi," I said awkwardly. "I need to talk to Gunnar."

"Yeah, yeah—he's inside."

He didn't look at me when he spoke, or take his hands out of his pockets, and I got the feeling that if I had asked to see Attila the Hun, his response would have been, "Yeah, yeah—he's inside."

The front door was open a crack. I pushed it all the way

open and stepped inside. Gunnar and Kjersten were in the living room—Gunnar was listening to an iPod so loudly I could hear the song all the way across the room. Kjersten sat on the sofa—but not in the way you usually sit on a sofa—she was sitting stiff and straight, like it was a hard chair. All at once I recognized this scene. This was the aftermath of a family fight. Mrs. Ümlaut was nowhere to be seen, but I suspected she was either upstairs in a room with the door locked, or in the basement violently doing laundry, or somewhere else where she could be alone with whatever emotions had gotten stirred. I wondered if this had anything to do with the car breaking down.

Kjersten noticed me first, but she didn't smile and say hello. In fact, she didn't seem happy to see me at all. Under the circumstances, I wasn't entirely thrilled to see her either, but I told myself not to judge things until I had all the facts.

"Hi," I said, trying to sound as casual as humanly possible, "what's up?"

"Antsy, this isn't a good time."

Well, call me callous, but I had a mission today and would not be put off by a family squabble. "Yeah, but I need to talk to your brother," I told her.

"Please, Antsy—just come back later, okay?"

"This can't wait."

Kjersten gave a resigned sigh, then threw a sofa pillow at Gunnar, getting his attention. He saw me and took off his earphones.

"Good, you're just in time to witness this pivotal moment of our family's history," said Gunnar, seeming resigned, disgusted, amused, and angry all at the same time—a combination of emotions I usually associate with Old Man Crawley. "Have a seat, and enjoy the show," he said. "You want me to get you some popcorn?"

Kjersten threw another pillow at him. "You're *such* an idiot!"

"I'm here to talk about Dr. G," I said, cutting to the chase. "Or should I say, Dr. Gigabyte?"

Then his cool expression hardened until he looked like a stubble-free version of his father. That's when I knew my suspicions were right. It was all there in that look on his face. "There's nothing to talk about," he said.

"I think there is."

He pushed past me. "Talk all you want to Kjersten—I'm sure you'd much rather talk to her anyway." And he was gone, bounding up the stairs. A second later I heard a door slam.

I turned to Kjersten, but she wouldn't look at me. Not that she was intentionally ignoring me, but she clearly had bigger things on her mind at the moment. Personally, I didn't think a family argument was bigger than her brother faking a terminal illness. It occurred to me that in my conversation with Gunnar, I never asked him the question directly. The answer was heavy in the air, but the question needed to be asked.

"Gunnar isn't really sick, is he?"

She looked at me for the first time since I had been alone with her. It was an odd look. I didn't understand it. She seemed bewildered.

"You're joking, right?"

"So . . . then he's actually sick?"

"Of course not!" She took a moment to gauge my seriousness, and her expression became a bit worried. "You mean you didn't know?"

That threw me for a loop. I stammered a bit, and finally shut my mouth long enough to control it and simply said, "No."

"You mean you weren't just humoring him? Playing along?"

"Why would I do that?"

"Because you're a good person."

"I'm not that good!"

"You mean all this time . . . all those contracts . . . you really thought he was dying?" said Kjersten. "I just thought it was a smart way to force Gunnar to snap out of it, and admit the truth!"

"I'm not that smart!"

She covered her mouth with both hands. "Oh no!" Her entire understanding of the situation was based on the premise that everyone knew Gunnar was faking. Now I could see all her thoughts cascading like dominoes. If I didn't know, then other kids didn't know, which meant the whole school believed Gunnar was dying. The fact that this was news to her made me feel sympathetic, and annoyed at the same time.

"Did you actually think Principal Sinclair was just 'playing along'?"

"Principal Sinclair?"

"Did you think that stupid time thermometer was all part of some practical joke?"

"What thermometer?"

I explained it all to her, because between tennis, debate team, and the static filling her family life, she had missed some crucial things. She never heard my Morning Announcement, never noticed the thermometer. She knew that time donations were pouring in, but she thought it was just from other kids. She had no idea that it had become "official," and that the faculty had begun donating months.

"There was a message on the answering machine, from Sinclair," Kjersten said. "But I erased it before I heard the whole thing—I thought it was one of those school recordings we always get." Which was understandable, since Principal Sinclair did sound like an automated message. I suspected there must have been more messages that Gunnar erased himself, knowing full well they were not recordings.

Then I thought about something Kjersten had said. She thought I was trying to get Gunnar to "snap out of it."

"Does Gunnar actually believe Dr. Gigabyte?" I asked. "Does he really think he's dying?"

The question just frustrated her. "How should I know? You know what he's like—no one can ever figure out what he's really thinking."

I was relieved to know that it wasn't just me. If he stymied his own sister, it meant he was more of a mystery, and I was less of a numbskull.

Out front I heard the scrape of metal on pavement, and glanced out of the window to see the tow truck leaving the driveway, scraping the underside of the Lexus on the curb as it did. Mr. Ümlaut just stood there and watched it go. I almost expected him to wave.

"So what's wrong with your car?" I asked, in an attempt to change the subject.

"It's not our car," Kjersten said. "At least not anymore." Then she got up and closed the blinds so she didn't have to look at her father standing in the driveway. "It just got repossessed."

This is something I knew a little bit about. When my parents got my brother Frankie a car, he was supposed to get a part-time job and make payments on it. He didn't, and the family fights all became about how they'd come and take the car away. Dad was going to let the bank repossess the car to teach Frankie a lesson, but it never got that far—Frankie got the job, started making payments, and the threatening phone calls and letters in red ink stopped coming. I wondered how many letters and phone calls you had to ignore until they actually showed up at your door.

"My father tried to stop them by ripping out some hoses so they couldn't drive it away. Then they sent a tow truck."

"I'm sorry," was all I could say to Kjersten. Now I felt like an idiot for dismissing the whole thing as just a family argument—but before I started beating myself up over it, I did a quick search for ultracool Antsy, who seemed to be easier to find these days. Even without thinking, I knew what he would do. I went to her, and gave her a gentle kiss. She kissed me back with a little bit of spark, so I kissed her again with slightly higher voltage, and she returned that with enough electricity to light Times Square, but before circuit breakers started popping, we shut it down, because we both knew this wasn't the time or place. Just my luck, right?

"Don't be too hard on Gunnar," Kjersten said.

"Hey, you're the one throwing pillows at him."

With a gust of cold air, Mr. Ümlaut came in and saw Kjersten and me standing a little too close. I made no move to back away from her. Sometimes a guy's gotta stand his ground.

"I thought your business was with Gunnar," he said.

"Yeah, well, I got lots of business."

He looked from me to Kjersten, to me again, like he was watching one of her tennis matches. Finally he settled his gaze on her, and he pointed the parental threatening finger.

"We'll talk about this later." Without looking at me again, he went to the back of the house and I heard the door to his study close. This was a house of many closing doors.

"We won't talk," Kjersten said. "He says that all the time, but we never do." Kjersten smiled at me, but there wasn't much joy in that smile.

"Yeah," I said, shaking my head in understanding. "Fathers and follow-through . . ." My own father didn't follow through on much of anything these days—threats *or* promises—since he started the restaurant. But Mr. Ümlaut did not have work as an excuse.

"I just wish things could be the way they were a couple of years ago," Kjersten said, "back when everything was fine—or at least when I was naive enough to think it was." Some warmth came back to her smile as she looked at me. I was glad I could have that effect on her. "You're lucky you're a freshman—you've got your whole life ahead of you."

That made me laugh. "And you don't?"

She kissed me gently on the forehead, then looked out to the grease spot on the driveway where her father's car had been. "My life is going to change very soon."

"Whoever it is, I have no intention of letting you in."

I knocked on Gunnar's door again. A more sensible guy

might have been satisfied with Kjersten's kisses and left, convincing himself that Gunnar was somebody else's problem, but I don't possess the self-preservation instinct. I've got the this-frying-pan-isn't-hot-enough-let's-try-the-fire instinct. I must have been Roadkyll Raccoon in a previous life.

I knocked again. This time there was no response, but I did hear the door being unlocked. I opened it to find Gunnar lying facedown on his bed, with a pillow over his head to shut out the world. This was quite a feat—because just a second ago he had unlocked the door. He must have hurried back to his bed at lightning speed, just so he could present himself to me in this state of anguish.

I sat at his desk chair, realizing he couldn't stay that way for long—he'd have to breathe eventually. Sure enough, he loosened the grip on the pillow, turned to see me for just a split second, then turned his face the other way.

"Go away," he said. But if he really wanted me to go away, he wouldn't have unlocked the door.

I said to him the one thing I could think to say under the circumstances. "I'm sorry you're not dying."

He sat up and faced me. He seemed insulted. "Who says I'm not? Just because it's a Dr. Gigabyte diagnosis doesn't mean it's not true."

"Well, then maybe my sister has leprosy."

He showed no sign of being surprised or confused by that, and I wondered if maybe he had, at some point, been given that diagnosis by Dr. Gigabyte, too.

"Have you seen any real doctors? What do they say?"

"I don't care what they say. *'The enlightened man knows the workings of his own body and soul.'*"

"Who said that?" I asked.

I could see him thinking and he said, "The Dalai Lama."

"You made that up!"

"So what."

And then I had a sudden revelation. "You made them *all* up!" Even as I said it, I knew it was true. Nobody could have so many quotes-for-all-occasions at their fingertips. "None of those people ever said those things, did they? Your quotes are all fake!"

He looked down at the pillow in his hands, and punched it like he was kneading a wad of dough. "That doesn't mean they *couldn't* have said them," he mumbled.

I laughed. Maybe it was the wrong thing to do, but the fact that even his pretensions were pretend struck me as funny. He didn't react well to that. He stood up, and went to the door. "I'd like you to leave now."

This time I think he meant it. "Well, for what it's worth, I'm actually glad you're not dying." I stood up and went to the door. "Do your parents have any idea you've been conning the whole school?"

"I'm not conning anybody," he said. "My life is over. Whether or not I actually die is just a technicality."

But before I could ask him what that meant, he closed the door between us.

The next day—the Friday before a desperately needed Christmas vacation—I was hauled into the principal's office again. This time he already had other guests—a man and a woman in expensive-looking business suits. When I walked in, they both stood up. I flinched, like you do when the cat jumps out in a horror movie.

"Ah," said Principal Sinclair, "here's the boy I've been telling you about." I shook their hands—but can't remember their names, on account of my brain was still processing the fact that they had been talking about me—but I'm pretty sure that the woman was the newly elected superintendent of schools.

"Anthony has been spearheading a schoolwide community-service effort to give hope to a terminally ill student."

"Uh . . . yeah," I said, looking anywhere but at the three of them. "Funny you should mention that . . ."

"I've heard all about it," said the superintendent. "We need more students like you."

That almost made me laugh.

"If you don't mind," the man said, "we'd like to donate time, too."

Call me a gutless wonder, but I didn't have the courage to let them know the truth about Gunnar and his "illness." I tried, but the words stuck in my throat and clung to my tonsils like strep, refusing to come out.

"Yeah, sure, why not," I said, and reached into my backpack, pulling out two blank time contracts for them to fill in and sign, with my principal signing as witness. Then, when it was done, Principal Sinclair sat on the corner of his desk, in that casual I'm-your-principal-but-I'm-also-your-friend kind of way. "Now, I'm sure you've heard that the student council has organized a rally for Gunnar during the first week of January," he said.

"They have?"

"Yes—and I think you should give a speech, Anthony."

There comes a moment in every really, really bad situation when you realize your canoe's leaking, there's no paddle, and you can hear Niagara Falls up ahead. There's nothing you can do but hold on and pray for deliverance. I don't mean the movie *Deliverance*, which is, coincidentally, about canoes—I mean real, Hail Mary, Twenty-third Psalm kind of deliverance.

"I'm not good at speeches."

"I'm sure you'll do fine," said the superintendent. "Just speak from the heart."

And the other guy said, "We'll all be there to support you."

"You'll be there?" I asked. The Falls were getting louder by the minute.

"This school," said the principal, "is under consideration as a National Blue Ribbon school. Academics are only a part of that. The school must also demonstrate that its students are committed to making the world a better place . . . and you, Anthony, are our shining star."

Kidnap Ye Grouchy Gentleman,
with Something to Dismay

13 In spite of what happened on the Double Date From Hell, my friendship with Lexie was back to normal. "I care about you too much to be anything more than mildly furious at you," she had told me, but even then, I could tell she wasn't furious at all.

The two of us kidnapped her grandfather as planned—the first Saturday of Christmas vacation. As usual, Old Man Crawley had no concept of what was in store for him today. "I don't want to do this!" he yelled as I fought to blindfold him. "I'm calling the police! I'll skewer you on the end of my cane!" But this was all part of the ritual.

By the time we got him out to his chauffeured Lincoln, he had stopped complaining about being kidnapped. Now he merely complained about the conditions.

"You forgot my winter coat."

"It's a warm day."

"I just ate. If I have digestive problems because of this, I won't be happy."

"When are you ever happy?" I asked.

"Your attitude does not bode well for your paycheck."

But I knew he paid me for my attitude as well. It was all part of the ambience of the experience.

"This one's special, Grandpa," Lexie assured him.

"That's what you always say," he grumbled.

Our Holiday Kidnapping Extravaganza was a zip line fifty feet off the ground through the treetops of Prospect Park—the largest park in Brooklyn. Lexie had arranged to have engineering students build the zip line for class credit. There were two platforms equipped with rope-and-pulley lift systems, because Old Man Crawley couldn't be expected to climb a ladder. Flying down the wire from one tree to the other, you reached a top speed of about forty miles an hour.

This was a good distraction from the Gunnar Debacle, as I was now calling it, since I figured I'd earned the right to be as pretentious as him. Still, it weighed heavily on my mind.

As the chauffeur drove to Prospect Park, I told Lexie everything.

"I knew it!" she said. "I knew something was wrong with that whole family. I could tell the way whatserface left that night without as much as a good-bye."

"You were pouting in the bathroom," I reminded her. "She couldn't say good-bye to you. And anyway, I'm not breaking up with her, if that's what you're thinking. The problem is with her brother, not her."

I had had enough time to really think about Gunnar's behavior, and realized that this wasn't just a simple con. He wasn't faking in the traditional sense. There's a fine line between being a hypochondriac and being a faker. I think Gunnar was speeding down that particular zip line at speeds in excess of forty miles an hour.

"Sounds to me," said Lexie, "that he's more miserable at the prospect of being healthy than being sick."

"Exactly! It's like he actually wants to have Pulmonary Monoxic Systemia." And I posed to her the question that had been rattling in my head for days. "Why would anyone WANT to be dying?"

"*Munchausen,*" said Lexie.

I was tempted to say "gesundheit," but I took the more serious route instead. "What's that?" I asked. "Sounds bad."

"It can be. It's a mental illness where someone lies about being sick, to get attention. There are people who give themselves infections, so they can go to the doctor. There are people who make their own children sick."

"All for attention?"

"Well," said Lexie, "it's complicated."

"Which means," grumbled her blindfolded grandfather, "that you're wasting your breath trying to explain it to him."

I thought about Gunnar. Did he want attention? He got a lot of it already. He was popular, girls liked him, everyone knew him. He wasn't starving to be noticed . . . but, on the other hand, he wasn't exactly the focus of his parents' lives these days. But, on the other hand, neither was I, and I wasn't telling everyone I had a dreaded disease, although I'm sure there are some people who are convinced I do.

We reached Prospect Park and walked Crawley, still blind-folded, to the first tree. When we took off the blindfold, Crawley made a move to run, but I caught him. This was a standard part of the ritual, too.

"This is too dangerous!" he shouted as we moved him onto a platform rigged with pulleys—probably more than were necessary, but after all, it was done by engineering students—they were trying to show off. "There must be laws against things like this!"

"That'll be a great quote for your tombstone," I said, but then I shut up, because it reminded me of Gunnar.

Crawley gave me the kind of gaze that knows no repeatable words, and we were hoisted up to the high platform, where one of the engineering students waited with sets of harnesses, helmets, and gear that looked like it was meant for space walks.

"How far is it to the other platform?" I asked the engineering guy next to me, but before he could answer, Crawley said bitterly:

"Lexie's boyfriend could probably tell you." And he made some clicking noises.

"Stop it, Grandpa."

Now that he was safely in his harness, I pushed him and he went flying down the zip line, screaming and cursing for all he was worth.

"So how *is* Raoul?" I asked Lexie.

"Raoul and I agreed it was best to end it."

"I'm sorry."

"No you're not."

"Yes, I am," I told her. "Because now you're going to want me to end it with Kjersten, just to keep the status quo."

"Status quo," she said. "Big words for you."

"I'm Catholic," I reminded her. "I get Latin." Then I gave her a gentle shove, and she shot down the zip line, toward her grandfather and the nervous engineering students waiting to catch her.

"It's a quarter mile," said the engineering student, who had been waiting all this time to answer my question, "but it feels a lot longer!"

I pulled up the rear, shouting and whooping as the landscape of Prospect Park shot beneath me. This kidnapping was a winner! The zip line did exactly what it was supposed to do—it filled our senses and souls with excitement. It reminded us what it meant to be alive. For twenty shining seconds there was nothing but me, the wind, and the fifty feet between me and the ground. The engineering guy was wrong. It felt too short!

By the time I arrived, Crawley had already recovered some of his usual demeanor.

"So, whaddaya think?" I asked.

"I'm only mildly impressed." From him, this was a five-star review.

"It was . . . exhilarating," Lexie said. I could tell she hadn't cared for it. When you're flying down a zip line, I suppose sight is a sense worth having.

The students lowered us from the platform, working hard on the pulleys like medieval sailors, and as we descended, Crawley said to me, "As usual, you're missing the obvious."

"Excuse me?"

"With regard to your not-quite-dying friend—you're missing the obvious."

I crossed my arms. "So tell us. We await your brilliance, O Ancient One."

For once he ignored my sarcasm. "It's not that he wants to die—it's that he needs to be sick. The sooner you find out why he needs to be sick, the sooner you can solve this mystery and return to your mediocre existence."

I didn't respond, because as much as I hated to admit it, I knew he was right.

"Now," he said, "take me back to the other tree, so we can do that again."

Crawley contacted the parks department shortly after the kidnapping and offered to build a zip line tourist attraction in Prospect Park. He got the blessing of the city, and wouldn't you know it, the zip line was already in place. Any minute he'll be making a hefty profit from it.

"The difference between you and me," he once told me, "is that when I look at the world, I see opportunity. When you look at the world, you're just trying to find a place to urinate."

When I got home that afternoon, I decided to play Sherlock Holmes and figure out why Gunnar needed to be sick. I did some in-depth research on Pulmonary Monoxic Systemia.

Although the disease is almost always fatal within a year of diagnosis, huge strides were being made in research recently, and there were early reports that test patients were living longer, healthier lives. The leading research and all the hopeful results were coming from Columbia University Medical Center, right in Manhattan.

I thought about Dr. G. The thing with the Dr. G website is that you can throw out the same basic symptoms, and each time it would diagnose you with something else. I wonder how many diagnoses Gunnar had gotten before he convinced himself that this is what he had.

And wasn't it convenient that all the hope for Gunnar's illness lay right here in New York?

Before I could think about it much further, I got a call from my father. He needed me to work at the restaurant. The Crawley kidnapping had exhausted me, and it was the last thing I wanted to do today.

"There are laws against child labor," I told him.

"Aren't you always telling us you're not a child?"

"What about my homework? Is your restaurant more important than my education?"

"It's *our* restaurant, not just mine—and didn't Christmas vacation start today?"

I knew he had me.

I showed up at seven and did my job, but the whole situation with Gunnar never left my mind entirely. Sure, it was vacation, but there was a big fat Gunnar-themed rally waiting for me when vacation was over. I was irritable, but maintained an air of professionalism for most of the evening. Things would have been fine if it hadn't been for the single certified idiot at table number nine.

He arrived at around seven-thirty with a scowling wife, and two kids who wouldn't stop fighting. From the moment he sits down, this guy starts complaining. His fork has spots on it; the wine isn't cold enough. The appetizer came out too late and the main course came out too early. He demands to see the manager, and my father comes over. I'm standing there, refilling water glasses, after having been chewed out by the guy for not having refilled them the instant he took a sip. For him I don't bother with skillful pouring.

"How can you call this a restaurant?" the guy complains while his kids kick each other under the table. "The service is lousy, the food came out cold, and there's a horrible stench in the air."

Well, first of all, the service was perfect, because my mother was his waitress, and she is the queen of quality control. Secondly, I know the food was hot, because I served it myself, and nearly burned my hands on the plate. And third, the horrible stench was coming from his son.

But my dad—he gets all apologetic, offering free dessert, and discounts off the guy's next visit, and such. That just makes me angry. See, my dad used to work in a big corporation, full of guys like this, so he had developed an idiot-resistant personality. I, on the other hand, had not. All I had going for me at the moment was a big pitcher of ice water.

This is why I could never get a job as a busboy in a restaurant my family didn't own . . . because, for the first time in my water-pouring history, I missed the glass. In fact, all the water in the pitcher missed the glass, and found the top of the guy's head instead.

After I was done pouring the pitcher of ice water on him, he finally fell silent, and stared at me in total shock. And I said, "I'm sorry—did you want bottled water instead?"

To my amazement, the rest of the restaurant started applauding. Someone even snapped a picture. I was ready to take a bow, but my father grabbed my arm. He grabbed it hard, and when I looked at him, the expression in his eyes was not one of gratitude. "Wait for me in the kitchen," he growled. Very rarely did my father speak in growls. When he was mad he usually yelled, and that was okay. Speaking in growls was not. I hurried off to the kitchen, sat on a stool, and waited, feeling more like a little kid than I had in years.

Christina came up to me. I don't know if she saw what happened, but I'm sure she guessed the gist. "I made a swan for you," she said, and handed me a folded napkin.

"Thanks," I said. "Got any Himalayan mantras I can recite for the occasion?"

"I'm beyond that now," she told me. "I'm into chakra points." She massaged some spots on my back that failed to relax me, then went to fold more napkins.

Dad did not come back to talk to me at all that night. He just let me stew on the stool. Mom would occasionally pass by to pick up orders and would scowl, shake her head, or wag her finger. Then eventually she gave me a plate of food. That's how I knew Dad was truly, truly angry. If Mom felt sorry enough for me to feed me, it meant I was in a world of trouble.

Eventually Mom just sent me home, because she couldn't stand to see me sitting there so miserably on that stool.

Before my parents got home that night, I got a call from Old Man Crawley, who must have had spies in the restaurant again.

"Did you actually pour a pitcher of water over a man's head?" he asked.

"Yes, sir," I replied. I was too exhausted to make excuses.

"And did it feel good to do so?"

"Yes, sir, it did. He was an idiot."

"Was this a premeditated attack on your part?"

"Uh . . . no, sir. It was kind of . . . spontaneous."

He paused for a long time. "I see," he finally said. "You'll be hearing from me." And he hung up. He didn't even bother to torment me with how much I had disappointed him—that's how bad this was. I couldn't help but feel that "you'll be hearing from me" were among the worst possible words to hear at the end of a conversation with Crawley. It was even worse than "you'll be hearing from my attorney."

This water incident might have meant a whole lot of bad things—including retribution against my father somehow—after all, it was Crawley's money that got my dad's restaurant going. Crawley could shut it down with a snap of his fingers, and I wouldn't put it past him to do it.

Dad did not punish me when he got home. He didn't punish me the next day. He just avoided me. It didn't feel like an intentional cold shoulder—it felt more like he was so disgusted, he just didn't want to have anything to do with me. It wasn't until Monday that I found out why.

On Monday the news had a headline that read:

BUSBOY BAPTIZES BOSWELL

And there it was, not on page four of the school paper, but smack on the cover of the *New York Post*—a full-page picture of the idiot from table nine, drenched in water, and me holding the empty pitcher. It was the picture taken by one of the other diners that night.

Getting your picture on the cover of the *New York Post* is never a good thing. It means that you're either a murderer, a murderee, or a humiliated public official. This time it was option three. The idiot from table nine was none other than Senator Warwick Boswell, and I was the one who had humiliated him.

That morning my father was already scouring the classifieds for job opportunities, as if he was expecting the restaurant to shut down in a matter of days.

"Dad, I'm sorry . . ." It was the first time I tried to breach the silence between us, but he put up his hand.

"Let's not do this, okay, Antsy?" He didn't even look up at me.

That's how it was for most of Christmas vacation. And it hurt. See, in our family we fought, we yelled, we gouged at one another's feelings, and then we made up. Our fights were fiery—never cold, and it got me to thinking about what my mom had once said about hell—how it's all cold and lonely.

Now I knew she was right, because I'd rather have fire shooting out of my dad's mouth like a dragon than suffer this nuclear winter.

My dad and I used to be able to talk. Even when something was bad, even when we were ready to strangle each other, we could talk. But not now.

Let's not do this, okay, Antsy?

Entire species died in that kind of cold.

Nobody Likes Me,
Everybody Hates Me,
Think I'll Eat Some Worms

14 Christmas came and went uneventfully, which, considering the previous set of events, was a good thing. For reasons that may or may not have been retribution for missing Thanksgiving, most of our relatives had other plans. We could have gone to Philadelphia to be with Mom's side of the family, but with Aunt Mona coming on Christmas Eve, we had to pass. Then Aunt Mona calls at the last minute to tell us she can't come till after New Year's. Typical.

"It wouldn't be a visit from Mona," Mom said, "if she didn't ruin the plans we made around her."

"She did us a favor," Dad responded, because he was simply too burned out to travel all the way to Philly anyway. Besides, he never spoke out against his sister, no matter what the situation. It was a sore spot with Mom.

"You watch," said Mom, "when she does come, she'll show up without any warning, and expect us to drop everything."

Christmas morning lacked the magic it usually had. At first I thought it was just me getting older, but the more I thought about it, the more I realized that wasn't the case. The tree was trimmed better than ever—but that was just because Christina and I worked hard to make it so. There were fewer presents under the tree, since there wasn't a horde of relatives—but that would have been okay. What really made it hard was that Dad was clearly not present in the moment, as they say. His thoughts were on the restaurant, his future, and I guess our futures, too. He was all preoccupied, and that made Mom preoccupied with him. I could tell that Mom resented the air of anxiety in our lives lately, but still did everything she could to get Dad to relax. I wanted to tell him to just get over it, but how could I? After all, I was the cause of his latest stress bomb.

The day after Christmas I went to give Kjersten her Christmas gift. Was it crazy for me to think we could have a somewhat normal relationship, in spite of all the abnormal stuff around us? Going there didn't feel right. I wasn't ready to face Gunnar—I didn't know how to talk to him, because I knew every word out of my mouth would be another way of asking why. Why did he *need* to be sick? Why did he let it go so far? Why did he have to draw me into it? The Great Gunnar Rally was planned for the day after we got back to school. The speech I was supposed to deliver hung over my head—and I resented Gunnar for putting me in that position.

When I arrived on their street that day, there was no denying the neighborhood's collateral damage. I moved past looming lawns of death, trying to gauge how bad it was. The dust bowl had already spread halfway down the block. All the evergreens were yellow, and everything that should have been yellow was that strange bruise shade of brown. Men were standing out front looking at the devastation, and their wives looked on, watching to see if their men would break.

The only thing green was, ironically, right on the Ümlaut door. A big green Christmas wreath . . . but when I got closer, I could see it was plastic.

Gunnar answered the door.

"I'm here to see your sister," I told him.

He looked at the wrapped package in my hands. "She's upstairs." Then he walked away. I should have let him go, but whether I like it or not, my mouth has a mind of its own.

"You're still not cyanotic," I said to him. "But if it's that important to you, you can buy some blue lipstick and pretend that you are."

He turned to me then. I could tell he was hurt, even though it didn't show in his face. Part of me felt glad about it, and another part of me felt ashamed for saying something so nasty. I found myself mad at both parts.

Gunnar gave me a cold gaze and said, "That would have been much more effective if you bought some for me as a Christmas gift," then he left.

"Wish I had thought of it," I shouted after him. Actually, I *had* thought of it, but I wouldn't sink so low as to get him a cruel gift. Besides, I didn't want to be seen buying blue lipstick. Even if no one saw me, there *are* surveillance cameras.

I found Kjersten up in her room watching *Moëba*, a zany cartoon about ethnically diverse single-celled organisms in Earth's primordial ooze. It seemed odd that she'd be watching this. In fact, she was so absorbed, it took her a moment to notice I was there.

"Antsy!"

"Hi." It came out sounding like a one-word apology.

She stood up and gave me a hug. "You're not having much luck with photographers lately, are you?" I could see the special Antsy edition of the *New York Post* on her desk.

"No," I admitted, "and now there's an animated version on the YouTube."

"Could be worse," she said, although downloadable e-humiliation is about as low as it gets.

The moment became awkward, and she glanced back at the TV, where Moëba was punching out a dim-witted paramecium.

"I used to love this show," she said.

"So did I," I told her. "When I was, like, eight."

She sighed. "Things were simpler then." Then she turned off the TV. "So, is that for me?"

"Oh . . . yeah," I said, handing her the gift. "Merry Christmas." Again, I sounded like I was apologizing for something. It was annoying.

"Yours is still under the tree," she said. I hadn't even noticed a tree downstairs.

She opened up her package, to reveal a NeuroToxin jacket.

"It's from their *Bubonic Nights* tour. Look—Jaxon Beale's autograph is embroidered on the sleeve."

"I noticed," Kjersten said. "I love Jaxon Beale!"

In case you've been living on a desert island, Jaxon Beale, former guitarist for Death Crab, is the guitarist *and* lead singer of NeuroToxin.

She thanked me, and put the jacket on. It looked good on her, but then, what didn't? It made me feel good that I could, at least for a few minutes, break her out of a world of repossessed cars, furious neighbors, and a brother on deathwatch.

"You want to do something today?' she asked.

To be honest, I hadn't given the day much thought beyond handing her the jacket. "Sure," I said. "How about a movie?"

"Something funny," she said. "Let's make it something funny."

"Why don't you pick—there's a whole bunch of new movies at the Mondoplex." Then I added, "You can even drive. I'm over that whole macho thing about riding shotgun with my girlfriend."

This was, I realized, the first time I used the word "girlfriend" with her. I watched to see if her reaction would be positive, negative, or neutral. It was negative, but not because of the word "girlfriend." Her problem was with the word "drive."

"We can't drive. My dad borrowed my car this morning."

I wondered if he had borrowed it to go gambling, but decided not to ask. "Your mom could drive us . . ."

"My mom's spending the holiday with family in Sweden, and she parked her car at the airport."

Why, I wondered, would she choose to pay for airport parking instead of just leaving her car for her husband to use? Again, I decided it was best not to ask. The whole family was a can of worms waiting to happen, and I, for one, was not going to supply the can opener.

"Sweden, huh?" I said. "Sounds like fun—why didn't you go with her?"

"It's Sweden, and it's winter—isn't that reason enough?"

"I bet there'd be snow."

"Snow, and ice, and eighteen hours of darkness. I hate it."

"Well, I'm sure it's a whole lot better than Christmas in Brooklyn." She shrugged gloomily, so I tried a different tack. "Well, I'm glad you didn't go, because now we can see each other all vacation."

That made her smile, and it wasn't just a polite smile, it was a real one. I silently reveled in the fact that she actually did want to spend time with me. We bundled up against the windy afternoon, braved the neighborhood dust bowl, and took a bus to the Mondoplex.

For several reasons, I will not give a blow-by-blow description of our darkened-movie-theater experience. First of all, it's none of your business, and secondly, anything you *think* happened is probably better than what actually did.

But for those of you who have never experienced the phenomenon called a movie-theater date, there are a few general things I can tell you:

1. Your hand completely falls asleep after about fifteen minutes around a girl's shoulder, especially if she's taller than you. It's better just to hold hands.

2. While holding hands, you can't manage both a tub of popcorn and a drink. One of them is bound to spill. Pray it's the popcorn.

3. If you ever come within six inches of actually kissing, you will suddenly become more interesting than the movie to the

entire audience, including one creep with a laser pointer, who you'll be ready to kill long before the credits roll.

As for the movie itself, it wasn't the movie I expected Kjersten to choose. I thought Kjersten might pick a love story, or a foreign film or something . . . instead she chose this lowbrow teen comedy that I might have gone to see with Howie and Ira, but never thought I'd see with her. It wasn't even one of the better lowbrow movies either. I mean, I've enjoyed my share of amazingly stupid movies, but this one was so bad, and so unfunny, it was embarrassing. This was a film that would actually insult Wendell Tiggor's "intelligence," and with every dumb, raunchy thing that happened on-screen, I kept expecting her to slap me for the mere fact that I was a guy.

Eighty-six agonizing minutes later, the movie was over and we were walking down the street holding hands—the first time we actually held hands while publicly walking. She didn't quite tower over me, but the difference was enough for me to be self-conscious about it. Every time someone nearby laughed, I involuntarily snapped my head around like maybe it was directed at us. Kjersten had no such worries.

"Did you like the movie?" she asked.

"It was all right, I guess."

"I thought it was funny," she said.

"Yeah." I searched for something worth saying. "When the fat guy got stuck in the Jell-O-filled swimming pool naked, that was funny."

"You didn't like it," she said, reading right through me.

"Well, it's just that . . . I don't know . . . you're on the debate team and everything. I thought you'd want to see a movie that would, uh . . . broaden my horizons."

"I'm happy with your horizons just where they are."

I should have felt good about that. After all, it was unconditional acceptance from my girlfriend . . . but like Gunnar's "acceptance," it was all wrong. Not that I wanted her to go through denial, fear, and anger while dating me—although a little bargaining might be fun. The thing is, I knew she chose the movie because she thought I would like it. What did that say about her opinion of *me*?

Yeah, yeah, I know, guys aren't supposed to think about stuff like that. I should be happy that I'm successfully playing out of my league, batting a thousand, and have earned bragging rights. I guess that was enough at first, but not anymore. I blame Lexie. She was the one who first broadened my horizons.

Kjersten's car was in the driveway when we got home, which meant her father was there. I would have gone in, but Kjersten didn't want to make any waves. She kissed me quickly at the door, ducked inside for a moment, and came out with a long, skinny box, wrapped perfectly, with a golden Christmas bow. "You can open it when you get home," she said. "I hope you'll like it."

And from inside I heard Gunnar shout, "It's a skateboard."

She growled in frustration, and handed me the box, accidentally knocking the wreath off the door. Quickly she scrambled to put it back up, but not quickly enough. I got a clear glimpse of the notice pasted to the front door that had been hidden by the wreath. She knew I saw it—but what could she do? She made sure the wreath was hung firmly on the nail, and pretended it hadn't happened. "See you tomorrow?" she said.

"Yeah . . . Yeah, sure, see you tomorrow."

Before she closed the door, I caught a glimpse of Gunnar

watching me from inside, his eyes filled with fatalistic doom, as unnerving as a dozen dying yards.

It was a nice skateboard. High-quality Spitfire wheels, cool design. I sat on my bed that evening, running my fingers over the grip tape surface, and the smooth polished back. I spun the wheels, and listened to the satisfying clatter of the bearings. It was everything you'd want in a skateboard, except for one thing. I didn't want a skateboard.

See, there's a time for everything in life—and everyone's clock is different. There are guys who use skateboards right up until they get their license—after all, it's a useful mode of transportation. Then there are guys like Skaterdud, to whom skateboarding is like a religion, and they'll do it all their lives. I'm sure the Dud won't just fall off that aircraft carrier, he'll roll off it. But my skateboard phase ended the summer before ninth grade. I kind of outgrew it—and everyone knows the second you outgrow something, it's like poison for a couple of years, until it becomes historically significant in your life and you can look back on it fondly.

It was all starting to make sense now. Especially after seeing that awful notice plastered on their front door.

HOUSE IN FORECLOSURE
RESIDENTS ARE HEREBY GIVEN THIRTY DAYS
TO VACATE PREMISES

It was far worse than any field of doom Gunnar and I had created. Thirty days. How do you cope with the world coming down around you, when your parents just seem to be running away? Is it easier to believe that it's the end of everything rather than face it, and start carving tombstones like Gunnar? Or maybe you just go into full retreat, like Kjersten—who wasn't interested in bringing me up to her level, but rather wanted to come down to mine—or at least what she *thought* was my level. Dumb movies, cool skateboards, and awkward fourteen-year-old advances. Because "things were so much simpler then."

Lexie had been right. Kjersten was dating "the idea" of me.

Could I be what Kjersten needed? Did I want to be? As I sat there running my hands along the edge of the skateboard, I realized that the Ümlaut can of worms was a big old industrial drum, and I was already inside, eating worms left and right.

What the Ümlauts really needed was time—and not the kind I could print out of my computer, but *real* time. And as for Kjersten, if I really cared about her—and I did—I realized the best I could do was to become "the idea of me" as much as possible for her. I couldn't give her time, but maybe I could give her a little time travel.

So I got on that skateboard and rode it around and around and around, trying my best, for the rest of Christmas vacation, to recapture the earliest days of fourteen.

Mona-Mona-Bo-Bona,
Bonano-Fano-Fo-Fona

15 "Hey, Kjersten—I can play 'The Star-Spangled Banner' in armpit farts; wanna see?"

"Antsy, you're so funny!"

There's something to be said for immaturity—acting your shoe size instead of your age, although in my case they're starting to get close. Once I gave in to it, it was fun. Dumb jokes, bathroom humor, pretending to care about stuff I gave up in middle school . . . who could have known dating an older woman could be like this?

"This is just, like, the coolest video game, Kjersten. You're driving a killer Winnebago, and everyone you run over becomes a soul trapped in your motor home. Isn't it totally great?"

"You play, Antsy. I'll just watch."

———

I was Kjersten's escape. It made her feel good, and that made *me* feel good. I even learned to make myself get red in the face and look all embarrassed, when I actually wasn't.

"See these scabs, like, on my elbows and stuff? They're from skateboarding. I've been, y'know, like, practicing my varial kick-flip and stuff. Like."

"So the skateboard I got you is a good one?"

"It's the best!"

The problem with stunting you own growth like that, though, is that it doesn't leave you with anything lasting. It's like eating cotton candy all day, although not quite as bad on your teeth. It's also exhausting. After a day with Kjersten, I'd just want to go home and read a newspaper or something—or even bus tables at the restaurant, just to gain back some basic level of age appropriateness. Unfortunately, I was still banned from the restaurant, and I didn't know if I'd ever be allowed back.

"What's with you?" Mom asked. I had just spent an energy-intensive day with Kjersten at the arcade and was now lying lumplike on the sofa, staring at the stock-market quotes scrolling on the financial network.

"Nothing," I answered, so Christina took it upon herself to elaborate.

"His girlfriend is using him to recapture her lost youth."

This confused Mom. "What do you mean 'lost youth'? She's only sixteen!"

"You know how it is," Christina says. "Everything starts younger and younger these days."

"It's not a problem," I told her. "I know what I'm doing."

Mom shook her head. "Lost youth! What is she gonna have you do? Wear diapers?"

"Yeah, and she burps me real good, too," I said.

Mom threw her hands up as she left the room. "I didn't just hear that."

My return to school after the holidays was met with much congratulations and pats on the back from friends and kids I didn't even know. At first I thought it was kudos for being publicly seen dating Kjersten, but it was all because of the *New York Post*. Dumping water on a senator and getting front-page exposure made me a school hero, but it was not the kind of fame I wanted.

"I could say 'I knew you when,'" Howie told me, as if this would launch me into full-on celebrity status. "Have you gotten any talk-show invitations?"

For a moment I imagined myself holding a pitcher of ice water next to Clicking Raoul on a talk show, but I shook the image away before it could do any damage.

People had no idea how the ice-water incident had affected my family. How it strained my father and the restaurant. I just wanted it to go away—why couldn't anyone understand that?

I also wanted Gunnar's rally to go away. A fake rally about

fake time, when real time was ticking away. Twenty-three days until he and his family had to be out. Were they even doing anything about it?

It actually snowed on Tuesday night—the first snow of the winter, and I hoped we'd have a snow day, postponing or even canceling the rally on Wednesday night. But who was I kidding? There's got to be woolly mammoth walking down the street before the New York City schools call a snow day.

Gunnar came up to me at my locker on Wednesday morning. Considering the looming foreclosure, I decided not to take my frustration out on him—even if he was at the root of it.

"What are you going to say at the rally tonight?" he asked.

"I don't know," I told him. "What do you think I should say?"

"You're not going to ruin it, are you?"

Did he really think I would tell everyone the truth now? How could I? I was like his partner in crime now—an accomplice. The only way to make this go away was to go through with it. Who knows, maybe as wrong as it was, it was the right thing to do. Didn't some famous dead artist say that everyone gets fifteen minutes of fame? Who was I to stand in the way of Gunnar's?

"Maybe I oughta turn the whole thing into a cash collection for your mortgage," I told him. I don't know whether he thought I was serious or just being sarcastic. That's okay, because I didn't know either.

"Too late for that," he said. "Knowing my father, the money wouldn't go to the mortgage anyway."

"Do your parents know about this rally? Do they have any idea how far this Dr. G thing has gone?"

Gunnar shrugged. Clearly they had no idea. "My mom got snowed in in Stockholm. She won't be back until late tonight. And my dad . . . well, I guess he cares more about his cards than his kids."

I was really starting to understand Gunnar's phantom illness. The Ümlauts were losing everything they owned; Gunnar's father was gambling away whatever was left and had practically abandoned his wife and kids in the process. In some ways it was probably easier for Gunnar to think he was dying than have to face all that. I thought about my father and how everything had gotten so frayed between us—but as bad as things were, deep down I knew it would all eventually blow over. We would recover. But there was no promise of recovery between Gunnar and his father. They were like the Roadkyll Raccoon danglers. Rescue was a slim hope, at best.

"I'm sure your father cares about you," I told Gunnar. "He's just messed up."

"He doesn't have a right to be messed up until he takes care of the messes he's already made."

I didn't know how to answer that, so instead I answered his original question.

"I'm going to give a speech about Pulmonary Monoxic Systemia, and thank everyone for their time donations. I'm going to say decent things about you. Then I'm going to call you up to the podium."

"Me?"

"It's your life. That thermometer's measuring years for you. You're the one who has to thank people—make them feel good about what they've done."

Gunnar couldn't look at me. He looked down, tapped the edge of my locker door with his foot. Then he said, "Dr. G isn't always wrong."

"Well . . . I hope he's wrong this time, because as screwed up as this whole thing is, I don't want you to die."

The bell rang, but Gunnar didn't leave yet. He hung around for a good ten seconds, then said, "Thanks, Antsy," and hurried off to class.

The rally was at six, on account of it couldn't interfere with class instruction or sports—but since it was approved by the district superintendent, who was up-and-coming in her political career, it was taken very seriously. I was hoping that since it was in the evening, a lot of kids wouldn't show—but then the principal offered every student who came extra credit in the class of their choosing. That was almost as good as free food.

I went home at the end of the school day, figuring I'd be home just long enough to shower, and change, and pray for an asteroid to wipe out all human life before I had to give my speech. When I got out of the shower, Mom accosted me in the hallway.

"Get dressed, we're picking up Aunt Mona at the airport."

I just stood there with a towel around me and a sinkhole opening beneath my feet.

"Don't give me that look," she said. "Her flight arrives in less than an hour." I could tell Mom was already at the end of her rope, and the visit hadn't even started. "Please, Antsy, don't make this any harder than it needs to be."

"But . . . but I got something I gotta do!"

"It can wait."

I laughed nervously, imagining an auditorium full of people waiting, and waiting and waiting. The one thing worse than having to give this speech was not showing up at all.

"You don't understand . . . I'm giving a speech tonight for that friend of mine." And this next part I had to force out, because it wasn't coming by itself. "The one who's dying."

That gave her a moment's pause. "You're giving a speech?"

"Yeah. The district superintendent is going to be there and everything."

"Why is this the first we're hearing about this?"

"Well, maybe if you two weren't at the restaurant all the time, you would have heard." I didn't mean that, but I chose to play the guilt card because this was serious, and I had to use every weapon at my disposal.

"What time does it start?" she asked.

"Six."

"Well, if you're giving a speech, we'll all want to be there. We can pick up your aunt and make it back by six."

"You can't be serious! LaGuardia Airport at this time of day? In this weather? We'll be lucky if we're back for the Fourth of July!"

But Mom wasn't caving. "Don't worry—your father knows shortcuts. Now go put on that shirt Aunt Mona bought you."

At last I lost all power of speech. Of all the days to have to wear that stupid pink-and-orange shirt—was I going to have to give a speech in front of the entire student body looking like a cross between a Barbie car and a traffic cone? My mouth hung open, something sounding like Morse code came out, and Mom said:

"Just do it," and she went downstairs to give the living room a final dusting.

I stewed all the way to LaGuardia.

"Stop pouting," Mom said, as if this was a mere childish expression of disappointment.

Well, you asked for it, I told myself. *You asked for an asteroid and here it is. Planetoid Mona, impact at 4:26 P.M., Eastern Standard Time.*

As much as I hated having to give a speech, I didn't want to be a no-show for Gunnar. All could be lost today if we didn't make it back. My good standing with the principal, my self-respect—even Kjersten, who did not approve of Gunnar's rally but would approve even less of me skipping out on him. And would Mona take the fall for this? Would my parents? No! It would all be on my head.

I cursed myself for not having the guts to say no and stick by it, refusing to go.

"Why do we all have to be at the airport?" I had said just before we left the house. "If the rest of you are there, why do *I* have to go?"

"Because I'm asking you to," was my father's response.

And as unreasonable as that was, I knew I had to go. Maybe Gunnar's dad has forfeited his right to be respected—but I still had to respect my father's wishes. Even if they screwed me royally.

By the time we got to the terminal, Aunt Mona was already waiting, and even before she hugged us, the onslaught began.

"Ugh! Where were you? I've been here for ten minutes!"

"Couldn't find parking," Dad said, kissing her cheek. "Your luggage come yet?"

"You know LaGuardia. Ugh! I'll be lucky if it comes at all." She looked at me and nodded approvingly. "I see you're wearing that shirt I got you. It's European, you know. I got it especially for you—the bright colors are supposed to make you look muscular."

Out of the corner of my eye I saw Christina grin, and I sniffed loudly to remind her she stunk of Mona's perfume. I looked at my watch—Mom saw me, and tried to rush everything along. Luckily the luggage came out quickly, and we hurried to the car, with less than an hour to make it to the rally.

Air travel was not a good thing for my aunt's mood. Our car ride was a veritable feast of unpleasantness—but rather than going through everything Mona said on the car ride, I'll offer you a menu of choice selections.

Moná

An all-you-can-stomach experience.

—————— APPETIZERS ——————

"I see you've still got the same old car.
Do they even make this model anymore?"

"Where are you taking us? You never had a sense of direction, Joe. Even as a boy he'd get lost on his bicycle and I'd have to find him."

"You should smile more, Angela.
Maybe then your children might."

———————— WHINE LIST ————————

"Ugh! I'm an icicle here—this heater gives no heat!"

"Toxic mold in your basement? Ugh!
You should have had the whole house torn down."

"Can't we stop and get something to drink?
I'm getting nauseous from the fumes. Ugh!"*

———————— SOUPS AND STEWS ————————

"Traffic? You don't know traffic until you've lived in Chicago.
Your traffic is nothing compared to mine."

"Stress? You don't know stress until you've run a perfume company.
Your stress is nothing compared to what I go through."

"Weather? You don't know how easy you have it!
Come to Chicago if you want to know what real weather is."

---

*(I SUGGESTED A PITCHER OF WATER, BUT MOM REACHED OVER CHRISTINA AND SMACKED ME.)

─────── **MAIN COURSE** ───────
(Served scalding hot, and taken with a grain of salt)

"You're taking me to *Paris, Capisce?* for dinner?
I thought we were going to a regular restaurant."

"It's on Avenue T? Couldn't you find a better location?
Well, I suppose you'll do better in a neighborhood
with low expectations."

"Once I move to New York, I'll be able to give you pointers
on the right way to run a business."*

─────── **LIGHTER SELECTIONS** ───────
for the calorie-conscious

"Angela, dear—I'll order Nutri-plan diet meals for you.
You don't have to thank me, it's my treat."

"Christina, you're very attractive, for a girl of your build."

"One word, Joe: 'Liposuction.'"

─────── **DESSERT** ───────

"What's this about stopping at a school?"

---

*(AT THIS POINT DAD REACHED TO THE DASHBOARD, AND FOR THE BRIEFEST INSANE MOMENT, I THOUGHT HE MIGHT BE REACHING FOR AN EJECTION BUTTON THAT WOULD SEND AUNT MONA FLYING THROUGH THE ROOF—BUT HE WAS JUST TURNING ON THE RADIO.)

"How long is this going to take?"

"I haven't eaten all day!"

"Can I just wait in the car?"

"On second thought, no. In this neighborhood I'll probably get mugged."

We walked into the rally five minutes late, to find an auditorium packed, standing room only. My parents were completely bewildered. They knew I'd been doing "something" for Gunnar, but I don't think they had any idea what it was, or how big it had become. They had never even seen my time contracts.

"Some turnout," said Dad.

"And on a school night," said Mom.

"This is how flu epidemics start," said Mona, zeroing in on one kid with a hacking cough.

"What's that up onstage?" my mom asked, pointing at the big cardboard thermometer.

"It's measuring all the time I collected for Gunnar."

"Oh," she said, with no idea what I was talking about. It was actually kind of nice to see my parents starstruck by something I had done—even if it was all a sham.

I had my speech in my pocket, and as nervous as I was to get up in front of all these people, I was relieved to actually be there. This wouldn't be so bad. It would be over quick, then we could get off to dinner and face a new menu of perspiration-inducing gripes from our own "relative humidity."

But it didn't happen that way. Not by a long shot. That night will be branded in my mind forever, because it was, without exaggeration, the worst night of my life.

The Day That Forever Will Be Known as "Black Wednesday"

16 The freezing rain had turned to sleet. It pelted the long windows of the auditorium with a clattering hiss like radio static. There were no seats for us—in fact, there were no seats for about a dozen people standing in the back, and even more were still filing in.

"This is very impressive," Mom said.

"Ugh," said Mona. "What is this, Ecuador? Do we need all this heat?"

She was right about that. Even though it was freezing outside, the auditorium was stifling hot. My father had taken off his coat, but there was nowhere to put it. He ended up holding his own and Mona's, which was made of so many small animals, my father looked like a fur trader. Mom took out a tissue and blotted his forehead since his hands were too full to do it himself.

"Antsy! Where have you been?" It was Neena Wexler, Freshman Class President.

"Airport."

Neena gave a nod of hello to my family. Mona fanned herself in response to point out the heat issue.

"Sorry it's so hot," Neena said, "but it's actually on purpose. We have a whole thermometer motif."

"Just remember to enunciate," Aunt Mona advised me. "I'm sure you'll do fine even with that speech impediment." She was referring to my apparent inability to pronounce her name "Moná."

I looked to Dad to make sure he was okay with all of this. Now that he had gotten over his initial bewilderment, he just looked tired and worried.

"Don't mind your father," Mom said. "He's just concerned because he left Barry in charge of the restaurant tonight." Barry is his assistant manager, who gets overwhelmed if there's too many salad orders.

With the clock ticking, Neena grabbed my wrist and dragged me toward the stage.

"We're all proud of you," Mom called after me.

Neena had led the entire thermometer campaign, and had done it with the brutal resolve of a wartime general. She did everything short of wrestling the entire time-shaving industry out of my hands in her attempt to make it a student-government operation. I wish I could have just left it in her hands and walked away, but I was as much a poster child for this Event as Gunnar—and make no mistake about it, this was an Event, with a capital *E*.

There were several chairs onstage, next to the thermometer. Balloons were strung to everything onstage, enough maybe to lift someone else up to the Empire State Building if you bunched them all up together. Gunnar was in one chair, and seemed to be enjoying this much more than I wanted him to. Principal Sinclair sat in another chair, and the third one was waiting for me. Some seats in the front row of the auditorium were taped off, intended for Gunnar's family, but Kjersten was the only one there. She smiled at me and I gave her a little wave. I could tell she wanted this over just as much as I did—it was good to know I wasn't the only one.

Neena whisked me past the superintendent of schools and her entourage. She shook my hand, and before I could say anything, Neena pulled me up onstage and sat me down in my preassigned seat, under bright lights that made it all the more hot.

"Interesting shirt," Gunnar said.

"'*True color coordination lies within,*'" I told him. "Tommy Freakin' Hilfiger." If Gunnar could do it, then so could I.

"Hey, Antsy," someone in the audience shouted. "You gonna baptize anyone today?"

People laughed. I couldn't find the heckler in the audience, but I did find my father, who showed no sign of amusement.

Neena approached the podium, tapped the microphone to make sure it was on, and began. "Welcome to our rally in support of our classmate and friend Gunnar Ümlaut." Cheers and whoops from the crowd. Gunnar waved; for the first time since I knew him, he seemed blissfully happy. He was milking it for all it was worth.

"You're not the homecoming king," I whispered to him. "Stop waving already."

He spoke back to me through a gritted-teeth smile, like a ventriloquist. "It would be suspicious to ignore the cheers."

Neena continued. "It's your heartfelt donations that have made this evening possible."

I pulled my speech out of my pocket, ready to give it, but Gunnar handed me a program, printed up special for the rally. "I'd put that speech away for a while if I were you," he said.

Neena, who I'm sure will grow up to plan weddings and Super Bowl halftime shows, had a whole evening of Gunnar-themed activities lined up. The program was four pages long, and "Speech by Anthony Bonano" was toward the bottom of page four. I groaned, and Neena said:

"Let's all rise for the national anthem, as performed by our jazz choir."

The curtain opened behind us to reveal the entire jazz choir wearing TIME WARRIOR T-shirts, like everyone else onstage except me and Gunnar. They delivered a painfully drawn-out rendition of "The Star-Spangled Banner," then someone in the audience yelled, "Play ball!" and the choir disappeared behind the closing curtain.

Next came an address from the principal. He talked up the school, the faculty, he kissed up to the superintendent, and then he went right into infomercial mode. "Let me just tell you about some of the many student organizations, clubs, and activities we have on our exceptional campus . . ."

Way in the back I could see Aunt Mona's lips moving and my dad nodding, taking in whatever she was spouting. I took a deep shuddering breath, and fiddled with my speech until it was all crumpled.

"I'm sorry you have to go through this," Gunnar said, "but look at how happy everyone is. They all feel like they've done a good deed just by being here."

"It doesn't get you off the hook," I reminded him.

Principal Sinclair sat down, and Neena took the podium again. "And now we're happy to present a short film made by our very own Ira Goldfarb."

"Ira?" I said aloud. I found him in the second row. He gave me a thumbs-up. I had no idea he was involved with this at all.

The auditorium darkened, and on the TVs in the corner we viewed a ten-minute documentary featuring interviews with students and teachers, candid moments of Gunnar that he didn't even know about, and a painfully detailed, animated description of Pulmonary Monoxic Systemia that would make most of my speech seem redundant. The whole thing was done to songs like "Wind Beneath my Wings" and "We Are the Champions." The fact that Ira had half the audience in tears after the last slow-motion sequence made me more impressed, and more annoyed, by his filmmaking skills than ever before. Gunnar was still grinning like an idiot, but I could tell he was getting embarrassed. This was too much attention, even for him.

When it was over, the lights came up, and Neena rose to the podium once more. "Wasn't that wonderful?" she asked, not expecting a response, although some bozo yelled that he wet his pants. "But before we go on," said Neena, "let's have a look at the thermometer." She pulled the microphone from its holder and crossed to the thermometer, which stood taller than she did. "As you can see our goal is fifty years. Right now, we only have forty-seven years and five months, but tonight we're going to reach our goal!"

The audience applauded with questionable enthusiasm.

"Who out there would like to help us reach our goal for Gunnar?"

She waited. And she waited. And she waited some more.

Gunnar and I looked at each other, starting to get uncomfortable. Neena, perfectionist that she is, was not willing to leave it at forty-seven years, five months. The thermometer had to be complete. There was a red Sharpie standing by for that very purpose, and no one—*no one*—was going anywhere until Gunnar had a full fifty years.

"Isn't there anyone out there willing to give the tiniest amount of goodwill to Gunnar?" urged Neena.

Principal Sinclair took to the microphone. "Come on, people! I know for a fact that our students here are more generous than this!" And that clinched it—because now filling up the thermometer was far less entertaining than making us all sit up there looking foolish.

Finally Wailing Woody rose from his seat and came down the aisle, high-fiving everyone as he passed. As he came up to the stage he raised his hands as if to quiet nonexistent applause. He gave a month, and was quickly followed by the superintendent and her entourage. The applause was getting weaker and less enthusiastic with each signature.

"Okay," said Neena. "That makes forty-eight years, even. Who's next?"

I leaned over to her. "Neena," I whispered, "this isn't a telethon, we don't have to reach the goal."

"Yes! We! Do!" she snapped back in the harshest whisper I've ever heard. I looked to Principal Sinclair, but he was intimidated by her, too.

No one was stepping forward, and I was beginning to wonder if maybe Neena might put the school into lockdown, and we'd be there until morning. Then, from the back of the room, I heard, "Oh, for goodness' sake!" And my salvation came marching down the center aisle.

My father!

I could not have been more grateful as he made his way to the stage. After all I had put him through, here he was saving the day!

Neena reached out to shake his hand, but his expression definitely lacked the spirit Neena was looking for, and she put her hand down.

"How much do you need?" he asked, getting right to business.

"Two years," Nina answered.

"You got it. Where do I sign?"

I took a time contract and handed it to my father, showing what to fill in, and where to sign.

"Thank you, Dad," I said. "Really."

"Your aunt is driving us crazy," he told me. "It was either this or a grudge match between her and your mother." He wiped sweat from his brow, then signed the document. The principal signed as witness, and Neena snatched the paper, holding it up to the audience.

"Mr. Bonano has given us two full years! We've reached our goal!" And the crowd went wild, whooping and hollering at the prospect of moving on to page three.

Dad shook Gunnar's hand, turned to leave the stage . . . then he hesitated. He turned to me, wiping his forehead again. It was the first time that I noticed he was sweating a bit more than anyone else onstage. He looked pale, too, and it wasn't just the stage lights.

"Dad?"

He waved me off. "I'm fine."

Then he rubbed his chest, took a deep breath, and suddenly fell to one knee.

"Dad!"

I was down there with him in an instant. A volley of gasps came from the audience, blending with the clatter of sleet on the windows.

"Joe!" I hear my mother scream.

"I'm okay. It's nothing. I'm fine."

But now he went all the way down, on all fours. "I . . . I just need someone to help me up." But instead of getting up, he kept going down. In a second he had rolled over and was flat on his back, struggling to breathe.

And still my father insists that everything's okay. I want to believe him. This is not happening, I tell myself. And if I say it enough, maybe I'll believe it.

From this moment on, nothing made proper sense. Everything was random shouts and disconnected images. Time fell apart.

Mom is there holding his hand.

Mona's on the stage, clutching her coat beside her, and gets pushed out of the way by the security guard who claims to know CPR, but doesn't seem too confident.

A million cell phones dialing 911 all at once.

"I'm fine. I'm fine. Oh God."

Gunnar standing next to Kjersten standing next to me, none of us able to do a damn thing.

The guard counting, and doing chest compressions.

The whole audience standing like it's the national anthem all over again.

Dad's not talking anymore.

The squealing wheels of a gurney rolling down the aisle. How did they get here so fast? How long has he been lying on that stage?

An oxygen mask, and his fingers feel so cold, and the crowd parts before us as the wheels squeal again, and me, Mom, Christina, and Mona are carried along in the wake of the gurney toward the auditorium door, where cold air rolls in, hitting the heat and making fog that rolls like ocean surf.

And in the madness of this terrible moment, one voice in the crowd, loud and clear, pierces the panic. Once voice that says:

"My God! He gave two years, and he died!"

I turn to seek out the owner of that voice. "SHUT UP!" I scream. "SHUT UP! HE'S NOT DEAD!" If I found who said it, I'd break him up so bad he'd be joining us at the hospital, but I'm pulled along too quickly in the gurney's wake, out the door and into the wet night. He's not dead. He's not. Even as they load him into the ambulance, they're talking to him, and he's nodding. Weakly, but he's nodding.

We pile into our car to follow, leaving Gunnar, and Kjersten, and the thermometer and the crowd. Now there's nothing but the sleet, and the cold, and the wail and flashing lights of the ambulance as we break every traffic law and run every red light to keep up with it, because we don't know which hospital they're taking him to, so we can't lose the ambulance. We can't. We can't.

My Head Explodes Like Mount St. Helens, and I'll Probably Be Picking Up the Pieces for Years

17 Our lives get spent worrying about such pointless, stupid things. Does this girl like me? Does this boy know I exist? Did I get an A, B, or C? And will everyone laugh when they see my ugly shirt? It's amazing how quickly—how, in the smallest moment of time, all of that can implode into nothing, when the universe suddenly opens up, revealing itself with all these impossible depths and dizzying heights. You're swept up into it, and as you look down, the perspective is terrifying. People look like ants from so far away.

I understand hell now, and you don't have to leave this world to get there. You can get there just fine sitting in a hospital waiting room.

Coney Island Hospital's emergency room didn't seem to have much to do with health. It seemed more like this sickly mix of bad luck, bad timing, and even worse news. My father got rushed in right away, and the rest of us were left to wait in the reception area, where people who weren't immediately dying waited for service like it was a deli counter.

"Did they have to bring him here?" says Aunt Mona. "What's wrong with Kings County, or Maimonides?"

There were a lot of people with bloody clothes, poorly bandaged wounds, and bloated, feverish faces—all hanging their hopes on a single overtired receptionist who was, in theory, calling names, although it was more than half an hour until I heard her call a single one. I tried to read a magazine, but couldn't focus. Christina played halfheartedly with a battered old Boggle game she got from a toy chest that smelled of small children. Mom seemed to be studying the pattern of the carpet.

"Why aren't they telling us anything?" says Aunt Mona. "I don't like how they run this hospital."

There was a huge fish tank filled with fake coral rocks and a plastic diver all covered with green tank scum. There seemed to be only three fish in the giant tank, and I'm thinking, *If this place can't take care of their fish, what does it say about patient care?*

"I don't know what this stain on this seat is," says Aunt Mona, "but I'm going to sit over there."

My phone rang. I didn't recognize the number, so I didn't pick up. But then it had been ringing a lot, and I hadn't picked up for anybody. Thinking of the phone reminded me of something.

"You gotta call Frankie," I told Mom.

Mom shook her head. "Not yet."

"You gotta call Frankie!" I told her more forcefully.

"If I do, he'll come driving all the way from Binghamton in

the middle of the night in this weather at a hundred miles an hour! No thank you, I don't need two in the hospital! We'll call your brother in the morning."

I was about to protest—but then I got it. Even though I couldn't see the look in her eyes, I got it. *You gather the whole family at a deathbed.* So as long as Frankie's not here, it's not a deathbed, is it? It's the same reason she hadn't asked to talk to a priest.

My phone rang again, and I finally turned it off. Did people think I would actually answer it? As if their need to know was more important than my need not to talk about it.

An hour later a doctor came out and asked for Mrs. Benini. I took no notice until Mom says, "Do you mean Bonano?"

The doctor looked at his chart and corrected himself. "Yes— Bonano."

Suddenly I think the heart attack might have spread to me. We all stand up.

"Mrs. Bonano," the doctor said, "your husband has an acute blockage of the—"

But that's all I hear, because I get stuck on one word.
Has.

Present tense! "Has" means "is," not "was." It means my father's alive. Never have I appreciated tense so completely. I swore I'll never take tense for granted again.

"He's going to need emergency bypass surgery," the doctor told us. "Triple bypass, actually." The fact that they had a name for it was a good thing, I figured. If they knew what they had to do, then they could do it, but Mom covered her mouth and found a new wellspring of tears, so I knew this wasn't so good.

"It's a long operation, but your husband's a fighter," the doctor said. "I have every hope that he'll pull through." And then he added, "There's a chapel on the second floor, if you'd like some privacy." Which is not something you say to someone if you truly believe their loved one is going to pull through.

The doctor said he'd keep us posted, and disappeared through the double doors. Mom said nothing. Christina and I said nothing. But Aunt Mona said, "It's all that cholesterol in his diet. I've warned him for years. Our father, rest his soul, went the same way, but did Joe listen?"

Back in eighth grade, I had a geology unit in science. We studied volcanoes. Some erupt predictably, spewing magma, and others just explode. The rock is so hot it actually becomes gas, and the blast is more powerful than a hydrogen bomb.

That's the closest I can come to explaining what happened to me next. I could feel it coming the moment Aunt Mona opened her mouth, and I had no way to control it.

Mom saw me about to blow. She tried to grab me, but I shook her off. There was no stopping this—not by her, not by anybody.

"Shut your freaking mouth!" I screamed. Everyone in the waiting room turned to me, but I didn't care. *"Shut your freaking mouth before I shut it for you!"* Mona gaped, unable to speak as I looked her in the eye, refusing to look away. *"You sit there and complain every day of your stupid life, passing judgment on everyone, and even now you won't shut up!"*

And then I said it. I said the words that had been brewing inside since the moment my father went down on that stage.

"It should have been you."

She looked at me like I had plunged a dagger through her heart.

"Anthony!" my mother said, losing all her wind with that single word.

I kept Mona locked in my gaze, feeling as if my eyes could just burn her away. *"It should be you in that operating room. I wish it was you dying instead of him."*

So now it was out. I meant it, she knew I meant it—everyone in the waiting room knew.

And from somewhere beside me, I heard Christina, in a tiny voice say, "So do I . . ."

Suddenly it felt like there was no air in that room, and the walls had closed in. I had to escape. I don't even remember leaving. The next thing I knew I was in the parking garage, searching for our car, and I found it. I didn't have the keys, but Mom, in her panic, had forgotten to lock it. Good thing, too, because I was fully prepared to break a window. I almost wanted to.

I sat in the car that smelled so strongly of Aunt Mona's perfume, and I pounded the dashboard. Mona was the one with all the anxiety. She was a human propeller churning up stress until everyone was drowning in it. Why couldn't it have been her? Why?

I was starting to cool down by the time my mom came, and sat in the car beside me.

"No lectures!" I yelled, even before she opened her mouth.

"No lectures," she agreed quietly.

We sat there for a while in silence, and when she finally did speak, she said, "Aunt Mona decided it was best if she took a hotel room across the street from the hospital. That way she can be close." Which meant she wouldn't be staying with us anymore. I wondered if I'd ever see her again. I wondered if I cared.

"Good," I said. I might have cooled down, but it didn't change what I said, or the fact that I meant it. But then my mother said something I didn't see coming.

"Anthony . . . don't you realize I was thinking the same thing?"

I looked to her, not sure that I had heard her right. "What?"

"From the moment I knew your father was having a heart attack, I had to fight to keep it out of my mind. *'It should have been her, not Joe—it should have been her . . .'*" Mom closed her eyes, and I could see her trying to force the worst of those god-awful feelings away. "But honey, there are some things that must never be said out loud."

Knowing she was right just made me angrier. I gritted my teeth so hard I thought I might break them—and then what? We'd have dental bills on top of bypass.

"I'm not sorry."

Mom patted my arm. "That's okay," she said. "Someday you will be, and you can deal with it then."

Somewhere in the garage a car alarm went off, echoing all around.

"No word from the doctor?" I asked.

"Not yet. But that's good."

I knew what she meant. It was a four-, maybe five-hour operation. There's only one reason it would end early.

"I'd better get back," Mom said. "Come when you're ready. We'll be in the chapel." And she left.

My anger at the unfairness of it all still raged inside, but some of that anger was bouncing off of Mona and sticking to me. Wasn't I the one who dumped that pitcher of water on Boswell, making life that much harder on my father? Wasn't I always talking back, creating problems, making things harder at home? Could I have been the one who pushed him one step too far?

And then I got to thinking about the time contracts, and how I, in a way, had been tempting fate—playing God. Was this my punishment? Was this, as they say, the wage of my sin?

My brain had already turned to cottage cheese, and now it was going funnier still. You can call it another volcanic burst, you can call it temporary insanity, you can call it whatever you like. All I know is that in my current dairy-brained state, the letters in my own mental Boggle game suddenly came together and started talking in tongues.

Fact: My father's heart attack happened within moments of him signing a contract for two years of his life.

Fact: It was my fault the contract even existed.

Fact: There was a fat black binder filled with almost fifty years sitting in Gunnar Ümlaut's bedroom.

. . . but I could get those years back.

Maybe if I got all those pages and brought them to my father—or better yet, brought them to the chapel and laid them down on the altar . . . Did a hospital chapel have an altar? If not, I would make one. I'd take a table, and sprinkle it with holy water. I'd renounce what I had done—truly renounce it, and those pages would be my bargain with God. Then, once that bargain had been struck, the morning would come, the operation would be a success, and I would still have a father.

This wasn't just an answer, it felt like a vision! I could almost hear the gospel choir singing the hallelujahs.

I left the car, my breath coming in fast puffs of steam in the midnight cold, and took to the street, searching for the nearest subway station.

Go Ahead . . . Tenderize My Meat.

18 There were things I didn't know, which I didn't find out until much later—like what happened in the auditorium after my father was rushed out.

My God—he gave two years of his life and he died!

It hadn't occurred to me that others had heard that—and even though news of my father's death had been greatly exaggerated, it didn't matter. What mattered was the possibility that he'd die. Just like my eruption at Aunt Mona, it was something everyone was thinking, but it was too dangerous to say aloud.

In the awkward, uneasy moments after we had left, Principal Sinclair tried to get things back on track—the show must go on, and all. It was no use. The crowd was murmuring up a cloud of worry—not about my father, but about themselves. Then someone yelled, "Hey, I want my month back," and all eyes turned to Gunnar.

In less than a minute, people were asking him, tugging at him, grabbing at him, demanding their time back—and when he didn't give it back right then and there, things started to get ugly. People were yelling, pushing one another, and then kids who didn't even care took this as their cue to make further mischief, by fighting, throwing stuff, and creating a general atmosphere of havoc. Mob mentality took over.

Gunnar and Kjersten escaped through a back door, along with the superintendent, leaving poor Mr. Sinclair and a skeletal faculty desperately struggling to bring back sanity, like that was gonna happen. In the end, Wendell Tiggor led about twenty semihardened criminals and delinquent wannabes on a rampage through the school. The rest was history.

But I didn't know any of this when I arrived at Gunnar and Kjersten's house at twelve-thirty in the morning.

I rang the bell and knocked, rang and knocked, over and over until Mrs. Ümlaut came to the door in a bathrobe. There was luggage just inside the door, and I knew she must have arrived home that evening. I didn't bother with pleasantries, I pushed right past her and bounded up the stairs.

"What are you doing? What do you want?" she wailed, but I really didn't have time for explanations.

Gunnar's door was closed, but not locked. The one thing I had going for me tonight was unlocked doors. I found a light switch, flicked it on, and Gunnar sat up in bed, blinking, not entirely conscious yet.

"Where is it?" I demanded.

"Antsy? Wh–what's going on?"

"The notebook. Where is it? Answer me!"

It took him a moment to process the question, then he glanced over at his desk. "It's there, but—"

That's all I needed to know. I grabbed the notebook—and noticed right away that it felt way too light. I opened it up and saw that it was empty. The pages were all gone.

"Where's all the time? I have to have that time!"

"You can't!" Gunnar said.

Wrong answer! I pulled him out of bed so sharply, I heard his T-shirt tear. "You're giving them to me, and you're giving them to me now!" I never muscled other kids to get what I want, but right now I was willing to use every muscle in my body to get this.

Behind me I heard Kjersten call my name, I heard their mother scream, and that pushed me all the more to push him. I slammed Gunnar hard against the wall. "Give them to me!"

Then something hit me. Mrs. Ümlaut had attacked me. She was armed, and swinging, wailing as she did. I felt the weapon connect with my back, the blow softened slightly by my jacket, but still it hurt. She swung it again, and this time I saw what it was. It was a meat tenderizer. A stainless-steel, square little mallet. She swung the kitchen utensil like the hammer of Thor and it connected with my shoulder right through my coat.

"Ow!"

"You stop this!" she screamed. "You stop this now!"

But I didn't stop. I didn't stop until Kjersten entered the battle, and with a single blow that bore the force of the dozen or so other Norse gods, her fist connected with my face and I went down.

You don't know this kind of pain—and if you do, I'm sorry.

Had it been my nose, she would have broken it. Had it been my chin, my jaw would have to be wired together for months. But it was my eye.

All those muscles that were, just an instant ago, ready to tear Gunnar limb from limb suddenly decided it was time to call it a night, and they all went limp. I didn't quite pass out, but I did find myself on the ground, with just enough strength to bring my hands to my eye, and cry out in pain.

My left eye was swollen shut in seconds, and in the kind of humiliation beyond which there is only darkness, I allowed Kjersten to guide me downstairs and into the kitchen. I had just been beaten to a pulp by my girlfriend in a single blow. Social lives did not get any bleaker than this.

"I had to do it," she said as she prepared a bag of ice for me. "If I didn't, my mother would have taken that meat tenderizer to your head, and knocked you silly."

"Silly works," I mumbled. "Better than where I was."

She seemed to understand, even without me telling her— after all, she was right there in the front row when my dad had the heart attack. I told her where things stood with my father, and she went out into the living room, explaining everything to her mother. She spoke in Swedish, which, I guess was the language of love in this family. I could see Mrs. Ümlaut glance at me as they spoke. At first she looked highly suspicious, but her distrust eventually faded, and her motherly instincts returned.

Gunnar joined me in the kitchen. It kind of surprised me on account of we now had a perp/victim relationship. He seemed unfazed by my unprovoked attack. Maybe because there were plenty of other things to faze him.

"I don't think we're going to be a National Blue Ribbon school," he said, and he explained to me the madness that ensued after my family and I had left the rally.

"I couldn't give anyone back their months," he said. "You can't have them either. Because last week my dad found them, and burned them all in the fireplace."

And there they went, all my hopes of redemption up in smoke. Without those time contracts, I could not undo what I had done. But I had already regained enough of my senses to realize getting those pages would not help my father.

Gunnar went on to tell me how his dad had officially left the minute his mom came home.

"They're splitting up," he told me.

I almost started to say how that wasn't such a big deal, considering—but realized that I would sound just like Aunt Mona. *Trauma? You don't know from trauma until your father's had a heart attack. And they're much worse in Chicago.*

I wouldn't invalidate his pain. Every problem is massive until something more massive comes along.

In a few moments Mrs. Ümlaut came in with Kjersten. Mercifully she did not have the meat tenderizer. Mrs. Ümlaut sat beside me, far more sympathetic than when I pushed through the front door.

"Your father?" she asked.

"They're still working on him," I said. "At least they were when I left."

She nodded. Then she took my both my hands in hers, looked into my one useful eye, and then Mrs. Ümlaut said something to me that I know I will remember for the rest of my life.

"Either he will live, or he will die."

That was it. That was all. Yet suddenly everything came into clear focus. *Either he will live, or he will die.* Simple as that. All the drama, all the craziness, all the panic, didn't mean a thing. This was a gamble—a roll of the dice. I don't know why, but I took comfort from that. There were, after all, only two outcomes. I could not predict them, I could not control them. It was not in my hands. I had been afraid to say the word "die," but now that it had been said, and with such strength and compassion, it held no power over me.

For the first time all night, I found myself crying like there was no tomorrow—although I knew there would be a tomorrow. It might not be the tomorrow I wanted, but it would still be there.

I could feel Kjersten's hand on my shoulder, and I let comfort come from all sides. Then, when my tears had gone dry, Mrs. Ümlaut said, "Come, I'll take you to the hospital."

When I got to the hospital, there were more familiar faces in the waiting area. Relatives we didn't get to see this holiday season, Barry from the restaurant, a couple of family friends—and in the middle of it all were Lexie and her grandfather. I went straight to Lexie. Moxie got up when he saw me, and so Lexie knew, even before someone called my name, that I was there.

"We came as soon as we heard," she said. "Where have you been?"

"Long story. Is there any news?"

"Not yet."

I looked around. Mona had come back, and Christina was asleep in her arms. I wondered if they had made up. Mona didn't look at me.

Crawley, who never came out of his apartment unless he was kidnapped or pried out with a crowbar, came up to me. "All expenses shall be covered," he said. "Either way."

For a second I felt like getting angry at that, but I had had enough anger for one evening. "That's okay," I told him. "We don't want your money."

"But you'll take it," he said, and then added with more emotion than I'd ever seen in him before, "because that's what I have to give."

I nodded a quiet acceptance.

"Your mother's up in the chapel," Lexie said.

I gave a quick greeting to relatives and friends, then went to find her.

The place wasn't much of a chapel—there were only four rows, and the pews seemed too comfortable to be effective. There was a small stained-glass panel, backlit with fluorescent lights. There was no cross on account of it was a spiritual multipurpose room, that had to be used by people of all religious symbols. The chapel's best feature was a huge bookshelf stocked with Bibles and holy books of all shapes and sizes, so nobody got left out. Old Testament, New Testament, red testament, blue testament. This one has a little star—see how many faiths there are. (This is the moment I realized how exhausted I really was.)

Mom was alone in the room, kneeling in the second row. It was so like her to take the second row even when she was alone in the room.

"Did you fall asleep in the car?" Mom asked, without turning around to see me.

"How did you know it was me?"

"I can always tell when you need a shower," she told me. Between her and Lexie, who needed sight? At least if she didn't look at me too closely, she wouldn't see my swollen eye.

"Come pray with me, Anthony."

And so I did. I knelt beside her, joining her—and as I did, maybe for the first time in my life, I understood it. Not so much the words as the whole idea of prayer itself.

I'll never really know if prayer changes the outcome of things. Lots of people believe it does. I know I'd like to believe it, but there's no guarantee. Some people pray and their prayers are rewarded—they walk away convinced that their prayers were answered. Others pray and they get refused. Sometimes they lose their faith, all because they lost the roll of the dice.

That night, as I prayed, I wasn't praying for my own wants and needs. I prayed for my father, and for my mother, I prayed for my whole family. Not because I was *supposed* to—not because I was afraid of what would happen if I didn't. I was doing it because I truly wanted to do it with all my heart, and believe it or not, for the first time ever, I didn't want it to end.

That's when I realized—

—and excuse me for having a whole immaculate Sunday-school moment here, but I gotta milk it since they don't come that often—

—that's when I realized that prayer isn't for God. After all, He doesn't need it. He's out there, or in there, or sitting up there in His firmament, whatever that is, all-knowing and all-powerful, right? He doesn't need us repeating words week after week in His face. If He's there, sure, I'll bet He's listening, but it doesn't *change* Him, one way or the other.

Instead, *we're* the ones who are changed by it.

I don't know whether that's true, or whether I was just delirious from lack of sleep . . . but if it *is* true, what an amazing gift that is!

I let my mother decide when it was time to stop. Like I said, I could have just gone on and on. I think she knew that. I think she liked that. Then I think she started to worry that I might become a priest. This wasn't a worry of mine.

It was still the middle of the night. Three-thirty, and no word. Mom looked at me, and seemed to notice my swollen face for the first time, but chose not to ask. Instead she said, "I think you were right. Maybe I should call Frankie now."

She took out her phone and called. When it connected, the sheer look of horror on my mother's face even before she said a word got me scared, too.

"What? What is it?"

But in a moment her terror resolved into something else I couldn't quite read. "Here," she said. "Listen to the message."

I took the phone just as the message started to repeat.

"Hello. You've reached the Kings County Morgue. Our offices are closed now, but if this is a morgue-related emergency, please

dial zero. Otherwise please call back during normal business hours."

I looked at her, gaping and shaking my head. This was my doing. Just like I said, I had programmed the morgue into her speed dial as a joke, and I must have programmed it over Frankie's number. What stinking, lousy timing.

"I'm sorry," I said. "I'm so, so, sorry."

My eyes started to well up, because right here, right now, it almost seemed like a bad omen, and she was getting all choked up, too. She turned away. Then I heard her give a little hiccup, and then another, and when she turned back, I could see that in the middle of tears, she had started laughing.

"You rotten, rotten kid."

And then I was laughing, too. I put my arms around her and held her, and both of us stood there laughing, and crying, laughing and crying like a couple of nutjobs, until the doctor came in, and cleared his throat to get our attention. Maybe he understood what we were feeling, maybe he didn't. Maybe he'd seen everything. He started to speak before we had the chance to brace ourselves.

"He made it through the operation," he said, "but the next twenty-four hours are crucial."

We relaxed just the slightest bit, and Mom finally got to call Frankie instead of the morgue.

I Love You, You're an Idiot,
Now Let's All Go Home

19 My father almost died again the next day, but he didn't. Instead he started to get better. By Friday, they moved him out of intensive care, and by Saturday, he was bored. He tried to squeeze news out of my mom about the restaurant, but all she would say was, "It's there," and she forbade anyone else to talk about it, for fear that talking business would send my father back into cardiac arrest.

With my dad on the mend, and more than enough people doting on him, my thoughts drifted to Kjersten and Gunnar. I went to visit on Sunday morning, to see how they were handling their own hardships, and give whatever support I could. The Christmas wreath was gone from their door, and the foreclosure notice glared out for the whole world to see.

"Good riddance," I heard one beer-bellied neighbor say to another as I walked down the block toward their house. "After what they did to our yards, let 'em go back where they came from. Freakin' foreigners."

I turned to the man. "No, actually *I* was the one who did that to your yards, and I ain't going nowhere. You gonna do something about it?"

He puffed on a cigarette. "Why don't you just move along," he said from behind the safety of his little waist-high wrought-iron fence.

"Lucky you got that fence between us," I said. "Otherwise I might have to go samurai on your ass." I have to say there's nothing more satisfying than lip delivered to those who deserve it.

Mrs. Ümlaut answered the door, and pulled me in like she was pulling me out of a blizzard instead of a clear winter day. She barely allowed Kjersten to hug me before she dragged me into the kitchen, practically buried me in French toast, and had me tell her all about my dad's condition. Now that I had fought various members of the Ümlaut household and had been struck repeatedly by a blunt object, I guess that made me like family.

I went upstairs to find Gunnar in his room, watching a black-and-white foreign film called *The Seventh Seal.*

"It's by Ingmar Bergman, patron saint of all things Swedish," he said. "It's about a chess game with death."

"Of course it is," I said. "What else would you be watching?" I sat down at his desk chair. There was dust on his desk, as if he hadn't done homework for weeks.

"What's that thing the Grim Reaper holds, anyway?" I asked.

"It's called a scythe," Gunnar said. "It's what people used to use to harvest grain."

"So does modern death drive a combine?"

Gunnar chuckled, but only slightly.

We watched the film for a few minutes. It was a scene where the main character was looking out of a high window, supposedly facing the horizon of his own mortality, and it got me thinking about the guy who fell from the Roadkyll Raccoon balloon on Thanksgiving. I wondered if he, like the guy in the film, saw the Grim Reaper waiting for him.

No one likes the Grim Reaper. He's like that tax auditor who came to our house a couple of years ago. He's just doing his job, but everyone hates his guts on principle. If there really is such a guy and he comes for me someday, I promised myself I'd offer him cookies and milk, like little kids do for Santa Claus. Then maybe at least he'll put in a good word for me. Bribing Death never hurts.

"It's good that you're reconnecting with your roots," I told him. "I should watch more Italian films."

He turned off the TV. "I don't need to watch this," he said. "I know the ending. Death wins."

I shrugged. "Doesn't mean you gotta go carving tombstones."

Gunnar tossed the remote on his desk. "I'm done with that." He flexed his fingers. "I think maybe it gave me carpal tunnel."

He looked at his hand for a while, and although his gaze never left his fingers, I know his thoughts went far away.

"My father's at the casino again," Gunnar said. "He hasn't found a place to live yet, so I guess that's where he's staying until he does. Maybe he'll just set up a cot underneath one of the roulette wheels. I really don't care."

That, I knew, was a lie. Keep in mind that I had almost lost my father a few days before, so I knew what Gunnar was going through. It was in a different way, but the concept was basically the same. Reapers come in all shapes and sizes. And they don't always clear-cut the field with their scythes—sometimes they just leave crop circles.

I really don't care, Gunnar had said—and all at once I realized that Gunnar was finally, *finally* in denial. For him this was the best thing that could happen, and it gave me an idea.

"I know they're taking away your house," I said to him, "but do you think you guys can squeeze out enough money to fill your mom's car with gas?"

Even if the answer was no, I knew that I had enough money if they didn't.

When someone's addicted, they have these things called interventions. I know about them because my parents had to intervene for one of my dad's high school buddies who got addicted to some designer drug. Like drugs ain't bad enough, they got designers involved now. Basically everyone the guy knew sat him down in a room, told him they loved him and that he was a freakin' moron. Love and humiliation—it's a powerful combination—and it probably saved his life.

That's what I thought we'd have with Mr. Ümlaut—a feel-good, huggy-feely intervention. But it didn't quite turn out that way.

The Anawana Tribal Hotel and Casino was located deep in the Catskill Mountains, on the grounds of an old summer camp, proving that times changed. Old crumbling cabins, yellow and brown, could still be seen from the parking structure. The place boasted a riverboat that, for a few dollars more, would tool around Anawana Lake while you gambled.

The hotel's main casino was patrolled by security, but I guess Kjersten, Gunnar, and I looked old enough to pass for gambling age—or at least old enough to be ignored for a while, because they didn't stop us from going into the casino. Kjersten was quiet, steeling herself for the ambush, which is pretty much what this would be.

"Do you really think this will make a difference?" she asked me.

I had no idea, but the fact that she asked at all meant that she still had hope. She held my hand firmly, and it occurred to me that I was no longer her gateway to a younger, simpler time. In spite of our age difference, she'd never see me as "younger" again. And yet still, she was holding my hand.

We found Mr. Ümlaut playing craps. Even before he saw us, I could tell by the look on his face, and the circles under his eyes, that this was not going to be a heartwarming Hallmark moment.

He was throwing the dice, and apparently doing well. Adrenaline was high among the gamblers at the table around him.

"Dad?" said Gunnar. He had to say it again to get his attention. "Dad?"

With the dice still in his fist, he saw us, and it was like he was coming out of a dream. "Gunnar? Kjersten?" Then he saw me, and glared at me like their presence here was all my fault, which it was.

"Sir," said the craps guy, quickly sizing up the situation, "your children can't be here."

"I know." Mr. Ümlaut threw the dice anyway. I don't know much about craps, but apparently eleven was good. The other gamblers roared.

"You shouldn't be here," Mr. Ümlaut said to us. "Your mother isn't here, is she?"

"Just us, Daddy," said Kjersten gently.

"You should go home."

The craps guy handed him the dice, but was reluctant about it. Mr. Ümlaut shook the dice in his hand while the others standing around the table waited anxiously. Realizing we weren't going to simply disappear, Mr. Ümlaut said, "Go wait for me in the lobby." Then he hurled the dice again. Nine. This time only a few of the gamblers were happy.

"Sir, I'm afraid I must insist," the craps guy said, and pointed to us.

In turn, Mr. Ümlaut pointed to the lobby. "You heard the croupier!" Which sounded a whole lot classier than "craps guy." It makes you wonder why they haven't come up with a better name for craps. Croups, maybe.

By now the suit who managed the whole bank of craps tables came over. This guy's title I knew. He was the pit boss. The croupier's croupier. "Is there a problem here?" the pit boss asked.

"No," said Mr. Ümlaut. Then he whispered to Gunnar and Kjersten, "Leave the casino before you create a scene." Kjersten quietly stood her ground, but Gunnar had enough lip for both of them.

"A scene," said Gunnar. "Right." He nodded and backed away. I thought we were going to wait in the lobby, but then

Gunnar turned around in the middle of the aisle. For a second I thought he might say something meaningful and thought provoking—like maybe a really well-chosen fake quote. But no. Gunnar decided it was time to sing. This wasn't a quiet kind of singing either. He belted out at the top of his voice, and the sounds that came out of his mouth were like no words I'd ever heard.

"Du gamla, Du fria, Du fjällhöga nord . . ."

As far as interventions go, this was taking on a whole personality of its own.

"It's the Swedish national anthem," Kjersten explained to me.

"Du tysta, Du glädjerika sköna!"

Mr. Ümlaut just stared at him with the kind of shock and embarrassment that can only come from a parent.

"Jag hälsar Dig, vänaste land uppå jord."

Kjersten joined in, and now it was a duet. Since I didn't know the Swedish national anthem, I improvised and began to sing the most Swedish thing I knew. I began to sing a song by that Swedish seventies group, Abba.

So now the croupier looks at the pit boss, the pit boss signals the manager, and the manager comes running.

"Din sol, Din himmel, Dina ängder gröna."

All gambling in the casino grinds to a screeching halt as we perform.

"You can dance! You can jive! Having the time of your life!" I sing at the manager, who's much less entertained than I believe he should be.

Kjersten and Gunnar complete their anthem, and although I've still got a couple of verses of "Dancing Queen" left, I figure it's wise to wrap it up early. Some of the gamblers applaud, and not knowing what else to do, we all take fancy bows, and the manager turns to Mr. Ümlaut and says, "I think you should leave now."

Mr. Ümlaut did not look happy as we crossed the casino toward the lobby. Gunnar, on the other hand, looked downright triumphant at his little victory. Even more triumphant than he did on the night of the rally. It was Kjersten who seemed worried, because she knew as well as I did that this was just one battle in a much bigger war. The security guard escorting us must have resented that look on Gunnar's face, because he was rough with him, and got rougher when Gunnar tried to pull out of his grasp.

"Are you gonna let this rent-a-cop beat me up?"

Mr. Ümlaut didn't look at him. He didn't say a word until we were off the casino floor, and the security guard returned to his duties, satisfied that we were no longer a threat.

"Proud of yourself, Gunnar?"

"Are you?" Gunnar answered, with such righteous authority that his father couldn't look him in the eye.

"There are things you don't understand."

"I understand a lot more than you think."

Rather than letting the two of them bicker, Kjersten cut it off. "Daddy," she said, "we want you to come home."

He didn't answer right away. Instead he looked at them, perhaps searching for something in their faces, but you couldn't read much in those two—in that way, they took after their father.

"Didn't your mother tell you?" he said.

"What?" said Gunnar. "That you're splitting up? Of course she did."

It surprised me that he hadn't told them himself. Even if they already knew, he had a responsibility to say it in his own words.

"I will let you know where I am, once I know myself," he said. "There's nothing to worry about."

"There's a lot to worry about," Gunnar said—then Gunnar got closer to him. All this time he had maintained a distance from his father, like there was an invisible wall around him. Now Gunnar stepped inside that wall. "You're sick, Dad." He looked at the casino, all full of whirring, blaring, coin-clanging excitement, then turned back to his father. "You're very sick. And I think if you don't do something about it . . . if you don't stop gambling, somehow it's going to kill you."

But rather than taking it in, Mr. Ümlaut seemed to just pull his wall in closer, so Gunnar was on the outside again. "Is that what your mother says?"

"No," said Kjersten. "We figured it out for ourselves."

"I appreciate your concern," he said, like he was talking to strangers instead of his children. "I'll be fine."

"What about *them*?" I said. Maybe I was out of line speaking at all, but I had to say something.

Suddenly I found all his anger turned against me. "What business is this of yours? What do you know about our family? What do you know about anything?"

"Leave him alone!" shouted Kjersten. "At least he's around when we need him. At least he's there." Which I guess is the best you could say about me. "At least he's not away day after day, gambling away every penny he owns. How much money have you lost, Dad? Then the car—and now the house . . ."

"You're not understanding!" he said, loud enough to snag the attention of another family waiting to check in. They peered at us over their luggage, pretending not to. Mr. Ümlaut forced his voice down again. "The car, the house—we were losing them anyway—if not this month, then next month. A few dollars gambled makes no difference."

I think he truly believed that—and for the first time, I began to understand what Kjersten and Gunnar were up against. Mr. Ümlaut had, once upon a time, been a lawyer. That meant he could create a brilliant and convincing argument as to why the hours, days, and weeks spent in a casino were the best possible use of his time. I'm sure if I sat there and let him make his argument, he might even convince me. Juries let guilty men go free all the time.

Then Gunnar dropped the bombshell. It was a bombshell I didn't even know about.

"Mom's taking us back to Sweden," he said. "She's taking us there for good."

Although the news shocked me, I have to say I wasn't surprised. Apparently neither was Mr. Ümlaut. He waved his hand as if shooing away a swarm of gnats. "She's bluffing," he said. "She's been saying that forever. She'll never do it."

"This time she means it," Kjersten said. "She has airplane tickets for all of us," and then she added, "All of us but you."

This hit Mr. Ümlaut harder than anything else that had been said today. He looked at them, then looked at me as if I was somehow the mastermind of some conspiracy against him. He went away in his own head for a few moments. I could almost hear the conversation he was having with himself. Finally he spoke with the kind of conviction we had all been hoping to hear.

"She can't do that." He shook his head. "She can't legally do that. She can't just take you from the country without my permission!"

We all waited for him to make that momentous decision to DO something. Anything. This is what Gunnar and Kjersten wanted. Sure, it wasn't reconciliation between their parents, but it was the next best thing—they wanted their father to see what he was losing, and finally choose to do something about it.

I felt sure Gunnar and Kjersten had finally broken through that wall. Until Mr. Ümlaut released a long, slow sigh.

"Perhaps it's all for the best," he said. "Have your mother call me. I'll sign all the necessary papers."

And it was over. Just like that, it was over.

There are some things I don't understand, and don't think I ever will. I don't understand how a person can give up so totally and completely that they dive right into the heart of a black hole. I can't understand how someone's need to gamble, or to drink, or to shoot up, or to do anything can be greater than their need to survive. And I don't understand how pride can be more important than love.

"Our father's a proud man," Kjersten said as we drove away from the casino—as if pride can be an excuse for acting so shamefully—and yes, I know the man was sick, just as Gunnar said, but that didn't excuse the choice he made today.

I felt partially to blame, because I was the one who convinced Gunnar and Kjersten to come. I honestly believed it would make a difference. Like I said, I come from a family of fixers—but what happens when something simply can't be fixed?

I thought about my own father, fighting for his life, and winning, even as Mr. Ümlaut threw his life away, surrendering—and it occurred to me how a roll of the dice had given me back my father, and had taken theirs away.

The day was bright and sunny as we drove home, Gunnar in the back, me shotgun beside Kjersten. I wished it wasn't such a nice day out. I wished it was raining, because the mind-numbing sound of the windshield wipers swiping back and forth would have been better than the silence, or all the false emotions of the radio, which had been on for a whole minute before Kjersten turned it off. Kjersten looked a little tired, a little grateful, and a little embarrassed that I had seen their seedy family moment. It made driving home now all the more awkward.

A lot of things made more and more sense now. Gunnar's illness, for one. I wondered when he first began suspecting they might move out of the country. But being sick—that would change everything, wouldn't it? It could keep his parents together—force his father to spend money on treatment instead of gambling it away. And since the best treatment was right here in New York, no one would be going anywhere. If I were Gunnar, I might wish I had Pulmonary Monoxic Systemia, too. Because the sickness of the son might cure the sickness of the father.

I held off filling our driving silence as long as I could, but there's only so long you can resist your own nature.

"I had this friend once," I told them. "Funny kind of kid. The thing is, his mom abandoned him in a shopping cart when he was five—and his dad treated him like he didn't even exist . . ."

"So, do all your friends have screwed-up families?" Gunnar asked.

"Yeah, I'm like flypaper for dysfunction. Anyway, he had it rough for a while, did some really stupid things—but in the end he turned out okay. He even tracked down his mom."

"And they lived happily ever after?" said Gunnar.

"Well, last I heard, they both disappeared in the Bermuda Triangle—but for them that was normal."

"I think what Antsy's saying," said Kjersten, sounding a little more relaxed than she did before, "is that we're going to be fine."

"Fine might be pushing it," I said. "I would go with 'less screwed up than most people.'" That made Gunnar laugh— which was good. It meant I was getting through to him. "Who knows," I said, "maybe your dad will turn himself around someday, and you'll hear his wooden shoes walking up to your door."

"Wooden shoes are from Holland, not Sweden," Gunnar said, but I think he got the point. "And even if he does come around, who says I will?"

"You will," I told him.

"I don't think so," he said bitterly.

"Yeah, you will," I told him again. "Because you're not him."

Gunnar snarled at me, because he knew I had him. "Now you sound like my mother," he said.

"No, it's much worse than that," I told him. "I sound like *my* mother."

The fact is, Gunnar and his father might have been a lot alike—embracing their own doom, whether it was real or imagined. But in the end, Gunnar stopped carving his own tombstone. In my book, that made him twice the man his father was.

Life Is Cheap,
but Mine Is Worth More
Than a Buck Ninety-eight
in a Free-Market Economy

20 On Monday I finally listened to my phone messages—they were all back from the night we first went to the hospital, because my voice mail maxed out in just a couple of hours. The messages were all pretty much the same; people wondering how my father was, wondering how I was, and wanting to talk. The wanting-to-talk part always sounded urgent, suggesting something that was, at least in their worlds, of major importance.

And so on Monday I finally went back to school for the first time since Black Wednesday, ready to take care of business.

At first people slapped me on the back, offered their support, and all that. I wondered who would be the first to say what was really on his or her mind. I should have guessed that Wailing Woody Wilson would be the first to cross the line of scrimmage, and go deep.

"Hey, Antsy, I'm glad your dad's okay and all—but there's

something I need to talk about." The awkward look of shame in his eyes almost made me feel bad for him. "About those months I gave Gunnar. I know it was just symbolic and all, but I'd feel a whole lot better if I could have them back. Now."

"Can't do that," I said, "but how about this?" Then I pulled a notebook out of my backpack, snapped open the clasp and handed him two fresh contracts, which I had already signed. "That's two months of *my* life," I told him. "An even trade for the ones you gave Gunnar. All you have to do is sign as witness, and they're yours."

He looked at them, considered it, and said, "I guess that works," and he left.

It was like that with everybody. Even easier with some. Sometimes people never got past "Listen, Antsy—" before I handed them a month, told them *vaya con Dios,* which is like French or something for "go with God," and sent them on their merry way.

I witnessed the true nature of human greed that day, because everyone seemed to be on the dole. Once people realized what I was doing, it became a feeding frenzy. Suddenly everyone claimed to have given multiple months, even people who never gave at all. But I didn't care. I was willing to go the distance.

By the time the bell rang, ending the school day, the feeding frenzy was over, and I had given away 123 years of my life. I told Frankie this when I got to the hospital that afternoon. I thought he'd call me an idiot like he always does, but instead he was very impressed.

"You had an Initial Public Offering!" he told me. Frankie, who was on the fast track to being a stockbroker, knew all about these things. "A successful IPO means that people believe your life is worth a lot more than it actually is." And then he added, "You'd better live up to expectations, though, otherwise you go bankrupt and gotta file chapter eleven."

And since chapter eleven was pretty annoying, I'd just as soon avoid it.

Of all the conversations I had that day, the most interesting was with Skaterdud, who was skating up and down my street when I got home from school. As it turns out, things were not well in the world of Dud.

"Bad news, Antsy. I'm reeling from the blow, man, reeling. I knew I had to talk to you, because not everyone couldn't understand like you, hear me?"

"So what happened?"

"The fortune-teller—the one who told me about my burial at sea. Turns out she was a fake! Wasn't even psychic. She's been ripping people off, and telling them stuff she just made up. Got arrested for it. She didn't even have no fortune-telling license!"

"Imagine that," I said, trying to hide my smirk. "A fortune-teller making stuff up."

"You know what this means, right? It means that all bets are off. There ain't no telling when I do the root rhumba. It's all free fall without a parachute until I meet the mud. Very disturbing, dude. Very disturbing. I could get hit by a bus tomorrow."

"You probably won't."

"But I could, that's the thing. Now I gotta restructure my whole way of thinking around a world of uncertainty. I ain't none too unhappy about this."

I thought I knew where Skaterdud was leading me, but with the Dud, conversational kickflips are not uncommon, and directions can suddenly change. "So I guess you want your year back, right?"

He looked at me like I had just arrived from someone else's conversation. "No—why would I want that?"

"The same reason everybody else does," I told him. "My dad's heart attack suddenly made you all superstitious, and you're afraid you're going to lose all that time."

He shook his head. "That's just stupid." He put a scabby hand on my shoulder as we walked, as if he was an older, smarter brother imparting deep wisdom. "Here's the way I see it: that fortune-teller's a crook, right? Tried and convicted. And in a court of law when someone is guilty of theft, they usually gotta pay damages to the plaintiff, right? And is there not justice in the Universe?"

"Probably, yeah."

"So there you go." And he tapped me on the forehead to indicate the passage of knowledge into my brain.

"Uh . . . I lost you."

He threw up his hands. "Haven't you been listening? That year will come from the *fortune-teller's* life, not mine. Damages, see? She pays cosmic, karmic damages. Simple as that."

In this world, there is a fine line between enlightenment and brain damage, and I have to say that Skaterdud grinds that line perfectly balanced.

We'll Always Have *Paris, Capisce?*

21 The Saturday before their flight, the Ümlauts had a garage sale. It was more than a garage sale, though, since official foreclosure was three days away, and everything had to go before the bank took possession of the house. Most of what they owned was either on the driveway or on the dead front lawn. The rest was in the process of being carried out. I added my muscle to the effort until everything that could fit through the front door was outside in the chilly morning.

They had advertised the sale in the paper, so scavengers from every unwashed corner of Brooklyn had crawled out from under one rock or another to pick through their belongings. No question that there were deals to be made that day.

Gunnar seemed less interested in the sale than he did talking about what lay ahead.

"We'll be staying with my grandma," he told me. "At least for a while. She's got this estate outside of Stockholm."

"It's not an estate," said Kjersten. "It's just a house."

"Yeah, well, if it was here, it would be considered an estate. She even paid for our plane tickets. We're flying first class."

"Business," corrected Kjersten.

"On Scandinavian Airlines, that's just as good."

That's when I realized that somewhere between yesterday and today, Gunnar had already made the move without anyone noticing. His head was already there at that Swedish estate, settling in. Getting the rest of him there was now just a shipping expense. I marveled that in spite of everything, Gunnar was bouncing back. Suddenly he was looking forward to something other than dying. He wasn't even wearing black anymore.

I helped Kjersten sort through things in her room, which felt kind of weird, but she wanted me to be there. I'll admit I wanted to be there, too. Not so much for the sorting, but just for the being. I tried not to think about how quickly the day was moving, and how soon she'd be heading out to the airport.

"There's a two-suitcase limit per person on the flight to Stockholm," Kjersten told me. "After that, there's an extra charge." She thought about it and said, "I think I might have trouble filling both suitcases."

I guess once you start parting with all the things you think hold your life together, it's hard to stop—and then you find out your life holds together all by itself.

"It's just stuff," I told her. "And stuff is just stuff."

"Brilliant," Gunnar said from the next room. "Can I quote you on that?"

Later in the day Mr. Ümlaut came by with a U-Haul to take

away what few things didn't sell, which wasn't much, and to say his good-byes.

It was cordial, and it was awkward, but at least it happened. A ray of hope for the danglers.

"He says he's got an apartment in Queens," Gunnar told me after he left—which I suppose was a giant step up from a room at a casino—so maybe our little visit did have some effect after all. "He says he's looking for a job. We'll see."

Later that day I got a call from Mr. Crawley demanding that I come to *Paris, Capisce?* I hadn't been there since my father's heart attack. Neither had my dad—he was still at home recuperating, and leaving restaurant business to everyone else, under threat of brain surgery by my mom.

"You will report at six o'clock sharp," Crawley said. "Tell no one."

Which of course was like an invitation to tell everyone. In the end, I only told Kjersten, and asked her to come with.

"For our final date, I'm taking you to a fancy restaurant," I told her. "And this time no one's grounded."

When we arrived, I discovered, to my absolute horror, that Crawley had installed something new to complement the ambience. On the restaurant's most visible wall was a giant framed poster of me pouring water over Senator Boswell's head. There was a caption above it. It read:

PARIS, CAPISCE?
French attitude, with a hot Italian temper.

It just made Kjersten laugh, and laugh and laugh. I tried to tell myself this was a good thing—that she needed to laugh far more than I needed, oh, say self-respect?

Wonder of wonders, Crawley was actually there—in fact, I found out he had been there on a regular basis, training the staff, through various forms of employer abuse, in how to run a top-notch restaurant. When it came to the poster of me and my victim, he was very pleased with himself. "I also rented several billboards around the city," he told me.

"Where?" Kjersten wanted to know. I was a little too numb to hear the answer.

"Are we done yet?" I asked Crawley. "Can we eat now?"

"Oh," said Crawley, "but the festivities are just beginning."

Waiting in the restaurant's second room was a film crew from *Entertainment Right Now,* a daily show that featured movie news and celebrities doing scandalous things. Today's celebrity in question was none other than—yes, you guessed it—Jaxon Beale, lead singer of NeuroToxin. He sat relaxing at a table with a plate of fake food in front of him. He looked shorter than he does in music videos.

Kjersten was instantaneously starstruck, and suddenly what began as humiliation became something else entirely. "You knew all about this, didn't you!" she said to me.

I neither confirmed nor denied it. Today I was getting more mileage from silence than from ignorance.

I wasn't quite sure what this was all about, or why Crawley had requested my presence, except to maybe show off the fact that he somehow dragged a celebrity in through our doors . . .

but then someone bodily grabs me, puts me in my white bus-boy apron, and someone else puts a pitcher of water into my hands. I stood there looking dumb, one episode behind the program.

"Roll camera," the director shouts, and Jaxon looks at me, doing the bring-it-on gesture with his fingers.

"C'mon, what are you waiting for? Do I get an official welcome, or not?"

I can see Crawley grinning and wringing his fingers in anticipation in the background like Wile E. Coyote, and I finally get it. So does Kjersten.

"Omigosh!" says Kjersten. "You're going to dump water on JAXON BEALE!"

It's the first time I ever heard Kjersten, star of the debate team, say "Omigosh." All at once I realized that, for this wet, shining moment, our roles were truly reversed. Not only was I Mr. Mature, but now she was the goofy fourteen-year-old.

"Well," I said, smooth as a Porsche on ice, "if my buddy Jaxon wants water, then water he shall have." I strode up to him as Kjersten squealed with her hands over her mouth, and I said, "Welcome to *Paris, Capisce?*, Mr. Beale." Then I emptied the pitcher over his head.

He stood up, shaking the water off, and for a second I'm worried that maybe he'll get mad and punch me out, but instead, he just starts laughing, turns to the camera, and says, "Now, *that's* celebrity treatment!"

From here, I didn't need a road map to know exactly where this was leading and why. Crawley had paid Beale a small fortune for this publicity stunt, and it was money well spent. Say what you want about Creepy Crawley, but the man is a marketing genius.

"It's all about spin," Old Man Crawley said while Jaxon Beale signed a waterlogged autograph for Kjersten, and other arriving guests. "There are lots of egos out there. Once this piece airs, celebrities, politicians, you name it, will be climbing over one another to get drenched by you."

Thanks to our celebrity encounter, it became a date to remember. Even more special, because I knew it would be our last. I tried not to dwell on that, though, because we'd shared enough sad occasions together. We deserved for this one to be happy. I ordered in Italian—I don't speak it all that well, but I can order like a pro. Still on her Jaxon Beale high, Kjersten was all gush, flush, and blush for a while. "I probably looked so stupid!" she said. "Like one of those lame adoring fans."

"Naa," I told her. "You're cute when you're embarrassed."

By the time dessert came, everything settled down, and the dating balance was restored. It was different now, though. For the first time, I felt more like her equal. Maybe now she saw me that way, too—and it occurred to me that a relationship isn't about being two distinct kinds of people—it's about feeling comfortable in whatever roles the moment required.

I guess that's why my friendship with Lexie survived through Norse gods and echolocation—we always seemed to be what the other one needed.

"Tell you what," Lexie told me as we sat in her living room one afternoon, planning her grandfather's next kidnapping. "If we both happen to be in between relationships, I see nothing wrong with going out to dinner, or a concert now and then."

I think it was good for both of us to know that as long as we were both there for each other, we'd always have a social life, even when we had no social life.

On the morning of the Ümlauts' flight to Sweden, we had a funeral.

I'd like to say it was symbolic, but, sadly, it was all too real. Ichabod, our beloved family cat, finally went to the great windowsill in the sky. We decided to bury him in the Ümlauts' backyard, since there was already a sizable gravestone available that otherwise would have gone to waste. Gunnar spackled over his own name, then chiseled out ICHABOD on the other side, and it was good to go.

Christina had written a heartfelt eulogy that I suspect she had been working on for months, the way newspapers start preparing obituaries the instant a celebrity gets a hangnail. With all the family pictures covering the little wooden crate, and the solemn air of the occasion, Ichabod's memorial service actually brought a few tears to my eyes. I didn't mind that Kjersten and Gunnar saw me cry over a cat. After everything I'd been through, I had a right. And realistically, who would they tell in Sweden?

With Ichabod laid to rest, we went inside to find Mrs. Ümlaut sweeping the empty kitchen, because "I don't want the bank to think we're slobs."

"She's just like our mother," Christina noted. I think all mothers are alike, regardless of cultural background, when it comes to illogical cleaning.

Christina wanted to go home and mourn privately, but I made her wait, because I wanted to see Kjersten and Gunnar off. The luggage was at the front door, waiting for the arrival of the taxi. Six pieces, and a couple of carry-ons.

Gunnar looked at his house with no outward show of emotion. "We had mice," he said. "And the drains never smelled right. It's just as well." I'm sure he felt a lot more than he let on, but it was his way. Kjersten, on the other hand, had moist eyes all over the place. Every corner seemed to hold a hidden memory. She looked fondly into empty places while Mrs. Ümlaut kept going around the house, up and down the stairs.

"There's something I forgot," she kept saying. "I know there's something I forgot."

Eventually Kjersten gently grabbed her, and gave her a hug to slow her down. "Everything's taken care of, Mom. Everything's ready." The two rocked back and forth for a moment, and I couldn't tell whether Mrs. Ümlaut was rocking her baby girl, or if Kjersten was rocking her anxious mother. Kjersten grinned at me over her mother's shoulder, and I offered her an understanding smile back.

There's no question I was going to miss Kjersten, but the kind of sadness I felt wasn't the kind that brings up tears, and I'm thinking, *Great, I cried for the cat, but I'm not crying for her*—but I think she was okay with that.

I think we both knew if she stayed, our relationship wouldn't have gone much further. Ours was like one of those fireplace Duraflame logs that burns big and bright, then drops dead an hour before the package says it will. I think it's best that we left it here, before it became useless.

"So," I asked her, only half joking, "once you get there, do you think you'll start dating guys your own age?"

She looked at me with a grin, then looked away. "Antsy, I think you've aged at least two years over the past few weeks," she told me. "No matter what, you're going to be a hard act to follow."

For that, I gave her the best kiss of my career—during which Christina said, "Oh! Is that why you brushed your teeth this morning?"

The taxi finally arrived, honking from outside in repeated little blasts like a fire drill. Gunnar and I brought the luggage to the cabdriver, who, like every New York cabdriver, acted like it was an insult to his profession that he had to load luggage.

Thanks to all the horn blasts, neighbors had come out onto their porches to watch the Ümlauts' departure. Then Mrs. Ümlaut threw up her hands "Ah! Now I remember!" She ran back into the house and came out with something in her hand. "This is for you," she said to me. "Someone wanted to buy it last Saturday, but I told them it wasn't for sale."

She handed me the stainless-steel meat tenderizer.

"To remember us by," she said with a wink.

This was the first hint that she had a sense of humor—and a twisted one, too. I was impressed.

"It'll be one of my prized possessions—I'll keep it with my rare paper clips," I told her, and she looked at me funny. "No, really."

"You must visit us!" she said, which I figured was about as likely as me visiting the International Space Station, but I nodded politely and said, "Sure."

Then I heard a gruff voice from somewhere down the block intrude on our tender farewell moment.

"What about our plants, hah?" I turned to see the same paunchy, beady-eyed man, who had made nasty comments before, peering down from his second-floor balcony. From this angle, the guy looked like what you might get if you crossed a human being with one of those potbellied pigs. "You gonna send us back some freakin' tulips?" he mocked.

Mrs. Ümlaut sighed, and Kjersten shook her head as she got into the taxi. "Why does everyone confuse us with Holland?"

"I know this guy," says Christina. "His kid's in my class. He eats pencil sharpenings."

"Go on," grunted the pig-man. "Get atta here! We don't need ya!"

I'm about to tell the guy off—but then I hear a bang, and I see that Gunnar has jumped up on the trunk of the taxi—and, to the driver's extreme chagrin, Gunnar climbs up so he's standing on the taxi's roof.

"You can't get rid of me!" he yells to the pig-man. Then he turns to address all the neighbors, speaking loud and clear: "I'll be everywhere—wherever you look. Wherever there's a fight so hungry people can eat, I'll be there. Wherever they's a cop beatin' up a guy, I'll be there. I'll be in the way guys yell when they're mad, an' I'll be in the way kids laugh when they're hungry an' they know supper's ready. An' when our folks eat the stuff they raise an' live in the houses they build—why, I'll be there."

I had to smile—I even applauded, because at last Gunnar had found a real quote. And with all due respect to John Steinbeck, as far as I'm concerned, Gunnar owns it now!

Gunnar took a long, elaborate bow, then hopped down from the roof, and did something very un-Gunnar-like. He gave me this sudden, death-grip hug that crunched my bones like a chiropractor. When he let go, we stood there for a moment, feeling stupid.

"Dewey Lopez didn't get a picture of that, did he?" I asked.

"If he did, it's your problem now." Then he jumped in the taxi. "Ciao."

Kjersten put her hand out the window for one final farewell grasp, and the taxi driver floored it, nearly leaving Kjersten's hand behind with me. I watched as they accelerated down the street and turned the corner.

"Someday," said Christina, "I hope to have friends as problematic as yours."

My thoughts were still on Kjersten. I wish I could have come up with a quote like Gunnar did—y'know, the absolute the perfect parting words to leave Kjersten with.

But what do you say to a Scandinavian beauty who's about to get on a plane and fly out of your life?

A Weed Grows in Brooklyn

22 Just as Old Man Crawley predicted, *Paris, Capisce?* had celebrities dragging their nails over one another's backs to get in the door. We ended up having to schedule celebrities—one per night—so they didn't all arrive at once. Dad, still recuperating, took the calls from home, chatting with agents, and the stars themselves. It was great! I got to meet more famous people than I thought I'd meet in a lifetime, then pour water over their heads.

With all this celebrity appeal, the restaurant was packed every night with people hoping to eat a fine meal, spot someone famous, and see them get drenched—either by me, or this guy they hired who looked and sounded like me, which I still find too creepy to talk about.

Christina even got into it, selling the pitchers we used on eBay for prices that could fund her college education someday.

Long story short, by the time Dad was ready to go back to

work, *Paris, Capisce?* was the hottest restaurant in Brooklyn. We were all realistic enough to know that trends pass, that it wouldn't last forever, but we'd also been through enough to know we gotta enjoy what we got, when we got it.

"It's gonna be different now," he told us. "Now that the restaurant's always busy, there's going to be a lot more work."

So he doubled his staff, and cut his own hours in half, leaving the stress for someone else. He even has time to cook at home with Mom again, and watch a game or two on the weekends with me.

"When I finally go, I'm sure it'll be a heart attack," he said to me. "But let's hope I go like your grandpa"—whose ticker didn't give out until he was pushing eighty-eight.

It's all about spin, Old Man Crawley had said. Spin makes a big difference, doesn't it? My father almost died, but spin it a little, and it's a life-changing warning that taught him to appreciate the important things in life. And the Ümlauts—they lost just about everything they had, but with the right spin, it becomes a shining opportunity to start fresh.

I went back to their block a few months later, out of curiosity more than anything else. The house was still empty, and still at the center of a dust bowl. The bank that now owned the home was still trying to find a buyer—but, see, my sister, in her attempt to keep Ichabod undisturbed, had started a rumor that the backyard didn't just contain a single cat grave—it was, in fact, a local pet cemetery, and the final resting place of a hundred neighborhood critters—not all of them resting in peace.

Funny thing about rumors, the harder a rumor is to believe,

the more likely it's going to chase buyers away. Serves the bank right.

As I approached the house that day, I saw a single weed trying to poke its way up through a crack in the pavement. The first sign that the dust bowl was over! Then, as I looked more closely at the yards all around me, I could see patches of little ugly weeds popping up everywhere. Life was coming back to the street, and I thought how appropriate that the first plants to come back will be the plants all the neighbors will kill with more herbicide. Thus is the cycle of life.

Me, I had better things to do than watch the weeds grow— because for my fifteenth birthday, my parents got me a passport, and a plane ticket. Brooklyn weeds may have their own unique charm—but I hear spring break is beautiful in Sweden!

APPENDIX 1

More Fake Quotes by Gunnar Ümlaut

"A family is a collection of strangers trapped in a web of DNA and forced to cope." —MARIA VON TRAPP

"No luncheon shall ever present itself free from payment in coin or pound of flesh." —WILLIAM SHAKESPEARE

"All right, I admit to having cursed the darkness once or twice." —ELEANOR ROOSEVELT

"Being rich is nothing when compared to being really, really rich." —BILL GATES

"What no one seems to realize is that there are no bathrooms on the moon." —NEIL ARMSTRONG

"I do not mourn the loss of my hearing, and in fact, I foresee a time when popular music shall cause entire populations to long for my affliction." —LUDWIG VAN BEETHOVEN

"Time is the unquantifiable commodity that greases the gear work of creation. But I prefer Russian dressing." —ALBERT EINSTEIN

"The fabrication of quotes is like the manufacture of polyester. It may pretend to be silk, but suffocates when the climate is hot." —MAHATMA GANDHI

APPENDIX 2

THE DEATH EUPHEMISMS OF SKATERDUD

Pushing Posies
Meeting the Mud
The Dirt Dance
Snooze Button Bingo
The Root Rhumba
Sucking Seaweed*
The Formaldehyde High
Visiting Uncle Mort
Sniffing Satin
The China Express
Bucket Soccer
The Last Lawn Party
Farm Finale
The Shovel Symphony
Chillin' with Jimmy
Box Potato
El Sayonara Grande

*FOR BURIAL AT SEA.

APPENDIX 3

ANTSY BONANO'S TIME CONTRACT
(IN ITS FINAL VERSION)

I, _____ being of sound mind and body, do hereby bequeath one month of my natural life to Gunnar Ümlaut, subject to the stuff listed below:

1. The month shall not be this coming May or June, or the last month of Gunnar Ümlaut's life, any leap-year Februaries, or the months of his high school or college graduations, or the month of his marriage, should he live to those dates, as those months are already reserved by others.

2. The month shall be taken from the end of my natural life, and not the middle.

3. The donated month shall be null and void if my own expiration date is less than 31 days from the date of this contract, regardless of the length of the month which is ultimately donated.

4. Should Gunnar Ümlaut use my month for criminal acts such as shoplifting or serial killing, I shall not be held responsible.

5. The month shall be reduced to two weeks should Gunnar Ümlaut become my enemy for any reason including but not limited to the following: familial feud, personal grudge, nonrepayment of debt, all forms of bad-mouthing, hallway bullying, refusing a reasonable request to share lunch.

6. Gunnar Ümlaut, and/or his next of kin shall have no claim on property, or chunks of time beyond those granted in this contract, and said month shall have no cash value, unless mutually agreed upon, in which case I shall share equally in the cash value, without limitation, with the exception of limitations rising from the verifiable end of Gunnar Ümlaut's life, either prior to or after aforementioned end.

7. Should any disputes arise from the exchange of this month, both parties agree to submit to binding arbitration by Anthony Bonano, who in this contract shall be known as the Master of Time.

_____

Signature

_____

Signature of Witness

The Complete Guide to Fundraising Management

SECOND EDITION

The Complete Guide to Fundraising Management

SECOND EDITION

STANLEY WEINSTEIN, ACFRE

John Wiley & Sons, Inc.

ISBN 0-471-20019-0

Printed in the United States of America.

10 9 8 7 6 5 4 3 2 1

AFP/WILEY FUND DEVELOPMENT SERIES

The AFP/Wiley Fund Development Series is intended to provide fund development professionals and volunteers, including board members (and others interested in the not-for-profit sector), with top-quality publications that help advance philanthropy as voluntary action for the public good. Our goal is to provide practical, timely guidance and information on fundraising, charitable giving, and related subjects. AFP and Wiley each bring to this innovative collaboration unique and important resources that result in a whole greater than the sum of its parts.

The Association of Fundraising Professionals

The AFP is a professional association of fundraising executives that advances philanthropy through its more than 25,000 members in over 159 chapters throughout the United States, Canada, and Mexico. Through its advocacy, research, education, and certification programs, the Society fosters development and growth of fundraising professionals, works to advance philanthropy and volunteerism, and promotes high ethical standards in the fundraising profession.

2001–2002 AFP Publishing Advisory Council

Linda L. Chew, CFRE, Chair
Associate Director, Alta Bates Summit Foundation

Nina P. Berkheiser, CFRE
Director of Development, SPCA of Pinellas County

Samuel N. Gough, CFRE
Principal, The AFRAM Group

Guy Mallabone, CFRE
VP, External Relations, Southern Alberta Institute of Technology

Robert Mueller, CFRE
Director of Development, Alliance of Community Hospices & Palliative Care Services

Maria Elena Noriega
Director, Noriega Malo & Associates

R. Michael Patterson, CFRE
Regional Director of Planned Giving, Arthritis Foundation

G. Patrick Williams, MS, ACFRE
Vice Chancellor of Development & Public Affairs, Southern Illinois University—Edwardsville

John Wiley & Sons:
Susan McDermott
Editor (Professional/Trade Division), John Wiley & Sons

AFP Staff:
Richard B. Chobot, Ph.D.
Vice President, Professional Advancement, AFP

Jan Alfieri
Manager, AFP Resource Center, AFP

Beyond Fund Raising: New Strategies for Nonprofit Innovation and Investment
Kay Sprinkel Grace, CFRE
ISBN 0-471-16232-9
Inspirational yet practical, this book teaches you how to "put away the tin cup" and take fundraising to a new level. An experienced fundraising consultant and volunteer, Grace shows you how to establish a true relationship between philanthropy, development, and fundraising. You will also get forms, checklists, and flow charts to help you understand, visualize, and incorporate this new philosophy into your own nonprofit organization.

Careers in Fundraising
Lilya Wagner, Ed.D., CFRE
ISBN 0-471-40359-8
Careers in Fundraising provides expert guidance on professional opportunities in the field of fundraising, including topics on professional development, on-the-job issues, and the significance of fundraising as a career. This comprehensive resource covers all aspects of the profession, and also addresses the personal mission and commitment necessary for success in the field.

The Complete Guide to Fund-Raising Management
Stanley Weinstein, ACFRE
ISBN 0-471-24290-X
This book is a practical management, how-to guide tailored specifically to the needs of fundraisers. Moving beyond theory, it addresses the day-to-day problems faced in not-for-profit organizations, and offers hands-on advice and practical solutions. The book and accompanying disk include sample forms, checklists, and grids that will help the reader plan and execute complicated fundraising campaigns.

Critical Issues in Fund Raising
Dwight F. Burlingame, Ph.D., CFRE, editor
ISBN 0-471-17465-3
Examines the most pressing issues facing fundraising professionals today. Extensive chapters cover donors, innovative fundraising, marketing, financial management, ethics, international philanthropy, and the fundraising professional. Written by a team of highly respected practitioners and educators, this book was developed in conjunction with AFP, the Council for the Advancement and Support of Education, the Association for Research on Nonprofit Organizations and Voluntary Action, and the Indiana University Center on Philanthropy.

Cultivating Diversity in Fundraising

Janice Gow Pettey

ISBN 0-471-40361-X

Cultivating Diversity in Fundraising offers an overview of cultivating successful fundraising and an enhanced understanding of philanthropic motivation in four selected racial/ethnic populations—African American, Asian American (Chinese, Filipino, Japanese, Korean, and South Asian), Hispanic/Latino (Cuban, Dominican, Salvadoran, Mexican, and Puerto Rican), and Native American. By understanding the rich philanthropic traditions of the individuals they are working with and soliciting funds from, fund raisers will be better equipped to serve their communities and their organizations.

Direct Response Fund Raising: Mastering New Trends for Results

Michael Johnston

ISBN 0-471-38024-5

This guide offers fundraisers, managers, and volunteers an excellent understanding of how to plan and execute successful direct response campaigns. The success of a nonprofit direct response program requires staying on top of recent trends in the field. These trends include appealing more effectively to aging baby boomers as well as tapping into powerful new databases, the Internet, CD-ROMs, diskettes, and videos. The book includes a CD-ROM, with all the full-color, complete examples from the book as well as many more.

Ethical Decision-Making in Fund Raising

Marilyn Fischer, Ph.D.

ISBN 0-471-28943-3

A handbook for ethical reasoning and discussion. In her provocative new book, Dr. Fischer provides conceptual tools with which a nonprofit can thoroughly examine the ethics of how and from whom it seeks donations. With the book's Ethical Decision-Making Model, the author explains how fundraisers can use their basic value commitments to organizational mission, relationships, and integrity as day-to-day touchstones for making balanced, ethical fundraising decisions.

The Fund Raiser's Guide to the Internet

Michael Johnston

ISBN 0-471-25365-0

This book presents the issues, technology, and resources involved in online fundraising and donor relations. A practical "how-to" guide, it presents real-world case studies and successful practices from a top consulting firm, as well as guidance, inspiration, and warnings to nonprofits learning to develop this new fundraising technique. It also covers such important factors as determining your market, online solicitation pieces, security issues, and setting up your web site.

Fund Raising Cost Effectiveness: A Self-Assessment Workbook
James M. Greenfield, ACFRE, FAHP
ISBN 0-471-10916-9
A comprehensive, step-by-step guide that will help nonprofit professionals ensure that their department and campaigns are as efficient and cost-effective as possible. It combines a thorough explanation of the issues critical to fundraising self-assessment with easy-to-use worksheets and practical advice. The accompanying disk contains all the sample worksheets plus software for downloading a nonprofit's fundraising data from major software products into charts, graphs, and P&L-like spreadsheet templates.

Fund Raising: Evaluating and Managing the Fund Development Process
James M. Greenfield, ACFRE, FAHP
ISBN 0-471-32014-5
Covering initial preparation in 15 areas of fundraising and the on-going management of the process, this book is designed for fundraising executives of organizations both large and small. Included are numerous examples, case studies, checklists, and a unique evaluation of the audit environment of nonprofit organizations.

International Fundraising for Not-for-Profits: A Country-by-Country Profile
Thomas Harris
ISBN 0-471-24452-X
The only comprehensive book of its kind, it examines and compares the fundraising environments of 18 countries around the world. Each chapter is written by a local expert and details the history and context of fundraising for the country, local and global economic factors, legal and fiscal practices, sources of funding, and what fundraising practices are considered acceptable by the culture and government.

The Legislative Labyrinth: A Map for Not-for-Profits
Walter P. Pidgeon, Jr., Ph.D., CFRE
ISBN 0-471-40069-6
Currently, only a fraction of the nonprofit community takes advantage of the legislative process in representing its members and furthering its missions. Nonprofits are missing a significant way to fulfill their mission of gaining visibility and attracting new members and funding sources. This book answers the questions of nonprofits thinking of starting a lobbying program.

The Nonprofit Handbook: Fund Raising, Third Edition
James M. Greenfield, ACFRE, FAHP
ISBN 0-471-40304-0
The Third Edition of this invaluable handbook provides a complete overview of the entire development function, from management and strategic planning to

hands-on, practical guidance for the various kinds of fundraising. Written by leading fundraising professionals and edited by James M. Greenfield, this invaluable resource brings together over 40 contributors who are vanguard experts and professionals in the field of fundraising.

Nonprofit Investment Policies: Practical Steps for Growing Charitable Funds
Robert P. Fry, Jr., esq.
ISBN 0-471-17887-X
Written in plain English by an investment manager who specializes in nonprofit organizations, *Nonprofit Investment Policies* explores the unique characteristics of nonprofit investing. Covered topics include endowment management, planned gift assets, socially responsible investing, and more. This book includes charts and graphs to illustrate complex investment concepts, tables and checklists to guide nonprofit managers in decision-making, and case studies of organizations of various sizes to show how to successfully develop and implement investment policies.

The NSFRE Fund-Raising Dictionary
ISBN 0-471-14916-0
Developed by NSFRE experts, this book provides clear and concise definitions for nearly 1,400 key fundraising and related nonprofit terms—from development & accounting to marketing and public relations. It also offers additional resource material, including a suggested bibliography.

Planned Giving Simplified: The Gift, the Giver, and the Gift Planner
Robert F. Sharpe, Sr.
ISBN 0-471-16674-X
This resource, written by a well-known veteran of planned giving, is a down-to-earth introduction to the complex world of planned giving, a sophisticated fundraising strategy that involves big money, complex tax laws, and delicate personal politics. This book shows charities, and in particular the charities' planned givers, how to understand the process—both the administration of planned gifts as well as the spirit of giving.

The Universal Benefits of Volunteering
Walter P. Pidgeon, Jr., Ph.D., CFRE
ISBN 0-471-18505-1
Volunteering is good for nonprofits, individuals and corporations because it builds strong interpersonal and professional skills that carry over into all sectors. A concise, hands-on guide to maximizing the use of business professionals in the nonprofit volunteer context, this workbook is a vital resource to all those involved in volunteering efforts. Included is a disk with all the worksheets and model documents needed to establish effective, successful, and ongoing volunteer programs.

This book is dedicated to the board members, volunteers, and staff members who help with fundraising. It is said that they have earned a special place in heaven—next to the martyrs.

About
the Author

Stanley Weinstein, ACFRE, EMBA, has spent 32 years in the non-profit sector. He served for nine years on the AFP's National Board of Directors. As a distinguished consultant and executive vice president of Hartsook and Associates, he has provided services and hands-on fundraising help for more than 200 not-for-profit organizations nationwide. Mr. Weinstein's capital campaigns have resulted in numerous major gifts ranging from $50,000 to $50 million. His experience includes strategic planning, board development, and capital campaigns for a broad spectrum of social welfare, healthcare, arts, and religious and educational institutions.

Acknowledgments

I want to thank all the people who helped create this book. Certainly, my wife, Jan, deserves the greatest measure of my love and gratitude. Not only was she a source of personal support during the writing process, she also helped by suggesting clear language, preparing the manuscript, and organizing the exhibits. Suffice to say, a great deal of this activity took place at odd hours. However, any errors due to sleep deprivation are mine alone.

My two sons, Rob and Steve, also helped. Rob has a good ear for language, and teases me unmercifully whenever I sound stuffy. Steve spoke up when he found something in the text to be unclear. Moreover, he spent quite a few early mornings typing manuscript corrections.

A number of friends and colleagues deserve special thanks. B. Jeanne Williams encouraged me to write this book. Susan D. Thomas and Lona M. Farr provided encouragement and ideas. T. Joseph McKay helped shape the planned giving chapter. Brian Knecht shared his ideas and provided valuable input. Beverly Peavler, a friend who happens to be a professional editor, helped keep me calm during the editing process. Mike Kroth, a friend and expert on organization development and adult learning theory, has influenced my life and many of the pages in this book. I am also deeply grateful to the clients I have served. I have learned something of value from each of them.

Let me also express thanks to the people and institutions that graciously granted permission to use their materials and ideas. I am especially thankful to Robin Stark of Starkland Systems for her gracious permission to use so many examples of reports generated by *DonorPerfect* fundraising software. Bob and Kay O'Connell, from Saint Bonaventure Indian Mission &

School, also deserve special mention. Together with their dedicated staff, they do marvelous work with the children and community elders they serve. Moreover, Bob and Kay have developed a sophisticated direct mail program that helped shape many of the thoughts expressed in Chapter 9.

Many volunteers I have had the pleasure to work with also taught me a great deal about resource development. Many keenly understand how to motivate others. Quite a few have extraordinary business acumen. All share a strong passion for the causes they represent. Among the volunteers who have influenced me the most are: Mary Langlois, Ray Zimmer, Adelaide Benjamin, Scott Sibbett, Curt Brewer, and Cleta Downey—all hold a special place in my heart.

Finally, I would be remiss if I did not thank two people who have had an enormous impact on my life—Kyozan Joshu Sasaki Roshi, a 94-year-old Zen Master, and Seiju Bob Mammoser. Their lives embody a devotion to selfless service that can serve as a model for all who work in the not-for-profit sector.

Contents

Foreword

By taking on the assignment of developing *The Complete Guide to Fundraising Management, Second Edition*, Stanley Weinstein has displayed both daring and dexterity. While attempting a less death-defying act than, say, H.G. Wells' composition of his two-volume *History of the World*, Stanley has, nonetheless, achieved a formidable task—condensing and organizing the world of fundraising into one manageable reference tool. With this new edition, Stanley has refined the original and included feedback received from his first printing in order to offer an updated, practical, and reliable source for development professionals.

From major gift philanthropy to strategies on solicitation and closing the gift, from special events to cause-related marketing, planned giving to policies and procedures—it's all there. Stanley has organized the book and the index in such a way that development professionals, even those new to the industry, can point and flip their way right to the information they need.

I first became interested in Stanley Weinstein and his company when I recognized that his professional values and emphasis on client service were quite in harmony with our own orientation. He has since joined Hartsook and Associates, Inc., a nationwide, full-service firm, and added his talent, his dedication to his clients' best interests, and his intelligent humor to our company.

Philanthropy in America has grown significantly over the past decade. At the same time, the Association of Fundraising Professionals has played a strong role in providing leadership, integrity, education, and professional status to the fundraising community. The AFP/Wiley Fund Development Series is a good example of the forward thinking our sector enjoys. And

certainly, the choice of Stanley Weinstein as the primary source for a comprehensive book about fundraising was a wise decision.

Robert F. Hartsook, J.D. Ed.D.
Chairman and CEO
Hartsook Companies

Preface

"Cheshire Puss," Alice began . . . *"would you please tell me which way I ought to go from here?"*

"That depends on where you want to go," said the cat.

—Lewis Carroll

Not-for-profit organizations need strong boards of directors, loyal supporters, and a keen sense of mission. Not-for-profit organizations also need cash.

So, this is a how-to book. *The Complete Guide to Fundraising Management, Second Edition,* provides a practical road map for fundraising success in a highly competitive philanthropic environment. Here are some of the ways this book will help you strengthen your organization and raise more money.

- *The Complete Guide* will help you gain an understanding of fundraising principles and practices. You will learn the time-tested truths that govern the resource development process—the fundamentals that lead to fundraising success.

- *The Complete Guide* will help you raise funds using the most cost-effective fundraising strategies.

- *The Complete Guide* will teach you how to put together a comprehensive approach that can dramatically increase your contributed income.

- *The Complete Guide* provides valuable time-lines and explores the chronological steps needed to establish and strengthen your organization's fundraising program.

- *The Complete Guide* also provides advice concerning ways to bolster your organization and assure that your not-for-profit institution is worthy of support—practical suggestions concerning board development, institutional advancement, strategic planning, and volunteer involvement.

- *The Complete Guide* teaches chief executive officers, development staff, board leaders, community activists, and volunteers how to organize their efforts, nurture meaningful relationships, and maximize their fundraising effectiveness.

This book is also about strategic management—the art of managing approaches designed to produce successful performance. Strategic management is especially important in times of rapid change.

Not-for-profit organizations confront numerous challenges. Many are facing reductions in government funding. Others see their United Way contributions heading south. At times, traditional or older funders change priorities or die without providing for the not-for-profit's future. To make matters even worse, all of this is occurring at a time when the demand for services is increasing.

A strategic yet nimble approach is also needed when presented with opportunities. Such opportunities often arise with little advance notice: A chance to purchase property needed to enhance the agency's mission. A matching grant with a pressing deadline. A potential major donor's expression of interest in your cause.

Not-for-profit agencies that monitor the environment are better prepared to respond effectively to the challenges and opportunities that are sure to arise. How they respond to the changing environment is called their "strategy."

Many factors determine which fundraising strategies are appropriate to the not-for-profit organization's circumstances. Some of these factors include: the amount of money that must be raised; how soon the funds are needed; whether the funds are for annual expenses, endowment funds, special projects, or for capital investments; the reputation of the not-for-profit organization; the popularity of the appeal; the number of affluent and

influential board members and volunteers committed to the cause; the experience levels of the development professionals; the number of active donors to the not-for-profit organization; the amount of donations the organization receives each year; the number of prospective donors who have been identified and with whom the organization has nurtured positive relationships; and a host of other factors unique to each organization.

Of equal importance is the not-for-profit agency's ability to respond to changing conditions. Are the services needed today the same as those that were needed five years ago? What services will be needed one year from today? In five years? Ten years? In short, what strategies are needed to prepare for the future? As important, what resource development strategies are needed to help the organization achieve its aspirations?

The Complete Guide to Fundraising Management, Second Edition, helps you answer these questions. This book will also help not-for-profit executive directors and fundraising professionals manage a comprehensive resource development program. Board leaders and volunteers will learn how they can help increase contributions for annual operating support, endowment funds, capital campaigns, and special projects.

The Complete Guide to Fundraising Management, Second Edition, is designed for you. Whether you read the whole book or only the chapters that most interest you, this book provides time-tested, practical advice. So, enjoy . . . and prepare your organization to serve and to prosper.

Stanley Weinstein, ACFRE
Albuquerque, NM

The Complete Guide to Fundraising Management

SECOND EDITION

Five Major Fundraising Principles

Truth, like gold, is not less so for being newly brought out of the mine.

—John Locke

To maintain a strategic edge, not-for-profit organizations need to remain flexible. Still, our action plans must be developed in accordance with the key principles that lead to fundraising success.

PEOPLE GIVE TO PEOPLE . . . TO HELP PEOPLE

"People give to people . . . to help people" is the most often quoted fundraising phrase. As well it should be. This wise and simple thought has three aspects, and it is prudent to remember all three.

"People give . . ." reminds us that real living and breathing human beings—not institutions—make the decisions to donate or not to donate. They make their decisions based on relationships and to what degree the appeal responds to the funder's interests. They also base their decisions on the quality of the organization's leadership.

Which brings us to the second part of the aphorism, "People give *to people.*" Donors are not in the habit of contributing in response to institutional needs. No rational person will buy a computer to help IBM recover from a weak earnings quarter. Similarly, few donors will give merely in response

to a not-for-profit organization's deficit. Donors make their investments based on their relationship to the asker. Donors give to people they trust. And donors invest in projects that have a positive impact on their community, nation, and world.

And so we come to the third aspect of the saying, "People give to people *to help people.*" From a donor's viewpoint, institutions do not have needs. People do. Donors know that their contributions constitute an investment . . . an investment in enhanced services for people in need.

At its heart, fundraising is the art of nurturing relationships. So, our first job is to build strong, mission-based organizations. Successful fundraisers also form relationships with people who can help garner the resources needed to carry out the organization's mission. We then *ask* for the support required to better serve those in need. Finally, we thank our donors so graciously that they continue their support.

People Give Relative to Their Means

The second major principle is one of the great keys to understanding the resource development process.

"People give in relation to their means and in relation to what others give."

For some people, $5.00 or $25.00 is a generous gift. We also know that there are people who can donate a million dollars or more without changing their lifestyles. Most folks tend to give in ranges between these two extremes.

Do you remember this biblical incident?

> . . . a poor widow came, and put in two copper coins, which made a penny. And He said . . ., "Truly, I say to you, this poor widow has put in more than all those who are contributing to the treasury. For they all contributed from their abundance; but she out of her poverty has put in everything she had, her whole living."

Many people have missed the point of this passage. They focus only on the small size of the offering—not the sacrificial nature of the gift. When professional fundraisers stress the importance of pace-setting, leadership gifts, some volunteers ask, "Why focus on large gifts? Aren't we sending

the wrong message? We must not forget what we learned from the widow's mite."

Again, the point of the widow's mite passage is not the size of the offering but rather the size *relative* to the widow's means. For the poor widow, the gift was huge—a sacrificial gift representing "her whole living." Too often nonprofit organizations do not offer more affluent supporters the opportunity to give at such significant levels. Rather than asking for pace-setting leadership investments, they ask for token support. Or worse still, they fail to ask at all.

Would you agree that rich people can afford to donate more than poor people? An understanding of this truism leads fundraisers to the firm conviction that any fundraising plan based on seeking an "average gift" is bound to produce sub-standard results.

Whenever you hear someone suggest that it is possible to raise $100,000 by seeking one hundred $1,000 gifts or one thousand $100 gifts, know that you are listening to a flawed plan—one that is likely to fail. Here's why. Let's say we plan to raise $100,000 by requesting $1,000 from each of its constituents in the hope of garnering one hundred donations to make the goal.

Will some of those approached say no? Of course they will.

Will some of those approached give less than the amount requested? Sure.

Can some of those approached give a great deal more than the amount requested? Definitely!

To make this point even stronger, it is important to remember that donors tend to give relative to what others give. If a not-for-profit organization announced that the region's largest financial institution donated $10,000, many donors would conclude that their contribution could be proportionately lower. Few think that they should donate more than the leading financial institution or the wealthiest person in town.

Professionals avoid schemes based on the "average gift." The plan they prefer resembles a pyramid. To raise $300,000, they might seek one donation of $45,000, two contributions of $30,000, three gifts of $15,000 each, four contributions of $10,000, eight $5,000 gifts, fifteen $2,500 gifts, thirty $1,000 donations, and so on. By creating various levels of gift opportunities, the development professional helps assure that everyone—rich, poor and everyone in between—has a chance to make a significant gift.

THOSE CLOSEST MUST SET THE PACE

"Those closest to the organization must set the pace."

The value of this principle becomes evident to anyone who spends a few moments reflecting on it. If those closest to the organization do not believe in the project enough to give generously, how can we expect others not as close to make significant contributions? When looking for financial leadership, some people in the not-for-profit sector seem to say, "It's not you, it's not me . . . it's the other fellow behind the tree." Unfortunately, there is no other fellow behind the tree. Leadership begins with the board, staff, and key volunteers. When they lead in giving, others follow.

SUCCESSFUL FUNDRAISING

"Successful fundraising is the right person asking the right prospect for the right amount for the right project at the right time in the right way." The word "right" was used six times in this sentence. These six "rights" are the six critical success factors in any fundraising campaign.

Begin by asking, "Who is the right person to ask for the contribution?" In *most* cases the best person to approach a prospective donor is a volunteer with a peer relationship with the prospective donor. In many cases the most suitable person to approach the prospective donor is the executive director or chief executive officer of the not-for-profit agency—again, someone with a peer relationship with the prospective donor. The ideal face-to-face solicitation occurs when a volunteer leader teams with a key staff member to visit the prospective supporter. The ideal signer of a mail appeal is the board president, agency executive director . . . or a well-known celebrity supporter of your cause.

Let's now turn to the question of the "right prospect." A nonprofit cannot succeed in fundraising without asking, "Who are our best prospects? Which supporters are most likely to make pace-setting leadership gifts?" The most likely gifts come from people who have been generous to the nonprofit in the past. Next, we look for people with the capacity to give generously who have a relationship with the organization—but have not yet given. We also look for people who have been generous to similar organizations. And successful fundraisers do not overlook board members, key volunteers, and their network of associates.

"What is the right amount to request?" Remember, you must *decide*

how much to request before mailing a solicitation, phoning a supporter, or going on any solicitation visit. Too often, people in the not-for-profit sector express thoughts such as, "Anything you give would be important and appreciated." The problem with this thought is that it demeans the organization's cause. The prospective donor may think you want a $50.00 contribution. This can be disastrous, especially if the donor has the ability to give $50,000. Serious fundraisers conduct meetings to decide how much to request from each of their prime prospects. Professionals segment their mail lists and personalize their request amounts.

The "right project" is always the one in which the prospective donor has the most interest. A university that requests funds for the history department from an alumnus who is a history buff will do better than a university that misses the mark and requests general operating support.

Determining the "right time" is not always easy. However, you cannot go wrong with the following rule. The best time to approach a prospective donor for a major gift is when you have nurtured a positive relationship.

The "right way" to ask for a contribution is with poise and grace. Put away your tin cup. You have nurtured a genuine relationship with the prospective donor. Now, you are offering an opportunity for the supporter to make a significant contribution—one that will have a positive impact on many lives for years to come.

THE 80/20 RULE IS BECOMING THE 90/10 RULE

"Often, 80 percent or more of the funds raised will come from not more than 20 percent of the donors." This is a variation on the second major principle, "People give in relation to their means and in relation to what others give." The result of this propensity is a variation of Pareto's 80/20 rule. Eighty percent of your results will come from 20 percent of your efforts. We see the truth of this observation in many facets of our lives. Twenty percent of all salesmen produce 80 percent of all sales. Twenty percent of all volunteers raise 80 percent of all funds. Twenty percent of a corporation's product line accounts for 80 percent of the corporation's profits.

And so it is with fundraising. In many capital campaigns and mature fundraising programs, the top 10 percent now donate 90 percent of the

amount raised. When the top 10 to 20 percent—those closest with the most resources—are encouraged to make leadership gifts, campaigns succeed.

THE NEED FOR BALANCE

Often, fundraisers stress one aspect of resource development rather than another. Even seasoned professionals sometimes say, "A major gift program is the most cost-effective fundraising strategy. We have got to work at the peak of the giving pyramid. I really can't be bothered with broad-based fundraising." Others say, "We have to broaden our base of support. If we rely on too few donors, our constituents will think we are elitists. It is dangerous to have too few donors. What if we lose several of them in one year? Besides, our organization produces nearly a million dollars a year net contributed income from our mail program."

I don't believe that we live in an "either/or" universe. Both points of view have validity. Mature fundraising programs rely on a three-part strategy: treat all donors and prospective donors with the utmost respect, broaden the base of support, and nurture personal relationships with major current and prospective donors. In conclusion, a comprehensive approach is respectful of major donors and modest givers.

Your Organization and the Not-for-Profit World

These Americans are peculiar people. If, in a local community, a citizen becomes aware of a human need which is not being met, he thereupon discusses the situation with his neighbors. Suddenly, a committee comes into existence. The committee thereupon begins to operate on behalf of the need and a new community function is established. It is like watching a miracle, because these citizens perform this act without a single reference to any bureaucracy, or any official agency.

—Alexis de Tocqueville

AN OVERVIEW OF THE SECTOR— BROAD RANGE OF SERVICES

The not-for-profit sector is vital to American society and to the world. Generous volunteers and donors band together to make a better world for themselves, their neighbors, and the larger community.

Education institutions foster self-reliance and a passion for lifelong learning. Social service agencies give the poorest of the poor a hand up, not a hand out. Healthcare and research institutions find new cures for disease and heal the sick. Cultural and arts institutions enrich our lives and illuminate the human condition. Conservation organizations preserve and protect our environment and wildlife. Churches, synagogues, temples, and mosques renew our spirit and sustain our faith.

7

Simply put, the not-for-profit sector addresses a broad spectrum of needs and is crucial to individual, family, and community well-being. Moreover, private not-for-profit organizations are essential to the national economy. Consider the following.

Economic Impact

Nonprofits play a significant role in the modern economy:

- The United States has more than 1.6 million not-for-profit institutions. Of these, more than 800,000 are classified as 501(c)(3), commonly called charities.
- Not-for-profit organizations provide 1.8 million jobs, employing 10 percent of the work force.
- Not-for-profit institutions have a payroll of $167 billion each year.
- Public charity revenue represents approximately 7.5 percent of the nation's gross domestic product.

Voluntary Support

In response to the pressing problems addressed by the nation's not-for-profits, Americans continue to be generous with their time, talent, and money.

- In one recent year, charitable contributions totaled nearly $200 billion.
- Approximately 84 percent of all charitable donations come from *individuals*, 76 percent from current contributions and 8 percent from bequests. An additional 10 percent of donations come from foundations; 6 percent are from corporations.
- Not-for-profit organizations nationwide engage more than 100 million volunteers and donors, representing 75 percent of all American households.

OPPORTUNITIES AND CHALLENGES

In the years to come, not-for-profit organizations will be offered significant opportunities to increase their resources and enhance their services. At the same time, several issues pose serious challenges to the not-for-profit sector.

Among the opportunities: the inter-generational transfer of wealth (and the concomitant opportunity to increase planned gifts), advances in technology, and an emphasis on collaboration.

Among the challenges: threats to the not-for-profit sector's tax-exempt status, the need for regulation to deal with the small percentage of tax-exempt organizations engaged in abuses, and federal budget cuts in domestic spending.

Here are some of the trends that will affect philanthropy in the United States:

- Americans are aging. In the next 10 years the number of people 50 years of age or over will increase 33 percent as the baby-boomers grow older. The over 65 age group will jump 76 percent between the year 2010 and the year 2030.

  As baby boomers grow older, their children will leave the nest. As the boomers begin to retire, they will have more time to volunteer. And volunteers are 66 percent more likely to make gifts to charity than non-volunteers.

- The number of retired Americans is larger than ever before, and they are wealthier. Retired Americans are looking for places to spend their hours helping others and engaging in lifelong learning experiences. This group of retired Americans will transfer $9 to $11 trillion to the next generation in the next 15 years. In anticipation of this huge intergenerational transfer of wealth, not-for-profit organizations are investing more of their resources in planned giving programs.

- Donors, especially foundations and corporations, are more interested in "outcomes." They want charities to prove that the programs they help support are effective in changing lives.

- Information technology will alter everyone's life. To flourish, not-for-profit organizations will need to learn to communicate effectively using the Internet and emerging electronic technologies.

- The not-for-profit sector will come under more scrutiny. Self-regulation and cooperation with federal and state legislative and regulatory agencies will be needed to preserve confidence in the integrity of our philanthropic institutions.

- There is a growing reliance on faith-based organizations to provide vital social services.

Successful not-for-profit organizations will continue to monitor their internal and external environments. In response, they will adopt strategic plans that recognize and respond to their rapidly changing circumstances.

WORKING TOGETHER

Effective not-for-profit organizations form strategic partnerships. Some examples: arts institutions that join together to develop joint marketing strategies, churches that make space available to social service providers, conservation and preservation organizations that share education facilities, not-for-profits that form alliances to promote planned giving, and healthcare providers that share resources.

Many not-for-profit organizations speak positively about the value of strategic partnerships and collaboration; however, they tend to act alone. Some executive directors, development directors, program heads, and marketing directors seem to think that opportunities for collaboration will appear magically. That is simply not the case.

People who believe in collaboration are willing to pay a price. They meet periodically—even when outcomes or expectations are not clear. These periodic meetings are essential to the process of developing trust and uncovering collaborative opportunities. Over time the process evolves. In the beginning, key personnel uncover small projects that they can do together. As the relationship matures, what began as a few joint projects evolves into a true strategic partnership.

In addition to strategic partnerships, not-for-profit organizations—especially healthcare institutions—will explore mergers during the years to come. Competition for philanthropic resources, reductions in government spending, managed care, and a host of factors will drive many small and inefficient not-for-profits out of business. Mergers have the potential for producing economies of scale. By eliminating duplication and overhead, more of the organization's resources can be devoted to programs and services.

Ideas for collaboration among not-for-profits are limitless. Donors do not like to support organizations that duplicate the work of other not-for-profits. In fact, there is a growing trend among corporate and foundation funders to make grants to collaborative projects. Successful collaborative

projects avoid duplication. They also exploit the synergy brought about by the collaboration.

Collaborations, strategic partnerships, mergers, and joint advocacy are examples of important organizational strategies. Before discussing other organization development and fundraising strategies, it might be helpful to step back and examine the key concepts related to strategic management.

THE IMPORTANCE OF STRATEGIC MANAGEMENT

Strategic management has several advantages over the drift, freewheeling improvisation, and crisis management characteristic of some not-for-profit organizations.

The benefits of strategic management accrue to the entire organization. Similarly, a strategic approach to fundraising helps assure that your organization will obtain the generous financial resources needed to carry out its mission.

Fundraising professionals and volunteers who think strategically monitor their environments. They anticipate change. They observe trends. They stay tuned in to the thinking of corporate and foundation decision makers. They are aware of the changing demographics of their supporters. They respond to opportunities. They diversify their funding sources. And they stay focused on those cost-effective strategies that produce high net contributed income for their institutions.

The Strategic Management Process

People tend to avoid change whenever possible. Yet, change is unavoidable. A strategic approach to management recognizes the reluctance to change . . . and the unavoidable need to respond to changing circumstances.

Because "business as usual" will not work in the twenty-first century, we hear a lot about "paradigm shifts." For a true paradigm shift to take place, strategic managers stop their organizations from focusing on the past and help them respond to a rapidly changing future.

This process is called strategic visioning and planning. There are many ways of thinking about the strategic planning process. For convenience, you might wish to think about it as a seven-step process (see Exhibit 2-1).

EXHIBIT 2-1 THE STRATEGIC PLANNING PROCESS

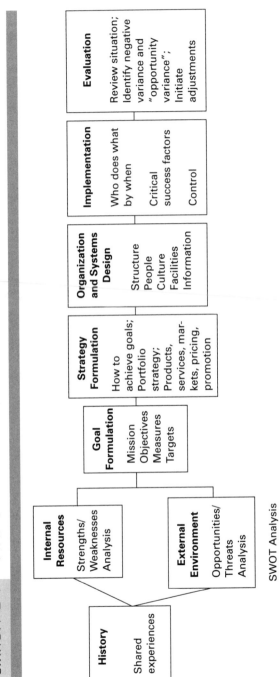

History

Shared experiences

Internal Resources

Strengths/ Weaknesses Analysis

External Environment

Opportunities/ Threats Analysis

SWOT Analysis

Goal Formulation

Mission Objectives Measures Targets

Strategy Formulation

How to achieve goals; Portfolio strategy; Products, services, markets, pricing, promotion

Organization and Systems Design

Structure People Culture Facilities Information

Implementation

Who does what by when

Critical success factors

Control

Evaluation

Review situation; Identify negative variance and "opportunity variance"; Initiate adjustments

1. *Recognize and celebrate the organization's history.* Even if many of the shared experiences are negative, one still must recognize that caring people gave birth to the organization and helped the institution through difficult times.

2. *Monitor the environment.* Examine the strengths and weaknesses of your internal resources. Look for the opportunities and threats presented by the external environment. This analysis of internal **s**trengths and **w**eaknesses and external **o**pportunities and **t**hreats is called a SWOT analysis.

3. *Define your organization's purpose and mission.* Reaffirm or revise your mission statement, in response to megatrends and environmental change. The mission statement should succinctly answer three key questions:

    • What is the organization—what is its business?

    • What does it do?

    • Whom does it serve?

4. *Develop long- and short-term goals.* Many of the key goals flow from the organization's mission statement. Other goals flow from the SWOT Analysis. Your organization will also want to develop broad goals dealing with each of the major planning dimensions: programs and services; governance and administration; facilities; human resources; technology; communications, marketing and public relations; fundraising and resource development; and financial security.

5. *Define strategies, objectives, and action steps—how the organization will achieve its goals.* During the planning process, state how success will be measured. Example: "Number of children served." The plan should then include specific measurable targets. Example: "Not less than 7,500 children served in the year 2005. Ten percent growth in the number of children served in each of the following three years."

6. *Implement plans.* Refine the organization design and systems. Decide who does what by when. Stay focused on critical success factors. The organization must decide on the ideal structure to achieve its goals. These solutions can be integrated into the plan by creating broad goals dealing with governance and administration. Each

action step and objective must be assigned to a responsible party. Inspect what you expect.

7. *Evaluate performance.* Track expected results. Review the situation. Look for negative variance. Also look for opportunity variance—unexpected good fortune. These latter variances often indicate a strength that could be built upon or a new source of income that might be continued. Initiate adjustments.

BE SURE YOUR INSTITUTION IS WORTHY OF SUPPORT

It is possible to have a modicum of fundraising success based on technique alone. Conversely, it is possible to have a strong not-for-profit organization that performs relatively poorly in the fundraising arena. However, the most effective not-for-profit organizations are strong, mission-based institutions with well-run fundraising programs.

So, as you think about strengthening your fundraising program, you can take the following steps to assure that your organization is worthy of support.

1. *Have a clear sense of mission.* Try this experiment. Have a friend or any independent observer interview a few of your organization's key people one at a time. Perhaps the interviewer could meet with your executive director, board chair, program head, development director, president of the auxiliary, marketing director, and several supporters. The interviewer can ask them about their understanding of the organization's mission. The key people can be asked to state the mission in their own words.

   Now, ask yourself, "How well understood is the mission statement?" "Is there agreement or disagreement about our mission?" "Are all key stakeholders familiar with the mission?" "Can all the key people articulate how the organization's services are related to our mission?"

   If the key people can't easily articulate your mission, your organization has one of two types of problems. First, the organization may have failed to define a clear mission. In this situation, the mis-

sion is not well understood because it is not well formed. Second, the organization has developed a clear mission, but has failed to communicate that mission to prime constituents. If the interviews were limited to a few people close to the organization, and they had difficulty in stating the organization's mission, chances are that the problem is of the first type.

Some years back, I interviewed a marketing director of a large institution. He said, "When we think in terms of increased income, we should remember that we are a museum. When we begin to behave more like a museum and open a gift shop, our income should show a healthy increase." My next interview was with the director of the institution's programs. She said, "The important thing to remember about our institution is that we are *not* a museum. Our mission is to preserve the materials entrusted to us and to make them available to scholars."

Surprisingly, such differing views of an organization's mission—while not always so dramatic—are commonplace. You get the point. Conduct the interviews and find out if your organization is laboring with similar unresolved issues.

2. *Strengthen your services.* Not-for-profit organizations exist to serve. Whether your agency is a social service provider, an arts institution, a church, a school, or a healthcare organization, its purpose is to provide some service for the betterment of your community. Whatever your service is, leaders of your organization should periodically ask themselves: Who are we serving? Are our services effective? Are we providing the services in the most cost-effective manner? Are there others who need our services whom we are not serving? Are there other services we should provide that we are not providing yet? Are there others working on the same problem with whom we can collaborate? Are we taking the steps necessary to recruit and train the best service providers possible? What steps can we take to strengthen our services?

Success in fundraising has a direct relationship to the quality of services the organization provides. In any strategic planning process, a focus on the needs of the people served will keep your organization on track.

3. *Strengthen the board.* Enhance the nominating process. Recruit people of affluence and influence. Provide early and effective orientation. Get people involved. Have an active board committee structure. Devote sufficient attention to your executive committee, nominating committee, finance committee, strategic long-range planning committee, and resource development committee. The last of these committees can be responsible for overseeing the personal solicitation, major gifts, and planned giving programs. You may wish to set up separate committees to deal with special events and membership. As uncommon circumstances arise, the board chair might appoint *ad hoc* committees to resolve the issue or make recommendations to the board.

   Keep meetings lively and timely. Start and end on time. Refer business to committees; but allow sufficient time for the board as a whole to discuss major issues. Conduct annual or bi-annual board retreats. Provide ample time for social activities.

4. *Remain tuned in to community perceptions.* Meet with constituents. Conduct focus groups. Conduct informal interviews. Survey your supporters. Build on positive feed-back. Eliminate negative perceptions. Be able to articulate the strengths of your organization.

5. *Develop an atmosphere of mutual respect between your board and staff.* Provide opportunities for interaction. Encourage open communication. Clarify roles: the board remains responsible for policy; the staff implements the policy. The board hires and evaluates the executive director; the executive director is responsible for managing the staff. The board works with the staff to formulate a budget; the board and staff have shared responsibilities for monitoring the budget.

6. *Develop an active volunteer pool.* Many organizations find it difficult to recruit and retain active volunteers. At times, staff members say that it is more timely and more cost-effective to do a task rather than recruiting and training a volunteer to do the work. No doubt this is true in many cases. However, the payoff for working with volunteers is twofold: (a) by increasing the number of volunteers close to your organization, the number of potential financial supporters is also increased; (b) individual, foundation, and corporate supporters often view volunteer involvement as cost-effective and

highly desirable. Organizations that invest in volunteer involvement often experience increased financial contributions. Volunteers are 66 percent more likely to make charitable contributions than non-volunteers.

A checklist of Key Indicators of Organizational Strength and Capability is included on the CD-ROM that accompanies this book.

Managing the Resource Development Function

Organizing is what you do before you do something, so that when you do it, it is not all mixed up.

—A.A. Milne

ANALYSIS AND PLANNING

When beginning any resource development assignment, staff and key volunteers can increase their effectiveness by devoting sufficient time and effort to analysis and planning. Planning will be discussed later; first, let's turn our attention to analysis. Early analysis focuses on four main areas: the case for support and the need for contributed income; donor history; fundraising strategies; and resources.

The case for support is discussed in greater detail in Chapter 4. Some of the preliminary questions that must be posed during the early analysis include:

- How well understood is the organization's case for support?
- Do the existing fundraising materials clearly describe the need for contributed income in terms of the people served—rather than from the point of view of institutional needs?
- How much contributed income is needed to sustain the annual operations of the organization?

- How much contributed income is needed for the organization's high-priority special projects?

- Has the organization established an endowment goal? What is it? How does the endowment goal relate to the organization's programs and aspirations?

- Has the organization established a capital fund drive goal? What is it? If the organization is not planning a capital fund drive, has it identified high-priority capital projects that might be accommodated without a formal capital campaign?

When gathering facts related to donor history, development professionals are often at the mercy of the information system. Some organizations maintain accurate and useful donor records. Some organizations are remiss in this area. And many emerging or grassroots organizations have yet to put in place any fundraising information system. This subject is covered in greater depth in Chapter 5; however, those responsible for fundraising—no matter what the state of the information system—must gather the most accurate information available concerning donor history and market forces. Here is a brief list of questions that form the basis of the early analysis:

- How many donors contributed in each of the previous three years?

- What was the total amount contributed in each of the previous three years?

- How many individual donors contributed? What was the total contributed by individuals?

- How many corporations and businesses contributed in each of the previous three years? What was the total contributed by corporations and businesses?

- How many foundations made grants to the organization in each of the previous three years? What was the total of all foundation grants?

- From which, if any, government agencies did the organization receive grants or contracts in each of the previous three years? What was the total amount of the government grants and contracts each year?

- Did the organization receive any funds from churches, professional associations, unions, or civic clubs during the last three years? How much from each?

- In the last three years, how many gifts, and what was the total amount received in each of the following gift ranges: $1–$24; $25–$49; $50–$99; $100–$249; $250–$499; $500–$999; $1,000–$2,499; $2,500–$4,999; $5,000–$9,999; $10,000–$24,999; $25,000–$49,999; $50,000–$99,999; $100,000–$499,999; $500,000–$999,999; $1,000,000 and above. (Adjust this scale for your organization's gift range; but be sure to extend the range upward to remind your organization of the possibilities of even greater major gifts.)

- What sources of names and lists are available to the organization? Have affluent prospective supporters been added to the fundraising database?

The ease with which an organization is able to extract this information tells a great deal about the quality of the organization's record keeping. The aim is to establish reliable baseline information. If this is a difficult task, one of the organization's highest priorities is to purchase dedicated fundraising software or strengthen the system it has.

One other bit of advice. If gift history must be reconstructed, be sure to start with the most recent year and work backwards. Start by cleaning up current year records. Next reconstruct the previous year's donor records. Then proceed with each previous year. This is the quickest way to have reliable and useable information.

If the organization is establishing a new system or switching from one dedicated fundraising software program to another, you will want to transfer the records electronically to the extent possible. However, some very old databases are constructed using obsolete operating systems or are formatted in a manner that does not lend itself to electronic transfer. Similarly, some records are so corrupt that the transfer makes no sense. In most cases, it makes economic sense to clean up the existing records as much as possible before attempting an electronic transfer. With any electronic transfer, there will be some anomalies. Inspect the results. Manually correct all special situations and faulty records.

When analyzing fundraising strategies, be sure to focus on *net* contributed income. Answer the following:

- In the last three years, how much did the organization net from each of the following: personal major gift solicitation, mail, telephone, special events, grants, bequests and other planned gifts?

When analyzing fundraising resources, start by examining the institution's human resources by asking:

- What fundraising staff members are in place? What are their experience levels? What are the strengths each person brings to his or her position? What is each staff member's job description?

- How many board members participate in the resource development process? How well do the board members understand their role? Are there sufficient numbers of people of affluence and influence serving on the board? Do board members contribute each year?

- What other volunteers participate in the fundraising process? Does the organization have an auxiliary or volunteer support group? Are there other volunteers who help with fundraising or special events? Is the volunteer pool growing? Are the volunteers motivated and enthusiastic?

Next examine your equipment, systems, facilities, and budgets. Ask:

- What equipment is available to the development office? Is a sufficient number of computers, printers, copiers, faxes, and telephone lines available?

- Is the fundraising information system well-maintained? Does the fundraising software meet your organization's needs? Are timely and accurate reports available?

- Are the facilities adequate?

- Have you developed a realistic budget for the resource development function? Is the amount budgeted for staff sufficient to attract and retain experienced professionals capable of helping the organization reach its fundraising goals? Does the budget allocate sufficient resources for fundraising materials? Does the budget adequately accommodate the need for up-to-date equipment and technology? Does it accommodate supplies and other general expenses? Does the budget correlate well with the need to maintain a cost-effective operation that maximizes net contributed income?

These questions form the basis of your organization's analysis. The reader may also wish to conduct a more thorough analysis by delving into the complete self-assessment and evaluation in Chapter 16.

Often, not-for-profit managers and development professionals avoid intense analysis and evaluation. With tight time-lines and limited resources, staff members view analysis as a burden. However, it is helpful to remember that analysis and evaluation are most time-consuming and difficult the first time they are addressed. The changes your organization makes in record keeping will serve it well for years to come. This type of analysis will provide valuable base-line information against which future results can be compared. As important, the analysis—if it includes data from several years—will indicate trends that your organization will want to track.

Once the analysis has been completed, the next task is to develop a comprehensive resource development plan that is responsive to your organization's unique circumstances. The plan's success will depend on two critical traits—effectiveness and efficiency.

EFFECTIVENESS: DOING THE RIGHT THINGS

Effectiveness focuses on high payback activities. When deciding which fundraising strategies to undertake, first determine what will produce the greatest payback for the time and resources spent. These are the activities to schedule and focus on. If your organization has a strong history of receiving grants, by all means continue and strengthen the grants program. If your organization is becoming bogged down by too many small-scale special events, plan more successful events, seek larger sponsorships, or cancel the events. If your organization has the potential to develop a successful mail campaign, but the data are not sufficient to quantify expected results, budget and schedule some test mailings. Also consider testing a combined phone and mail program, if such a program seems appropriate for your not-for-profit organization. By all means, consider implementing or strengthening your organization's major gift program.

Thus, effectiveness always involves some basic *decisions*. What undertakings and areas of concentration will produce the most desired results and greatest impact? Remember, your goals are to:

- Maximize net contributed income
- Increase the number of donors and sources of contributed income
- Nurture positive relationships with all supporters and potential

supporters; nurture personal relationships with those capable of pace-setting leadership contributions

- Continually strengthen the organization and enhance its reputation

Earlier we mentioned Pareto's 80/20 rule. Vilfredo Pareto, Italian sociologist and economist (1848–1923), observed that 20 percent of all effort produces 80 percent of all results. How can your organization put this powerful observation to work?

Fundraising professionals know that personal contact and relationship building activities precede any consideration of major gifts. Yet, how many professionals and volunteers devote nearly enough time to nurturing these relationships? Effectiveness is setting the right goals and following through with your plans.

As individuals and professionals, fundraisers have multiple roles. Development officers wear several hats: planner, writer, volunteer trainer, communicator, project organizer, and ombudsman. Personal and family roles are equally complex. We also must not ignore our spiritual needs as we plan for effective and balanced lives. A burned-out staff member or volunteer is of little value to your not-for-profit organization.

The first task in getting organized is to list *all* of the fundraiser's roles. Following this you can ask the basic questions: "What are the goals for each of these roles? What critical factors can I monitor to make sure that I stay on target?" Once you have answered the basic questions you can improve your chances for success by nurturing the traits most commonly associated with effectiveness:

- *Understanding and control of time.* Effective people understand time and know how they spend this valuable resource. They log their time periodically. They evaluate how they use their time in light of their priorities.

  Very often, development professionals are hired because they are generalists. They have strong people and communication skills. Often they are viewed as people who can serve the organization in a broad range of capacities. Many times these development professionals are called upon to perform work that is not strictly related to fundraising. Many professionals find that they are spending only a small percentage of their time devoted to resource development. Most find that

they spend far too little time meeting with key supporters and prospective major donors.

- *Focus on Results.* Ask, "What results are expected of me? What can I do that will have the greatest impact?"

  Remember that the only results that really count are outside the organization rather than within the organization. Ask, "Am I, as a development professional or volunteer, focusing on activities that will bring prospective donors closer to my organization? Will the development office's activities enhance the long-term reputation of our organization in our community? Will our activities motivate donors and maximize net contributed income?"

- *Build on Strengths.* It has been said before, but it is worth repeating: Concentrate on the fundraising strategies at which your organization excels.

  On a related point, effective people staff from strength. Management expert Peter Drucker points out that effective executives never focus on weaknesses. Their question is always, "What can I do uncommonly well?" Drucker advises us to ". . . look for excellence in one major area and not for performance that gets by all around."

  This book recommends a comprehensive approach to resource development. Do not, however, misinterpret this advice. If your organization has great strength in its mail program, special events, or grants programs, build on those strengths. Then add new initiatives as resources allow.

- *Recognize Responsibility, Take Initiative.* Effective people are alert. They are planners. They also implement preventive measures. To be effective self-starters, not-for-profit executive directors, development directors, key staff, and key volunteers must *schedule and perform* their real priorities.

- *Have Vision.* Effective people set goals. They have the ability to envision a future of their creation.

- *Develop Interpersonal Competencies.* Effective people have "people skills." They are effective communicators. They understand other points of view and nurture *empathy.* They remember that all human beings need *recognition.*

Above all, development professionals must understand *motivation*. They must know what motivates donors to give and what motivates volunteers. They must understand what motivates colleagues and staff. Working alone they accomplish little. Effective people learn the power of *team building.*

In fundraising, as in life, the highest payoff activities are: planning, setting goals, doing what needs to be done, evaluating and refining our strategies and methods, employing preventive measures, eliminating bad habits and low payoff activities, and building positive relationships. By their nature, these very high-priority activities do not have their own deadlines. To actually occur, they must be scheduled. The two models in Exhibit 3-1 illustrate this.

Assembling and prioritizing the daily do list is not enough. Development professionals must use daily and longer-term planning calendars to actually schedule blocks of time for the very high payoff endeavors. To occur, cultivation and friend-raising activities must be scheduled. To occur, program review and evaluation must be scheduled. To occur, prospect research must be scheduled. To gain the time to perform the high-priority activities that have been scheduled, you will want to eliminate low payoff activities and learn the time-saving techniques associated with efficiency.

EFFICIENCY: DOING THINGS RIGHT

Once we have established our priorities and goals, we must pursue our aspirations in the most competent, practical, and productive manner. This is efficiency. Does producing a routine letter take more than an hour? Can't we speed up many of the simple chores and communications and save our time for the high-priority work?

A cautionary note: efficiency is not the same as effectiveness. If in our effort to be productive we make a prospective donor feel rushed or unimportant, we may gain 10 minutes but lose $10,000.

With this cautionary note in mind, we can turn our attention to internal efficiencies. Take stock of how things are done in the office. Try this simple exercise. Pretend you are a donation check. Follow yourself from the incoming mail through the record keeping process to the deposit. What did you learn? Who opens the mail? Are there any bottlenecks? Are

EXHIBIT 3-1   **TWO TIME MANAGEMENT MODELS**

Model #1: A popular and common conceptual model. This closely represents reality, but it focuses on "high payoff/*do now*" activities. This view of time management fosters crisis management and reactive behaviors.

High Payoff

Medium Payoff

Low Payoff

Do Now   Do Soon   Can Wait

Model #2: Illustrates Weinstein's Law . . . **The highest payoff activities do not have their own deadlines.**

Weinstein's corollary . . . **To occur, non-deadline driven very high payoff activities must be pro-actively scheduled**.

Very High Payoff   CHANGE TO "DO NOW" ◄——————

Relationship building
Planning
Discarding bad habits
New initiatives
Evaluation
Prevention
Etc.

High Payoff

Medium Payoff

Low Payoff

Do Now   Do Soon   Can Wait

there points in the system where the gift entry is redundant? Are the controls adequate? Does the system result in a gracious acknowledgment letter being sent within two business days of receipt? How long does it take to thank each donor? Are major donors also thanked with a phone call?

After this simple analysis, you may wish to refine your gift handling procedures. Consider adopting a gift handling policy based on models provided by colleagues. Also be sure to have an accountant look at your gift handling policies and procedures.

Policies and procedures should be kept as simple as possible—but not too simple! We should think through all the implications of our policies. Systems have their own cost/benefit ratios. The aim is to maximize the benefit while minimizing the cost. After eliminating unnecessary steps and reports, policies and procedures can be documented. Thoughtful documentation is tangible evidence that on-going activities have been reduced to simple-to-administer routines.

BUDGETS AND FINANCIAL RESOURCES

Resource development professionals and board members have two concerns related to the organization's budget: the not-for-profit institution's overall budget and fiscal health, and the budget and cost-effectiveness of the fundraising program.

The institution's fiscal health is of paramount concern to donors. This concern is manifest in a range of issues:

- Donors focus on institutional credibility and accountability. Thoughtful donors support organizations with strong budget processes and reputations for fiscal responsibility.

- Donors want to know how their contributions will be used. They focus on projects that match their philanthropic interests. They want to know that their funds are being used wisely. And prospective donors are often motivated to make major contributions in response to specific projects and budget projections that generate named-gift opportunities.

- Donors recognize the benefits of a thoughtful budget process. Thoughtful budget processes give decision-makers an opportunity to focus on priorities and impact. Moreover, the process gives all involved a chance to buy into the program.

  Budgeting gives management an overall view. Each activity is fit into a general plan. Budgeting sets performance goals for each activity. Budgeting regulates spending within the limits of income.

With careful monitoring of the budget process, management can determine in advance to what extent contributed income is especially urgent or when financing might be needed. (At times, cash-flow projections can be a powerful fundraising tool. Few events create a sense of urgency as strong as a pending cash-flow crisis.)

Budgeting is imperative for the board and management to anticipate unfavorable situations and to take timely corrective action. Budgeting also allows the board and management to identify unexpected favorable variance. Unanticipated positive cash results can signal a fundraising or earned income opportunity on which to build.

Executive directors of not-for-profit organizations, key staff, and board leaders should be thoroughly familiar with the institution's budget process. If the organization has not yet adopted a formal budget process, or if the institution wishes to refine its process, the board's finance committee may wish to examine the sample budget process outlined in Exhibit 3-2.

The executive director, finance director, treasurer, and the board finance committee have responsibility for monitoring the performance of the not-for-profit organization's overall budget. The development director has the primary responsibility of monitoring the budget for fundraising and resource development.

EXHIBIT 3-2   SAMPLE NOT-FOR-PROFIT AGENCY BUDGET PROCESS

1. Reexamine mission—develop preliminary goals, objectives, and recommendations.
   a. Study options
      Evaluate on-going programs.
      List and evaluate potential new programs.
   b. Make preliminary recommendations for next fiscal year programs.
      Develop a sense of priority, significance, and impact.
      Remember, total agreement is not necessary at this stage.
      Final agreement on goals, objectives, and programs takes place during the reconciliation process.
2. Estimate expenses
   a. Use previous fiscal year's actual expense information to serve as a point of departure for budget estimates of ongoing programs. Refine data and improve forecasts.
   b. Staff should carefully estimate the costs of any potential new programs.
   c. Carefully estimate aggregate costs of the preliminary program recommendations. Preserve line-item detailed expense estimates for all programs.

(continued)

EXHIBIT 3-2   (CONTINUED)

3. Estimate income
   a. Carefully examine all revenue sources:
      Government (city, state, federal)
      United Way
      Endowment
      Annual fund (This should never merely be a plug number. Rather, the
         institution must develop objective means of estimating the potential and
         expected results. Realistic estimates are mandatory.)
      Special events
      Fees, contract services, ticket income, admissions, payment for services,
         tuition, sales of goods . . . or other measures of "earned income"
         appropriate to the individual agency, detailed analysis on a per-project
         basis.
      Unrelated business income
      Auxiliary or guild income
      Program advertising
      Interest
      Miscellaneous and other income sources unique to the individual agencies
   b. The revenue estimates must be detailed and based on the specific program
      recommendations.
4. Reconciliation
   a. Examine income vis-à-vis the expenses. **Expenses must not exceed income!**
      Once the institution adopts the notion that planned deficits are permissible
      under certain circumstances, the floodgates will have been opened. The
      ultimate result can be an agency's drowning in its own sea of red ink.
   b. Adjust program goals and objectives to appropriate levels.
   c. Make the hard decisions and double-check your revised figures.
5. Board approval
   a. This is not just a formality; the budget must be carefully presented to and
      reviewed by the ratifying body.
   b. Once ratified, all involved must be committed to the resulting plan of action.
6. Monitor and administer the budget
   a. Administer the budget correctly but not inflexibly.
   b. The overall plan must not be sacrificed in order to keep one item on line.
   c. The appropriate decision makers must be prepared to explain to the board any
      planned deviation.
   d. Break down the budget into periods corresponding to periodic financial
      statements. Estimate income and expenses on a monthly or quarterly basis.
      (To the extent possible, plan income-producing activities or fundraising
      strategies to help alleviate the organization's cash-flow difficulties, if any.
      Also, be cautious of large contributed income projections late in the fiscal
      year when little time remains to correct any adverse conditions.)
   e. Statements must be prepared on a timely basis and compared with budget
      projections.
   f. Board must act—it must take action in cases of significant adverse deviation
      from the approved budget plan.

The Fundraising Budget

Before we can address the issue of monitoring the resources and results, the fundraising team must first develop its annual budget. Let's tackle that chore now.

The budget format in Exhibit 3-3 focuses on fundraising strategies. To construct the budget using this format, the development staff or key volunteers must make careful estimates of income and expenses based on each

---

EXHIBIT 3-3   SAMPLE DEVELOPMENT OFFICE BUDGET

INCOME

Prospect mailings (5,000 × 16 × 1.5% × $26)=1,200 new donors	$ 31,200
In-house Mail Renewals and Upgrades (5,000 × 83% × $55=228,250)	
+(25% × 5,000 × $55=50,000)	297,000
Telephone Solicitations (15 days × 7 callers × 3 hours × 2 donors/hr × $29)	18,270
Grants	185,000
Fund Raising: Special Events (Art Auction and Testimonial Dinner)	
Sponsorships (2 events: 1 generates $25,000; the other $35,000)	60,000
Other Income	52,500
Art Auction (275 people × $50 tik=13,750)	
+(110 people × $100 purchase=11,000)=24,750	
Testimonial Dinner ($75 × 370 people)=27,750	
Board Campaign (24 members: 1@10K; 2@5K; 4@2.5K; 7@1K;	
5@.5K; 4@.3K; 1@.1K)	40,800
Personal Solicitation (40K board / 15% = 266,666)	
Individuals	165,000
Corporations	117,000
Unsolicited Contributions	14,500
United Way Donor Option	21,000
Bequests	20,000
TOTAL CONTRIBUTED INCOME	**$1,022,270**

EXPENSES

Staff (Director of Development@60K; Data Entry/Records@24.5K;	
Promotions-Special Events@32K)	
Salaries	$116,500
Benefits (15%)	17,475
Taxes (12%)	13,980
Professional Associations	550
Publications and Reference Materials	130

(continued)

EXHIBIT 3-3   (CONTINUED)

Training and Conferences	
Fees	375
Travel, Food, Lodging	1,000
Other Travel, Food, Lodging	1,000
Equipment, Maintenance and Software Support	3,000
Office Supplies and General Printing	2,500
General Postage	2,700
Relationship Nuturing Activities	
Volunteer and Donor Acknowledgment Events	3,000
Open House	500
Social/Informative Gathering(s)	750
Miscellaneous Entertainment	600
Acknowledgment Mail	2,680
Acknowledgment Items, Plaques, and Benefits	4,000
Prospect Mail	
Postage (40K × 2 × .09)	7,200
Printing (80K × .25)	20,000
List Rental ($60/1000 × 80)	4,800
Consultant, Copy, Artistic	2,000
Mail-house Services (80K × .07)	5,600
In-house Mail (renewals and upgrades)	
Postage (12K × 7/yr × .10)	8,400
Printing (12K pieces × 7/yr × .36)	30,240
Consultant, Copy, Artistic	4,500
Mail-house Services (12K × 7/yr × .15)	12,600
Telephone Prospecting	
List Rental (12 × 75)	900
Service Provider Fees	14,700
Telephone Renewal and Upgrade	0
Service Provider Fees	
Special Events (expenses from each event budget)	43,000
Personal Solicitation Materials	
Case Statements and Other Presentation Materials	4,500
Presentation Folders	2,500
Video Case Statement	7,000
Pledge Cards and Call Report Cards	250
Planned Giving	
2 Seminars	600
Thank You Inserts	150
Mail Brochures (2,000 × 2 × .20)1postage (4,000 × .11)	1,240
TOTAL EXPENSES	**$340,925**
NET CONTRIBUTED INCOME	**$681,350**

of the fundraising strategies employed by the not-for-profit organization. The format also reminds the reader to include a board campaign and a personal solicitation program. Direct mail, telephone, and special events may not be appropriate for every organization; but board giving and person-to-person contact can benefit any organization. If resource development staff and volunteers do not have experience in some of the fundraising strategies included in the sample budget format, the appropriate chapters of this book can provide preliminary help in estimating results. However, when implementing and budgeting a new fundraising strategy, development professionals may wish to employ a consultant or confer with colleagues from other not-for-profit organizations.

The Sample Development Office Budget (see Exhibit 3-3) was constructed largely around staff expenses and fundraising strategies. At times, development professionals start by setting goals based on programmatic or institutional needs. For example, the board finance committee for a grassroots organization might calculate that the organization needs $225,000 for annual operations, $7,500 for new computer equipment, and $50,000 for an intensive advocacy campaign. In this case, the organization's executive director, who is the person mainly responsible for fundraising, figures that the organization can approach several foundations and a local computer manufacturer for the equipment. The executive director can also approach affluent individuals and additional foundations for the advocacy campaign. The $225,000 is quite a bit more than previous years, but still must be raised through the organization's direct mail, phone, and special events. The executive director may also consider initiating a major gifts club—thus encouraging $250 and $500 a year annual donors to consider contributions of $1,000, $2,500, $5,000, or more.

Alternatively, a mature institution with a $10 million annual budget may be contemplating a $6 million capital/endowment campaign to build a new facility and endow the maintenance of that building. In this case, the chief development officer prepares the annual budget, but also includes expenses in preparation for the capital/endowment campaign: consultant fees, more intensive prospect research, and enhanced cultivation activities. In either case, the reasoning should bring the planner back to the fundraising strategies that will produce the income needed for the project or programs.

Some resource development budgets and plans have been constructed around the organization's programs, with inadequate planning regarding

fundraising strategies. One such plan listed three program initiatives and enhancements to annual operations. The plan and budget for the first program initiative listed several foundations to be approached. The plan also included a special mail appeal, and concluded that the remainder of the funds needed would be solicited from interested individuals and corporations. The second and third program initiatives were similarly "planned." The plans for increased annual funds included vague enhancements to the annual campaign and overly optimistic budget projections. There are many problems with this approach. The first is that the planning for each fundraising strategy becomes fragmented. The second major problem is that budget projections should never be based on need alone. Thoughtful planning calls for the ability to set realistic goals.

Setting Fundraising Goals

Experienced professionals focus on cost-effective fundraising strategies, and they employ five methods for setting fundraising goals: (1) summarize old and new gift potential, (2) create a goal based upon board of directors' donations, (3) perform a feasibility study, (4) prepare comparative statistics, and (5) use an analysis of each prospect and request amount.

The first—as well as most common and effective—method of setting goals is to summarize trends and recent gift history, adjust for known losses, and project an organization's goals based on this analysis (see Exhibit 3-4). The score-keeping reports in Chapter 16 will help you project trends and focus on *net* contributed income.

The second method of setting goals works well if an organization relies heavily on a person-to-person major gift initiative. In such a case, a rough estimate of potential can be based on giving by board members. One general rule in fundraising is that the Board of Directors donates approximately 15 percent of the contributed major gift income. This observation can be expressed algebraically:

$$\text{Board Contributions} = .15 \times \text{Major Gift Total}$$

With this belief—and a simple algebraic adjustment—the major gift goal can be projected once the board's gift total is known.

$$\text{Board Contributions} \div .15 = \text{Projected Major Gift Income}$$

EXHIBIT 3-4	SUMMARY OF OLD AND NEW GIFT POTENTIAL

Last Year's Fund Drive (all contributed income)	$_____
Minus Known Nonrepeatable Amount	-$_____
New Base of Support	$_____
1.1 × New Base of Support = Base + Increased Gifts	$_____
(This assumes a 10% rate of growth. Use historical rate of growth based on recent trends.)	
Plus Value of New Prospect Pool	+$_____
(Conservative estimates of increased prospecting and fundraising strategy initiatives)	
Estimated Goal for New Fiscal Year Fund Drive	$_____

Also carefully estimate the expenses. **Track *net* contributed income.**

To illustrate, assume that the board donates $41,000. When we divide $41,000 by .15, the result is $273,333. This figure can serve as the major gift goal. One must remember, however, that no mathematical formula should be followed blindly. Gifted managers make decisions. They adjust the projections based upon additional analysis or information that may not be reflected in the projection.

The third method of setting goals listed above is the feasibility study. Many consultants choose to avoid that term because of the negative connotations associated with the word "feasibility." At Hartsook and Associates, we simply refer to this process and report it as a campaign assessment.

Whether it is referred to as a feasibility study, a market study, or a philanthropic planning study, a campaign assessment or pre-campaign study, an experienced consultant conducts confidential interviews with prospective pace-setting donors to the proposed campaign. Capital campaigns are almost always preceded by a planning study. Consultants are important to the process because they bring objectivity to the analysis. Someone not closely associated with the organization is better equipped to ask sensitive questions about the not-for-profit organization's reputation. Using consultants also allows the potential donor to speak candidly about their interest in the project and their potential financial participation.

The feasibility or planning study contains findings, conclusions, a summary of strengths and weaknesses, as well as recommendations concerning

leadership, campaign structure, timing, and goals. The financial goals are established based on the possible and probable levels of support indicated by the study participants.

The fourth method of establishing goals is to gather and analyze comparative statistics—sources of income, expenses, number of donors, and totals raised through each fundraising strategy. This is often difficult because quality data is not always available. And when data is available, the factors leading to the comparative results may very well be quite different from your organization's circumstances. Still, gathering and analyzing data is a worthwhile exercise.

Some associations such as the American Symphony Orchestra League and others collect and publish useful statistics. Even if you work in a field that does not have readily available statistics, it is still possible to gather such data. For example, let us say that you work for a social service agency. With a bit of effort, you can form an *ad hoc* alliance with several similar agencies. The agencies chosen should have budgets similar to yours. And the agencies should be in cities with demographics and population size analogous to your organization. It's one thing to meet a challenging goal in Chicago. It's quite another to achieve the same results in Yazoo City.

By gathering statistics, whether from published sources or through *ad hoc* alliances, it becomes possible to compare annual fund and capital campaign results. This information can help you set goals. If most of the other organizations out-perform your agency's results in annual giving, you may wish to call representatives of each of the organizations to find out what they are doing differently. Armed with this new knowledge, the organization's goal can be adjusted upward as you institute recommendations from your colleagues.

The fifth method of setting goals is a name-by-name analysis of the prospect pool. This technique is especially helpful in preparing for capital campaigns. To employ this name-by-name analysis, list the top donors and prospective donors, those with the capacity to donate at leadership levels. Then, decide how much your organization will request from each donor and prospect.

The director of development then fills in the percentage probability of attaining each contribution based on experience and on these general guidelines: donors who have given in the range to be requested for several years, 80 to 90 percent; donors who gave last year for the first time, 60 to

70 percent; donors who have skipped a year, 40 percent; new prospects (with a well-assigned solicitor), 20 to 30 percent; long shots, but with some rational expectation, 10 percent. If a representative of your organization has had a conversation with the prospect, and he or she indicated interest in donating at the levels discussed, the development director can rate the probability higher. The value assigned to each prospect equals the request amount multiplied by the percentage probability (see Exhibit 3-5). The accuracy of these subjective judgments is surprising.

The accuracy of the last column comes from its cumulative power, rather than from the individual amounts. For example, if five prospects on the list are to be asked to donate $1,000 each and each is rated at a 20 percent probability, you might expect to raise $1,000 total from that group of five. It would be a statistical anomaly if you were to receive $200 from

EXHIBIT 3-5	PRIORITY EVALUATION FORM

NOTE: This form is useful in establishing the value of a priority prospect list. The longer it is, the more accurate its predictive qualities become. The two main uses of this form are: to check whether a prospect pool is adequate for fundraising needs and to establish goals and predict how much can be raised.

PROSPECT	AMOUNT TO BE REQUESTED	% PROBABILITY OF SUCCESS	VALUE OF SOLICITATION
ABC Corporation	$5,000	80	$4,000
M/M Gotbucks	10,000	20	2,000
Mega Foundation	150,000	60	90,000
Etc. (Many lines, many prospects)			
Total Requested	$X,XXX,XXX		$XXX,XXX (Amount List is Most Likely to Produce)

At least 100 prospects are required for this form to be predictive; 300 to 400 prospects are preferable. Very large institutions can identify even more prospects for leadership gifts. The larger the list, the more predictive the model. Of course, the prospects must be visited and asked to consider the amounts requested.

(*continued*)

EXHIBIT 3-5   (CONTINUED)

PRIORITY EVALUATION FORM

PROSPECT	AMOUNT TO BE REQUESTED	% PROBABILITY OF SUCCESS	VALUE OF SOLICITATION
Total Requested	$		$ (Amount List is Most Likely to Produce)

each of the prospects as the form seems to indicate. Rather, you might receive $1,000 from one and nothing from the other four. Alternatively, you might receive $600 from one, $200 from two others, and two might donate nothing. Once again, the longer the list, the more accurate the results.

With an understanding of this last method of establishing goals and predicting contributed income comes a number of insights concerning ways of increasing total donations: we can increase gifts by increasing the number of requests we make, we can ask our donors to consider larger donations, or we can increase the probability of receiving larger donations by strengthening our case for support and by nurturing closer relationships with our supporters.

Increasing total contributions is one thing. Maximizing net contributed income is another. The next section discusses cost-effectiveness and the expense side of the puzzle.

Cost-Effectiveness of Various Fundraising Strategies

Exhibit 3-6 summarizes the cost-effectiveness of each major fundraising strategy. However, caution and managerial judgment are needed in evaluating fundraising programs. Each institution's circumstances are unique. A one-year-old not-for-profit agency might very well have higher startup costs. An organization with strong name recognition and wide appeal may have lower fundraising costs. Most organizations fall somewhere in the middle.

EXHIBIT 3-6   COST-EFFECTIVENESS OF VARIOUS FUNDRAISING STRATEGIES

Fundraising Method	Typical Expense Range
Direct mail acquisition	$0.95–$1.25 per $ raised
Direct mail renewal	$0.25–$0.38 per $ raised
Telephone acquisition	$0.90–$1.20 per $ raised
Telephone renew and upgrade	$0.27–$0.40 per $ raised
Special events	$0.45–$0.55 of gross proceeds
Grants: Corporate and foundation	$0.03–$0.20 per $ raised
Planned giving	$0.05–$0.25 per $ raised
Major gift personal solicitation programs	$0.02–$0.15 per $ raised
Capital campaigns	$0.03–$0.10 per $ raised

A mature and comprehensive resource development program might require an investment of $0.16 to $0.37 per dollar raised. The most important point is to evaluate the overall effort. Individual components of fundraising programs often require significant startup investments. Do not be overly concerned if acquisition programs cost more than they bring in. The purpose of donor acquisition programs is to increase an organization's number of supporters. As these new donors renew and upgrade their support, the initial investment pays for itself. Besides, the larger base of support will, over time, bolster the organization's major gift and planned giving programs.

Monitoring the Budget

If an organization's fundraising plan and timing of activities is similar from year to year, a budget format that compares year-to-date performance to last year's year-to-date may work well (see Exhibit 3-7). Alternatively, if fundraising activities are fairly evenly spread throughout the year, you may wish to adopt a budget reporting format that compares the year-to-date performance to the budget expectations based on the percentage of the year completed (see Exhibit 3-8).

A better approach is to compare actual results to planned results. There is a formula that helps with this:

(year-to-date actual) − (year-to-date budgeted amount) + (amount budgeted for the entire fiscal year) = revised fiscal year projection

This mathematical formula should not be followed blindly. Management judgment can be employed to refine the projections. With or without adjustments to the projections, this formula suggests a very usable budget reporting format (see Exhibit 3-9).

For the budget reporting format illustrated in Exhibit 3-9 to work, the fundraising team must first create its annual budget, then break it down into monthly or quarterly expectations. The task of making such projections is not a simple matter of dividing the year into twelve or four periods. Rather, the projections are made based on the schedule of activities. For example, if a large special event is scheduled in the third quarter, we would not expect to see one-fourth of the special event income in the first

INCOME	Year to Date	Last Year to Date	Annual Budget
Prospect mailings	4,600	2,100	$ 31,200
In-house mail	127,690	120,360	297,000
Telephone solicitations	17,300	0	18,270
Grants	46,500	51,700	185,000
Special events	53,750	41,790	112,500
Board campaign	38,700	35,500	40,800
Personal solicitation	98,300	100,150	282,000
Unsolicited contributions	3,600	3,850	14,500
United Way donor option	5,200	6,210	21,000
Bequests and memorial gifts	30,590	22,150	20,000
TOTAL CONTRIBUTED INCOME	**426,230**	**383,810**	**$1,022,270**

EXPENSES			
Staff	49,610	46,650	147,955
Association fees	0	0	550
Publications	270	130	130
Training/conferences	210	0	1,375
Other travel, food, lodging	270	210	1,000
Equipment/maintenance	970	2,400	3,000
Supplies/printing	1,120	970	2,500
General postage	840	900	2,700
Cultivation and acknowledgment	3,210	2,500	11,530
Prospect mail	5,520	2,850	39,600
In-house mail (renewals and upgrades)	19,100	18,750	55,740
Telephone prospecting	15,750	0	15,600
Special events	24,600	23,450	43,000
Personal solicitation materials	2,100	570	14,250
Planned giving	475	525	1,990
TOTAL EXPENSES	124,045	99,905	**$340,925**
NET CONTRIBUTED INCOME	**302,185**	**283,905**	**$681,350**

quarter. All of the income and expenses would be projected for the third
quarter. The benefit of this budget reporting format is that the reports
compare the results to this year's fundraising plan. Comparisons to last year
are of little value if the plan is substantially different, or if the activities are

EXHIBIT 3-8	YEAR-TO-DATE BUDGET REPORT— PERCENTAGE-OF-YEAR BASIS JULY 1, 2002–OCTOBER 31, 2002 (33% OF YEAR)

INCOME	Year to Date	% Annual Budget	Annual Budget
Prospect mailings	4,600	14.7	$ 31,200
In-house mail	127,690	42.9	297,000
Telephone solicitations	17,300	94.6	18,270
Grants	46,500	25.1	185,000
Special events	53,750	47.8	112,500
Board campaign	38,700	94.8	40,800
Personal solicitation	98,300	34.8	282,000
Unsolicited contributions	3,600	24.8	14,500
United Way donor option	5,200	24.7	21,000
Bequest and memorial gifts	30,590	152.9	20,000
TOTAL CONTRIBUTED INCOME	**426,230**	**41.7%**	**$1,022,270**

EXPENSES			
Staff	49,610	33.5	147,955
Association fees	0	0	550
Publications	270	207.7	130
Training/conferences	210	15.2	1,375
Other travel, food, lodging	270	27	1,000
Equipment/maintenance	970	32.33	3,000
Supplies/printing	1,120	44.8	2,500
General postage	840	31.1	2,700
Cultivation and acknowledgment	3,210	27.8	11,530
Prospect mail	5,520	13.9	39,600
In-house mail (renewals and upgrades)	19,100	34.3	55,740
Telephone prospecting	15,750	101	15,600
Special events	24,600	57	43,000
Personal solicitation materials	2,100	14.7	14,250
Planned giving	475	23.8	1,990
TOTAL EXPENSES	124,045	36.38%	**$340,925**
NET CONTRIBUTED INCOME	**302,185**	**44.3%**	**$681,350**

scheduled at different times from those in the previous year. Comparisons to the percentage of the year completed have little meaning if the events and fundraising program elements are not evenly distributed throughout the year.

EXHIBIT 3-9   YEAR-TO-DATE BUDGET REPORT—
ACTUAL VIS À VIS PLAN
JULY 1, 2002–OCTOBER 31, 2002

INCOME	YTD Actual	YTD Budget	Fiscal Year Budget	Fiscal Year Projection
Prospect mailings	4,600	4,100	31,200	31,700
In-house mail	127,690	120,000	297,000	304,690
Telephone solicitations	17,300	18,270	18,270	17,300
Grants	46,500	49,000	185,000	182,500
Special events	53,750	52,500	112,500	113,750
Board campaign	38,700	37,500	40,800	42,000
Personal solicitation	98,300	104,000	282,000	276,000
Unsolicited contributions	3,600	3,000	14,500	15,100
United Way donor option	5,200	5,500	21,000	20,700
Bequests and memorial gifts	30,590	10,000	20,000	30,590
TOTAL CONTRIBUTED INCOME	**$426,230**	**$403,870**	**$1,022,270**	**$1,034,330**

EXPENSES

Staff	49,610	49,320	147,955	148,245
Association fees	0	0	550	550
Publications	270	75	130	325
Training/conferences	210	590	1,375	995
Other travel, food, lodging	270	340	1,000	930
Equipment/maintenance	970	1,000	3,000	2,970
Supplies/printing	1,120	600	2,500	3,020
General postage	840	750	2,700	2,790
Cultivation and acknowledgment	3,210	2,750	11,530	11,990
Prospect mail	5,520	5,000	39,600	40,120
In-house mail (renewals and upgrades)	19,100	18,000	55,740	56,840
Telephone prospecting	15,750	15,600	15,600	15,750
Special events	24,600	22,000	43,000	45,600
Personal solicitation materials	2,100	3,000	14,250	13,350
Planned giving	475	450	1,990	2,015
TOTAL EXPENSES	**$124,045**	**$119,475**	**$340,925**	**$345,490**
NET CONTRIBUTED INCOME	**$302,185**	**$284,395**	**$681,350**	**$688,840**

FUNDRAISING MODES

Like generals preparing for battle, fundraisers must be sure that they are gearing up for the right war, using the appropriate strategies for the situation. How often do volunteers prepare for a capital campaign by examining all of their special event fundraising options? This strategy is simply inappropriate and ineffective for a capital campaign. Similarly, it would be overly optimistic or just plain unrealistic to believe that a foundation grantsmanship program could sustain the not-for-profit organization's annual operations. (Although, a multiyear grant of seed funds might get the organization started.)

To be sure that your organization employs the appropriate fundraising strategies for its circumstances, it is necessary to have a firm understanding of various fundraising modes or states.

The Annual Campaign

The term *annual fund* can be misleading. As stated throughout this book, one major goal of not-for-profit organizations is to encourage supporters to make multiple gifts throughout the year. Some supporters misinterpret the term *annual fund* to imply that the organization expects just one gift a year.

To further confuse the issue, many not-for-profit organizations conduct what they call membership drives. Unless membership fees are closely associated with tangible and exclusive benefits, those responsible for fundraising can view the membership fee as a contribution. In fact, most memberships are unrestricted annual fund gifts. In return for the membership fee, donors usually receive a newsletter that they might have gotten anyway. The main advantage of conducting membership drives is that donors are encouraged to repeat their membership contribution on an annual basis. Additional special project appeals create the feeling that the member is also helping support the valuable work of the not-for-profit organization.

Characteristics of annual fund drives are:

- Annual funds are really operating funds. The contributions received are unrestricted.
- The strategies are designed to produce a broad base of support.
- The emphasis is on single-year contributions and pledges.
- The strategies used most frequently are: direct and select mail,

telephone solicitation, and special events. The results can be strengthened by adding a major gift component and by seeking special project support.

- Annual fund drives rely on a large number of requests. Response rates and gift levels increase when list selection improves, segmentation techniques are mastered, and the message is honed.

The Capital and Endowment Campaign

Capital and endowment drives are discussed in Chapter 14. However, it would be helpful at this point to understand the main characteristics of capital campaigns. Too often volunteers go into their capital campaigns with plans shaped by their successes in their annual fund drives. But experienced professionals know that direct mail, telephone solicitations, and special events are inappropriate strategies to emphasize when planning and implementing a capital campaign.

Characteristics of capital and endowment campaigns are:

- The emphasis is on visionary capital projects. Endowment fund campaigns frequently are combined with the capital campaign—often to endow the building project or to endow the programs associated with the building.

- The emphasis is on pace-setting leadership contributions. (Often, the top 10 investments will produce one-third to one-half of all capital funds raised. The top 110 investments will produce from two-thirds to four-fifths of the total raised.)

- Donors are encouraged to make multiyear pledges.

- Most capital campaigns are preceded by a planning study.

- Capital campaigns are intense. The campaigns are organized in a sequential manner. A quiet or advancement phase focuses on stretch gifts and lead gifts from those closest to the organization. An intermediate phase focuses on major gifts from the philanthropic community. A public phase encourages generous and modest gifts from a broad base of supporters.

- The most effective fundraising strategy for capital campaigns is person-to-person visits and solicitations. Intense relationship nurturing activities are integral to the process.

Special Project Support

Seeking special project support is a mode of fundraising that falls somewhere between annual fund drives and capital campaigns. Certainly, seeking special project support lacks the characteristics of intensive campaigns, either for operating or capital purposes. The appropriate strategies are grantsmanship and major gift fundraising. The major gifts can come from affluent individual supporters or from corporate donors.

Seeking special project support offers three advantages:

- Regular donors often make second or third gifts in response to special project appeals.
- Foundations, affluent individuals, and corporate donors often view attractive components of the organization's core activities as funding opportunities.
- Special project support encompasses the larger investments needed for new project seed funds, modest-scale capital purchases, and existing program enhancements.

Hybrid Models

Not-for-profit organizations rarely engage in a single fundraising mode. What organization will abandon its annual fund drive to concentrate solely on its capital campaign? What organization is so well off that it can conduct annual fund drives but never has to seek special project support? How often are the not-for-profit organization's fundraising efforts geared *solely* to a capital campaign?

Clearly these are uncommon situations.

So, to be effective, not-for-profit leaders must learn to manage a mix of fundraising activities. Effective resource development professionals must become comfortable with providing leadership for a visionary capital campaign while maintaining strong annual fund drives—with their time-consuming mail appeals, phone campaigns, and special events. At other times, the resource development staff must maintain their annual drives while meeting multiple grant application deadlines for special project support.

Annual & Capital Campaigns

The most common questions asked of resource development professionals are: "How can we sustain our annual fund drive while conducting a

capital campaign? Won't the capital campaign take funds away from the annual drive?"

There is a simple answer to these questions. With the proper approach, the capital campaign actually will strengthen the annual fund drives. Here's why. First of all, a well-planned capital campaign captivates the imagination. It inspires. The campaign engages people in a cause bigger than themselves, and it brings people closer to the organization. Second, the capital campaign focuses on the importance of leadership giving. Donors are inspired to make major multiyear commitments. The $1,000 per year donor may make an additional three-year pledge of $15,000, $30,000, $100,000 or even more when approached for an investment in the capital campaign. When the pledge period is completed, such donors frequently increase their annual giving levels.

What, then, is the proper approach? Well, there are several. One approach is the two-envelope metaphor. In churches and synagogues, members of the congregation make weekly offerings, pledge a specific amount for the year, or fulfill annual membership obligations. During capital campaigns, congregation members are reminded to continue their regular support, and are encouraged to make a generous multiyear pledge for the capital campaign. In many cases, this is more than a metaphor. In actuality, there are two types of envelopes: one for the regular offering, another for the capital campaign.

During capital campaigns, the presentation materials stress the importance of "gifts in addition to your annual support." Campaign leaders remind donors to continue their annual support. Major donors understand that their capital campaign contributions are in addition to the on-going support. Thus, the two-envelope metaphor.

Another approach is the comprehensive campaign. With this approach, the organization states the case for an all-encompassing campaign that embraces the institution's annual operating, capital, endowment, and special project needs. In reality, the organization's leaders still need to use the appropriate strategies for raising annual, capital, endowment, and special project support. In other words, the modest donors still receive their mail appeals and invitations to special events. Foundations can be approached for special project support or capital funds. Major donors are asked to continue their annual support and also to consider a multiyear pledge to the capital/endowment drive. Many gift opportunities are developed. Supporters and prospective supporters are asked to consider components of the

campaign that interest them the most. The endowment-building component of the campaign may encourage planned gifts in addition to the current gifts received during the pledge period.

With this level of activity, the key management task is to track the relationship-building activities and coordinate the requests. The university School of Medicine's development officer should not approach a key donor for a $10,000 piece of equipment during the same week that the university president and chair of the board approach that person for a $10 million contribution to the $120 million Campaign for Excellence. The left hand must know what the right hand is doing.

With thorough prospect research and genuine concern for building relationships, it becomes possible to match the ideal gift opportunity to the right prospect. The aim is to offer each donor and prospective donor an opportunity to make a significant investment—an investment that will pay dividends for the people the organization serves.

Annual Fund and Special Project Support

Two strategies are common to most experienced resource development offices. The first is to write program descriptions and grant applications for attractive parts of the operating budget. An essential quality of money is that it is fungible. When an organization acquires underwriting for one of its on-going programs, this augments the organization's unrestricted gifts. The second strategy is to conduct vigorous annual campaigns and also seek major support for your organization's initiatives, special projects, seed funds, and non-recurring endeavors.

To illustrate the first strategy, an organization may approach a foundation to provide multiyear support for an established Learning Center at a homeless shelter. You need not stress that the Learning Center is established. Rather, you might stress enhancements to the program or reasons the program is particularly needed at this time. Other examples include symphony concert sponsorships, underwriting for popular on-going museum exhibits, and adopt-an-animal plans at zoos. At this point, the line between gift opportunities (where the focus is on how the gift will be acknowledged) and special project support (where the focus is on how the funds are accounted for and used) becomes murky. However, the result is that special project support augments annual operating contributions.

The second strategy—vigorous annual campaigns with funding requests

for non-recurring special projects—is also commonplace. A problem occurs, however, when the staff is so small or too poorly organized to get to the grant applications and major gift visits. The answer to this problem is to schedule blocks of time for grants research and writing. Simultaneously, fundraisers can eliminate low-payoff time wasters and devote more time to nurturing relationships and visiting major donors.

The Comprehensive Approach

The strategy, or fundraising mode, that successful not-for-profit organizations pursue most of the time is to conduct vigorous annual campaigns while seeking, encouraging, and accepting capital, endowment, and special project investments. An organization does not have to be in a capital campaign mode to accept capital gifts. An endowment can grow through bequests or other planned gifts. Moreover, generous current donors can be encouraged to make a lifetime gift to the endowment fund.

To manage the complexity of the comprehensive approach, organizations will need to observe the following principles:

1. Stagger activities so that they can be handled even with small staffs (see Exhibit 3-10).

2. Time fundraising activities based on response rates. (Example: prospect mailings in early November and December are far more likely to produce positive results than summer mailings.)

3. Schedule major cultivation events such as open houses and annual dinners.

4. Devote blocks of time to time-consuming tasks such as grant research and grant writing.

5. Build on strength. Focus energies on the fundraising activities that maximize long-term net contributed income. Eliminate low-payoff activities.

SPECIAL ISSUES RELATED TO SMALL AND LARGE OPERATIONS

A great deal has been written and said about the challenges faced by the small development office. Mostly it boils down to common complaints. Too much to do. Too few people. Too little time to do it.

EXHIBIT 3-10 COMPREHENSIVE DEVELOPMENT PLAN

KEY ACTIVITIES	JUL	AUG	SEP	OCT	NOV	DEC	JAN	FEB	MAR	APR	MAY	JUN
Government grants/ contracts and underwriting	gggggg	gggggg	gggggg	gggggg	gggggg	gggggg	gggggg	gggggg	gggggg	gggggg	gggggg	gggggg
New grants research	xx!											xoxoxo
Newsletter fiscal year 1	xoxoxo!											
Fundraising letters fiscal year 1	xxxxxxxx!											
Planned-giving seminar/ estate planners 1		ooooooooto!										
Fall special event fundraiser		aaaaaaaaaaaaaaaaaadta!									aaaaaaaaaaaaaa	
Planned-giving prime prospect brochure			oooooo!									
Young Professionals club fundraising event		++++++++++++++++++++++++++dt++!										
Newsletter fiscal year 2				xoxoxoxox!								
Planned-giving seminar/ prospects 1				oooooooooot!								
Year-end mail— prospects and in-house					xxxxxxxxxxx!							
Open house or annual dinner					xoxoxoxoxoxoadt!							
Personal solicitation, lists and gift opportunities preparation						xxxoxodt!						
Newsletter fiscal year 3							xoxoxoxx!					

Activity	Marking
Planned-giving seminar/estate planners 2	ooooooo!
Volunteer phone-a-thon	xxxxxxxxxadt!
March prospect and in-house mail appeals	xxxxxxxxxxxxxxx!
Directors and trustees 100% campaign	xodtxoxoxodt!
Spring special event fundraiser	aaaaaaaaaaaaaaaaaaaaaaaaaaaaaaaaaxxaaaaaaxxaaaaaaa!
Planned-giving prime prospect brochure	ooooooo!
Mail appeals fiscal year 4	xoxoxoxoxoxox!
Luncheon for Legacy League	otooooo!
Planned-giving seminar/prospects 2	ooooooot!
Joint meeting directors, trustees, & auxiliary officers	xtataxotda!
Personal solicitations—many gift opportunities	dtxtdxodtxxdtxoxxx!
Planned-giving annual interviews	ooooooooooooooooooooooooooo!
Preparation fiscal year final report meeting	xodtaxo!

Key:

The majority letter for each key activity represents the prime responsibility.

g = grants writer responsibility; x = development director; o = planned giving specialist; d = board of directors participation; t = foundation trustees participation; a = auxiliary participation; + = Young Professionals Club project; ! = Event, milestone, or activity wrap-up

However, experienced development professionals know that the issue just stated misses the point. No one has the time to do everything. Everyone feels understaffed. The task for development professionals is to make decisions. They must decide what to do, when to do it, and what the expected outcomes are.

They also must decide what *not* to do. Too often in one- or two-person development shops the development director spends his or her time shopping for t-shirts, stuffing envelopes, and choosing decorations for a special event that hardly pays for itself—let alone for the staff time. At other times, the small staff gets wrapped up in designing and printing materials that are never used in the solicitation process.

Another problem occurs when the development staff is given responsibility for public relations. Have you ever seen a job title such as "Director of Development and Public Relations"? Chances are that whatever comes after the word "and" gets done. For a variety of reasons—fear of rejection, perceived risk involved with measurable outcomes, and discomfort in discussing money—the director of development responsibilities get lost in the shuffle.

Again, the answer is focus and concentration. The professional must ask, "What public relations activities will have the greatest impact on the institution? What fundraising strategies will maximize net contributed income?"

The answers to these two questions overlap in significant areas. A strong case for support, a sustained effort at nurturing relationships, and the ability to segment constituencies and target our messages are essential to both the resource development and public relations programs. The public relations program should have clear objectives. Name recognition is not enough. Not-for-profit organizations need strong public relations and marketing efforts to help recruit volunteers, increase earned income, and create an environment where contributed income can be maximized.

By remaining focused, one- or two-person offices—even those with public relations responsibilities—can handle two acquisition mailings; at least four mailings to the in-house list annually (these four mailings are segmented); a personal solicitation program; one volunteer phone-a-thon; a cost-effective planned giving program; one or two major special events annually; at least two newsletters annually; a simple-to-administer grants program; and a vigorous cultivation and acknowledgment program.

When these activities begin to produce substantial net contributed income, expanding the staff may make economic sense. However, your analysis must demonstrate that the opportunity cost (i.e., the lost funds that might have been earned by having additional staff) is far greater than the expense related to the additional staff.

As an institution grows and the development staff expands to meet the demand for increased contributed income, a new set of challenges come into play: issues related to control, coordination, and evaluation. The fund-raising staff that started with a director of development and an assistant/data entry person may grow with the addition of a mail campaign professional, a special event coordinator, a grants writer, a major gift officer, a director of gift planning, or any combination of personnel that can respond to the institution's unique circumstances. At the same time, data entry and other support personnel are added as the volume of contributions and gift levels increase.

Here are some general guidelines for large development offices:

- The staff should include one development officer for every 200 prospects capable of contributions of $25,000 or more.
- A development officer should help close at least 25 commitments per year. Each commitment should be for not less than $10,000.
- Prospective supporters are assigned to only one development officer. The name may not appear on more than one development officer's list!
- Development officers are responsible for identifying new prospects, nurturing relationships, and assuring that the prospects are offered an opportunity to make significant investments.
- Senior development officers develop and monitor a system that quantifies key information concerning the donors and prospects on each development officer's list. This information includes proposed request amounts, the probability of receiving the request amount, estimate of when a pledge might occur, and where each prospect is in the cultivation cycle. In a numeric system, you might assign the following cultivation cycle indicators: 0 = Suspect; 1 = Viable Prospect; 2 = Relationship Nurturing Underway; 3 = Request But No Response; 4 = Agreed to Gift; 5 = Closed. To understand how this is useful, please see Exhibit 3-11.

EXHIBIT 3-11 PROSPECT ASSIGNMENTS AND SUMMARY INFORMATION

DEVELOPMENT OFFICER: C. BYBEE
JULY 31, 2003

PROSPECT	VOLUNTEER	CULTI-VATION LEVEL	PLEDGE TARGET DATE	REQUEST AMOUNT	PROBA-BILITY (%)	VALUE
C. Davis	A. Smith	5	7/03	$500,000	100	$500,000
B. Wentworth	A. Smith	5	6/03	150,000	100	150,000
A. Quigley	D. Barnes	5	6/03	25,000	100	25,000
D. Coppermine	B. Farmer	4	9/03	50,000	50	25,000
F. Harding	A. Smith	4	9/03	50,000	60	30,000
B. White	D. Barnes	4	9/03	30,000	20	6,000
J. Baxter	J. Meyers	4	9/03	30,000	50	15,000
S. Smith	T. West	4	12/03	100,000	80	80,000
M. Liggett	B. Farmer	4	12/03	50,000	40	20,000
M. Dell	A. Smith	3	9/03	25,000	80	20,000
F. Winston	T. Downey	3	9/03	50,000	40	20,000
H. Packard	D. Barnes	3	9/03	10,000	80	8,000
W. Payne	J. Meyers	3	12/03	10,000	60	6,000
A. Maynard	T. West	2	3/04	100,000	40	40,000
R. Ambrose	T. West	2	3/04	250,000	50	125,000
Numerous other names and ratings						
TOTAL				$1,430,000		$1,070,000

In addition to monitoring the performance of each development officer, senior staff also evaluate the effectiveness of each person responsible for a specific fundraising function or strategy. Each functional area—grants, annual fund, major gifts, and planned giving—is evaluated on the basis of return on investment. As important, the senior staff should monitor each functional area to quantify the net contributed income generated each year. By monitoring this over time, development staff members are naturally encouraged to find ways to improve performance of each of the institution's fundraising strategies.

ETHICS

The not-for-profit institution's ethical standards have an impact on re-source development. The public expects not-for-profit institutions to be held to the highest ethical standards, and when those standards are breached, donors withhold their support.

Ethics is not an exact science. To be sure, there are many gray areas. Mechanical decisions are not possible, but decisions must be made. There is wide-spread agreement on a broad range of ethical responsibilities. Not-for-profit organizations are recognized as having both internal and external ethical responsibilities. The external responsibilities include:

- Stating the truth in fundraising, marketing, and public relations.
- Meeting obligations to donors, vendors, and external stakeholders.
- Providing service recipients with services of the highest possible quality.
- Ensuring product safety.
- Protecting the environment.
- Observing the letter and spirit of all laws that pertain to the non-profit's external activities.

The not-for-profit organization's internal responsibilities include:

- Ensuring worker health and safety.
- Ensuring fairness and equal opportunity in all human resource activities: hiring, firing, and promotion.
- Nurturing moral common sense within the institution: prevent harm to others; respect the rights of others; do not lie or cheat—be honest and fair; keep promises and contracts; help those in need; encourage others to live this way.
- Observing the letter and spirit of all laws that pertain to the non-profit's internal activities.

Many people wonder why conversations about ethics get so sticky. If we are dealing with common beliefs and moral common sense, how can there be so many disagreements?

Ask a room full of resource development professionals if there is a donor from whom their organization would not accept a $1,000,000 contribution. Whose gift would your organization refuse? Respondents to this type of question generally split into three roughly equal camps. Some point to the good that the funds will accomplish. Others focus on the evil that may have generated the funds and the harm that the gift will do to the organization's reputation. Still others take a pragmatic approach and ask if the gift must be acknowledged generously through naming opportunities. Pragmatists also estimate whether the projected lost income from dissatisfied current and future supporters is less or more than the actual gift being contemplated. Clearly, there are no right or wrong answers.

Communication about ethical issues generally falls into three main areas:

1. Descriptive Ethics—factual accounting of what actually is occurring.

2. Metaethics—abstract discussions concerning issues such as cultural differences, the pursuit of objectivity in ethics, the differences between scientific and religious ethical systems, and so on.

3. Normative Ethics—ethical judgments concerning right and wrong, and attempts to describe "what ought to be."

To facilitate communications about ethics and to clarify thinking, it is essential to understand the point of view of the speaker or writer. After all, statements can be read or heard from the standpoint of any of the three fields just listed.

> Example: "The XYZ Charitable Institution considers it wrong to pay a finder's fee to a financial planner who brings forward a planned gift; the ABC Non-profit Agency has been known to pay a finder's fee on several occasions."

One reading of the sentence above simply states what is occurring. This is an example of descriptive ethics.

On a second reading, it might be concluded that different organizations have different standards. Therefore, there is no absolute right or wrong. Practice and custom may be viewed as the guiding principles. Others might disagree. This is an example of a discussion dealing with metaethics.

On a third reading, one might say, "The XYZ Charitable Institution has adopted a high ethical standard. The ABC Non-profit Agency is wrong when it pays a finder's fee." This example deals with normative ethics.

EXHIBIT 3-12   COMPARATIVE ETHICAL
STANDARDS

Ethical Principles	Included In
Obey letter and spirit of laws and regulations.	CASE, NAIS, AFP, NCPG
Truthfulness, fairness, free inquiry.	DBR, CASE, AFP, NCPG
Compensation: appropriate and disclosed.	
No percentage fundraising or finder's fees.	DBR, NAIS, AFP, NCPG
Confidentiality and privacy.	DBR, CASE, NAIS, AFP
Avoid conflicts of interest.	CASE, AFP, NCPG
Use funds as designated by donor; disclose use of funds.	DBR, NAIS, AFP
Accurately describe organization and mission.	DBR, CASE, AFP
Stewardship financial disclosure.	DBR, NAIS, AFP
Disclose professional experience and qualifications.	AFP, NCPG
Inform donors about tax implications of gift.	AFP, NCPG
Encourage consultation with independent advisors.	NAIS, NCPG
Respect for cultural diversity and pluralistic values.	CASE, AFP
Uphold professional reputation of other advancement	
officers, credit for ideas, words, and images.	CASE
Receive acknowledgment and recognition.	DBR
Primacy of philanthropic motive.	NCPG
Gift made "not in lieu of tuition or other charges."	NAIS
Affirm through personal giving a commitment	
to philanthropy.	AFP

Key
AFP: Association of Fundraising Professionals Code of Ethical Principles and Standards
   of Professional Practice
CASE: Council for Advancement and Support of Education Statement of Ethics
DBR: Donor Bill of Rights (Developed by the American Association of Fund Raising
   Council, the Association of Healthcare Philanthropy, CASE and AFP)
NAIS: National Association of Independent Schools Principles of Good Practice for
   Member Schools—Fund Raising
NCPG: National Committee on Planned Giving Model Standards of Practice for the
   Charitable Gift Planner

Codes of ethical standards are normative statements—judgments of right and wrong.

An examination of ethical standards (see Exhibit 3-12) developed by various not-for-profit sector institutions such as the National Committee on Planned Giving (NCPG), Association of Fundraising Professionals (AFP), Council for Advancement and Support of Education (CASE), National Association of Independent Schools (NAIS), and others shows that they

tend to rely on moral common sense and a point of view that individual rights guide our ethical standards—especially the rights of the donor!

EVALUATION

Chapter 16 contains comprehensive self-evaluation tools, forms, and questionnaires. It may be helpful now, however, to place the big picture in focus.

The philosophy of this book is to encourage resource development professionals to monitor a broad range of key success factors. The aim is to continually make improvements in as many of these areas as possible. By monitoring and improving the number of donors contributing each year, the percentage of board members who contribute each year, the number of donors contributing at each gift level each year, and the number of people personally contacted each year, an organization's contributed income will continue to increase over time.

One cannot observe a system without changing the system. This is as true in fundraising as it is in physics.

Monitoring trends and making improvements to your fundraising systems and strategies are central themes of this book. With this focus, readers also need a clear view of their organization's most important resource development objectives: to maximize net contributed income and to diversify sources of funding.

Not-for-profit institutions need cash with which to carry on their programs. For this reason, the most important figure to monitor is *net contributed income*. To assure sustainable cash flow, not-for-profit organizations must also monitor the number of contributors and sources of funding. Two million dollars a year in contributed income may be adequate for many organizations. But if those funds come from only one or two sources, the organization's very existence may be in danger. For this reason, not-for-profit organizations must not become overly dependent on too few major donors or funding sources.

By implementing the recommendations in the chapters ahead, fundraisers can help their organizations achieve their two main resource development objectives—raising more net income and developing a larger base of donors.

The Case for Support and Fundraising Materials

All work is empty save when there is love.

—Kahlil Gibran, *The Prophet*

THE CASE STATEMENT

The first task of fundraising is to understand the rationale for the appeal. Fundraising professionals call this rationale the case for support or the case statement. It might be more helpful to think in terms of scripts—a body of language that tells any prospective supporter how the funds will be used and who will benefit from the programs and services.

So, a not-for-profit organization's case statement answers the questions "How does this agency help people?" "Who do we help?" "What vital services do we offer?" "What is our agency's track record?" "What are the organization's plans for the future?" "Why does this agency merit support?"

From the donor's perspective, institutions do not have needs . . . people do. Too often not-for-profit appeals are based on statements such as "As the winter months approach, our organization is facing a mounting deficit. We need your support to keep our doors open. . . ."

Such appeals say little or nothing to the donor.

Imagine IBM running an advertising campaign that sounds like this: "Our last two quarters were the worst in our company's history. Please buy our computers to help our cash flow as we enter the critical months ahead." Would anyone purchase a computer—or any product—based on such an

appeal? Of course not. And yet many not-for-profits continue to state their needs from this internal perspective. Mounting deficits might loom large in the thought processes of people with key roles in their agency. Still, to the donor, what matters most is how the agency helps people in need.

By way of example, a homeless shelter might do well by saying "The winter months are harsh for people like John—a homeless person traumatized by circumstances too horrible to even imagine. At XYZ Homeless Shelter, we address the root causes of homelessness and restore broken lives. Your contribution will help us get people like John back into the work force with a fresh foundation and a home of his own."

Case statements expressed from the donor's point of view are vital to the fundraising process. Such case statements are essential to major gifts programs, grantsmanship, planned giving programs, capital/endowment campaigns, and strong annual programs.

THE COMPREHENSIVE FORMAL CASE STATEMENT

The comprehensive formal case statement is a written document that states the major reasons for supporting a not-for-profit organization. It forms the basis for all other communications. This most important document answers the following questions:

- What is the organization's history?
  - —Founded when and by whom
  - —Major accomplishments of the organization
  - —Milestones in the organization's history
- Whom does the organization serve?
  - —Demographic information: age, ethnicity, gender, geographic, socio-economic background, religious affiliation
  - —Describe a real person who benefits from the organization—share testimonial or anecdotal true-life experiences
- What needs confront the people served by the organization?
  - —What pressing problems does the organization address?
  - —What challenges do the people served face?

- How does the organization address these challenges?

    —What programs does the organization offer?

    —What services are provided for people in need?

- What is the organization's reputation for managerial and business acumen?

    —What evidence can be offered pertaining to the organization's stability?

    —What evidence can be offered pertaining to fiscal responsibility—for example, years of deficit-free operations?

- How is the planning process described?

    —Who participated in the planning process (especially helpful when well-known community leaders played a key role in your organization's strategic planning)?

    —How broad-based was the process?

    —How thorough was the planning process?

- What are the goals for the future? (This is the most important section of the case for support.)

    —What are the program, financial, facility, technology, administrative and governance, and human resource and diversity goals?

    —How will those in need be served better?

- How will the donor's investment be used?

    —Why is the fundraising campaign being conducted?

    —What are the organization's key budget items?

    —How do these expenditures relate to the organization's mission and services to people in need?

- How will the donor's involvement be acknowledged?

    —Describe gift opportunities

    —Describe the intangible benefit the donor receives by this philanthropic investment

Development planners who answer all of these questions will have created a comprehensive formal case for support. Some bureaucrats and a few foundation officers appear to be impressed by weightiness. They seem to

"fund by the pound." Most people, however, dislike wordiness. They prefer to read summaries—if they read at all.

Still, going through the process of writing the formal case for support is most helpful. It clarifies the organization's thinking. It gets everyone rowing in the same direction. A well-prepared case statement also prepares fundraisers to answer questions posed on grant applications. It provides key staff members and volunteers with useful language. And the case statement contains important phrases and themes that are included in the organization's phone and mail campaigns.

Once the comprehensive case statement has been written, edit it. Reduce it to four, five, or six pages of the best and most compelling language. This new version—when personalized—can become the basic presentation tool for major gift solicitations.

The Case Statement Process

The process by which the case statement is arrived at, like the process by which the organization's strategic long-range plan is created, is of paramount importance. Board members and community leaders are most likely to support a plan they helped create.

It is not recommended that the case statement be written by a committee. On the contrary, it is strongly recommended that it be written by one writer—but with lots of input from key leaders.

The process for writing a case statement involves a number of steps. First, interview several key leaders of the organization. Next, gather and review the organization's written promotional and planning materials. The organization's strategic long-range plan must be understood clearly. Examining promotional materials and case statements from similar organizations also may be helpful.

Now, synthesize the material. Answer the questions in the preceding outline. Develop new language. Then prepare and circulate a draft case for support. Listen to the feedback. Afterward, revise the case and present it to the appropriate committees for review, revision and final approval.

Every organization has only one opportunity to make a first impression. By developing a thoughtful case for support, fundraisers can ensure that donors and potential supporters receive clearly written materials. In most

cases not much money needs to be spent on the presentation package. Attractively word processed materials are enough in most cases. The expensive brochures and booklets can be saved for the end phases of capital campaigns—if they are used at all.

The point here is that the case for support must, to be well written, be motivational, and even poetic. Statistics and logic may be helpful. But emotion and passion lead to commitment. Until the donor believes in your organization's mission, the written case statement has no value. A conversion process must take place. The case for support must become part of the donor's belief system. Supporters give freely of their time, talent, and treasure when they understand and embrace a cause.

MARKET AND SITUATION-SPECIFIC CASE STATEMENTS

Once the comprehensive formal case for support is written, presentation materials can be tailored to specific markets. Elements of the case that resonate with specific donors and prospective donors should be highlighted.

For example, when approaching corporate leaders, development professionals may wish to stress the economic benefits brought about by the organization's programs. If the organization is a university approaching an engineer, programs that benefit the school of engineering might be highlighted. A health care provider approaching the mother of a child with a hearing impairment may focus on the institution's services for the hearing impaired.

Customization is not limited to these examples. A religious order establishing a spiritual center in the Southwest might stress the critical shortage of clergy in the area served. However, when approaching supporters from other parts of the country, the materials might take on a broader focus: historical links, geographic ties, or the relationship of spirituality to the nation's social fabric.

PRESENTATIONS AND PRESENTATION MATERIALS

Once developed, an organization's case statement can exist in many formats. Let's look at some.

Printed Materials

Personalized formal case statements are comprehensive formal cases for support with personalized cover sheets prepared for each prospective donor. The attractive cover sheets might have the organization's name, the campaign slogan or campaign name . . . and a phrase such as "Information Prepared for Mr. & Mrs. I.M. Ready" (see Exhibit 4-1).

Brochures are helpful. Their small size makes them convenient for volunteers to keep on hand. They can fit easily inside envelopes and make convenient enclosures for mailings. Their brevity makes them useful for the vast majority of people who do not take the time to read lengthier documents.

Every not-for-profit organization will find it useful to produce a general-purpose brochure that briefly states the case for support. The

EXHIBIT 4-1   CASE COVER PAGE

Northern South Dakota
Regional Hospital

VISION 2000

Information Prepared
for

Mr. and Mrs. I.M. Ready

brochure might contain a response device for contributions and volunteer commitments.

Unfortunately, many not-for-profit organizations produce expensive brochures but fail to develop the more effective and less costly case for support. Most prospective major donors are more motivated by the *personalized* materials than by expensive generic printed materials. So while attractive printed materials, such as brochures, are important, they should not be relied on for major gift solicitations. Enclose the brochure and other promotional materials in a presentation folder along with a personalized case for support. There is something about human nature that makes prospective donors feel important when they see their name printed in larger letters than the organization's name.

One- or two-page versions of the case for support are quick to absorb and come in handy in many situations. Containing all the main points, these background or fact sheets are helpful for volunteer orientations. They are great for briefing telephone solicitors. And prospective supporters find them easy to understand.

Sometimes the short version is written in paragraph form. If this format is used, keep the paragraphs short and punchy. The sheet also should include a call for action and end with a clear statement of how the funds are to be used.

At other times the case statement is presented as a *fact sheet*. These usually are printed on a letterhead with the word FACTS in large type at the top of the page. Below the heading are a series of bullets that make up the case for support.

Videos and DVDs

Video and DVD case statements are powerful fundraising tools. They have the power to bring prospective donors to the cause. Indeed, no other presentation strategy has the ability to bring about the conversion process as quickly. Upon viewing a well-produced video case statement, many prospective donors readily embrace the organization.

Before producing a video case statement, write your case for support. Some language from the case for support may be used as part of the narration for the video case statement. Often the main themes used in the

written material can be presented as attractive visual images in the video case statement.

The steps for producing the video case statement are as follows:

1. Decide on the communication goals for the video case statement.
2. Decide on the audience for the video case statement.
3. Determine the length—usually 6 to 9 minutes.
4. Determine a few key messages.
5. Describe possible images or interviews that might correspond to each key message.
6. Outline a sample script and/or run sheet (see Exhibit 4-2).
7. Determine the budget. (Count on spending $1,000 to $2,000 per finished minute for a quality video. Alternatively, find a video producer—such as a TV station, a university communications department, or other provider of pro bono services—to donate all or part of the work.)
8. Allow the video producer and copywriter great flexibility in shaping the video case statement. They know their business best. However, work closely with them to ensure that the main points of the case for support come through clearly and powerfully.

Whenever an opportunity to view a video or DVD case for support arises, do so. The more videos watched, the more ideas will be available for your organization's case statement.

If video case statements seem too expensive and too time-consuming, consider the following story.

A development officer was working for the homeless shelter that produced a video very much like the one just described. She called six times to meet with a potential supporter. Six times the supporter failed to return her call. The development officer then called a seventh time—with a difference. This time she told the prospect's secretary a bit about the homeless shelter, mentioned that the prospect had been supportive in the past, and promised that the meeting would not take more than 15 minutes. The prospective supporter called back and made the appointment.

When the visit took place, the development officer and the board president arrived with a video case for support. In this situation, the development officer and board president used the brief meeting to introduce

EXHIBIT 4-2   NOTES FOR VIDEO OR DVD CASE STATEMENT

XYZ HOMELESS SHELTER
Preliminary Notes for Video or DVD Case Statement

Goals of the Video or DVD

- Indicate to the donor public why the XYZ Homeless Shelter deserves their financial support.
- Create an emotional bond with major donors.
- Let prospective donors understand the need for the Homeless Shelter's capital campaign.
- Tell prospective donors how the capital project will help the shelter address long-term solutions to homelessness.

Audience

- Affluent individuals
- Corporate and foundation leaders
- Church leaders: Pastors and mission committees

Maximum Length:

7 to 8 minutes

Key Messages

Homeless people have needs—like you and I
   Potential Images and Interviews:
      * Food line—tell of 80,000 meals served out of small kitchen
      * Sleeping facilities
      * Medical room
      * Clothing room—show how small it is

Education is needed. Our goal is to help the people who come to us resolve the root causes of their homelessness. We strive to establish each person in a permanent job.
   Potential Images and Interviews:
      * Learning center
      * Interview one of the men using a computer

A Spiritual Component is also needed
   Potential Images and Interviews:
      * Service/gospel—show face of someone listening to the gospel
      * Interview the director of the XYZ Shelter's education program

Day Services and Facilities Needed
   Potential Images and Interviews:
      * The executive director walking around new building
      * Executive director or board president—show crowded current facilities
      * Show blueprints and architectural drawings
      * State what day services will be offered
      * Show line outside—state how the reception area in the renovated building will help the neighborhood and help the men get into the warmth sooner.

(continued)

EXHIBIT 4-2 (CONTINUED)

Request for Support
 Potential Images and Interviews:
   * Any relevant uplifting finale
   * Board president: "Your contribution constitutes an investment—an investment in the XYZ Homeless Shelter's ability to serve those most in need. In each lifetime, few opportunities present themselves where we can truly make a significant difference in the lives of others. Now is one of those times. Your time, talent, and treasure will help restore broken lives—now and for generations to come."

Sample Script Outline

TIMES	SCENES
20 seconds	Titles—Music Opening: Scenes of homelessness, lines forming outside, street people, etc.
40 seconds	Scenes of homelessness continue as narrator begins. "The homeless have the same needs you and I do. . . ."
	State the problem: "We know the enormity of the problem."
2 minutes	Scenes of shelter services: food, clothing, sleeping facilities. Show current programs; stress the tight space.
	More is needed: Education (interview concerning the Learning Center); day support services and a strong spiritual grounding
3 minutes	Capital project explained: Blueprints, walk around building (selected shots)
1 minute	Expanded services needed: Stress spiritual component and expanded hope; mention new chapel
30 seconds–1 minute	Appeal for support: "Your gift and support is an investment . . ." followed by uplifting and/or celestial closing shot.

Random Observations and Notes to the Video or DVD Producer

- These video or DVD case statements work well when the producer/director is given broad leeway to create an artistic work.
- One narrator works well. However, some interviews or testimonials may be useful.
- "Talking heads" tend to become boring if the segment is too long. It is far better to state the message with pictures and dramatic shots. Example: A scene with a homeless person learning to use a computer is more powerful than a person saying "We teach computer skills."
- Go for emotion.
- Music used well is a must.

themselves and summarize the case for support, and left the video case statement.

The next morning the supporter called and made a $75,000 pledge.

Considering that the prospect manifested great resistance to the solicitation process, as evidenced by his reluctance to return phone calls, a remarkable conversion must have taken place. In all probability, such a dramatic turnaround was due to the power of the video case for support.

Group Presentation Techniques

Group presentations make it possible to present the case for support to gatherings of potential supporters. Briefings, slide shows, overheads, flip charts, computer-generated presentations, participation routines, group discussions, structured note taking, demonstrations, and role playing are all valuable group techniques.

As always, begin by organizing the material. The written case for support contains all the main points. The key to success in any verbal presentation is to prune the material. Keep it short. Don't go over the predetermined time limit. Remember the cardinal rule: "Thou shalt not bore thine audience."

Whole books are written on presentation techniques. Read several. Find ideas that work. Here are a few points to consider:

- Start with a strong introduction.
- The presentation style should sound warm and natural.
- When possible, use a variety of presentation techniques to keep the group involved.
- Humor helps—but only when the humor is appropriate and supportive of the main messages.
- When using overheads, keep the text simple and readable—mostly 24-point type and larger.
- When using flip charts, allow 1 inch of letter size for each 15 feet from the back row.
- Remain focused on a few main points.
- Prune the material. Every little point cannot—and should not—be covered.
- Conclude with a motivational ending.

Managing Information

To err is human, but to really foul things up requires a computer.

—Anonymous

Many not-for-profits have reaped great benefits from their dedicated fundraising software. Some have purchased a powerful software package but have yet to unleash its power. Others have purchased software that simply does not work well. Still others have yet to invest in this most basic tool of the modern development office.

Unless a group is a very small grassroots organization, it is foolish to enter into a fundraising effort without dedicated fundraising software. A sophisticated information system with managerial "buy-in" is central to the success of any resource development program. And with computer prices continually falling, even the smallest organizations can computerize their fundraising efforts.

All can gain by better understanding the power of a properly functioning information system. Too often development personnel view the information system as little more than a glorified mail list. They simply have not thought through the strategic uses of the fundraising information system.

In reality, the system should help development professionals identify, cultivate, and solicit current and prospective donors. The system should support and simplify many fundraising strategies. And the system should provide valuable scorekeeping, attention-directing, and problem-solving reports.

Dedicated fundraising software facilitates the development function in five ways:

- Record keeping
- Direct support of fundraising strategies
- Acknowledgments
- Reports
- Targeted communications

RECORD KEEPING

Accurate and complete records are at the heart of any successful development program. A well-designed software package will permit users to record and retrieve easily the following information: names, addresses and phone numbers of current, past, and prospective donors; a history of every donation indicating the amount of the contribution, the solicitation method, and any gift restrictions; the form of the contribution (cash, stock, in-kind, or other); a history of pledges and pledge payments; comments and memos containing vital information concerning the prospective donor; volunteer solicitor assignments; deadlines and contact dates; memorial and honorary giving; and a great deal more information concerning the prospect's interests and relationship to the organization.

SUPPORTING FUNDRAISING STRATEGIES

Dedicated fundraising software directly supports resource development efforts in a number of ways. Surely, sophisticated direct mail campaigns would be unthinkable without mail-merge capabilities and powerful databases.

But stop and think a minute about all the other ways software can help raise more money. Some examples:

- Fundraising software helps users track who was invited and who came to each cultivation activity. The software also allows you to track volunteer solicitor assignments. This information is crucial to major gift and personal solicitation programs.
- Fundraising software allows users to print phone-a-thon forms complete with donor history and other information useful to the caller.

- A flexible software program will allow users to support special events by selecting the best prospects, accounting for ticket sales, and even tracking seating assignments.

- Software can help track important grant deadlines and other information vital to the grantsmanship program.

- Not-for-profits with membership drives use their software to track membership categories and renewal information. As important, the software simplifies the entire renewal and upgrading process.

- Annual and capital campaigns are strengthened when lists are segmented. The aim is to match the approach and message to each constituency. For example, the broad base of modest givers may be approached through mail and phone; potential pace-setting donors could be approached through a personal solicitation program. Similarly, the message can be tailored to each group.

- As mentioned, dedicated fundraising software is at the heart of any sophisticated direct mail program. Mail-merge capabilities, segmentation, personalization, testing, tracking and analysis are needed to refine and improve the direct mail fundraising program.

ACKNOWLEDGMENTS

The mail-merge capabilities of a flexible software program make it possible to automate and highly personalize acknowledgments.

Some development professionals are reluctant to automate the acknowledgment process. They fear that the thank-you letters will sound too institutional or general. Of course, as the volume of gifts received increases, it becomes more difficult to write individual notes to all contributors. So, what can be done?

The answer is to compose a series of thank-you letters. Some examples include: the thank-you letter to modest donors; the "Thank you for your very generous contribution of $_____" letter to donors of $1,000 or more; the "Your contribution combined with your service as a member of our board represents a unique level of commitment" letter to board contributors; the "Thanks for your generous pledge" letter; the in-kind gift thank-you letter; the sponsorship thank-you letter; the letter written to donors who

contributed to a special project appeal; and a host of other highly personalized letters in response to the organization's unique circumstances.

Various offices handle this automated personalization differently. Some have a development officer assign a thank-you code to each gift received. The data enterer or person responsible for acknowledgments then uses the dedicated fund-raising software and word processing software to ensure that each contributor receives the appropriate letter. A better approach is to train the gift entry specialist to recognize the nature of each gift and to code each appropriately. If users are not sure how to automate the acknowledgment process with more than one thank-you letter, the fundraising software support team can explain how.

If the volume of gifts received is not too daunting, the thank-you letters should be hand-signed and perhaps further personalized with a handwritten note written at the bottom of the letter.

At any rate, the system should allow a thank-you letter to be sent within 48 hours of receiving the contribution. No thank-you letter should languish on anyone's desk. Dedicated fundraising software is integral to a system that ensures the personalization and timeliness of every thank-you letter.

Reports

Dedicated fundraising software comes with many standard reports. The best programs also make it easy for development staff to create their own reports. Fundraising reports can be grouped in three main categories: scorekeeping, attention directing, and problem solving. As many reports serve more than one purpose, these distinctions are not always clear. But all these reports can support your fundraising strategies.

Scorekeeping Reports

Scorekeeping reports tell how much has been donated. These reports also let users count the number of donors who support the organization.

Scorekeeping reports (see Exhibit 5-1) can be generated for any time period. Most development professionals like to track fiscal year-to-date contributions. The reports also can be subdivided in a number of ways. For example, scorekeeping reports indicate how many individuals, businesses,

EXHIBIT 5-1 INCOME ANALYSIS XYZ NOT-FOR-PROFIT ORGANIZATION

INCOME ANALYSIS: BY GENERAL LEDGER CODE, FOR PERIOD ENDING 04/30/2003

	Apr # Gifts	Apr $ Amount	# of Gifts YTD	LY	% Var	$ Amounts YTD	LY	% Var	Avg. Gift YTD	LY
Capital Campaign										
$ 0	0	0.00	1	0	0	25	0	0	25	0
$ 50	1	50.00	4	0	0	200	0	0	50	0
$ 100	3	700.00	26	15	73	5,974	3,674	62	229	244
$ 500	0	0.00	8	3	166	4,300	1,500	186	537	500
$ 1000	1	2,000.00	36	29	24	68,728	47,166	45	1,909	1,626
$ 5000	0	0.00	9	8	12	48,256	41,085	17	5,361	5,135
$ 10000	0	0.00	5	7	-28	76,402	88,642	-13	15,280	12,663
$ 25000	0	0.00	2	2	0	59,000	58,000	1	29,500	29,000
$ 50000	0	0.00	4	1	300	338,631	150,000	125	84,657	150,000
Total:	5	2,750.00	95	65	46	601,517	390,068	54	6,331	6,001
Memorial										
$ 0	0	0.00	20	0	0	465	0	0	23	0
$ 50	0	0.00	9	2	350	450	100	350	50	50
$ 100	0	0.00	16	0	0	2,005	0	0	125	0
$ 500	0	0.00	1	0	0	500	0	0	500	0
$ 1000	0	0.00	3	0	0	4,455	0	0	1,485	0
Total:	0	0.00	49	2	2350	7,875	100	7775	160	50
Unrestricted										
$ 0	89	1,679.50	265	325	-18	4,885	5,123	-4	18	15
$ 50	29	1,485.00	87	54	61	4,435	2,730	62	50	50
$ 100	19	2,400.00	75	49	53	9,175	6,920	32	122	141
$ 500	0	0.00	4	2	100	2,000	1,000	100	500	500
$ 1000	0	0.00	1	1	0	1,000	1,000	0	1,000	1,000
Total:	137	5,564.50	432	431	0	21,495	16,773	28	49	38
Grand Total:	142	8,314.50	576	498	15	630,887.08	406,942.04	55	1,095	817

Reprinted with permission from DonorPerfect-Starkland Systems.

foundations, government agencies, churches, and associations have supported the institution . . . and how much was contributed by each of these
types of donors. Scorekeeping reports can show how many donors increased their donations and how much more they contributed. They also
track how many donors contributed more than once each year and the
total number of gifts received. Additionally, scorekeeping reports enable
users to track renewal rates and indicate how many new donors are attracted each year and how much they donate.

These scorekeeping reports should be generated, reviewed, and filed on
a regular and timely basis.

Attention-Directing Reports

Attention-directing reports help users focus on opportunities. For example,
a report can show the prime prospects who have yet to be assigned a volunteer solicitor. (For this to work, development staff and key volunteers
identify prime prospects. A computer code is then entered into the prospect's record indicating that he or she has the capability to make a major
gift. Later, when volunteer solicitors assume responsibility for making the
visit, these volunteer assignments also are entered into the system. After
these steps have been taken, it is a simple matter to generate a report showing which prime prospects do not have a solicitor.)

Other examples include: cash-flow projection reports (see Exhibit 5-2),
solicitor reports (see Exhibits 5-3A and B) that indicate which volunteers
have performed their assignments successfully and which must be urged to
complete their tasks, and follow-up date reports that focus attention on key
deadlines and contact dates (see Exhibit 5-4).

Problem-Solving Reports

Problem-solving reports help the development staff make better decisions.
Perhaps the most helpful, but underutilized, example of a problem-solving
report is the Solicitation Analysis of Fundraising Methods. (See Exhibit
5-5.) Such a report indicates the amount spent on each component of the
fundraising program—mailings, special events, phone campaigns, and other
strategies. The report also shows the total funds raised by each method, the
corresponding response rate, and other statistics. This information is crucial
to the evaluation of the fundraising program. Such analysis encourages

EXHIBIT 5-2 CASH-FLOW PROJECTION REPORT

XYZ Not-for-Profit Organization
Cash Flow Projection Report for Final Six Months 2003

Donor	Jul	Aug	Sep	Oct	Nov	Dec	Total
ABC Corporation, Inc.						1,000.00	1,000.00
Mr. & Mrs. L. R. Arnold	1,333.00						1,333.00
Mr. C. J. Biggers					2,500.00		2,500.00
Mr. & Mrs. Daniel Bolton						700.00	700.00
Mr. & Mrs. Peter M. Chubs	2,500.00						2,500.00
Mr. Clarence Cortez	125.00			125.00			250.00
Mr. & Mrs. Andrew Ellwood				500.00			500.00
Mr. & Mrs. Michael L. Fairchild						5,000.00	5,000.00
Mr. & Mrs. Don E. Farr	12,500.00					12,500.00	25,000.00
Mr. & Mrs. Herbert C. Farris, III			400.00				400.00
Mrs. Jan Garcia	250.00					250.00	500.00
Mr. & Mrs. Richard D. Gonzales						10,000.00	10,000.00
Mr. & Mrs. Robert Gruber	250.00	250.00	250.00	250.00	250.00	250.00	1,500.00
Mr. & Mrs. Edward T. Holliday						1,000.00	1,000.00
Dr. & Mrs. Frederick J. Peters					750.00		750.00
Mr. & Mrs. Thomas A. Swindle						1,000.00	1,000.00
Mr. Edward L. Weakland, Jr.				5,000.00			5,000.00
TOTALS	**16,958.00**	**250.00**	**650.00**	**5,875.00**	**3,500.00**	**31,700.00**	**58,933.00**

EXHIBIT 5-3A SOLICITOR REPORT (VOLUNTEER MADE THE VISITS—NOTE PLEDGES)

SOCIETY FOR THE WIDOW OF THE UNKNOWN SOLDIER
SOLICITOR ASSIGNMENTS

Solicitor: Irma Bailey

Prospect(s)	3-Year Request Amt

Mr. & Mrs. Paul T. Butler   3,000.00
1946 Washington St.
Little Rock, AR 72205
(H): (501) 666-4394
(W): (501) 666-4395

FLAGS: PCL,AB*,MAL,CCP

```
PREVIOUS GIVING HISTORY:

Total Previous Giving:
Most Recent Amount:
  Most Recent Date:      /  /
  Campaign Pledge: 3000.00
```

Ms. Martha Cooley   250,000.00
3009 Spruce St.
Little Rock, AR 72215
(H): (501) 567-3746
(W): (501) 798-5014

FLAGS: PCL,AB*,MAL

```
PREVIOUS GIVING HISTORY:

Total Previous Giving:
Most Recent Amount:
  Most Recent Date:      /  /
  Campaign Pledge: 250000.00
```

Mr. and Mrs. Mark Letterman   7,500.00
7531 Main St.
Little Rock, AR 72213
(H): (501) 834-7234
(W):

FLAGS: AB5,AL5

```
PREVIOUS GIVING HISTORY:

Total Previous Giving:500.00
Most Recent Amount: 500.00
  Most Recent Date: 12/30/1997
  Campaign Pledge:
```

Mr. and Mrs. James Shelby   15,000.00
1497 Madison St.
Little Rock, AR 72215
(H): (501) 837-4738
(W): (501) 837-2938

FLAGS: PCL,AB*,AL5,ML5,MAL,CCP,CMA

```
PREVIOUS GIVING HISTORY:

Total Previous Giving:
Most Recent Amount:
  Most Recent Date:      /  /
  Campaign Pledge:  7500.00
```

TOTAL REQUEST AMOUNT: 275,500.00

Reprinted with permission from DonorPerfect-Starkland Systems.

SOCIETY FOR THE WIDOW OF THE UNKNOWN SOLDIER
SOLICITOR ASSIGNMENTS

Solicitor: Christopher Meyers

Prospect(s)	3-Year Request Amt
Mr. and Mrs. Mark Ascher 3116 Bluffside Place Little Rock, AR 72215 (H): (501) 643-2938 (W): FLAGS: HR1,AB*	7,500.00

PREVIOUS GIVING HISTORY:

Total Previous Giving: 500.00
Most Recent Amount: 500.00
   Most Recent Date: 02/01/2000
   Campaign Pledge:

Dr. & Mrs. Thomas Kelly 1234 Persimmon Court Little Rock, AR 72219 (H): (501) 374-2983 (W): FLAGS: AB5,AL5	7,500.00

PREVIOUS GIVING HISTORY:

Total Previous Giving:
Most Recent Amount:
   Most Recent Date: / /
   Campaign Pledge:

Mr. and Mrs. Max Miller 3874 South Monroe Little Rock, AR 72214 (H): (501) 387-2938 (W): FLAGS: AB5,AL5,CCP	10,000.00

PREVIOUS GIVING HISTORY:

Total Previous Giving: 1000.00
Most Recent Amount: 1000.00
   Most Recent Date: 11/14/1999
   Campaign Pledge:

TOTAL REQUEST AMOUNT:	25,000.00

Reprinted with permission from DonorPerfect-Starkland Systems.

development staff to eliminate low-payoff activities and focus on high-payoff endeavors.

TARGETED COMMUNICATIONS

Most not-for-profits have the ability to generate labels and mail-merge personalized letters. Still, too few have integrated the power of "minimarketing" into their development programs.

EXHIBIT 5-4   CONTACT MANAGEMENT REPORT

CONTACT MANAGEMENT REPORT — 11/07/03

Development Officer: Steve Crisman

Mr. and Mrs. Arnold Wiley   Last Contact: 09/06/01   Contact Type: Visit
1234 35th Street   Next Contact: 11/12/01
Austin, TX 78710   Next Action: Make appointment
(512) 244-3074
Notes: Mr. Wiley expressed interest in the scholarship fund. Mrs. Wiley is interested in journalism. Speak to the Wileys about a named scholarship fund for the School of Journalism. They have been on a trip to the Bahamas. They are scheduled to return during the first week of November.

Charles and Marlene Baxter   Last Contact: 05/10/01   Contact Type: Telephone
2522 North Adams Ct.   Next Contact: 11/14/01
Austin, TX 78711   Next Action: Visit
(512) 244-9364
Notes: Chuck is expecting a visit. When we last spoke, he asked that we get together mid-November. He recently sold his business and wants to discuss his gift to the university prior to the end of the year.

Willy Lohman   Last Contact: 10/24/01   Contact Type: Telephone
3874 Character Lane   Next Contact: 11/17/01
Austin, TX 78700   Next Action: Telephone
(512) 234-3874
Notes: Willy seemed a bit depressed the last time we spoke. Prospect research indicates that Mr. Lohman is not in a position to make a major gift. However, he does have some assets that he might leave to the university. He doesn't appear to be getting along well with his sons at this time.

Sophisticated software allows the segmentation of lists in a seemingly infinite variety of ways. Rather than limiting fundraising programs to mass mail campaigns, more personal contact can be fostered and a greater number of highly personalized communications can be encouraged. For example, gracious follow-up letters can be written to the 20 or 30 people who came to recent cultivation activities. Or personalized friend-raising letters can be written to civic leaders. Alternatively, you might consider helping that physician on your board send personalized fund-raising letters to the 25 or so doctors he doesn't have time to visit personally. Many experienced

EXHIBIT 5-5 SOLICITATION ANALYSIS

DATE	SOLICITATION	NUMBER CONTACTED	RESPONSE #	RESPONSE %	TOTAL INCOME	AVG GIFT	EXPENSE Printing	EXPENSE Other	EXPENSE Total	NET PAYOFF RATIO INCOME	NET PAYOFF RATIO $ Returned per $ Spent
2/14/01	St. Valentine Event	2,130	197	9.25	25,350.00	128.68	2,270	9,230	11,500	13,850	2.20
3/7/01	Test List #1	5,000	48	0.96	1,306.00	27.21	765	1,024	1,789	(483)	0.73
3/7/01	Test List #2	5,000	97	1.94	3,027.00	31.21	765	1,024	1,789	1,238	1.69
3/7/01	Test List #3	5,000	64	1.28	1,781.00	27.83	765	1,024	1,789	(8)	0.99
3/30/01	Board Campaign	23	23	100.00	47,460.00	2,063.48	54	0	54	47,406	878.89
5/14/01	18 Month Lapsed	1,957	33	1.69	695.00	21.06	297	359	656	39	1.06
5/14/01	In-house > $100	596	56	9.39	8,797.00	157.09	108	119	227	8,570	38.75
5/14/01	In-house < $100	3,629	435	11.98	24,367.00	56.02	515	719	1,234	23,133	19.75
6/30/01	02-06 Major Gifts	65	37	56.92	101,790.00	2,751.08	127	23	150	101,640	678.60

fundraising professionals and volunteers review "top donor" lists of supporters who gave during the same month last year. They use these lists and contact information to stay in personal touch with top donors and to renew their support. In summary, fundraising software offers endless possibilities for targeted communications.

THE SYSTEM

Whether fundraising professionals are contemplating a software purchase or seeking to unleash the power of their current system, an examination of fundraising strategies is crucial to their success. A well-designed fundraising system can support and enhance a comprehensive approach to resource development.

Simply put, decide how you wish to raise funds, then purchase software and design your system to support the most cost-effective means of achieving your goals.

Perhaps it might be helpful to see where you are before you decide where you are going. Where do you fit in the categories below?

- Ad hoc record keeping (some combination of multiple mail lists in word processing programs, one or more separate database files, file cards, or handwritten lists, personal memory of staffers and key volunteers, etc.)

- Reliance on a general-purpose database program. Frequently programmed by someone with little understanding of fundraising. Always time-consuming, rarely successful.

- Purchase of dedicated fundraising software . . . but with little oversight or management "buy-in." (The powerful tool has become little more than a mail list.)

- In-house record keeping combined with contracted outside record keeping services. (This model is used most often by those who rely heavily on a mail house service provider. When done well, the service provider is capable of providing valuable reports and analysis. However, this somewhat fragmented approach does not maximize the fundraising potential.)

- Purchase of dedicated fundraising software . . . with managerial oversight and "buy-in." The best of all worlds.

When a not-for-profit organization purchases dedicated fundraising software and the development staff uses the full powers of the system, the software then becomes a powerful tool that can help dramatically increase contributed income.

In summary, management "buy-in" is crucial to a strategic approach to information management. Development directors, senior staff, and key volunteers are reminded to "Inspect what you expect." Monitor the accuracy of data entry. Look at the reports. Avoid duplicate accounts. Use the full power of the system.

ESTABLISHING THE INFORMATION SYSTEM

It is helpful to think of an institution's dedicated fundraising software as its main communication tool. Rather than using the system exclusively to track donor information, staff can enter names, addresses, phone numbers, and other crucial information pertaining to prospects, volunteers, and other constituencies. In this way, you can avoid the difficulties of maintaining multiple mailing lists.

By keeping all names on one database, the development staff can communicate more easily with potential supporters. In fact, all communication becomes simpler. And when the staff updates information in a record, they will not have to search out the same name and make the identical update in numerous other databases.

With the development of the personal computer, many people within an organization have the ability to maintain their own mail lists. The person responsible for fundraising can transfer periodically all these separate lists into one master database. By using various "sort codes," the list can be segmented, and volunteers or staff can communicate with any desired grouping.

With these thoughts in mind, the first step in establishing or refining the record-keeping system is to identify all the sources of names and addresses available, keeping track of the sources of all names and lists. As these names are entered or transferred into the fundraising software system, source codes that identify each record's relationship to the organization also are entered.

Next decide whether the system needs enhancement using current fundraising software or by purchase of a new software package.

New Software Purchase

Follow these steps when deciding which software package to purchase:

1. Determine what fundraising strategies are most likely to be employed. Remember that we recommend a comprehensive approach. Plan for future growth.

2. Ask: "What information is tracked now? What information will be tracked in the future?"

3. Examine other development office reports. Decide which reports are needed to manage the fundraising program.

4. Summarize inputs and expected outputs.

5. Contact a number of leading fundraising software suppliers. Examine their demo versions, literature, and arrange to "test drive" an actual working version of the full software system.

6. When evaluating dedicated fundraising software, look for: (a) service and support, (b) user-friendliness, (c) flexibility, (d) features, (e) standard and custom reports, and (f) price. (When examining price also ask about annual support contracts, training, and other expenses. Calculate the cost to use the package over a five-year period.)

7. Review all selection criteria. Make your choice. Then allow adequate time for transitions, training, setup, data transfer, and testing.

Procedures, Entry, and Reporting

All organizations will find it helpful to have a certified public accountant (CPA) review their gift-handling and gift-processing procedures. Organizations should be made as embezzlement proof as possible.

An effective fundraising information system is closely linked to the record-keeping function of the finance department. If there is no direct computer link to the financial records, regular and periodic reconciliation of contribution totals is most helpful. Records should be reconciled as frequently as possible. Otherwise, untold hours could be spent trying to find the cause of a $50 differential. Even more disconcerting is an unexplained $100,000 difference in the records of the fundraising office and the organization's finance office.

Inconsistent campaign totals drive volunteers crazy. So, a thoughtful process for confirming and reporting fundraising totals must be designed, indicating who's in charge, what numbers are being used, and who's responsible for accuracy.

Above all, the danger of double-counting pledges and gifts must be eliminated. Be sure that pledge payments reduce pledge balances.

Also, think through the special issues related to sponsorships and special events. The goal is to have each donor record complete with all giving history—regular gifts and sponsorships. The amount each special event raised also should be tracked. Organizations can double-count income unless they are careful. Or the system could show the special event income but fail to have the sponsors' records complete with their regular giving and their sponsorship contributions. There is no one best way of handling this. But with thought, a record-keeping system that accomplishes both goals can be developed. Every organization is different. Someone in the organization simply must take the time to figure this out.

Integrity of Data

Drift in record-keeping systems can be counteracted by making some fields in the software system "must enter" fields. One approach might be to make the type, gift date, appeal code, and use of funds "must enter" fields.

No matter where staff members are in the information management process, they can begin to strengthen their system by focusing on the most important elements of data entry. Begin by capturing the name, address, and phone number of each donor. This is bankable information. Next record the five most important data points pertaining to gift entry: (1) donor; (2) the gift amount; (3) gift date; (4) how the gift was obtained (the appeal code); and (5) how the gift is to be used.

In many cases the gift is unrestricted. In such a case, the data processor enters a code that means unrestricted contribution in the use of gift field. In all other cases, the data processor enters the appropriate code for the restricted use. Examples might be "CC" for a capital campaign contribution and "SF" for scholarship fund.

Don't be too general when developing appeal codes. "M02" meaning 2002 mail campaign is insufficient if multiple mailings are done throughout the year. The results of each appeal have to be tracked. A system with

more complete information in the coding system is necessary. One such solution might include: "MP0302" for the March 2002 prospect mailing; "MD0302" for the March 2002 donor renewal mailing; "MD0502" for the May 2002 donor special appeal letter; "MD0902" for the September 2002 donor mailing; "MP1002" for the October 2002 prospect mailing; and "MD1102" for the November 2002 year-end appeal to donors. As such user-defined codes are created, be sure to enter the explanation, description, or translation of the codes in the utilities database or other appropriate place in the fundraising software system.

Periodically clean up the records. Check for duplicate records. Have someone familiar with donor activity look over hard copies of fundraising reports and lists. Make any corrections noted. Look for ways of improving the system in order to prevent mistakes.

Most fundraising software systems allow for the creation of user-defined codes. Such codes typically are used in fields for: solicitation method, general ledger code (use of funds), type, division and source. Such fields are meant to contain mutually exclusive categories. For example, the "type" field allows users to classify donors and prospects as individuals, businesses, foundations, government agencies, churches, or associations. The type field usually uses something similar to the following coding system: I = individual; B = business or corporation; F = foundation; G = government agency; C = church or synagogue; A = association or union; S = service clubs such as Kiwanis, Rotary, Lions, or Civitan.

Problems arise when data processors make up their own codes. If the system allows this to be done without the definition in the fundraising software system being entered, the result can be lots of codes that no one can interpret. Another issue comes up when the data processor enters codes that are not mutually exclusive in fields designed for mutually exclusive categories. For example, if users print out user-defined codes for "type" and find that I = individuals; R = retired board member; T = teacher; C = church; M = Methodist church; G = government agency; and S = state government agency, they have a real mess on their hands. They will not be able to count how many individual donors there are simply by sorting on "type" = I, because the classifications are not mutually exclusive. Retired board members and teachers are individuals. If that kind of information must be recorded, use a field other than "type."

Check each field that is intended to include mutually exclusive classifications. Eliminate user-defined codes that are not mutually exclusive.

Some fields—often called flags, sort codes, or promotion codes—allow multiple nonmutually exclusive entries within one field. These codes frequently are separated by commas. These codes are highly flexible and allow the organization to define multiple relationships. Examples might include: FBD = former board member, ROT = Rotarian, ALM = alumnus, STA = staff, and so on. While these are not mutually exclusive categories, the system allows sorting on any of these classifications even if many of them are entered into a single record.

When checking the integrity of an information system, users must check to see that the names of contact persons are listed in records for organizations and businesses. It is not enough to have XYZ Corporation entered in a system. Mr. I. Make Decisions, CEO, must be in the records also. Remember the old principle, "People give to people." To communicate with real decision makers, ensure that records are complete with contact names.

File Systems and Procedures

Establish a logical filing system to further enhance the power of the dedicated fundraising software.

- File periodic standard reports.
- Establish appropriate hard-copy files of major individual, corporate, and foundation donors.
- File final reports of every major fundraising activity (special events, mail campaigns, special appeals, etc.).
- Establish "tickler" file systems that ensure that no deadline is missed.

Among the hard-copy files that might be maintained in fundraising offices are: alphabetical files of individual major donors and prime prospects including the donor history, relationship information, and prospect research materials; alphabetical files of foundations including giving history, relationship, major philanthropic interests, grant guidelines, annual reports, grant limitations, gift ranges (high, low, average); alphabetical files of corporate funders with information similar to the foundation files; event reports indicating plans, time lines, committee assignments, attendees, and income

and expense reports; final reports pertaining to each appeal (users can decide whether to file a hard copy regularly or rely on computer-generated reports as needed); periodic and annual scorekeeping reports; an ideas file; and other files unique to your circumstances.

Should checks be photocopied, with the copies filed? Small and emerging organizations may want to, many not-for-profits still do. Organizations with strong computer systems and backup procedures may rely on computer records to check numbers, dates, amounts, use of funds, and donor information. The key here is the ability to extract the information quickly . . . combined with the integrity of the backup procedures.

Remember, computer mail lists and donor records are among a not-for-profit organization's most important assets. So, BACK UP, BACK UP, BACK UP! Periodically store a recent backup off site.

Prospect Identification, Research, and Segmentation

Different strokes for different folks.

—Anonymous

Earlier we discussed the importance of a strong case for support. We then established an information system to record the key information about our donors and prospective donors. Now would be a good time to step back and figure out who is most likely to support our cause.

Ultimately fundraising professionals will want to adopt a highly personalized approach. When they write, their letters should sound as if the appeals are written from one person to one person—not to a group of supporters. When they put together presentation materials for face-to-face visits, they personalize the cover sheet and tailor the case for support to the individual interests of the prospective supporter.

However, before they can get to these highly personalized approaches, development professionals must put together a master list that identifies all potential supporters. Most often, not-for-profit organizations can seek support from the following broad classifications of donors:

- Individuals
- Businesses/corporations
- Foundations

- Government agencies
- Associations (professional associations and unions)
- Service clubs (Rotary, Kiwanis, Lions, Civitan, etc.)
- Churches and synagogues

(Remember the "type" code in the last chapter? These are the most common classifications to code and enter into the "type" field in your fund raising software.)

Now that the broad classifications and markets have been considered, attention can be turned to the task of identifying those most likely to support the organization.

THE BEST PROSPECTS

Board members and other key volunteers can help identify prospects and important contacts. A Community Relationships Survey is included on the CD-ROM that accompanies this book. The best prospects will vary from organization to organization, but most not-for-profits find success in garnering support from: constituents, board members, staff, current and lapsed donors, vendors, people generous to similar organizations, and affluent peers of organization members.

Constituents

Universities look to support from their alumni. Hospitals seek support from former patients. Symphonies raise funds from season subscribers. Churches raise funds from members of the congregation. Wildlife refuges receive donations from conservationists. Not-for-profit organizations should make an effort to record the names, addresses and phone numbers of their prime constituents—the people who use their services.

Perhaps the only not-for-profit organizations that cannot rely on financial support from their constituents are social service agencies that serve the poor.

Current and Former Board Members

The people who make policy and guide the not-for-profit organization are often the organization's best supporters. Chapter 1 stresses that those closest to the organization must set the pace. Not-for-profit organizations find

it helpful to stress the importance of this maxim. Gracious ways of encouraging current and former board members to give generously are discussed in Chapter 8.

Key Volunteers

People who volunteer for the organization are involved. This involvement gives volunteers an in-depth understanding of the nonprofit's services. The volunteers often know the most moving stories about the people the organization serves.

Some volunteers view financial contributions as a natural extension of their commitment to an organization. Others feel that their volunteer time is as much as they can afford to donate. The job of those responsible for fund raising is to encourage contributions from volunteers—but never make anyone feel uncomfortable if they cannot contribute.

Staff

Please don't overlook staff members as potential contributors. All staff members are familiar with the organization's services and programs. All staff members, by definition, are employed. The best prospects are people who are familiar with a not-for-profit's services and have the capacity to make a financial contribution. So, staff members meet the most fundamental criteria for consideration as prospects.

Staff contributions are among the most important contributions that can be received. Board members and other contributors are impressed when they become aware of generous staff contributions. Such donations bolster confidence in the philanthropic community. Donors know that if the staff is generous, the organization has inspired confidence in those most likely to know its weaknesses and strengths on an intimate basis.

Still, staff solicitations must be approached with sensitivity. As with volunteers, staff members must be comfortable with their decision to donate . . . or not to donate.

Current Donors

The most likely future supporters are current donors. One myth about fundraising is "We can't keep going back to the same people." Fundraisers

would be foolish to follow this advice. Professionals don't want to solicit the donor so frequently as to upset him or her. But donors who believe in the cause expect to be asked for contributions more often than once a year. Most organizations tend to ask too few times, not too often.

Lapsed Donors

A donor who supported an organization in the past but has not contributed in the most recent 12- or 18-month period is generally considered a lapsed donor. Some fundraising professionals estimate that as many as 20 percent of these lapsed donors can be persuaded to donate again. A thoughtful and highly personalized approach helps. Phone solicitations combined with mail appeals often work well. To be effective, development professionals will want to restate the case for support and handle any objections that might come up. Most of all, they can let the supporter know that his or her past contributions made a big difference and the people served by the organization miss that support and involvement.

Vendors

Businesses that sell goods and services to not-for-profit organizations often donate when asked.

Those Generous to Similar Organizations

A generous sponsor of one arts organization is often a good prospect for other arts institutions to approach. Likewise, people who support one environmental organization are frequently supporters of many other such causes.

Successful fundraisers find the names of generous philanthropists in their communities through symphony program books; hospital annual reports; university publications; on the walls of churches, libraries, hospitals, museums, and private schools. Donor lists are easy to come by. Addresses and phone numbers take more work. However, dedicated volunteers often can help look up readily available information. As important, many board members have the names, addresses and phone numbers needed on their personal contact lists.

Fundraisers should take the time to discover information about people generous to similar organizations and add that information to the fund-

raising software system. Record any information about their giving history to other organizations. Find someone in the organization who knows the new prospect. Proactively nurture relationships with these potential supporters.

Affluent Individuals with Whom Someone in the Organization Has a Peer Relationship

When the subject of potential pace-setting donors comes up, volunteers often think about the wealthiest people they have ever heard of. Knowledge that someone is wealthy might be meaningless. The aim is to identify and nurture relationships with affluent people who might be expected to support the organization. As mentioned, the prospect's rationale for supporting a specific organization might be an interest in similar causes. Sometimes the rationale for supporting an organization is merely a close relationship with a board member or major supporter.

People give to people. A variation of this point is to remember that a wealthy person might be a "suspect" at best. That person does not become a "prospect" until someone close to the organization with a peer relationship with the philanthropist is identified. Equally important, the person close to the organization must be willing to make the introduction.

PROSPECT RESEARCH

Some mature not-for-profit institutions have a sophisticated prospect research office. Some small emerging not-for-profit organizations have only one staff member to do everything including: service delivery, fundraising, public relations, and general administration. Whether the organization is a grassroots agency or a large institution, those who wish to raise money must focus on four key areas of prospect research:

1. The prospective supporter's relationship to the organization
2. The prospect's interests and hobbies, especially as they relate to the organization
3. Networking—who in the organization is close to the prospect
4. Capability—net worth, ability to donate, and challenging contribution amounts to request

At the early stages of prospect research, fundraising professionals should identify as large a prospect pool as possible, capturing and recording the names of everyone who has a direct or indirect relationship to the organization. Board members and other key community leaders must be debriefed and asked whom to include on the master list of people to keep informed about the organization.

As the master list is compiled, remember to get the names of decision makers at the corporations and foundations you wish to approach. To be effective, the fundraising database should include names of key contacts. People make decisions. No one succeeds in raising funds from General Motors by standing outside corporate headquarters yelling "Hey, General Motors, please make a contribution to this worthwhile cause." And yet numerous fundraising databases do not contain contact names.

As fundraisers develop more information about potential supporters they segment the list based on capacity to give. As stated earlier, donors who already have given at generous levels are the organization's best prospects. But segmentation is not based on giving history alone. A key aim is to identify wealthy people who have a relationship to your organization.

Next, the list must be divided into potential giving levels. Prospects have vastly differing giving capacities. More research time should be spent on those prospective donors at the very top levels—the major gift prospects.

Every organization has its own definition of a major gift. The institution with a $60 million goal might consider contributions of $1 million or more major gifts. The not-for-profit agency with a $100,000 fundraising goal might consider any donation of $1,000 or more to be a major gift. In general, fundraisers consider any gift of 1 to 1.5 percent of the goal to be a major gift.

It is especially important for small not-for-profit organizations to develop cost-effective prospect research methods. Larger institutions can afford personnel dedicated to prospect research because the stakes are so high. Stakes are high for smaller not-for-profit organizations as well, but funding is very limited for prospect research. So, the research has to be highly focused and not too time consuming, given the organization's other priorities. The following is a prospect research strategy that even the smallest not-for-profit organization can use. Although streamlined, this method yields extremely useful information.

Prospect Ratings and Evaluations

Many not-for-profit organizations with relatively small fundraising staffs find it difficult to conduct effective prospect research. Presuming that unlimited resources for prospect research are *not* available, the following technique may be helpful to the research and major gift process.

First create a cover sheet, Prospect Rating Form, and key page (see Exhibits 6-1, 6-2, and 6-3). The cover sheet is a way to comfort volunteers who are supplying the information. It also provides an opportunity to summarize the case for support. The key explains how the volunteers are to fill in the columns on the prospect rating form.

Volunteers should be reminded to put their names at the very top of the first page in the space provided. The information is somewhat useless without knowing who supplied it. When dealing with the column about maximum capacity, it is helpful to say something like "If this were the prospect's favorite charity, perhaps their church or university, what might be the most they could contribute? Please do not fill in a number that represents what you expect the prospect to donate. Rather, focus on the

---

EXHIBIT 6-1   SAMPLE COVER PAGE FOR RATINGS FORMS

PROSPECT RATINGS FORM

ABC Not-for-Profit has embarked on a Major Gift Initiative to strengthen all of our programs for the people we serve . . . while at the same time maintaining our reputation for financial stability and sound management. The information gathered on this form will help us refine our plans. The campaign can succeed only with the generous support of a limited number of pace-setting contributors.

The information derived from this and other ratings and evaluations activities will be kept confidential and treated with the utmost discretion. The final decision concerning the correct amount of contribution to request will be based on the prospective donor's capacity, philanthropic nature, and relationship to ABC Not-for-Profit. The correct choice of solicitor can be determined only with knowledge of the prospect's network of associates.

When rating capacity to give, keep in mind the prospect's total means rather than past giving patterns. In other words, please indicate the *maximum* potential.

Thank you for your help. Your opinions are valuable to us.

EXHIBIT 6-2　SAMPLE PROSPECT RATING FORM

Staff fills in 300–400 names prior to the Volunteer review

VOLUNTEER'S NAME_____

Donors & Prospects Name/Company	Maximum Capacity	Interest in Our Organization	Your Relationship	Willing to Visit?
Mr. Ronald P. Abelson				
Mr. Thomas N. Ackerly				
Dr. & Mrs. Arthur Q. Adelle				
Mr. & Mrs. Harry B. Allen III				
American Widgets, Inc.				
Mr. Stanley W. Ammson, Jr.				
Aphorism Industries Paul Epigram, President				
Mr. & Mrs. Robert O. Baxter				
Mrs. Evelyn T. Carter				
Harold Charles, Esq.				
Mr. & Mrs. Russell Clinett				
Mr. & Mrs. Steven Darnit, Jr.				
Mr. & Mrs. William Derby				
Mr. & Mrs. Frank Desstitute				

maximum amount the person could afford to contribute." It is also helpful to explain that a number of factors will help determine how much the
organization will request. In some cases—especially when the prospect has
a very close relationship to an organization and when the organization is

EXHIBIT 6-3   SAMPLE "KEY" PAGE

PLEASE USE THE FOLLOWING KEYS WHEN FILLING IN THE FORM

MAXIMUM CAPACITY
(Base Solely on Prospective Donor's Means)
Enter number 1 to 8 based on your best guess. Leave blank only if you have no knowledge whatsoever.
1 $300,000 or more 3-year pledge (100k a year)
2 100,000 or more 3-year pledge (33k a year)
3 75,000 or more 3-year pledge (25k a year)
4 30,000 or more 3-year pledge (10k a year)
5 15,000 or more 3-year pledge (5k a year)
6 7,500 or more 3-year pledge (2.5k a year)
7 3,000 or more 3-year pledge (1k a year)
8 Less than $1,000 a year pledge potential

LEVEL OF INTEREST IN OUR ORGANIZATION—AND PHILANTHROPIC TENDENCY
Enter letter A through E based on your best guess. Leave blank if you have no knowledge of prospect.
A High level of interest in ABC Not-for-Profit
B Moderate level of interest (probably donates or attends organization activities)
C Low level of interest but with potential for cultivation (doesn't give or participate yet but is interested in the goals of the organization)
D Little known interest in the goals of the organization but has demonstrable civic pride
E No interest and no concern for community

YOUR RELATIONSHIP TO PROSPECT
Enter number 1 to 5 to indicate the phrase that best describes your relationship.
1 Best of friends, relative, or close business associate
2 Acquainted and friendly
3 Met once or twice
4 Never met
5 Hostile relationship

engaged in a visionary campaign—the request amount will be equal to the maximum capacity. In other cases, the appropriate request amount may be somewhat less than the maximum the prospect can afford.

The column that deals with interest in the organization and philanthropic tendencies is self-explanatory based on the key. The staff might wish to fill in information about a prospect's closeness to the organization prior to having volunteers fill out the form.

Having created the forms, the next step is to have the staff or a dedicated volunteer fill in the names of 300 to 400 top "suspects." The list is composed of those thought to be likely prime prospects. Included are current generous donors; the largest local or national corporations likely to be approached; those who are generous to similar causes; wealthy individuals who have a relationship to a volunteer or board member; and other affluent constituents.

Now that the 300 to 400 names are filled in, the list should be taken to the board of directors or to a special committee composed of people who know the community, especially professionals who are knowledgeable about relative net worth of many of the prospects. To recruit such a committee look to bankers, real estate brokers, insurance agents, stock brokers, and attorneys. Also recruit people who have lived in your city a long time as well as community or national leaders. In short, recruit affluential and influential "movers and shakers" to serve on the rating committee.

Since keys are being used—numbers and letters rather than dollar amounts and specific information—many of the financial advisors find they can participate in the process without violating any ethical codes. If, for instance, a committee member put a "1" in the maximum capacity column, signifying that the donor is capable of making a $100,000 or more annual contribution, no specific information about the donor's net worth has been revealed. After all, the prospective donor might have a net worth of $6 million, $25 million, $60 million, or more. All that is known from the rating is that one committee member estimates that the prospect is capable of a contribution at the level indicated.

Anyone who has ever participated in a "talking" prospect rating meeting will recognize the benefit of using this silent method of forms and keys.

Traditional prospect rating sessions usually turn out like this. The meeting begins with an explanation of the importance of gathering information about prospective supporters. Everyone is assured that the information will be kept confidential. People are also told to please stay focused because there are numerous names to review. Now the fun begins. Mrs. Abercrombie is the first name discussed. Someone in the room knows her. All agree that she might well be capable of a $10,000 contribution, and surely Mabel will call on Mrs. Abercrombie. Next the committee discusses

Mr. and Mrs. John Bennett. Someone asks if those are the Bennetts who live on the hill. No one is sure. Next come Mr. and Mrs. James Bigheart. Mabel informs the committee that the Bighearts are getting a divorce. "No!" exclaim the committee members. Next follows a ten-minute discussion of what led to the divorce. The committee chair brings the committee's attention back to the list. The next name is Thomas Boswell. There is general agreement that Mr. Boswell had a good year and should be approached for a $20,000 contribution. Feeling confident, the chairman moves on to the next name, Thelma Carswell. At this point it is discovered that Mrs. Carswell is living with James Bigheart. The committee never gets back on track.

While this may be an exaggeration, it is safe to say that ratings committees rarely get through more than 25 to 50 names in an hour-and-a-half meeting. On the other hand, by using the forms in this book, a board of directors or committee can review up to 400 names in 20 minutes.

This 20-minute concentrated period is among the most important times in an organization's history. By staying focused—and by not being swayed by extraneous comments—an organization can quickly discover who on its list is most capable of generous gifts. Perhaps the most helpful information obtained through this process is the knowledge of which volunteers have close relationships to the organization's best prospects.

Once development planners know who has a positive relationship with potential supporters, they can recruit volunteer solicitors more readily. To broaden the knowledge about supporters, development officers also can phone or meet with the committee members who have the relationship with the supporter. Now is a good time to debrief the volunteers. The goal is not to gather titillating information; rather, it is to be sure to avoid embarrassment and approach prospects graciously. Thus it is best to gather some information in private rather than in group settings.

After the volunteers fill in the forms, the staff collects the forms, summarizes the committee's work, and creates the Compiled Prospect Rating Form (see Exhibit 6-4).

Once the committee's work has been summarized in the Compiled Prospect Rating Form, it becomes relatively easy to determine preliminary request amounts and volunteer assignments. There are a few commonsense ways of going about this.

EXHIBIT 6-4   COMPILED PROSPECT RATING FORM

Name/Company	Maximum Capacity	Interest in Organization	Your Relationship	Willing to Visit?
Mr. Ronald P. Abelson				
Mr. Thomas N. Ackerly	6(Carr) 5(Harrison)	B(Carr) C(Harrison)	2(Carr) 2(Harrison) 3(Hagard) 2(Mitchem) 2(Whitt)	
Dr. & Mrs. Arthur Q. Adelle	4(Carr) 3(Herring)	D(Herring)	2(Carr) 2(Hagard) 2(Herring)	
Mr. & Mrs. Harry B. Allen, III	7(Carr)		3(Carr) 3(Hagard)	
American Widgets, Inc.	2(Harrison)	C(Harrison)	2(Harrison) 3(Hagard)	
Mr. Stanley W. Ammson, Jr.	7(Liddy) 8(Mitchell) 8(Carr) 8(Harrison)	C(Liddy) C(Mitchell) C(Harrison)	2(Liddy) 2(Mitchell) 2(Carr) 2(Harrison) 3(Hagard) 2(Michel II)	Y(Mitchell) Y(Carr)
Aphorism Industries Paul Epigram, President	1(Liddy) 2(Carr) 2(Hagard)	B(Hagard) A(Liddy) A(Carr)	2(Hagard) 2(Liddy) 4(Carr)	
Mr. & Mrs. Robert O. Baxter				
Mrs. Evelyn T. Carter				
Harold Charles, Esq.				
Mr. & Mrs. Russell Clinett	8(Harrison)	C(Harrison)	2(Harrison) 3(Hagard)	
Mr. & Mrs. Steven Darnit, Jr				
Mr. & Mrs. William Derby				
Mr. & Mrs. Frank Desstitute	8(Liddy)	D(Liddy)	5(Liddy)	

Determining the "Ideal" Volunteer Solicitor

Using the forms and the compiled information, this step-by-step approach to choosing the volunteer solicitor can be followed:

1. When only one volunteer fills in the "Willing-to-Visit?" column for a specific prospect, the assignment becomes automatic.

2. When two or more volunteers fill in that column, recruit the volunteer who rated the prospect's giving capacity higher. That volunteer will be more comfortable requesting a more generous contribution.

3. If two or more volunteers filled in the "Willing-to-Visit?" column and several rated the giving capacity equally high, choose the volunteer who knows the prospective supporter better.

   (One note of caution: If the volunteer places a "1" in the "Your Relationship" column, that means that the prospective supporter is the volunteer's best friend or a family member. This is *not* the ideal volunteer solicitor. It is possible to be too close to the prospect for a comfortable solicitation. Volunteers who place a "2" in this column generally make the very best volunteer solicitors. Again, seek people with peer relationships with the prospective supporters.)

4. If all factors are equal, assign the prospect to the volunteer with fewer assignments. The volunteer with many people to visit may not be able to make all the face-to-face solicitations. And the volunteer with few names has a smaller psychological hurdle to overcome in beginning to make the visits.

Ideally, when this process is through, each volunteer will have three to five prospective supporters to visit. Also remember that, to the extent possible, team visits are to be encouraged. The most effective solicitations involve a key staff member and a dedicated volunteer calling on a generous prospect or generous couple.

Often the "ideal" volunteer solicitor for a particular prospect was not part of the team that filled in the prospect ratings forms. In such cases speak with one of the people on the ratings team who knows the prospective supporter. The team member can tell you who knows the prospect well. The volunteer could be asked: "Who are some of Mr. Prospect's good friends? Who on our team is close to Mr. Prospect? Who believes in our cause that has the right 'chemistry' to approach Mr. Prospect for a contribution to our cause?"

Once the ideal solicitor has been determined, the next concern is how best to recruit him or her. Assuming that the volunteer is already a believer in the organization, a gracious yet direct approach is appropriate. Someone with a peer relationship with the prospective volunteer solicitor calls and makes an in-person appointment. Use the appointment to strengthen your

bond with the volunteer. Ask if the volunteer would be comfortable in a personal solicitation setting. Help these volunteers find their comfort levels. Some will be comfortable allowing their name to be used when seeking an appointment with the prospective donor. Others are willing to go on the call but will want a staff member or fellow volunteer to ask for the contribution. Still others are willing to make an appointment, go on the visit, and ask for a contribution at the predetermined level.

Determining the Capacity to Give

Using the Compiled Prospect Rating Form (Exhibit 6-4), it is easy to follow the steps for choosing the volunteer solicitor. A more difficult task is determining the appropriate request amount. Mastering this art is one of the keys to fundraising success. The aim is to determine a challenging, yet appropriate, gift amount or gift range to request *prior to* any solicitation visit with a prospective supporter.

What first must be considered is how much the prospect can afford to give. (The development professional and the team members may wish to discuss ways of judging giving capacity before committee members fill out the Prospect Rating Form.) Later what to request and what to expect can be discussed. Capacity to give is one matter. Willingness to give is quite another.

When considering capacity, remember that many people tithe and contribute 10 percent of their earnings to their church or charity. Independent Sector, an advocacy coalition for the nonprofit sector through its "Give Five" campaign, encourages people throughout the United States to donate 5 percent of their earnings to charity and to donate at least five hours to the not-for-profit sector each week. Many figures indicate that Americans tend to donate between 1.5 and 2.5 percent of their annual income to charity. Other studies indicate that Americans tend to donate one-fifth of what they can afford to donate. Stated another way, most Americans can afford to give five times as much as they currently are giving without substantially changing their lifestyle.

From this information it might be assumed that a prospect with a family income of approximately $100,000 might be capable of donating anywhere from $7,500 ($100,000 × 1.5% × 5) to $12,500 ($100,000 × 2.5% × 5) to a not-for-profit organization. However, people tend to give

not more than $1,500 ($100,000 × 1.5%) to $2,500 ($100,000 × 2.5%). So, what should be requested? Are gifts asked for at the levels the people currently are giving? Does one ask for as much as they can afford? Or are there times when what seems to be more than the gift levels being discussed are asked for?

So far the focus has been on annual income and annual contribution amounts. However, many people find it possible to make much larger contributions to campaigns that encourage multiyear pledges. Additionally, committed donors frequently make contributions from their assets. They believe so much in the cause that they donate generously from their life savings or from their inheritances.

When discussing capacity to give, annual income *and* assets must be considered. The prospective donor's net worth is a better indicator of giving capacity than his or her current earning level. Not-for-profit organizations sometimes receive six- and seven-figure contributions from supporters with modest careers. In one case, a retired schoolteacher donated $250,000. The not-for-profit organization had discovered that the teacher had inherited a large block of stock in a successful company. The legacy allowed the inheritor to do what she loved best—teach.

Here are some general guidelines that can help determine *capacity* to give:

- A person with a net worth of $40 million can afford to donate $2 million without changing his or her lifestyle.

- A person with a net worth of $25 million or more can afford to donate $1 million.

- A person known to have contributed $5,000 to a political candidate can afford to donate $100,000 to a multiyear capital campaign (20 times the political donation amount).

- Most donors can afford to donate at least five times as much as they are currently giving. If the donor's name appears on another organization's donor listing, it can be expected that he or she can donate at least five times the amount being donated to that organization. In other words, if a donor is giving your organization $100 a year, it can be assumed that he or she can donate $500 a year; however, if the donor has donated $1,000 to another organization, it is reasonable to believe that he or she might be able to donate at least $5,000 to a cause.

- Committed supporters often can afford to donate an amount equal to 10 percent of their annual incomes. At times, they may be able to donate even more. Such pace-setting leadership gifts are given from the donor's assets rather than from current income.

- Committed supporters often can afford to donate an amount equal to three weeks of their salary.

- When planning a capital campaign with a three-year pledge period, current donors to your organization often can afford to donate an amount equal to 20 times their annual gift. Thus a $500-a-year donor might be asked to consider a three-year pledge of $10,000 to the capital campaign.

The ratings team can help determine how much a prospective supporter can afford to donate. However, to ascertain the true upper limits of capacity, committee members must themselves be generous people. The sad truth is that miserly people cannot imagine others donating generously. So, all the talk at the committee about how to rate maximum capacity falls on unreceptive ears. *Generous* people with knowledge of the community provide the best assessment of giving capacity.

Help refine the information by looking at the organization's records. Determine the largest amount the donor has given, then multiply that amount by at least five to determine his or her capacity. As already mentioned, committed supporters frequently can afford as much as 20 times their annual giving. By gathering information about salary ranges in your area, development professionals can get a good sense of the donors' annual salaries. Also, don't forget reference materials. For example, corporate annual reports or the SEC 8-K reports contain information about executive remuneration and stock control.

Determining the Request Amount

Once information about capacity to give has been gathered, the next step is determining the appropriate amount to request.

Consider this most important premise: *When deciding how much to ask for, it is far better to err on the high side than to ask for too little.*

People aren't insulted to be asked for a larger gift than they feel they can afford. In fact, many people find it flattering that they are thought affluent enough to make pace-setting significant contributions.

There are two things worse than asking too little. The first is not being specific in the request. As mentioned, frequently donors have no way of knowing if $50 or $500,000 is needed. Such important issues must not be left unresolved. Offer the donor an opportunity to make a significant investment in your cause.

The second—and most fatal—mistake is to not ask at all.

So, decide to always request a specific gift amount or gift range. Use the information obtained on the Prospect Rating Forms and the Compiled Prospect Rating Form to help determine the *appropriate* request amount.

Here are the general guidelines for determining the request amount:

- If the prospective donor has a close relationship to the organization, and it is engaged in a visionary campaign with a large goal, request an amount equal to the donor's maximum capacity.

  These donors are the 1-As on the rating forms. Volunteers put a "1" in the maximum capacity column, indicating extraordinary affluence. They or staff also put an "A" in the relationship to the organization column, indicating a close connection to the organization. The 1-As are those closest with most assets—the organization's very best prospects.

  Imagine conducting a $6 million capital campaign. A leadership donation of $1 million is needed. By all means, graciously request that sum from someone who has bonded with the organization who can afford to donate the pace-setting investment.

- If the donor has a close relationship to your organization, and it is engaged in an annual campaign or other routine fundraising effort, request an amount equal to the organization's largest giving club or gift level.

  Imagine conducting a $400,000 annual campaign. Perhaps the top giving level is the $50,000 Founders Circle. Even if one of the closest supporters can afford a $1 million contribution, he or she can't be asked for that every time. In such a case, request the $50,000 contribution. Of course the relationship should be developed further with the supporter informed about the not-for-profit's visionary plans for the future.

- If the donor is not already closely associated with the organization, intensify the relationship nurturing activities and wait to request a

higher level gift. If the campaign has a pressing deadline and momentum is needed, consider requesting an amount one or two levels below the prospective donor's capacity.

• If the prospective supporter is a foundation, request an amount in its general or average gift range—preferably an amount closely tied to a realistic project budget. If the foundation sometimes donates amounts greater than its average gift range, form a relationship with the giving officers and seek their help in securing grants at the higher levels.

• If a strong volunteer with a peer relationship with the prospective supporter has been recruited, ask for the maximum amount that the volunteer is comfortable requesting. Encourage such volunteers to "think big." Even when prospective supporters have not yet developed a close relationship to an organization, they can be encouraged to donate at their maximum capacity levels if they have a strong relationship with the community leader who asks for the contribution.

KNOW THE PROSPECTIVE DONOR AS A PERSON

Speaking of suspects, prospects, ratings, and evaluation sounds somewhat analytical—maybe even clinical. All that fundraising jargon is helpful when describing the "nuts and bolts" of the research process. However, it really misses the heart of the issue. We must know our supporters as people. We must understand their likes, dislikes, and philanthropic motivations. We must know what each prospective supporter cares about.

A lot has been written and said about sources of information. Professional prospect researchers know how to access a great deal of library and on-line information. An alternative available to all not-for-profits is to develop a small network of people who can be relied on for background information. Community leaders who are long-term residents of the region tend to know a great deal about prospective supporters. With this in mind, the prospect researchers' best tool is the telephone. The amount of prospect information three to five plugged in confidants can provide is amazing.

After getting information through telephone contacts, the next step is additional research with corporate reports. The annual report gives a broad overview of the corporation's business and economic condition. The 10-K

report is a detailed annual financial report that also shows salaries and other compensation for principal officers. The proxy statement gives detailed information on executive compensation and control of stock. The 8-K report details sales of large blocks of stock.

A plethora of information about foundations is available at each state's foundation center. Look at foundation reports, *The Grants Index,* and a variety of foundation directories.

Information on individuals can be found in *Who's Who in America* and with various electronic databases available on-line. Several consulting firms also offer electronic screening services that enable not-for-profit institutions to identify prime prospective supporters who are already on the in-house list but who have not yet given at leadership levels.

One final point before leaving this discussion of prospect research. All of the prospect research in the world is of no value if it does not directly support the solicitation process. During a tour of the administrative offices of a not-for-profit institution on the West Coast, this author was shown a large room with file cabinets filled with prospect research information. In response to a positive comment about the organization's prospect research, the tour guide said, "We don't do much prospect research anymore. For years we collected and stored a lot of information about wealthy people. But no one from the development office ever seemed to use this information, so we stopped collecting it."

In summary, focus on the key information that will help determine the challenging yet appropriate amount to request, the right solicitor to go on the call, and the project the prospective donor would be most likely to support. And see that the volunteers and staff members making the visits use the prospect research information.

Nurturing Relationships

If a man does not make new acquaintances as he advances through life, he will soon find himself left alone.

—Samuel Johnson, quoted in Boswell's *Life of Johnson*

FRIEND-RAISING ACTIVITIES

Friend-raising activities are essential to any fundraising effort. As people become more involved, they become more committed. Their donations increase as their sense of belonging grows.

Activities designed to nurture relationships are not driven by deadlines. When schedules get tight, these relationship-building meetings and gatherings get pushed back or canceled. How unfortunate. An organization's future is shaped by the number and quality of quiet, seemingly inconsequential encounters—moments when people have the opportunity to speak with those who can help the organization.

Friend-raising activities might include any or all of the following.

Newsletters and General Mailings

As cultivation strategies, printed materials and mailings are never enough by themselves. Personal contact is needed. However, newsletters and printed material do constitute an important first step in the relationship-building process. Newsletters ensure that the organization has contact

information and up-to-date mail addresses. When planning a communications strategy, include prospects, not just donors, on the mail list. And don't be attracted to false economies; mail to as many people as possible.

Include simple planned giving appeals in every newsletter. Also acknowledge donors in newsletters. This increases awareness of the importance of contributed income . . . and stimulates even more donations.

Newsletters can include response forms and appeals for funds, but the focus should be on the institution's accomplishments. Testimonials and poignant stories are effective ways of telling your case for support.

Many successful charitable organizations send a simple information publication immediately after receiving the first contribution from a donor. This public relations piece strengthens credibility. As this mailing does not directly ask for funds, it serves well to help the donor bond with the organization.

Highly Personalized Mailings that Do Not Request Funds

These friend-raising mailings tell of some important activity at the organization. For example, a letter might begin: "As an important member of San Francisco's business community, you may be interested to know that the XYZ Institution recently completed a study on ways of strengthening our city's economy. . . ."

Development officers—and other professionals who value relationships—write frequent short personal notes. Sometimes the note is a brief thank-you. At times it is a brief congratulatory note. Indeed, there are unlimited reasons for writing these friendly notes. Professionals who make this a habit in their lives will be amazed at the unexpected rewards that come their way.

Invitations to Tour the Not-for-Profit Organization's Facilities

Supporters often enjoy an opportunity to see behind the scenes at an institution. If appropriate, invite donors and potential donors to the organization's offices or facilities. This is especially helpful if the visit helps the donor better understand the good works that the organization does.

As supporters become more familiar and more at home with the organization, they become more likely to make generous contributions to its cause.

Social and Informative Gatherings

Relationship-building events are not directly fundraising in nature. Rather they should be social and informative. A gracious and fun buffet dinner with a guest speaker describing the organization's accomplishments and aspirations is ideal. A development staff member can prepare a simple run sheet and script for the presenters (see Exhibit 7-1).

Many volunteers and donors become involved with not-for-profit organizations as a means of building new and meaningful friendships. One not-for-profit agency held a social and informative gathering at the home of a prominent Austin, Texas, family. The agency invited influential people from the community—even several who were active with other organizations. One well-known philanthropist, who was closely identified with a leading institution in the region, attended. Apparently she recently had begun to feel unappreciated at the other institution. She asked questions about the organization sponsoring the social gathering; she also asked questions about who was on the board—and if any of the board members played bridge. She was very open in stating that she wanted to get involved with another organization . . . and with people she would enjoy. Her involvement later led to substantial financial support for the new organization.

Breakfasts and Luncheons

Informal get-togethers with the executive director, chair of the board, board members, or key staff are useful tools in the cultivation process. Many business leaders enjoy breakfast meetings, which tend to be less disruptive of the workday. Lunch is still a favorite of many folks who find it enjoyable to meet and eat.

Focus Groups

This technique is popular with marketing experts, who find the information gathered through such groups helpful in understanding the attitudes of key constituencies. From a fundraising perspective, focus groups not only provide useful information about attitudes but also prove to be very valuable cultivation activities. The participants—donors and prospective donors—

EXHIBIT 7-1   XYZ NOT-FOR-PROFIT ORGANIZATION

RELATIONSHIP-BUILDING EVENT
Social Gathering
The Home of Mr. and Mrs. I. Gotinfluence
Friday, August 8, 2003

Presentation Notes and Sample Language

6:30 PM   People begin arriving

7:10 PM   Presentation begins
(approx)   Board President (welcoming remarks—see sample text)

Welcome . . . For those of you who haven't met me, I'm Thelma Goodneighbor, President of the XYZ Not-for-Profit Organization Board of Directors. Thank you all for coming tonight. We will keep this part of the evening short so that you can enjoy the fine food and fellowship.

I'd like to begin by thanking my fellow board members and our campaign cabinet members for their hard work in helping create a safe and compassionate environment for abused and neglected children. Let me also take this opportunity to thank our campaign chair, Ed Roberts. I especially want to thank Jan and Stan Gotinfluence for their support and graciousness in opening their home and overseeing the arrangements for this gathering. **Jan and Stan, would you like to say a word or two?** *(Make hand gesture calling Jan or Stan forward to speak.)*

Jan or Stan's remarks. (We are proud to be associated with this project. We would like to personally welcome you and thank you for coming tonight.) *(At end of the remarks, turn attention back to Thelma Goodneighbor.)*

(Thelma's remarks continue.) Many of you know about the importance of the XYZ Organization, our shelter for children in crisis and our comprehensive counseling services for children and families. I suppose you wouldn't be here if you weren't convinced of the vital role the XYZ Organization plays in providing for compassionate services for abused and neglected children. You also know how we have seen a dramatic increase in the requests for services during the last five years.

As we look to the future, we know that one part of the solution is to stress the importance of prevention. And, I'm sure you will be pleased to know that our board has identified preventive services as a priority in our strategic long-range plan.

The other part of the solution is to strengthen the counseling services. That's an important part of prevention also. But the sad truth is that we will need improved facilities for the children who are entrusted to our care.

Our plans call for renovating our existing buildings. This will allow us to take care of the growing number of children being sent to the agency. As important, the enhanced facilities will be brighter, safer, and will allow us greater flexibility in how we use the space available to us. The children deserve the best our community can envision.

I will say a bit more about our vision for the future in a few minutes. But now I would like to introduce our guest, Donald Celebrity. (Thelma's own words to introduce Mr. Celebrity)

EXHIBIT 7-1 (CONTINUED)

7:15 PM Sample Remarks for Donald Celebrity . . .

Thank you, Thelma. I'd like to add my personal thanks to every one of you who came tonight. You are the leaders who mean so much to XYZ Organization's future.

Let me also express my appreciation to the board and staff for their outstanding contributions to the children who are sent to us for care. Very few people are aware of the sacrifice and tenacious commitment your leaders have made to this cause. Here are some facts you might not know:

- Volunteers at the XYZ Organization devote, on average, 300 hours each month to help run the agency and take care of the children
- Of course, many of you know that nearly 500 children spend some time at the XYZ Organization shelter each year. These are children who have been abused or neglected. And make no mistake about it, the level of abuse is at times horrific.
- The XYZ Organization begins the healing process. Our aim is to begin the process of recovery and to show each child that adults can be trusted. There are people in the world who love and care for children. And the XYZ Organization is staffed with compassionate people who make a difference in these kid's lives.
- (Other personal observations Mr. Celebrity would like to share.)

When we started this presentation, Thelma Goodneighbor told you we would be brief. Let me summarize why I feel that your presence is so important tonight.

The board, staff, and volunteers at XYZ Organization have looked beyond our short-term needs. Their vision will provide for the needs of children—children who are innocent victims of circumstances beyond what any child should endure. The plans you will be hearing more about in the months to come stress prevention, counseling, and adequate resources to care for the kids—now and for generations to come.

In the months and years ahead, I hope many of you will support the XYZ Organization with your time, talents, and treasure. Your work and wisdom combined with a healthy investment of financial resources will help the XYZ Organization realize its vision. I came tonight to meet with you and to let you know that my personal prayers and best wishes are with the entire XYZ Organization as we work together to prepare for years of service to children living in our city and state.

7:21 PM Thelma Goodneighbor . . .
Thank you, Donald. Again, I want to thank each one of you for coming tonight. (*Executive director's remarks.* Briefly review plans and case for support.)

7:25 PM Thelma wraps up. Again thanks, Jan and Stan, Ed Roberts, and all the guests for coming. Encourage everyone to get back to the food and conversation.

NOTE: The entire presentation should take 15 to 20 minutes, not more!

explore their attitudes toward an organization. The focus discussions offer them an opportunity to state the case of support in their own words. And if they have any concerns, the process allows them to voice their opinions. Again, involvement leads to commitment.

Invitations to the Annual Meeting

If potential donors are invited to the annual meeting, every possible step must be taken to ensure that the meeting is not a boring, perfunctory affair. Use the annual meeting to stimulate enthusiasm. Celebrate victories. Thank donors. Keep the meeting fast paced.

Individualized Strategies

If a donor or prospective donor enjoys being in front of groups, invite him or her to speak at an organization event. Whenever possible, recruit the best prospects to serve on an ad hoc task force or special committee. The simplest cultivation strategy is to meet face to face and seek advice from the supporter. People are flattered to be asked their opinion.

Publish Names and Photographs of Donors and Potential Donors

Don't underestimate the value of this relationship-building technique.

Donor lists and more highly personalized acknowledgments in newsletters, annual reports, and other publications help organizations bond with the philanthropic community.

Use photographs liberally in your newsletters. Take photos at special event fundraisers. Take photos at committee meetings. Take photos of people receiving awards from your organization. Take photos of volunteers. Send people copies of their photos. Whenever possible publish these photos.

Prompt and Generous Acknowledgment of Every Contribution

Every contribution should be acknowledged with a polite note or letter, ideally within 48 hours of the gift receipt. Development professionals feel strongly that it should never take more than seven days to acknowledge a contribution.

One cautionary note: Many well-intentioned people make a special effort to thank their largest donors in a highly personalized, gracious manner. This is as it should be. However, the danger arises when the person responsible for sending the thank you pulls the gift information out of the

usual acknowledgment process. What can happen is that the person the organization wanted to thank most graciously becomes the person whose gift
acknowledgment is delayed—or even worse, lost in the black hole of the
responsible person's in box. So, keep the large donors in the regular loop.
Then send a second highly personalized letter. Also, be sure to call and
thank the most generous supporters.

A Host of Other Personalized, Genuine Contacts

One good indication that the organization's cultivation activities are going
well is when prospective donors begin inviting key representatives of the
not-for-profit to enjoyable get-togethers. After all, the goal is to develop
true friendships. Professionals do not manipulate people; they nurture
strong relationships.

People responsible for fundraising should think for a minute about all of
the nice things they can do for people they really like. Prospective supporters should be treated in this manner. That's all there is to it.

RELATIONSHIP-BUILDING ACTIVITIES MUST BE SCHEDULED AND MONITORED

People who adopt a strategic and professional attitude toward fundraising
track information concerning who has been invited to which gatherings,
who came, and their reactions to the programs. Moreover, most people
view the act of visiting people only when asking for money as rude. So,
be sure that every prime prospect has been invited to a social and informative gathering—where no money will be requested—at least once every
six months.

The fundraising activity with the highest payoff possible is building relationships with people capable of making major contributions. And yet
there is never a deadline for inviting someone to visit the organization.
There is never a deadline to create a social informative gathering to which
to invite them. For these cultivation activities to occur, those responsible
for fundraising must proactively create and schedule them.

From a professional point of view, a code can be created for everyone
invited to each cultivation activity. This coded cultivation information is
then recorded in the fundraising database. Another code should be used to

indicate who actually came to each event. Record information about conversations or other encounters in the comments field.

"MOVES" MANAGEMENT—CULTIVATING REAL RELATIONSHIPS

Many development professionals find it helpful to summarize their prospect research information, develop a relationship-nurturing strategy, and track the cultivation steps, or "moves," as they are called in the jargon of the business. A move might be as simple as sending a birthday card . . . or as significant as a luncheon meeting with the president of the institution. Tracking involves recording the activity and making notes about the prospect's response and readiness to support the institution. Small organizations can track their top 25 to 50 prime prospects using a simple form (see Exhibit 7-2). Larger institutions use their dedicated fundraising software to track donor information and cultivation moves. Do remember, however, that while the process is being managed, the real goal is to nurture warm and respectful relationships.

DONOR ACKNOWLEDGMENT

The most effective way to ensure continued support for an organization is to express gratitude *promptly* and appropriately for the donor's investment in the organization's mission and programs. Appropriate, generous, and timely acknowledgment is essential to nurturing positive relationships with your donors.

Gracious thank-you notes also are called for after a meeting with a prospective supporter. The person should be thanked for the time he or she took to meet with the organization's volunteers and staff—whether the visit resulted in a pledge or contribution or not.

Of course, donors should be thanked for all pledges and contributions promptly in writing. After seven days, acknowledgment letters have a greatly reduced impact. Well-run development offices are able to thank all donors within 48 hours of receiving the pledge or contribution. Automated yet personalized letters are possible and absolutely essential to larger operations. Most dedicated fundraising software systems allow for the composition of multiple versions of thank-you letters. The person responsible for generating the letters can be trained to select the appropriate one.

EXHIBIT 7-2   PRIME PROSPECT TRACKING FORM

XYZ NOT-FOR-PROFIT ORGANIZATION
PRIME PROSPECT TRACKING FORM

Prospect: _____
              (Last)   (First)   (Middle)

Address: _____
             (Street)   (City)   (State & Zip)

Business Address: _____

Phone: (Work) _____ (Home) _____ (Fax) _____ (Email) _____

Giving History:

Grand Total	# Gifts	1st Gift Date	Most Recent Gift Amt	Most Recent Gift Date	Largest Donation
$_____	_____	_____	$_____	_____	$_____

Family: _____
     (Spouse)

     _____
     (Children)

     _____
     (Other significant relationships)

Interests: _____

Key Relationships with Your Organization: _____

_____

Capability: _____   _____
     (Estimate net worth)   (Form of wealth)

     _____
     (Other factors & information)

Rating: _____   _____
     (Preliminary)   (Final)

Network:

_____
(Closest friends)

_____
(Those close to your organization that have common bond w/prospect)

Solicitor(s) of Record: _____

(continued)

EXHIBIT 7-2   (CONTINUED)

Cultivation Strategy: _____

_____

_____

_____

Gift Opportunity or Project: _____

_____

Next Step: _____

_____

By: _____   _____   _____
            (Target date)   (Entered tickler)   (Done)

Summary Comments: _____

_____

_____

Next Step: _____

_____

By: _____   _____   _____
            (Target date)   (Entered tickler)   (Done)

Summary Comments: _____

_____

_____

Of course, acknowledgments can be handled promptly only if the check-handling system is designed well with no bottlenecks. The development director, working with an accountant, can examine the current check-handling system and eliminate all obstacles to expeditious contribu-

tion processing. Not-for-profit organizations must maintain adequate controls to avoid embezzlement. The gift-handling system also should ensure the accuracy of the donor history and accounting information.

No single gift-processing system can work for all organizations. However, it is essential that the system be designed so the gifts can be acknowledged promptly. Avoiding unnecessary duplicate steps and moving the process quickly to the data entry stage can help in the process.

Many organizations not only write thank-you letters but call to thank generous donors. In some institutions a $500 contribution triggers a personal call. In others, a $10,000 contribution may be the trigger point. Every institution has its own definition of what constitutes a generous gift.

Any not-for-profit organization can refine its acknowledgment policies by first agreeing on a list of giving levels and the corresponding donor benefits for each such level (see Exhibit 7-3).

Once the giving categories and donor benefits are agreed on, this information can be used to determine commensurate acknowledgments for special event sponsors or underwriters, corporate sponsors, underwriters of capital purchases, other special contributors, and generous annual donors. In other words, the donor benefit list can serve as a general guideline for an organization's auxiliary, support group, or supporting foundation. The aim is to acknowledge various levels of support in a flexible yet consistent manner.

The suggested benefits listed in Exhibit 7-3 rely heavily on an annual dinner and an annual report. While these might not be the right approach for every organization, many not-for-profit organizations find them helpful in their overall cultivation strategy.

FOUR PARTS TO AN ACKNOWLEDGMENT PROGRAM

Resource development professionals view the mature acknowledgment program as having four components: donor recognition, donor benefits, permanent recognition, and involvement opportunities.

Donor Recognition

Donor recognition begins with the letters and phone calls discussed earlier. Some organizations also find it helpful to develop lapel pins for donors.

EXHIBIT 7-3   DONOR BENEFITS

XYZ ORGANIZATION
SUGGESTED GIFT CATEGORIES AND DONOR BENEFITS

NOTE: We have listed modest and higher-level giving categories in order to put the giving levels in the context of a comprehensive annual giving and capital/endowment acknowledgment program. When promulgating this information, use language that makes the benefits sound as attractive as possible. Also, use common sense when administering the program and interpreting the phrase "all the above." For example, one would not expect to receive a certificate in addition to an attractive plaque. These donor benefits are merely guidelines. The aim is to have commensurate acknowledgment for the organization, the support foundation, and the auxiliary's gift clubs, sponsorships and comprehensive resource development programs.

Friend   **$25**
   Newsletters and listing in an annual report
Supporter   **$100**
   All the above plus—A special invitation to the annual open house
Sustainer   **$250**
   All the above plus—A certificate of appreciation
Patron   **$500**
   All the above plus—An invitation to the XYZ Organization's annual dinner
Fellow   **$1,000**
   All the above plus—An attractive fellow plaque acknowledging your generosity to XYZ Organization. (In future years, donors who have already received a plaque can be given differing acknowledgment gifts each year.)
Sponsor   **$2,500**
   All the above plus—Generous acknowledgment of your support at a special event (signage and acknowledgments on programs and printed material) (Higher- and lower-level sponsors receive fewer comp tickets and slightly smaller signage; more generous sponsorships receive more comp tickets and more generous signage.)
Invitations to special social events
Guardian   **$5,000**
   All the above plus—An attractive guardian plaque for the donor and placed permanently on a donor recognition wall at the XYZ Organization.
Good Samaritan   **$10,000**
   All the above plus—An attractive Good Samaritan plaque or limited-edition special commemorative gift. Permanent acknowledgment on a recognition wall at the XYZ Organization and published in perpetuity in the annual report.
Humanitarian   **$50,000**
   All the above plus—An architectural feature of the XYZ Organization can be named in honor or in memory of a loved one. Alternatively, a permanent endowment fund can be named.
Benefactor   **$100.000**
   All the above plus—An endowment fund can be named in perpetuity in honor or in memory of a loved one. The fund may have a restricted or designated purpose.
Philanthropist   **$250,000**
   All the above plus—A room or larger architectural feature can be named in honor or in memory of a loved one.
Gifts of $500,000, $1,000,000, or more can be used to name a wing or building. The general rule is that the donation must cover _not less than_ one-half the actual cost of construction. However, the existing buildings of XYZ Organization can be named with less concern for the construction costs.

Some pins recognize various gift levels; others signify that the supporter has made a planned gift to the organization.

Plaques and certificates also play a role in donor recognition and actually have a dual benefit. The very act of hanging an attractive plaque on a wall strengthens the donor's ties with the institution. When visitors see the plaque, they are reminded of the importance of the organization.

In addition to lapel pins, plaques, and certificates of appreciation, many not-for-profit organizations send their donors various tokens of appreciation: paperweights, key chains, pens, business card cases, and a host of other acknowledgment gifts. Donors especially appreciate such gifts when they are engraved with the donors' name.

How the organization presents the pins, plaques, certificates, and other tokens of appreciation to the donor is even more important than the gift itself. Gracious, highly personalized letters accompanying the gift let donors know how very important and appreciated they are. If such presentations can be made in public or at a private get-together, the impact of the gift is even greater.

Donor Benefits

Many not-for-profit organizations create membership categories. At the lowest level, the member receives newsletters and announcements of events and programs sponsored by the institution. At the higher levels, the member may be invited to an annual dinner or to other social events. At times, membership perquisites include discounts to the organization's gift shop, reduced entrance fees, or other discounts of value to the donor.

Some organizations offer various premiums for contributions of different sizes. A contribution of $35 may entitle the donor to a coffee mug. Contributions of $120 might entitle the donor to a signed book or a tape of a popular program. This strategy appears to work well for public television stations.

A cautionary note may be helpful here. When the donor benefits become substantial, not-for-profit organizations must inform donors of the value of the quid pro quo donor acknowledgment gift. Only the portion of the contribution in excess of the acknowledgment gift is tax deductible.

A closely related concept is the gift club. Sometimes these are merely categories or gift levels published in an annual report or in a program book.

These clubs include bronze, silver, gold, diamond, and platinum circles, and also president's clubs and founder's clubs. Donors at the highest levels often are listed as benefactors, humanitarians, or philanthropists.

Gift clubs are most effective when they get beyond the published list stage. Some organizations develop special letterhead for communicating with their upper-level gift clubs. Exclusive invitations to social and informative gatherings allow gift club members to network with each other and bond to the not-for-profit organization. Other acknowledgment strategies can be combined with gift clubs. For example, lapel pins, plaques, certificates, and other tokens of appreciation can be tied to gift club levels. And gifts at the highest levels may result in permanent recognition at the not-for-profit organization.

No discussion about donor benefits would be complete without mentioning sponsorships. Individuals can be called on to sponsor a child or a family. In this case, the donor benefit often comes in the form of letters or direct contact with the child or family. Similarly, individual donors may contribute to scholarship funds to be used for a specific category of students. A donor may get a thank-you letter from the student who got the scholarship. The donor might even be invited to an annual dinner and be seated with the student.

Another entirely different type of sponsorship is the corporate sponsorship, which works particularly well for special events, performing arts groups, exhibits, highly visible public programs, and athletic gatherings. When seeking sponsorships, it is most helpful to put together a generous benefit package. The benefits may include: banners and signs at the event; prominent inclusion of the company name and logo in all related printed material (the sponsorship proposal should state how many times the company name will be included and how many people will be made aware of the sponsorship); complimentary tickets to the event; a pre- or postevent reception for the sponsors; and a host of other benefits unique to the specific sponsored activity.

Again, how membership, gift club, sponsorship, and other tangible benefits are bestowed may be more important than the intrinsic value of the benefits. Each donor—at whatever level—must know that he or she is important and appreciated.

Permanent Recognition

Permanent recognition often is reserved for those who make major investments in the institution. Buildings can be named for a donor who contributes at least 50 percent of the construction cost. Some institutions establish a 75 percent guideline. Similarly, wings and rooms of buildings offer very significant permanent named gift opportunities.

When planning any capital campaign, it is customary to create a number of permanent named gift opportunities equal to the number of gifts needed at each leadership level. For example, for a $10 million campaign, it may have been determined that the following gifts are needed: one of $1.5 million, one of $1 million, two of $500,000, four of $250,000, and so on. In such a case, the organization would need to create gift opportunities, such as the naming of a wing for $1.5 million; naming the lobby for $1 million; naming a large conference room and a small auditorium in recognition of $500,000 contributions; and naming four prominent rooms for contributions of $250,000. It is even helpful to create more gift opportunities than are needed, so donors can select the named gift opportunities that appeal most to them.

In addition to named gift opportunities related to capital projects, some organizations create permanent recognition for major current gifts or in recognition of cumulative giving. In one institution, supporters contributing $10,000 or more in a single year have their names added to a permanent wall display in the main lobby. In another organization, donors whose cumulative giving reaches $50,000 have a permanent plaque placed on the donor wall; the donor also becomes a member of the president's club.

Donor walls usually are divided by gift level. Alternatively, some donor walls feature a Tree of Life, in which leaves represent one gift level and stones and acorns may represent other giving levels. When these sculptures are placed in prominent locations, they stimulate additional supporters to contribute at the $5,000, $10,000, and $25,000 levels. Of course, some organizations encourage gifts at lower levels, while others encourage gifts at higher levels.

When designing the overall acknowledgment program, it is most important that recognition be handled consistently. The gift levels should be

widely publicized. And donors to one aspect of the institution's programs should not receive extravagant acknowledgment while others donating the same amount to another campaign receive little or no recognition. Acknowledgment need not be identical, but it should be commensurate.

Involvement Opportunities

From the not-for-profit organization's point of view, involvement opportunities are the most effective donor acknowledgments. Donors who are invited to join a founder's circle or advisory council can be made to feel important and appreciated, when their advice and participation is genuinely sought.

When the not-for-profit organization creates gift clubs, planners also include a number of social and informative gatherings to which the members may be invited. The social aspect of the gift club allows donors to form stronger relations with the not-for-profit organization's leaders. The informative aspect of the gatherings provides donors with the opportunity to learn more about the organization's vision of the future.

By establishing a gift club made up of people who have provided for an institution in wills or estate plans, an organization strengthens its ties to these key benefactors. Often named Codicil Club, Legacy League, or Angels, the planned gift club—which might be named for a prominent and respected person closely associated with the organization—might host an annual luncheon, an estate planning seminar, or other pleasant social functions throughout the year. It is important to stay in touch with supporters who have remembered the organization in their wills and estate plans. After all, these are the people who are closest to the organization. Besides, many planned gifts are revocable.

The greatest donor benefit is being asked to serve. Donors feel honored and privileged to be asked to play a leadership role in the organization. Not everyone can be asked to serve on the board, but most major donors can be offered an appropriate volunteer opportunity. They may say no, but they will be flattered.

Those who do accept an invitation to participate are drawn closer to the organization as they become more involved.

Major Gift Programs

Let me tell you about the very rich. They are different from you and me.

—F. Scott Fitzgerald, *The Rich Boy*

Yes, they have more money.

—Ernest Hemingway,
rejoinder on hearing the Fitzgerald quote

Major gift fundraising encompasses the identification, cultivation, and solicitation of people capable of making significant contributions to a cause. Most often the relationship-nurturing activities and the solicitations are conducted in face-to-face settings.

Major gift fundraising is the most cost-effective resource development strategy. Moreover, a major gift initiative gives an organization an opportunity to tell "movers and shakers" about its programs and services to people in need.

As important, such an initiative requires little expense. Major gift programs require only inexpensive presentation materials, a series of meetings to generate prospect names and make assignments, patience as relationships are cultivated, a method of tracking assignments, training sessions, and volunteers or staff members willing to ask for contributions.

Often it is difficult to recruit volunteers willing to solicit funds. Therefore, it is recommended that the executive director, development personnel, and a few key volunteers work to become comfortable about asking

for contributions. Then they can ask volunteers to make appointments with potential donors and explain the value of the organization to the community, nation or world.

Volunteers who are comfortable with the solicitation process can ask for contributions; otherwise, a staff member or a bolder volunteer can ask for the donation. All volunteers can help with prospect identification, nurturing relationships, and making introductions.

WHEN MAJOR GIFT STRATEGIES ARE APPROPRIATE

Major gift fundraising—with its emphasis on face-to-face contact and solicitation—is effective for sponsorships, funds for special projects, pace-setting operations contributions, and capital and endowment campaigns.

Sponsorships

Many not-for-profit organizations conduct special event fundraisers—golf tournaments, testimonial dinners, fun runs and races, auctions, and a host of other events. Often these activities net low or modest amounts of contributed income. However, when the organization stresses the importance of high-level sponsorships, the events can net substantial funds.

In addition to special event fundraisers, many not-for-profits—especially arts organizations and institutions that conduct athletic events—find it helpful to seek sponsorships for their concerts, plays, and exhibits or for their teams and competitions.

An effective sponsorship program relies on personal contact. Higher-level sponsorships are available when the organization builds relationships with the funder . . . and solicits the sponsorship in person.

Funds for Special Projects from Individuals or Corporations

One traditional method of seeking funds for special projects or for nonrecurring high-priority organizational investments is to apply for foundation grants.

However, it is also possible to approach local corporate leaders or affluent individuals to support an organization's special projects. The donor

who contributes $250 in response to a mail appeal might well donate $2,500 to help with some special need—if he or she is visited in person. Conversely, the corporation that makes a $2,500 annual contribution to an organization might well consider a $25,000 contribution in response to a well-reasoned appeal—if the decision maker is visited in person.

Pace-Setting Repeatable Contributions for Operations

Major gift solicitations are not limited to special projects. Every organization needs healthy levels of ongoing, operational support. People responsible for fundraising can visit the organization's regular modest supporters personally and encourage them to consider increasing their annual support.

One strategy that works especially well is to create and seek pace-setting gift club contributions. People who embrace the organization's mission enjoy the opportunity to support it as a $1,000, $2,500, $5,000, $10,000, $25,000, or more member of the founder's circle, golden circle, or whatever the top-level gift club is called.

Capital and Endowment Campaigns

Major gift fundraising is the sine qua non of capital and endowment fund raising. Generally people do not make six- and seven-figure contributions to organizations unless they have a close relationship with them. Most often this close relationship comes about after years of relationship building. And while years of relationship building are helpful, personal contact is essential. Capital campaigns succeed when early pace-setting investments are secured in face-to-face settings.

PREPARING FOR A MAJOR GIFTS INITIATIVE

The early chapters of this book discussed the essential preparation for major gift fundraising. The first step in preparation is to strengthen the organization. Be sure that it is worthy of support. Then carry out the suggestions dealing with prospect identification and nurturing relationships in Chapters 6 and 7. These are the vital early steps in the major gift process. When these essentials are under control, the not-for-profit organization must then focus on the best prospects and refine its research.

Research, Ratings, and Solicitor Assignments

First, identify those individuals, corporations, and institutions most likely to support the organization generously. Also gather the information needed to support an effective solicitation. The four crucial points of research are the prospect's relationship to the organization, interests and hobbies, capacity to support the organization, and network of associates.

Remember the old adage: Successful fundraising is the right person asking the right prospect for the right amount for the right project at the right time in the right way.

Here is how prospect research supports this truism.

To recruit the most suitable volunteer solicitor, developmental professionals need to know something about the prospective supporter's network of associates. Who are the prospect's best friends and close associates? Who is close to the organization who also is close to the prospective supporter? If someone related to the organization who is associated with the prospective supporter cannot be identified, perhaps someone close to one of the prospect's friends or associates can be. Is that person willing to make introductions?

To identify the best prospects, fundraisers must explore their relationship to the organization. Consider these questions: Of all the people who might support the organization, which already have a close relationship to it? Which donors already have supported the organization generously? Which affluent prospects are most likely to become the newest generous supporters?

Determining an appropriate request amount often is difficult. Knowing the prospect's precise net worth isn't necessary, but it is important to determine the prospect's relative level of affluence and to decide on a challenging amount to ask the prospect to consider.

Finally, the more that is known about each prospective supporter, the more likely fundraisers are to choose a funding opportunity that will appeal to a particular prospect's interests. Knowledge of the supporter also will enable fundraisers to determine the best timing for the solicitation and will help them make the most gracious approach.

Chapter 6 outlines a process for gathering the information needed to determine the best prospects, assign a request amount to each, and determine the "ideal" solicitor. Now the information can be summarized (see

EXHIBIT 8-1   SUMMARY OF PROSPECT ASSIGNMENTS

VOLUNTEER	PROSPECT	REQUEST AMOUNT	GIFT OPPORTUNITY
A. Smith	Mr. & Mrs. Carl Davis	500,000	Name East Wing
A. Smith	Mrs. Beatrice Wentworth	150,000	Establish permanent endowment named after late husband Frank
A. Smith	Dr. & Mrs. Fred Harding	50,000	Endowment fund or executive director's office
A. Smith	Mr. & Mrs. Martin Dell	25,000	Underwrite lecture series
A. Smith	Dr. & Mrs. A. Lively	10,000	Good Samaritan
D. Barnes	A. Quigley	25,000	Fountain in meditation area
D. Barnes	B. White	30,000	Underwrite outreach
D. Barnes	H. Packard	10,000	Good Samaritan
B. Farmer	D. Coppermine	50,000	Endow 2.5K annual support
J. Meyers	J. Baxter	30,000	Playground equipment
L. Winston	Susan Smith	100,000	Name waiting room
L. Winston	Al Maynard	100,000	Name playground
L. Winston	Mr. & Mrs. Richard Ambrose	250,000	Name auditorium
T. Downey	Frank Winston	50,000	Endowment
T. Downey	Martha Washington	5,000	Guardian on gift wall
Numerous others at more modest gift levels also			

Exhibit 8-1) and the appropriate gift opportunity or project to offer the prospective donor determined.

Solicitation Timing

The precise timing of a request for funds is as much an art as a science. A few broad guidelines can be helpful.

- In general, solicit board members and those closest to the organization prior to approaching people not as close to the organization.

    Marketing experts tend to view this process as a series of concentric circles indicating primary, secondary, and tertiary markets. (See Exhibit 8-2.)

EXHIBIT 8-2   PRIMARY, SECONDARY, AND
                TERTIARY MARKET

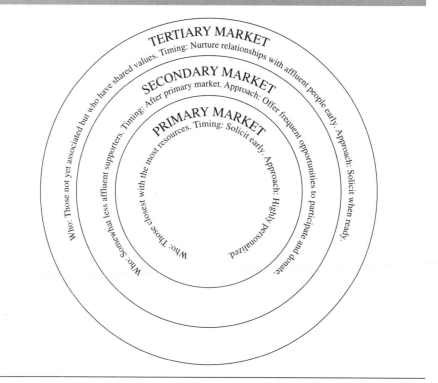

- Approach affluent members of the planning team soon after the conclusion of the planning process . . . or soon after the needs become
  manifest. A supporter who has participated in the organization's planning process has become familiar with its needs. Often such a team
  member expects to be asked for financial support. It is prudent to
  strike when the iron is hot.

- It is best to approach prospective supporters after they have had an
  opportunity to attend one or two informative relationship nurturing
  gatherings or events.

- Be sensitive to milestones or major events in the prospective supporter's life. If the prospect's daughter is being married in two weeks,
  the family may be in a good mood . . . but it probably is too busy to
  consider the request at this time. On the other hand, the fundraiser

could call and make an appointment. If a volunteer solicitor is familiar with the prospective supporter, inside knowledge can help the organization avoid the embarrassment of calling soon after a death or some other inopportune time.

- Someone familiar with the prospect's assets can time a funding request to a moment when the stock or asset is valued at a high level. Conversely, solicitations may be avoided after a sharp decline in the value of the prospect's holdings.

- Invest more time in the cultivation process during campaigns with longer planning periods and with multiyear pledge payments. In such situations it is easier to fine-tune the timing of the request. However, the danger of losing momentum by failing to ask must be avoided.

- Don't delay in approaching any prospect who has stated that he or she expects to be solicited. Often people who become familiar with not-for-profit organizations tell a board member or key volunteer, "I heard a lot about your campaign and expected someone to meet with me for a contribution, but no one ever called." After a cultivation event, fundraisers might hear that someone said, "After that party at Mrs. Gotinfluence's house, I expected someone from your team would call on me."

  As soon as such a remark is heard, someone should call on the prospect to make an appointment. Then the records should be checked to see if others who attended the event have been approached. Poor follow-up will seriously damage the fundraising effort. Some organizations plan and implement motivational cultivation events; they even make intelligent solicitor assignments. Many even get as far as determining the appropriate amount to request—but too often, the campaign falters when the organization fails to ensure that the solicitations actually take place.

- Solicit contributions from major gift prospects relatively soon after recruiting the "ideal" volunteer solicitor. Few volunteers are comfortable adopting a lifelong case worker model. They don't mind helping the organization nurture a relationship with a prospective supporter. However, annual campaigns are time-line driven and capital campaigns need to maintain a sense of momentum. A gracious solicitation can be part of a long-term relationship-building strategy. A donor

who has been offered an opportunity to make a significant investment—and who is pleased with the use of the funds—often will increase his or her contributions over time. Each successful solicitation and each successful project inspires confidence.

Materials Preparation

Once the ideal volunteer solicitor has been recruited and the appropriate amount to request and the appropriate time to solicit the funds have been determined, attention can turn to preparing the presentation materials. At this stage of the resource development process, a written case for support should be available. The organization might even have a video version of your case statement. Since a great deal more is now known about the organization's best prospects, the development team can personalize the case statement for each crucial presentation.

The campaign volunteers will also need pledge cards for the board campaign (see Exhibit 8-3), regular pledge cards (see Exhibit 8-4), and a Call Report Card (see Exhibits 8-5A and B).

A simple plan to follow involves the use of a presentation folder. Here are some of the materials that may be placed in an attractive solicitation folder:

- *A personalized case for support.* The cover sheet could have words such as "Information Prepared for Mr. & Mrs. Joseph Samplename" typed attractively on it. When using presentation folders, the cover

---

EXHIBIT 8-3   BOARD PLEDGE CARD

YES! As a member of the Board, I want to help the XYZ Not-for-profit *save lives and avert tragedies.*

I pledge: $_____ .   I will make my pledge Payment(s) on _____
                                                                                  date(s)

Please complete your Fiscal Year 2003 contribution by June 30, 2003.

Name: _____

Company: _____

Address: _____

City, State, Zip: _____   XYZ Not-for-Profit
                                                                                               123 Board Lane
Home Phone: _____ Business Phone: _____   Southern, MS 39200

_____   _____
Signature   Date

Thank you for your generous support of the XYZ Not-for-Profit

EXHIBIT 8-4   REGULAR PLEDGE CARDS

COMMITMENT CARD

YES! I want to help All Faiths Receiving Home provide loving care and protection for abused and neglected children. I pledge: _____ $2,500   _____ $1,000   _____ $500 $_____ Other

I have enclosed my tax deductible check made payable to All Faiths Receiving Home in the amount of
$_____ and wish to pay any balance _____ monthly, _____ other

Name: _____
Company: _____
Address: _____
City, St, Zip: _____

All Faiths Receiving Home, Inc.
1709 Moon St., NE
Albuquerque, NM 87112
(505) 271-0329

Please fill in your contribution amount and return this form with your check in the envelope provided. Thank you for your generous support of All Faiths Receiving Home.

Reprinted with permission from All Faiths Receiving Home.

XYZ NOT-FOR-PROFIT PLEDGE CARD

XYZ NOT-FOR-PROFIT
P.O. Box 3749
Austin, TX 78711
(512) 877-3742

I hereby pledge to _____ the sum of $_____. I would like my contribution
to (check one) ❑ be used for general purposes   ❑ be restricted to _____
I have enclosed $ _____ and I intend to pay any remaining balance as follows (check one):
❑ monthly ❑ quarterly ❑ semi-annually ❑ annually

Name _____ Address _____
City _____ State _____ Zip _____
Signed _____ Date _____
Comments _____

This statement of intent may be revised or canceled should circumstances require.

---

sheet can be designed so that the personalized inscription appears above the folder flap. In this way, the prospective supporter's name is prominent.

The content of the case for support also can be personalized. As stated in Chapter 4, reformat the materials and stress the points that resonate with the specific donor.

- *Financial data.* Many major gift prospects are people with business acumen. They want to know that a project is well planned. They feel assured when the organization has been operating without deficits for some time. For some donors, pie charts and summary financial information is sufficient. Others require more detailed information, such as

EXHIBIT 8-5A   CALL REPORT FORM, SHORT VERSION

XYZ Not-for-Profit Call Report Form

Volunteer or Staff Name: _____

Person Visited: _____

Date of Visit: _____

Notes:

Follow-up Action Needed:

By When:

Please return to Development Office. Use other side for additional notes.

Note: Volunteers and staff keep these 3" × 5" cards with them all the time.

audits, financial statements, project budgets, and multiyear projections. With major capital projects, many businesspeople especially appreciate multiyear projections that include the income and expenses related to the capital project as well as to the organization's operations. Such donors want to be assured that the project has been planned well and that the increased operational expenses related to it have been anticipated. They want to know that the project can be sustained once it is established.

- *Project description.* If the specific project that funds are being requested for is not integrated into the case for support, a separate document describing the project must be included. State the project benefits in terms of the people helped rather than from the perspective of the organization's needs. And, whenever possible, choose a project that appeals to the specific prospect being approached.

- *Other promotional materials.* Don't overload a presentation package. It should not be stuffed and difficult to handle. Do, however, include the latest newsletter, a positive press article, or a well-produced brochure. The case for support should be the most important piece in the presentation folder; the other promotional materials should be attractive and should support the case statement.

EXHIBIT 8-5B   CALL REPORT FORM, LONGER VERSION

XYZ NOT-FOR-PROFIT ORGANIZATION
INTERACTION SUMMARY

XYZ Representative: _____   Person Visited: _____

Date: _____   Time: _____Phone: _____

Meeting Place: _____Address: _____

Near Major Cross Streets: _____   _____

Goals of Meeting: _____

_____

_____

If Solicitation, Request Amount: $ _____   Gift Opportunity, If Any: _____

Results of Interaction

1. General Summary: _____

_____

_____

2. Follow-up Actions: _____   By When: _____ Check If Done: _____

_____   _____   _____

_____   _____   _____

_____   _____   _____

_____   _____   _____

3. Pledge Total: $ _____ Over: _____ years including 2002, 2003, 2004, 2005

   Initial Gift of: $ _____ to be contributed _____ (date)

   Reminder Statement Information: _____

   Other Comments: _____

   _____

4. Sent Meeting Thank You: _____ or Sent Pledge Thank You: _____

5. Next Contact Dates and Meeting Comments Entered into Database: _____(check if done)

- *Donor benefits and/or gift opportunities.* If the organization has established gift clubs and benefits, by all means include this information in the presentation folder. One note of caution, however: Customize the gift club information to the gift amount or range you are requesting. In other words, if the prospect will be asked to consider a

contribution of $5,000, do not include a gift page that shows gift amounts ranging as low as $100 or $500. A sheet that shows all the gift levels from $2,500 to the top gift category—perhaps $25,000—may be included. Psychologically, this gives the prospect a bit of wiggle room slightly below the target range. As important, it lays the groundwork for the prospect to consider larger requests.

- *Request for funds.* There are many ways to customize a presentation package and include a specific request for funds. Some organizations include a personalized letter to the prospect in their presentation materials. The letter summarizes the case for support and includes a phrase such as "Because of your outstanding leadership in our community, we are honored to offer you an opportunity to participate in our Founders' Circle with a contribution of $1,000 or more."

    Other organizations include a specific request for funds in their Case for Support. The final section in that document might be titled "Our Request to Mr. & Mrs. Specific Prospect Name." (See Exhibit 8-6).

    Still other not-for-profit organizations include a separate sheet with a title such as "Our Request to Mr. & Mrs. Specific Prospect Name." This format works especially well with presentation folders with staggered sheet sizes. (See Exhibit 8-7.)

    Another option is simply to include a gift opportunities page. Again, be careful not to include gift levels substantially below the tar-

---

EXHIBIT 8-6   SAMPLE REQUEST TO INCLUDE AS SECTION OF PERSONALIZED CASE STATEMENT

Our Request to Mr. and Mrs. I. M. Ready

The early years of the 21st century have proven to be very difficult for children facing emotional challenges. Government cutbacks, changes in health care, and pressures put upon traditional support systems can have an adverse impact if we don't act now.

As people who care about the XYZ Not-for-Profit Organization, you have a deep understanding about the important work we do. You know that your contribution is an investment . . . an investment in children who need the best possible therapy and emotional support.

Please consider a leadership contribution of $5,000, $10,000 or even more if you are able.

We will acknowledge your generosity by placing a graciously worded thank-you plaque on the Wall of Honor in our lobby.

get amount. When using a gift opportunities page with gift levels higher than the target amount, the solicitor can be trained to say "We need gifts at all of these levels. Where do you see yourself participating?" It is surprising how often donors choose amounts greater than the solicitation team anticipated.

The most important thing to remember is that the presentation package should include information about the gift range requested and amounts greater than the requested amount. Often volunteers and key staff members hesitate to request specific contributions. However, presentation materials go a long way toward overcoming that reluctance. When the materials request $25,000, the prospect is not left wondering whether a $500 gift or a $250,000 contribution was expected.

Even though the presentation materials tell the case for support and contain a request for funding, the materials cannot stand on their own. These presentation packages are not to be mailed to the prospects. Volunteers and staff members bring the folders with them to their appointment with prospective donors.

EXHIBIT 8-7   **CASE FOR SUPPORT AS CUT SHEETS IN PRESENTATION FOLDER**

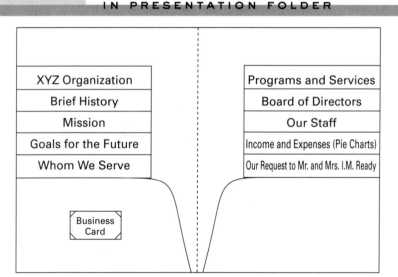

Solicitor Makes Financial Commitment

Prior to requesting funds from others, the members of the volunteer solicitation team—board members and other key volunteers—make their own financial commitment. Those closest to the organization must set the pace. This question bears repeating: If those closest to the organization are not committed enough to give generously, how can others be expected to give?

An increasing number of major donors are becoming tuned in to a not-for-profit organization's critical success factors. They want to know if 100 percent of the board has donated. They want to know if the person requesting funds is a donor. They want to know that the organization is strong . . . and if the people involved are committed.

Getting the Appointment

More money is lost during the process of getting appointments than at the actual solicitation visits. If fundraisers succeed in getting a face-to-face appointment, the chances are quite favorable that they also will receive a financial contribution. However, if the appointment is not gotten, most likely the organization will receive nothing or only a token contribution.

Here is some advice for increasing the odds of getting the appointment:

- Whenever possible, recruit a volunteer to whom the prospective supporter cannot easily say no.

- Offer the prospective donor a choice of dates. Example: "We can get together late this week or late afternoon on Monday or Tuesday. What works best for you?"

- Remember, the most important objective now is to get the appointment. If the prospect asks, "Are you going to solicit me for the campaign?" reply, "The most important thing now is that key people such as yourself have a good idea of what's happening. Should you decide to invest in the campaign later, that would be your decision. And I won't take more than 20 minutes of your time. Which works best for you, Monday or Tuesday?"

- Define success as getting the appointment. Let it be known, in all volunteer training and everything done and said that the organization's most important indicator of success is the ability to get face-to-face appointments with potential major donors. Track how many actual

solicitations occur. Does the number of solicitations increase from year to year? Once this information is tracked and the importance of obtaining appointments is stressed, the not-for-profit organization will experience a dramatic increase in contributions.

THE SOLICITATION INTERVIEW (HOW TO ASK FOR A MAJOR GIFT)

There are six steps to a "model" solicitation:

1. Build rapport
2. State the case for support
3. Encourage involvement
4. Summarize benefits and close
5. Be quiet
6. Respond appropriately

Build Rapport

Take the time to relax and reestablish the relationship or ask some easy open-ended question to break the ice. This is a very natural process. However, some people who are uncomfortable with the solicitation process might forget this step. A nervous volunteer or staff member might even jump into the solicitation without even saying "Hello, how are you?"

If there is an opportunity to meet at the prospect's home or business, it will be easy to find an easy opening question just by looking around. What looks interesting? Perhaps a football signed by a famous coach or player. Perhaps a collection of cut crystal. Every prospect's environment offers clues as to what is important to that person.

Simply say "That's a beautiful collection [or what-have-you]. There must be a story there." Then be quiet and be prepared to hear an interesting story.

At solicitations, spend more time listening than talking. Don't try to top a prospect's story. When a prospect is through with the story, he or she might say something like "Oh, but enough about that. You must have something to say about your organization." The words won't always be the same, but the prospect usually indicates that the story is over and now would be a good time to hear about the agency.

State the Case for Support

Use this opportunity to refer to the written materials. Many experienced fundraisers find it helpful to hold onto the presentation packet and the case for support, pointing out highlights while they speak. In this way, they avoid the awkwardness of speaking while the prospect is reading and thumbing through the materials.

More than anything, fundraisers must speak from the heart and tell the prospective donor why they believe the organization deserves support. Volunteer solicitors should focus on the stories and facts that moved them. The prospect will sense the volunteer's sincerity and enthusiasm.

Everything said about the written case also applies to any spoken presentations. The case must revolve around the problem being addressed— and the people being served—rather than focusing on the organization addressing the problem. When fundraisers speak about an organization, they should focus on the organization's strengths and abilities to address the community needs rather than institutional needs. Focus on how the organization serves people.

Encourage Involvement

As fundraisers state the case for support, they should pause from time to time to ask the prospective supporter questions.

Someone raising funds for a preventive health care program might ask; "Do you think it makes sense to try to prevent disease rather than putting all of our resources into treating illness?" Someone raising funds for an educational institution might ask: "Where does education fit into your philanthropic priorities?" If the agency has touched the lives of most people in the region, the donor might be asked: "Do you know of anyone who has been helped by—or whose life has been touched by our organization?" Volunteers or staff members might also ask open-ended questions such as, "Does any part of our organization's case for support especially appeal to you?"

Often questions such as these encourage the prospective supporter to state the case for support in his or her own words.

One more crucial bit of advice: Listen. Listen. Listen.

When the prospect is speaking, fundraisers must set aside their concerns. Don't try to anticipate what the prospect will say. Don't make judgments

about the prospect's observations. Don't give rise to autobiographical responses: Related life experiences are unnecessary. As Stephen R. Covey, the author of *The 7 Habits of Highly Effective People*, says, "Seek first to understand then be understood." As he explains in his writing about empathic communication, "Most people do not listen with the intent to understand; they listen with the intent to reply. They're either speaking or preparing to speak. They're filtering everything through their own paradigms, reading their autobiography into other people's lives."

Feel what the prospect feels. Hear what the prospect says.

If the prospect has a positive impression of the organization, move forward with the summary of benefits and the request for funds. To the extent possible and natural, use the prospect's own words and thoughts to state the case for support.

If the prospective supporter has concerns or objections, handle these with grace and poise. Do not argue with the prospect. Fundraisers never win arguments with prospects. Communications experts also say that "Yes . . . but . . ." phrases and replies should be avoided. Most humans never hear a word after the word "But." It's a complete turnoff. Those whose thinking patterns go in this direction can practice using "Yes . . . and . . ." phrasing. Example: "Yes, I have heard your concern before. And the organization has made considerable progress addressing that issue."

Many people with exceptional communication skills find it helpful to use the "Feel, Felt, Found" model for responding to objections. Here's an example of how the model might work. Suppose a representative of a not-for-profit agency that helps homeless people is visiting a prospective supporter who says, "I've got to tell you, I'm suffering from compassion fatigue. Lots of folks you help don't do anything to lift themselves up."

Using the "Feel, Felt, Found" reply, the representative of the homeless agency might say, "You feel distressed that so many homeless people cause their own problems and don't seem to do much to help themselves. I can tell you that you're not alone. Others felt that way. What they found out was that at our homeless shelter, we have more than 100 people in programs that address the root causes of homelessness. Some are learning to use computers. They're all enrolled in programs that teach them job skills."

The benefit of this model is that fundraisers begin with a statement that indicates that they understand how the prospect feels: "You feel that . . ." The "felt" phrase has two subtle benefits: (1) It assures the prospect that he

or she is not alone, that others share that point of view; and (2) it places the concern in the past tense. The "found" phrase allows people to supply new information and respond graciously to the concern.

At times a prospect may raise an objection or a concern for which the fundraiser has no ready reply. In such cases it might be helpful to use the "bottom-line" reply. Here's how it works. Imagine a volunteer solicitor raising funds for a rural hospital who hears for the first time something like "I've heard that the emergency room at your hospital is a nightmare. People have to wait a long time. And I've even heard some say that the quality of care there is not what it should be."

In situations such as these, the volunteer can begin by acknowledging the seriousness of the issue and the depth of emotion. He or she might say something like "I haven't heard that before. It surely sounds like a serious issue. I'll try to find out more about that for you."

Now the volunteer transitions to the "bottom-line" reply by saying: "Everyone I know on the management team is dedicated to continuous improvement and quality control. So I know they'll want to hear about your concerns. I speak to a lot of people about this hospital. And their bottom-line is that this hospital is the only one within 75 miles. It is crucial to the health care of people in our region. We've got to work together to make it as strong as possible."

By bringing the conversation to the organization's strongest points, often objections can be overcome—and prospects can be recruited into the efforts to improve the organization and provide the financial resources needed to keep it strong.

In addition to asking questions and handling objections, asking for advice may be helpful. Questions such as "What can our organization do to better address the needs of the people we serve?" "Are there any services we should be offering that we are not currently offering?" are helpful when the organization truly is open to new ideas. Questions such as "Do you have any advice on how we can recruit more volunteers?" "Do you know of other people who might be interested in our organization?" "Would you be willing to introduce our organization to some of your friends or business associates?" are always helpful.

Perhaps the most important advice that could be sought concerns the solicitation itself. Questions such as "What is the best way to approach your company?" "We were thinking about requesting $25,000 from your com-

pany; is this a realistic amount to request?" are positive ways of getting the prospective donor to support the cause.

Summarize Benefits and Close

Learn to recognize the words and body language that indicate that the prospective supporter is moving toward acceptance of the case statement. One clear sign is when fundraisers have asked an open-ended question and the prospect has replied with positive comments about the organization. Other signals may be more subtle. One positive sign is when the prospect shifts body position and leans closer. If the prospect's arms had been folded across the chest and he or she adopts a more open attitude, that too is a positive sign. Also note if the person is beginning to ask positive questions about the organization. Just listen and watch. Soon fundraisers will develop a sixth sense about the prospect's attitude toward the pending request for funds.

Some people with fundraising responsibility get so wrapped up in their case for support that they continue speaking well after the prospect has indicated a willingness to support the cause. A better approach is to summarize the case and graciously request the contribution soon after the prospect has indicated a positive attitude toward the cause.

When speaking with prospects who have affirmed their support for the case, you say something such as "You have a good grasp of how much our organization does for the people of our region. And to continue our programs, we are going to need gifts at these leadership levels." (Bring forward the gift opportunities page indicating investments at the rated range and higher.) "Where do you see yourself participating?"

Alternative language might sound something like this: "You know that a great city needs a strong symphony orchestra. Such an organization is crucial to the cultural and economic life of our community. So I hope you are in a position to consider membership in our Golden Circle with a contribution of $1,000 or more."

When speaking with a long-term, loyal supporter of the organization, close with the following: "You have been so important to our organization. And you know how much this project will mean to so many people. Our campaign leaders want to offer you the opportunity to make a significant investment in this campaign. Your $1 million contribution will allow

us to have the strongest possible start to the campaign and also will allow us to name the new center in memory of your husband, Ralph."

Before going on any call, have in mind what closing to use. Of course, be flexible. If in the course of the conversation the prospect indicates an aversion to large named gift opportunities, do not emphasize the naming opportunity. Rather, focus on the level of investment needed to better serve the people who rely on the organization. Again, the ability to listen is the key to success.

When training volunteers, summarize the benefits of the three closings illustrated here.

1. *"To better serve those who come to us for help, we will need gifts at these levels. Where do you see yourself participating?"*

   This closing allows the volunteer or staff member to rely on the gift opportunity page that has been customized for the individual prospect. Those planning to request $5,000 or more may show the gift opportunities page with all of the investment levels from $2,500 to the top ranges. Many prospects will choose an amount greater than their rating.

   The other benefit of this approach is that many people can never bring themselves actually to ask for a specific gift amount or range. The "Where do you see yourself participating?" question avoids any direct mention of the dollar amount. Therefore, many volunteers find this a very comfortable and gracious way of indicating the gift request range.

2. *"I hope you are in a position to consider a pledge of $X,XXX or more to help us . . ."*

   Please notice that this phrase has every conceivable word to soften the impact of the direct request. The phrases "I hope," "you are in a position," "to consider," when strung together, create the impression that the volunteer solicitor has not judged the prospect's capability to give. Moreover, there is even an implication that the volunteer solicitor hopes that the person is doing so well financially that he or she can make a significant contribution.

   This golden phrase is a priceless addition to anyone's fundraising vocabulary. It is well worth memorizing and practicing until it sounds entirely natural.

3. *"We would like to offer you an opportunity to make a significant investment in . . . Your pledge of $XXX,XXX will allow us to . . ."*

Douglas M. Lawson, Ph.D., author of *Give to Live*, likes to stress the importance of the two Os—offer opportunities. Significant projects grow out of a sense of involvement. Donors who want to make a wholehearted investment in your cause appreciate being offered an opportunity to manifest their spiritual kinship with your institution.

Be Quiet

After the closing question or closing statement has been posed, be quiet. Wait for the response.

If ever there were a time when the expression "Silence is golden" made sense, this is it. Salespeople like to say "After the close, whoever talks first loses." Prospective supporters never lose by stating what's on their minds. However, many contributions have been lost because the volunteer or staff member spoke too soon.

What might happen if the fundraiser were to speak too soon? What is the fundraiser likely to say?

In role-playing situations, observers note that it is human nature to project one's greatest fear and even put forward a response to a concern that the prospect never even mentioned. Volunteers may say something like this: "I hope you are in a position to consider a pledge of $25,000 or more. (*very slight pause*) But I know you are very generous to so many other charities and anything you can do would be appreciated."

In this case, the fundraiser talked himself out of the gift before the prospect even had a chance to think about the request.

Some people find it very difficult to wait for a response in utter silence. They become very uncomfortable. Seconds seem like hours. Still, don't speak.

If, in the rare event that the prospective supporter appears also to have decided not to speak first, and the tension gets to be too much, the fundraiser might say, "My mother always told me that silence means consent. Can I safely assume that your silence means that you have decided to contribute the amount we have requested?" In this rare situation, words like these can break the ice. The prospect might even laugh and contribute what was requested.

Respond Appropriately

To respond appropriately, fundraisers must know what the prospect is thinking. After the closing, the prospect's response is usually yes, no, or maybe.

If the prospect's response to the request for funds is yes, repeat the understanding and tie down all of the details. Say: "Thank you so much, that's very generous. Let me make sure I have all of the information correctly. You are pledging $2,500 a year for three years. Would you expect to be making your contributions monthly, quarterly, semiannually, or annually? By the way, do you prefer your acknowledgments as Mr. and Mrs. Harvey Generous or would you prefer we list you as Harvey and Gladys Generous?"

By repeating the understanding, discussing pledge payment schedules, and reaffirming acknowledgment details, the fundraiser is also taking a most important first step in cementing the relationship with the donor and ensuring pledge fulfillment.

If the answer is no, first determine what the no refers to. Say you said something like "I hope you are in a position to consider a contribution of $2,500 to our annual campaign." If the prospect says "I don't think I could do that," a moment's reflection will indicate that the person has declined to donate at the level requested. A fundraiser might respond "What level of support would you be comfortable with?" or "Of course we need gifts at all levels. Might you be more comfortable with a contribution of $500 or $1,000?"

If the prospect appears to be saying no to a contribution, suggest a pledge that might be contributed later in the year. Of course, when a final no is heard, the fundraiser should graciously thank the prospect for his or her time and say something like "I hope you will be in a position to help sometime in the future."

Most "maybe" responses come in the form of requests for time to consider the contribution. In such cases, the solicitor might say "I thought you might want some time to think about this contribution. That's why I put together these materials for you to look over. When do you think you might make your decision? I can call you in two or three weeks to discuss this. Would that work for you?"

At this point, remember one of the keys for fundraising success: DO NOT LEAVE A PLEDGE CARD!

Anyone who leaves a pledge card has lost control of the situation. Prospects who say "Give me a pledge card and I'll send something in" rarely do.

Many contributions are lost because of a lack of follow-up. Keep the solicitation process moving forward by pinning down the date or time frame to call back for a follow-up meeting or decision. Then be sure to follow through by contacting the prospect again.

AFTER THE SOLICITATION

Whether the prospective supporter said yes, no, or maybe, send a brief note of thanks for the visit. Of course, if the prospect said yes to the request, also acknowledge the contribution or pledge. If the prospect is undecided, use the thank-you letter to remind him or her of the request amount.

If the prospect said no, use the thank-you note to serve as a bridge to the organization. Phrases like "Thanks for your time and advice yesterday. I know that this is not the best time for you to consider a contribution to XYZ not-for-profit organization. However, let me send you some information from time to time. The work we do is so uplifting, I believe you might enjoy hearing about the organization as it moves forward with its services to people in our community."

The more personal the thank-you or other follow-up note sounds, the better. Most not-for-profit organizations with mature fundraising programs find it necessary to automate the acknowledgment process. However, even computer-generated thank-you letters can be written to sound warm and personal.

After writing the thank-you note for the visit, think of ways to involve the supporter in the life of the organization. Is there a committee on which the supporter might serve? What upcoming activities might the supporter be invited to? Whenever possible, recruit the supporter for an active role. In all cases, keep him or her well informed about the organization.

SOLICITATION TRAINING AND ROLE PLAYING

Let's start with the premise that the people serving on the campaign team or on the board of directors are intelligent people with a reasonable degree of interpersonal competency. Most likely they are community leaders and people dedicated to your cause.

EXHIBIT 8-8   ADVICE TO THE VOLUNTEER OR
STAFF SOLICITOR

Steps for Securing Major Gifts

Please consider going on your calls with a team member. If you decide
to go solo, the following suggestions might prove helpful.

Before the Solicitation

1.   When calling for the appointment, offer the prospective donor a choice of dates.
Example: "We can get together late this week or late afternoon on Monday or
Tuesday. What works best for you?"

2.   Please do not slip into a solicitation when you are calling for the appointment.
The most important objective now is to get the appointment. If the prospect
asks, "Are you going to solicit me for the campaign?" reply, **"The most important
thing now is that key people such as yourself have a good idea of what's happening. Should you decide to invest in the campaign later, that would be your
decision."**

3.   *KNOW YOUR FACTS.*   Be familiar with the case for support. Be sure to read the
literature in your solicitor's kit. More important, decide on a few key points that
move you personally.

4.   *KNOW WHAT YOU ARE GOING TO ASK YOUR PROSPECT.*   Please review the
request amount on your prospect list. Additionally, the presentation materials
contain customized gift opportunities for each prospect. Practice saying a closing line based on this information.

Some examples of the most gracious way to ask for the gift are: "I hope you
are in a position to consider a gift of $2,500 to help us move forward." OR
"For this campaign to succeed, we will need gifts at these levels (*present gift
opportunities page*). Where do you see yourself participating?"

Please memorize the closing sentence that works best for you. Remind yourself
about the **SILENCE** after the ask.

At the Solicitation

1.   First relax. Build rapport. Chat about the prospective donor's interests and any
common interests you may share.

2.   Then speak about the campaign and how the projects will help your organization continue to better serve the community. Ask some involvement questions.
Listen to the prospective donor's thoughts about your organization.

3.   As soon as you have heard the prospect state a positive opinion, *CLOSE.*

Present the gift opportunity page and ask for a contribution suggesting a specific amount or say, **"For this campaign to succeed, we're going to need pledges
at these levels. Where do you see yourself participating?"**

Silence. Wait for prospect to reply.

EXHIBIT 8-8   (CONTINUED)

4. TIE DOWN any loose ends. **(Never leave a pledge card!)** Repeat your understanding of the total commitment and the approximate anticipated pledge payment schedule (annually in December, quarterly, or any special arrangements).

    If the prospective donor needs more time to think about his or her decision, set up a date for a follow-up meeting or reconfirm when the decision will be made.

    Again, thank the prospect for his or her time.

After the Solicitation

1. Use the Call Report Form to record the total gift or pledge and expected payment dates. If the prospect has not yet made a firm commitment, use the Call Report Form to indicate the follow-up date. Send the Call Report Form to the office with the results of the meeting.

2. If time permits, please send a short personalized thank-you note to the person you visited. Of course, all pledges and contributions will be promptly thanked.

If there is something you don't understand or are unsure about, don't hesitate to call the office at any time. If you wish, you can give the director a call, for advice and encouragement, a day or two before going on any solicitation visit.

If you want a team member to make the solicitation with you, please let us know.

Good luck!

With this in mind, development professionals must be careful not to "overtrain" team members or undermine their confidence. Most community leaders don't need to be taught how to build rapport. The actual solicitation is a natural process that can be handled any number of ways. The most important aspect of training is to stress the importance of getting the appointment. Next devote as much time to role playing as possible to increase everyone's comfort level. Keep training materials concise. The sample Advice to the Volunteer or Staff Solicitor (see Exhibit 8-8) might form the basis for the orientation session. Again, keep it simple. Inspire confidence. And reap the rewards.

Direct and Select
Mail Fundraising

Of all those arts in which the wise excel,
Nature's chief masterpiece is writing well.

—John Sheffield, *Essay on Poetry*

Mail campaigns serve four functions: (1) to acquire new donors—solicitations sent to people who have never donated to your organization; (2) to encourage current donors to give again and increase their gifts; (3) to renew lapsed donors—solicitations sent to previous donors who have not donated during the most recent 12- or 18-month period; and (4) to bolster public relations and provide information.

ACQUISITION MAILINGS

Frequently donor acquisition mailings do not pay for themselves. However, as donors renew and increase their contributions, the donations from mail can grow to significant levels. Moreover, any in-house list will suffer from attrition over time. Some donors lose interest in the cause. Some move away. People die. In order for the number of donors and contributed income to increase, not-for-profit organizations must actively promote their donor acquisition programs.

A few words about the economics of donor acquisition might be helpful at this time. For simplicity's sake, consider a 10,000 piece mailing to nondonors as our example. (Larger not-for-profits may test seven mailing

lists with 5,000 names as a first step—thus mailing 35,000 test pieces with the expectation of mailing hundreds of thousands of letters to the best lists.) Suppose creative, production, and postal costs total $.50 per piece. In this instance, it costs the organization $5,000 for the project. Now assume that there is a 1 percent response rate; this means that of the 10,000 pieces sent, 100 respondents send in a contribution. Further assume that the average gift is $36. Multiplying the $36 by the 100 donors, it is learned that $3,600 in income has been received. To summarize:

$3,600 (income from 100 gifts @ $36 per average gift)
−$5,000 (expenses from 10,000 pieces sent @ $.50 per piece)
($1,400) (net loss from the project)

Does this make economic sense?

Many key volunteers, board members, or inexperienced staff may be quick to reply that such results do not justify the effort involved in mass mailing to prospects. To make matters worse, the results look even bleaker when larger-scale mailings are contemplated. However, don't be too quick to judge. This is one of the few cases in fundraising that is counterintuitive. Surface impressions and intuition can lead us astray.

In this case, $1,400.00 was "lost," but the organization *gained* 100 new mail-responsive donors. Are the names of people who are interested in the cause and who are mail responsive worth $14 each? Remember that between 50 and 80 percent probably will donate again. So, with an aggressive renewal program and mailings several times a year, costs can be recovered within one or two years. And these new donors can stay on the mail list for years to come. Many will increase their gifts. A few may even remember the organization in their wills or estate plans.

To sum up, never make decisions based on one mailing alone. Examine the mail program with a multiyear view. With such an outlook, donor acquisition programs can become very significant.

Still, mail programs should be cost-effective. Ask "What is a reasonable amount to invest in a donor acquisition program?" Several rules that might help are: If net income is gained from donor acquisition mailings, the program is highly successful. Donor acquisition mailings that break even are still way ahead. If costs exceed income, calculate the cost to acquire each new donor (net loss ÷ number of new donors = cost to acquire a new donor). If the cost to acquire a new donor is $15 or less, probably the range

is acceptable. Costs can be recovered quickly and net contributed income increases as the list grows. Another way of calculating the effectiveness of an acquisition program is to monitor the ratio of the income to the total expenses. If 85 percent or more of the costs are recovered, the program is doing very well. If between 70 and 85 percent of the costs are recovered, it is doing well. If results aren't this favorable, carefully analyze them to determine if continued investment is justified.

Another question arises. How many donor acquisition pieces should the organization mail each year? A number of factors enter into this decision, including the number of mailable households in the market, the funds available to invest, and how significant the mail program is to the overall development effort. Still, some general rules might be helpful.

Assume that the goal is to increase the number of donors by 10 percent next fiscal year. For simplicity's sake, assume that there are 1,000 active donors this fiscal year. Of course, not all of these donors will renew. An organization is doing well if 85 percent of the donors renew their support from year to year. So, if an organization does nothing other than communicate with existing donors, the 1,000 donors will decline to 850 donors. This is not good. Besides, the goal is for the number of donors to increase 10 percent, to 1,100 donors. Thus, if no one engages in donor acquisition, the organization may be 250 donors short of the goal (1,100 − 850 = 250 donors short). Therefore, to increase the number of donors 10 percent, those lost through attrition must be replaced *and* even more new donors must be gained. What can be done to gain 250 new donors? Remember, typical response rates for donor acquisition mailings range from 1 to 2 percent. Someone with access to a very productive prospect list and who has a strong message with a fine creative presentation might achieve the 1.5 percent response rate. Even with this favorable response rate, 16,667 pieces would have to be mailed to acquire the 250 new donors.

Consider: The organization started with 1,000 donors; a 15 percent attrition rate is anticipated; a goal of 1,100 donors was set; 250 new donors must be acquired (150 donors to replace the normal attrition + 100 new donors); and a 1.5 percent response rate was assumed. Algebraically, $1.5\% \times X = 250$, where X equals the number of pieces that must be mailed. Changing the expression: $250 \div .015 = 16,667$. Thus, more than 16 times the number of original donors must be contacted to achieve a 10 percent increase in the number of donors supporting the organization.

Even readers who do not understand the math can remember this rule: *The number of acquisition pieces mailed each year should be at least 16 times the number of active donors to the organization.*

An organization with 1,000 donors should mail at least 16,000 acquisition letters each year; one with 5,000 active donors should mail at least 80,000; and an organization with 20,000 active donors should mail at least 320,000 acquisition pieces each year. As with all rules, use common sense when designing and implementing your program. If response rates are higher than 1.5 percent, perhaps not so many letters must be mailed. Organizations with other sources of new donors each year may not need to mail as much. Similarly, if income does not justify the long-term investment or if cash flow cannot handle the acquisition program, modify the program. If the number of names available in the market does not equal 16 times the current donor base, consider writing to the best prospect lists two times a year—as long as response rates are favorable. For this rule to work, production costs must be as low as possible and the organization must continue to strive for even higher response rates and gift levels.

The most important factor in the success of any program is the quality of the prospect lists. Of course, professional guidance in selecting lists and designing the acquisition program will help.

In addition to careful list selection, be sure that the message is clear and compelling. To achieve this aim, the organization may wish to work with someone experienced in direct mail copywriting. Be sure to address the reader as an individual. A powerful mail appeal that produces a high response rate and that garners a high average gift level is used as the organization's control package. All new acquisition mailings are tested against this control. When a mail appeal out-performs the control package, it becomes the new control.

In summary, acquisition campaigns are designed to attract new donors, *not dollars*. If an organization is netting income from acquisition mailings, consider a more aggressive approach. Perhaps not enough donors are being added to the in-house list each year. Try new lists. Expand the number of people to whom the organization writes. Consider expanding the program to the break-even point. The increased number of new donors should reward the effort. After several years, net income from the mail program should increase dramatically.

RENEW AND UPGRADE

Once a person or business has contributed to the organization, it is most important to renew that support. First of all, thank each donor promptly—preferably within two days of receipt of the donation. Request another contribution within three or four months. It might be useful to wipe the phrase "annual support" out of fundraisers' vocabulary. The phrase implies that one contribution a year is expected. In fact, the goal is to encourage multiple donations throughout the year.

Now, how is this accomplished?

In the first place, personalize mailings to donors. A "Dear Friend" mailing with a labeled envelope may make economic sense for donor acquisition mailings. However, such letters are inappropriate when mailed to people who already have contributed to the organization. Imagine receiving a mass-produced letter from your mother, brother, sister, or best friend. It just doesn't make sense. And yet some not-for-profit organizations don't realize that the people who voluntarily contribute time, talent, and treasure are their best friends.

Since the mailings to people on the organization's donor list are being personalized, the list can be segmented to create a much more individualized feel to each letter. In every case the donor can be made to feel special. The appeal also should sound grateful but should assume continued support. The letter should sound confident; the recipient is a friend. And he or she is being offered an opportunity to serve and help. But the list also is segmented by recency, frequency, and dollar amount. (See Exhibit 9-1.)

The donors in the top left segments of the grid—those in the top left boxes—receive the most personalized letters. Perhaps the appeal envelope has a first-class stamp. Perhaps the executive director, board president, or chief development officer will write notes on these appeals. Alternatively, these donors may be invited to participate in a major gift club.

Donors who are mail responsive donate frequently throughout the year. They should receive the most appeal letters. Many not-for-profit organizations find that it makes economic sense to mail 8, 12, or 13 direct mail appeals to their most responsive donors. Others create a special program with specialized mailings to donors who have indicated that they wish to contribute each month. In organizations with dedicated fundraising

EXHIBIT 9-1   MAIL SEGMENTATION

Frequency	Dollar Amount		
	High: $100+	Medium: $25–$99	Low: $1–$24
High: 3 Gifts or more	Mail 9 times/year Highly personalize Visit (Reduce mailings if notified by donor)	Mail 5 times/year	Mail 5 times/year
Medium: 2 Gifts or more	Mail 5 times/year	Mail 5 times/year	Mail 3 times/year
Low: 1 Gift	Mail 5 times/year	Mail 3 times/year	Mail 2 times/year

Recency	Dollar Amount		
	High: $100+	Medium: $25–$99	Low: $1–$24
Most recent gift: Within 3 Months	Mail 8 times/year	Mail 4 times/year	Mail 4 times/year
Most recent gift: Within 6 Months	Mail 4 times/year	Mail 4 times/year	Mail 2 times/year
Most recent gift: Within 12 Months (after 12 months, place in lapsed donor program)	Mail 4 times/year	Mail 2 times/year	Mail 2 times/year

software, a special code might be created for those who expressed a desire to receive fewer mailings. Most fundraising software packages allow for "promotion" codes that specify which and how many mailings a prospect receives.

When multiple appeal letters are sent each year, the messages may vary. One might stress the organization's food program. Another might talk about the winter cold. Yet another might stress the organization's education and outreach programs. In every case, share poignant stories about the people you help.

The goal is to renew and upgrade the level of support. Which brings us to the most important rule in direct mail fundraising: YOU GET WHAT YOU ASK FOR. Be sure to ask for an appropriate yet challeng-

ing gift range for the prospect to consider. Find several ways to ask throughout the letter.

Once an organization has established the habit of upgrading donors, the most generous donors should be moved into a personal solicitation program. First, establish upper-level gift clubs that can be promoted by mail. Then intensify the relationship-nurturing activities involving prime prospects. Visit the best prospects. Get them involved. Finally, when appropriate, offer them an opportunity to make a significant investment in the organization.

LAPSED DONORS

Direct mail specialists often think about lapsed donors in the following ways: 12-month lapsed donors—past donors who have not contributed in the most recent 12-month period; and 18-month lapsed donors—past donors who have not contributed in the most recent 18-month period. Some also track and communicate with 24-month and 36-month lapsed donors.

Lapsed donor lists are valuable assets for not-for-profit organizations. A carefully crafted appeal that lets past donors know that they are important, appreciated, and missed almost always produces net income. (Of course, the letter should sound as if it were written directly to one individual.) The general rule most mailers follow is to continue mailing to lapsed donor lists until the lists prove to be unprofitable. This rule can be modified; perhaps an organization will continue to mail to lapsed donors as long as the list is at least as productive as other prospect lists. Put another way, periodically send mail appeals to lapsed donors as long as results are as good as or better than mailings to people who have never donated to the organization. Be very cautious about taking any name of a past donor off your in-house list. As long as the name and address are valid, removing information rarely, if ever, makes sense. Ninety-eight out of 100 such donors might never give again. But a 2 percent response rate can prove profitable. Besides, the lapsed donor might be unable to provide current support but may have remembered the organization in his or her estate plan.

If names must be removed from an in-house list, remember that some experts recommend not removing a record until it becomes a 60-month lapsed donor.

In addition to mailing, lapsed donors may be contacted by telephone. Combined mail and phone campaigns are particularly effective for renewing support from lapsed donors.

PUBLIC RELATIONS AND INFORMATION

A well-crafted direct mail program can be an important component of an organization's public relations strategy. To accomplish this, consider the following questions: Does the message of each appeal reinforce the organization's public relations and communications goals? Does the look, feel, and tone of the letter enhance the image of the organization? Is the timing and frequency of the letters consistent with relationship-nurturing goals?

Once these questions have been answered, consider these: Does the organization have an educational goal that can be addressed effectively in the context of a fundraising mail campaign? Will the educational message detract from fundraising effectiveness? If the answer to the first question is yes and the answer to the second question is no, educational and fundraising goals can be accomplished with the mail campaign. Most people have seen this strategy at work: the health care institution that includes the seven warning signs of cancer or a brief tract on coronary risk factors in its fundraising mail; the homeless shelter that explains the root causes of homelessness in its appeal; the religious institution that incorporates an inspirational message with its request for support. When done well, these educational messages strengthen fundraising appeal.

FREQUENCY

The question of how often to mail fundraising requests to the in-house list is one of the most sensitive areas of resource development. On the one hand, there is no benefit in offending loyal supporters by seeming to be greedy. On the other hand, mail-responsive donors make frequent contributions, and no one wants to lose the opportunity to raise more funds for the organization's valuable mission.

Some not-for-profits take the term "annual fund drive" too literally. They mail only once a year—usually a year-end mailing in November or December. Other not-for-profits with aggressive mail campaigns mail 12 or 13 times a year.

What is right for a particular organization?

A once-a-year mailing schedule is almost always a mistake. Donors enjoy hearing about the organization and appreciate the opportunity to help. Four mailings a year—especially when the approach varies—are rarely offensive to the vast majority of donors. And organizations with a refined cultivation strategy for major donors always can code the mail list to remove prime prospects from routine fundraising appeals. One cautionary note: If prime prospects are excluded from the ordinary fundraising mail, be sure that they are invited to special event fundraisers they may enjoy. Also, be sure that they are approached in person or through a highly personalized mail or phone appeal. Far more money is lost because fundraisers never get around to asking than is lost because they ask too often.

With proper segmentation, those who are highly mail responsive can receive more letters than less responsive contributors. Contributors who make multiple gifts throughout the year are the best prospects for the 8- to 12-times-per-year mailing schedule. Assuming that an organization has a strong mail appeal and a mail-responsive constituency, expect a 5 to 10 percent response rate from the in-house list, each time, even if the organization writes 12 times a year. In such a case, it is difficult to imagine a reason *not* to mail frequently.

Fundraisers who adopt a strategy that calls for multiple mailings throughout the year must create a number of promotion codes for their database. With a thoughtful approach, a number of objectives can be achieved. The most mail-responsive donors will receive the most appeals. People who complain about frequency can receive far fewer letters. Those who are about to be approached for a major gift can be excluded temporarily from the mail campaign. Longer-term lapsed donors can receive just one or two mailings per year plus a phone call. Monthly donors can be put on a special track—and receive thank-you letters, reminders, and envelopes.

ENSURING SUCCESS

A number of factors can help ensure the success of any campaign. Fundraising professionals estimate that the list itself accounts for 50 percent of the effectiveness of a mail program, the message accounts for 30 percent

of the response, and the creative presentation accounts for 20 percent of the results.

Not-for-profit organizations need a compelling case for support and a strong appeal. But the most important success factor for a mail program is *list selection*. It doesn't matter how strong the appeal is if it is sent to people who are not interested . . . or who are not mail responsive.

A proper creative presentation ensures that donors are more likely to open the envelope and consider the appeal. A sense of urgency should be conveyed. A decision that can be put off for a period of time sometimes is forgotten. For this reason many letters say "Please send in your contribution today." If funds are needed to shelter the homeless right now, say so. If matching funds must be raised right now, say so.

Most of all, ensure the long-term success of a mail program by tracking results continually. Make incremental improvements. What are the response rates for each appeal? What is the average gift from each appeal? What is the return on investment (ROI) for each appeal?

Most fundraisers have heard the direct mailer's mantra: Test. Test. Test.

This mantra doesn't apply only to sophisticated direct mailers. Rather it should be the guiding principle of every development professional. Testing is not difficult. For example, to learn which of two prospect appeals is stronger, test mail several thousand pieces using each package. In this way a highly effective control package can be created and chosen. This control package will be the basic direct mail acquisition appeal until a variation or appeal that outperforms the control package is discovered. At this point the organization will have a new control.

Once a strong appeal is created, make every effort to test only one variable at a time. To learn if your appeal is stronger with or without teaser copy on the outside envelope, for example, test the two kinds of envelopes; leave everything else identical. Similarly, to know if a single letter signer is more effective than multiple signers, alter the signature part of the letter only; leave everything else identical. If the letter has a new second paragraph and the response card also is altered, no one will know if the test results are due to the language or to the response card.

In summary, select effective lists, develop a strong appeal, enhance creative presentation, and convey a sense of urgency. Test, track, and analyze results. Finally, make the incremental improvements that will help garner dramatically increased contributed income.

ELEMENTS OF THE APPEAL PACKAGE

A typical fundraising appeal package has the following elements: outside envelope, the appeal letter, the response device, the return envelope, and additional possible enclosures.

Outside Envelope (see Exhibit 9-2)

Besides serving to hold the package together, the outside—or carrier—envelope has one main function: to get the recipient to open the package. A number of techniques help. Teaser copy on the outside envelope stimulates interest with a short question or phrase. Examples may include: "Important survey enclosed," "Photo enclosed, do not bend," "A letter from

---

EXHIBIT 9-2   OUTSIDE ENVELOPE

Reprinted with permission from St. Bonaventure Indian Mission & School.

[celebrity's name]," the organization's slogan . . . or, better yet, a brief phrase that arouses interest and hints at the main message of the enclosed letter. A first-class stamp on letters to high-end donors helps; and not-for-profit stamps tend to do a bit better than metered mail. Whenever possible, use a window envelope or directly imprint (mail-merge) the outer envelope; these formats tend to do better than labels. Vary the look of mail appeals by using snap packs, telegram look-a-likes, or creative artwork on the outer envelope.

Use the more expensive techniques (stamps, personalization, etc.) for mailings to the best prospects—those who give larger amounts more frequently. When designing mass donor acquisition appeals, concentrate on list selection and message . . . but do everything possible to keep production costs as low as possible. For acquisition mailings, the "Dear Friend" labeled mail is just fine.

The Appeal Letter (see Exhibit 9-3)

A great fundraising letter is one that elicits a high response rate and a relatively high average gift. Too often development professionals get caught up in personal likes and dislikes as well as thoughts concerning what a proper business letter might be. Instead, successful letters should be examined to determine what they have in common. Exhibit 9-4 provides a brief checklist of effective mail strategies.

Response Device (see Exhibit 9-5)

Response devices or forms have two main purposes: to convey the donor's name, address, and gift amount, as an aid to record keeping; and to repeat the main message and encourage the mail recipient to respond with a contribution.

Here are some rules to remember when creating a response form:

- Tie the response device to the letter. For example, if an appeal letter told the story of Jimmy, a child in need, the response device might say: "Yes! I want to help children like Jimmy. Enclosed is my contribution of $ _____ ."

- Separate the response device from the main letter. Once a letter with a perforated response form at the bottom was tested against a letter

EXHIBIT 9-3   APPEAL LETTER

St. Bonaventure Indian Mission & School

Eastern Navajo Reservation   Mission Director Robert D. O'Connell

P.O. Box 610, Thoreau. NM 87323-0610   Operating Blessed Kateri Tekakwitha Academy
Phone (505) 862-7847   P.O. Box 909. Thoreau. NM 87323-0909
Fax (505) 862-7029   Grade School (505) 862-7465 • High School (505) 862-7466

December 11, 2001

Mr. Stanley Weinstein
1111 Kentucky St NE
Albuquerque, NM 87110-6923

Dear Stanley,

Conditions on the Eastern Navajo Reservation cry out for your help! Lack of employment, substandard housing, language barriers, and inability to attend school are just a few of the challenges the Navajo people face every day.

Many live in poverty and know the despair that accompanies such conditions. Loss of hope can be seen in children who at mid-school or even younger say, "It won't matter anyway, I'm not smart at (math, or spelling, or reading...)." It's heartbreaking to think they've already given up on themselves.

People come to St. Bonaventure Mission for help every day. And we're able to provide that help thanks to your support.

They come for food; for clothing; for warmth. For help for their families. For transportation money. For safety. And for education.

It broke my heart to read the letter that Sister Natalie received from sixth-grade Jennifer's mother.

Sister Natalie asks parents of elementary school children to come to the school to pick up their child's report card. In the letter to Sister, Jennifer's mom said that she could not take the time from work to come.

The letter explained that Jennifer's dad had lost his job and the family car had broken down and was towed away. Jennifer's mom was now leaving home each morning at five to hitchhike 40 miles to work so the water and electricity would not be turned off and the family could get food. Her mom told Jennifer and her brother to eat as much as they could at St. Bonaventure for breakfast and lunch because there was so little to eat at home.

Because of donors' generosity, I was able to give Jennifer's family money for a down payment on a car and to buy some food. Jennifer's mom is now able to get to work, and Jennifer, a very good student, can focus on her schoolwork.

(over)

"I am the Good Shepherd. I seek out My sheep who are lost. I have come that they may have life and have it abundantly." (John)

(continued)

EXHIBIT 9-3   (CONTINUED)

Another mother tearfully told me at graduation, "This is the first high school graduate in our family. Thank you and the teachers and people who paid to help these students get through school. My son wouldn't be graduating if this school didn't do so much to help him and keep him in school."

Your loyal, faithful support kept us operating in 1996.

But the needs continue. My Christmas prayer and wish list begins with enough food, water and heating fuel for all on the Eastern Navajo Reservation. And for each child to have an opportunity for a good education. And jobs for the unemployed.

Recently a donor wrote, "It's good to know there are people like your Mission volunteers with the courage to try to make a difference."

Yes, we are blessed with generous volunteers. But without generous donors who care about the less fortunate, none of it can happen! Only when you help us with book money and food money and money for gas to transport the children to and from school and deliver food and water can Christ's mandate to love the poor be lived in Thoreau, New Mexico.

If you haven't already included the Indian boys and girls in your Christmas giving, please send your tax-deductible gift before December 31.

What greater gift can we provide to the elders and families than the basic necessities you and I take for granted? What greater gift for the children than opportunity... the opportunity to learn skills for all their lives long?

Please help me and all of us at St. Bonaventure Mission to do Christ's work. It can't happen without you!

In Christ's love for Native American children,

Bob O'Connell

Bob O'Connell
Director

P.S. I hope the smiling faces of the third graders on the Christmas card warm your heart as they do mine. These beautiful children, dressed in traditional Navajo attire, were part of our school's holiday program.

In this holy Christmas season, I join them and all our staff in sending you holiday greetings, our thanks and deep gratitude. You make our school and all the work at St. Bonaventure Mission possible. God bless you!

EXHIBIT 9-4   CHECKLIST FOR EFFECTIVE FUNDRAISING LETTERS

☐ Effective letters use the word "you" more than the words "I" or "we."

☐ Effective letters use strong or dramatic opening paragraphs.

☐ Effective letters use short paragraphs—often one-sentence paragraphs. Few, if any, paragraphs longer than five lines.

☐ Effective letters sound as if they are a letter sent from one person to one person—never to a group or mass of mail recipients.

☐ Personalized computer-generated mail-merged letters produce higher return rates than label and "Dear Friend" letters.

☐ Longer letters tend to produce greater response rates than short letters. But there have been many great one-page letters.

☐ Letters that *suggest a specific donation amount* produce larger average gifts.

☐ To be effective, fundraising letters must arouse interest, state a problem, tell how the contribution will help, and ask for the contribution.

☐ Effective fundraising letters reflect the personality of the organization or writer.

EXHIBIT 9-5   SAMPLE RESPONSE DEVICE

Dear Bob,

( ) In this holy Christmas season, I want to share with the Indian boys and girls and the elders served by St. Bonaventure Mission. Here's my tax-deductible gift:

( ) $25 ( ) $50 ( ) $100 ( ) Other $ _____

( ) Enclosed is my check or money order $ _____

( ) Please charge Credit Card $ _____

( )MC ( ) Visa Expires _____

Card # _____

Cardholder's Signature _____

ST. BONAVENTURE INDIAN MISSION AND SCHOOL
EASTERN NAVAJO RESERVATION
25 Navarre Vista Boulevard West P.O. Box 610
Thoreau, New Mexico 87323-0610

Reprinted with permission from St. Bonaventure Indian Mission & School.

with a separate response slip. The separate response slip produced a 1.3 percent higher response rate and a $38 average gift as opposed to the $36 average gift produced by the perforated form. This difference translated into more than $7,000 greater net income per mailing for the not-for-profit organization.

• A response device on a contrasting paper or card stock tends to produce slightly higher results than one that matches the organization's stationery.

- Personalize the request amounts whenever possible. A person whose last gift was $250 should not receive a letter with a response device that requests $15, $25, or $50. Gift categories of $150, $250, $350, or $500 would be more appropriate.

- Try listing gift amounts in reverse order—starting with the highest gift levels on the left proceeding to the lower gift levels as the eye moves to the right.

- Include "other" as a gift option.

- Always include the name and mailing address of the organization on the response card. Some donors lose their return envelopes and need the information to send in a contribution.

- Whenever possible, send response forms with the name and address filled in by the computer system. In that way, the donor doesn't even have to fill out the form unless there are corrections.

Return Envelope (see Exhibit 9-6)

Most not-for-profits find that the postage-paid business return envelope (BRE) is crucial to the success of their direct mail. The BRE's simplicity is its strength. Donors don't have to find a stamp; they don't even have to address the return envelope.

EXHIBIT 9-6   RETURN ENVELOPE

An alternative to the BRE is the wallet-flap return envelope with an extra-long flap. The response form and other promotional copy is printed on the flap. These are less popular than in years past. However, fundraisers might want to test the wallet envelope against the more traditional BRE if the extra copy might make a difference in response rates—or to see if expenses can be reduced significantly by avoiding the separate response form.

Another issue related to the response envelope is whether to use a postage-paid envelope or to print a "your stamp here helps too" message in the square where the stamp normally would be. For acquisition mailings, a postage-paid envelope is recommended, because the response rates will be significantly higher. Test the in-house list to see if the savings from the switch to donor-supplied stamps is greater than the potential lost contributions. Be cautious. Don't omit the postage-paid response envelope without testing.

Once decisions have been made on which type of response envelope to use and whether to use a postage-paid envelope, focus on design issues related to the response envelope. By and large, it should be kept simple. However, creative copy can serve to reinforce the message and encourage contributions. Phrases such as "challenge grant matched gift enclosed," "emergency response enclosed" may increase response rates.

The post office will supply the artwork for a simple BRE. This layout comes with a bar code that can save money on mass mailings. (To get the lowest postal rates, the carrier and return envelope must be bar coded.)

Additional Possible Enclosures

At times any of the following additional enclosures might improve response rates.

- Lift notes are shorter letters or notes that accompany the main letter. Often they are signed by celebrities. At times they contain a brief but punchy call to action.
- News articles about the organization can add credibility to the appeal.
- Petitions are helpful for political action groups.
- Brochures can tell a lot about the organization in an attractive format. Be careful, however. Some tests indicate that mailings may receive a

lower response rate when a brochure is enclosed. Besides, a brochure can add substantially to the mail costs. To say more, use a longer letter.

- Surveys have the potential to increase response rates and average gift substantially.

- Decals or other premiums are helpful with some donors and for some organizations. However, if such devices are used, clearly state that the donor is under no obligation to contribute or return the decal or premium. It is unethical to send out unordered merchandise without such language. Moreover, some mail experts find that premiums attract only small gift amounts, and the donors may be difficult to upgrade or convert to repeat contributors without premiums.

As always, test these elements to see if they are a cost-effective addition to the overall mail appeal package. And remember to test only one variable at a time.

MAIL LISTS

It's been said before but it is worth repeating. The list is even more important than the message and appeal package.

A productive list for an organization consists of mail-responsive people who share the values and have an interest in the cause. It is difficult to go wrong with such a list. Conversely, an unproductive list would be one with undeliverable names and addresses, people who are not mail responsive, and people who have no interest in your cause. With such a list it is virtually impossible to do anything right.

There are four main sources and types of mail lists: in-house lists, lists provided to an organization, rented lists, and exchanged lists.

In-house List

- *Current and past donors.* An organization's most important asset is its list of current and past donors. A person who already has donated to the organization is far more likely to donate again than someone who has never contributed. Maintain accurate records. Keep the list up to date. Back up computer files frequently.

- *Prospective donors with a relationship to your organization.* People who have had a positive relationship with the organization—alums, season

subscribers, patients, members of the congregation, vendors to your organization, volunteers, board members—are much better prospects than people with no relationship to the organization. Yet many not-for-profits never take the trouble to gather all of the in-house lists—and make these lists available to the development office or to the people responsible for fundraising. Few investments are as valuable as the time and effort devoted to compiling a comprehensive in-house list of potential supporters.

- *Other prospective donors.* Fundraising professionals find it helpful to gather lists of affluent individuals or businesses that have not yet donated to the organization. The names on this list are of people who have been generous to other causes or have been identified as being capable of cultivation. The letters these people receive may result in a contribution. Even if the appeal letter doesn't result in a gift, the potential donor will have heard more about the organization and the people it serves. While the most effective relationship-nurturing strategy involves highly personalized face-to-face encounters, putting the most affluent potential donors on the in-house mail list is almost always fruitful. The fundraising letters and newsletters they receive can serve as an important adjunct to the cultivation process.

Lists Provided by Supporters or Otherwise Made Available

- *Friends or board members' Rolodexes.* Key volunteers and board members can be encouraged to furnish names, addresses, and phone numbers of acquaintances and business associates. Keep track of the source of each prospect gathered by using the "Source Field" or other appropriate field in the database system to record the name of the volunteer who furnished each prospect's name. If the source of the name is recorded, special appeal letters for each volunteer can be mail-merged. Then volunteers can sign or personalize the fundraising letters to people they know. Similarly, if a board member or a key volunteer asks if any of the prospects he or she suggested ever donated, a report selected by the "Source Field" can be run.

- *Clubs, affluent groups, professional associations.* At times someone will offer membership lists of athletic clubs, civic organizations, professional associations, private schools, and the like. These may be fruitful.

But not always. Before adding such directories to the in-house list, ask the person furnishing the list to mark the best prospects for the organization. Alternatively, conduct a very small-scale test. Put 200 to 400 of the names on the in-house list, and check results after several mailings. If a 1 percent or better response rate has been received, add the remaining names to your in-house prospect list. Be careful to place an appropriate code in each record indicating the nature or source of the list that the name came from.

Lists Rented from List Brokers

Virtually no large-scale, sophisticated direct mail program is possible without the use of rented lists. If an organization has the potential for a large-scale regional or national direct mail program, list brokers can provide access to hundreds of thousands—even millions—of prospects. Not-for-profits with a more local appeal also can turn to list brokers as a source of tens of thousands of qualified prospect names and addresses.

List brokers deal with three main types of lists.

- *Compiled lists.* These lists are composed of names and addresses of people who have something in common. They are brought together from various sources such as newspapers, directories, or voter lists. Such lists are among the least expensive—and among the least productive—to rent. Just because someone lives in a "good" zip code doesn't mean that he or she is mail responsive or has any interest in your cause.

- *Commercial lists.* Some magazines and some catalog sales companies rent their lists. These lists can be useful if the magazine or catalog is of interest to the kind of people who support your organization.

- *Donor lists.* These lists are your best bet. The results of sending appeal letters to people who donate to similar organizations will outpace almost all other donor acquisition strategies. The results even will compare favorably to writing to modest income and affluent nondonors who have a relationship with your organization.

List Exchanges

It is fair to say that the idea of exchanging donor lists is anathema to many not-for-profit organizations. They dislike the idea with a passion. And yet,

leading direct mail authorities consistently recommend that not-for-profits consider exchanging lists when possible.

Opponents of list exchanges fear that their donors who receive multiple competing appeals may become irritated at receiving more direct mail solicitations and may even stop contributing to their organization. Direct mail experts point out, however, that list exchanges make economic sense. In the first place, the organization saves money on list rentals. Second, the not-for-profit organization has the potential to receive thousands of names of people generous to similar causes. Third, there is a good chance that the donor will receive many mail appeals, with or without the list exchange. And finally, the potential for dramatically increased income far outweighs any potential loss.

MAIL PREPARATION: WHAT TO DO IN-HOUSE, WHAT TO DO WITH A MAIL HOUSE

Preparing a mass mailing is a labor-intensive job with many tasks: database cleanup and list preparation; segmentation decisions; obtaining accurate counts of the number of pieces to be mailed; refining the budget; copywriting; design; choosing a printer, ordering stationery and envelopes, printing specialty material; choosing and communicating with the mail house; preparing the database for the mail house; mail-merge; stuffing and matching the envelope (if window envelopes aren't being used) and response cards (if imprinted) to the appropriate letters (if personalized); bundling and preparation for the post office; and finally, delivering the mailing to the post office.

One key task is deciding what work to perform in house and what should be contracted out to a mail house.

Mail houses are sometimes referred to as lettershops. Often they are listed under "Mailing Services" in the Yellow Pages. Some are expensive; some are extremely reasonable. Some provide shoddy or mediocre services; some are excellent—and can be significant strategic partners with an organization. When starting out, ask around. Get recommendations and visit the mail houses being considered.

It is possible for not-for-profit organizations dealing with mailings of perhaps as many as 10,000 or 20,000 pieces to handle the entire project in house. Whether it is prudent to do so is another question. While an

organization can save on mail-house preparation costs, the value of the staff and volunteer time must be considered, as should the costs related to wear and tear on office equipment. Additionally, a well-run mail service—with its specialized knowledge of postal regulations—can save an organization thousands of dollars each year in postage.

With these thoughts in mind, many fundraising professionals recommend that mailings of more than 2,000 or 5,000 pieces be handled as much as possible by a mail house. Of course, much larger mailings—50,000, 100,000, or perhaps 1 million pieces—are virtually always handled by a qualified mail house.

Organizations that mail fewer than 5,000 pieces per mailing tend to have small to medium-size development staffs—people who are stretched with too much to do and too little time to do it. The internal development staff should be devoting its time as much as possible to major gifts, planned gifts, seeking sponsorships for the special events, preparation and support of capital and endowment campaigns, grant writing, and other high-payoff activities. A gifted person who is a good copywriter and understands direct mail solicitation can be a plus for any staff. But such a person should not be spending days and weeks each month overseeing the preparation of mail. Again, this work can be done more economically by a qualified mail house.

Among the services offered by all mail houses are:

- Mail-merge: personalized letters, envelopes, labels, signature scan
- Merge/purge
- Postal automation to generate lowest possible postal rates: presort, Coding Accuracy Support System (CASS) certification, bar coding
- Metering or stamping
- Advice in all matters dealing with postal regulations
- Collate, fold, insert, and seal mail package components
- Prepare postal reports
- Deliver the mailing to the post office

Additionally, some mail houses provide the following services:

- Design and copywriting
- Mail list maintenance
- List provision

In working with a mail house, the responsibilities of a development professional include:

- Obtaining the not-for-profit bulk rate permit and establishing the business reply mail account well in advance of the mailing.

- Cleaning the in-house list and preparing it in the format needed by the mail house. Some service providers prefer a fixed ASCII format; some want a comma-delimited format; other service providers might have other specific requirements.

- Communicating with the mail house. The lettershop will need to understand the order of fields in the database or ASCII files. Perhaps a special situation exists, such as a database that has the company name in the last name field but automatically flipflops the two fields to produce an appropriate-looking label or direct printed address. In any case, the fundraiser should communicate with the mail house to be sure that the database and merge instructions are completely understood.

  The fundraiser also might need to communicate with the mail house concerning other issues such as: salutations (some databases have more than one salutation field or other related issues that must be dealt with); references in the body of the letter to past or largest gifts; and other fields used in the letter.

- Sending a sample package and written instructions concerning how the appeal contents should be inserted in the carrier envelope. The mail date must be stated clearly.

- Helping ensure that the coded response forms are appropriate for test mailings. When testing multiple lists or conducting other split tests, it is imperative that the response forms be coded for the appropriate list. That way the data enterer can enter the appropriate list code when the gift is recorded.

- Ensure that a responsible person at the mail house inspects the first mail-merged letters to make sure they are as expected. This single step can save more grief than any other.

POST OFFICE

Postal regulations are constantly changing. And a wide range of postal rates are available to not-for-profit organizations. CASS certification, zip +4,

bar coding, presort—all contribute to lower postal rates. Moreover, the post office will not accept a bulk mailing that is not properly prepared and bundled.

If the organization is dealing with a mail house, the service provider will monitor postal regulations and do most of the work needed to get the lowest postal rate. Still, it is best to stay aware of postal regulations and communicate with the mail service provider early in the production process. These early consultations can help ensure a successful outcome and significant savings.

NEWSLETTERS AS PART OF THE DIRECT MAIL PROGRAM

Newsletters are an important adjunct to an organization's fundraising and friend-raising plan. Every newsletter should have a donor response device and/or a contribution return envelope. Each one should generously thank donors and volunteers and restate the case for support by covering important program and service developments. Poignant stories are more effective than a bland recitation of statistics. Of course, the organization's newsletter should include constant reminders of the importance of planned gifts. If nothing else, consistently remind your donors to remember the organization in their wills or estate plans. Periodically print sample codicil language.

Two, three, or four newsletters per year may be enough. Organizations that do not mail a donor appeal letter to contributors each month may wish to mail newsletters during the months when mail appeals are not sent. Please know, however, that newsletters rarely if ever achieve as high a response rate as a direct-mail appeal.

Telephone Solicitations

If you utter words that are not intelligible, how shall it be known what is spoken? For you will be speaking into the air.

—I Corinthians 14:9

Telephone solicitation is a powerful and effective fundraising strategy. Too often, however, even experienced fundraisers avoid telephone solicitations because of a personal aversion to the technique. They don't want to be bothered at home, so they conclude that others will be bothered by the telephone solicitation.

But let's question this perspective.

A fellow named Bob once joined a table occupied by senior development professionals attending a national conference. The subject turned to telephone fundraising. Several said that they never donate in response to telephone calls. Bob recalled that over the years he had donated to a public television station, a symphony orchestra, and a Red Cross appeal following a well-publicized disaster—all in response to telephone calls. Bob asked the group if perhaps he was some kind of rare exception—a telephone-responsive donor. At that point the conversation took a strange turn. Each of the senior fundraisers remembered donating in response to a call from his or her favorite not-for-profit organization. Some had donated to their universities in response to a telephone call. Others also donated to the public television station in their region in response to a telephone call. In short, each of the professionals who moments before said

that he or she would *not* use telephone solicitations recalled donating in response to a well-crafted telephone appeal from a respected not-for-profit organization.

In fact, surveys indicate that relatively few people are annoyed by telephone solicitations from well-respected charities. They are annoyed by credit card companies, telephone service providers, and other commercial establishments that phone *ad nauseam*. Besides, the few people who complain about telephone calls from not-for-profits are in all probability misanthropes who rarely donate to any cause, no matter how worthy.

In short, many not-for-profit organizations find that phone solicitations are highly productive. Moreover, telephone fundraising is a cost-effective resource development strategy.

The subject of telephone fundraising covers a broad spectrum of approaches. Often volunteers too busy to visit each prospect in person simply telephone and solicit contributions. Some not-for-profit organizations conduct periodic volunteer phone-a-thons. And a great many such organizations stage well-organized year-round or multimonth professional phone solicitation campaigns. Any of these methods can be—and often are—combined with mail solicitations for maximum impact.

VOLUNTEER TELEPHONE SOLICITATIONS

Volunteer phone-a-thons are most effective when calling current and past donors. The strategy can work for prospecting, but volunteers find it very frustrating to call larger numbers of nondonors. The success rate is simply too low to keep volunteers motivated over time.

Here is a simple way to figure out if a volunteer phone-a-thon might work for your organization, how many volunteers are needed, and how many evenings of calling can be sustained. Assume that calls are planned from 6:30 P.M. to 9:00 P.M. Monday through Thursday. Assume further that the organization has access to a donated site with at least seven outside phones available.

1. Obtain a count of all current and past individual donors to the organization.

2. Volunteers can dial 40 names per hour, so divide the number of current and past individual donors by 40.

3. Compare the number of volunteer hours needed to the number available. If there is a reasonable match, proceed with the phone-a-thon.

To illustrate these steps, imagine that an organization has 2,800 current and past individual donors suitable for calling. When 2,800 is divided by 40, the result indicates that we can sustain 70 volunteer hours of calling. If the phoning site has seven phones and calling lasts for 2.5 hours each night, a four-evening volunteer phone-a-thon can be planned—if the seven volunteers needed each night can be recruited. To summarize, 7 volunteers per night × 2.5 hours per night × 4 nights × 40 names per volunteer hour = 2,800 names needed to call.

A staff member or a well-trained volunteer should be available each night to provide orientation and training for the volunteers and to manage the evening's operations.

Phone-a-Thon Overview

If an organization has clean donor and prospect lists and dedicated fundraising software, a volunteer phone-a-thon is a relatively simple activity to organize. While most special event fundraisers require six months or more lead time, a phone-a-thon can be organized in three months or less. The following time line outlines the main steps.

- *Three months prior to phone-a-thon.* Secure a location with many telephones and good group dynamics.
- *Two and one-half months prior to phone-a-thon.* Decide on database segmentation criteria. Focus on annual "regular" donors and new prospects who have a strong relationship to the organization.
- *Two months prior to phone-a-thon.* Recruit volunteers
- *One and one-half months prior to phone-a-thon.* Prepare tips, scripts, instructions, and follow-up letters.
- *Two weeks prior to phone-a-thon.* Send reminder notices to all volunteers.
- *Three days to one week prior to phone-a-thon.* Use computer system to print phone-a-thon forms that include giving history and information about the prospect's relationship to the organization. Print out 40 names and forms per volunteer hour.

- *Each night of the phone-a-thon.* Provide orientation and training. Smile and dial. Separate forms into five stacks: (1) Yes; (2) No; (3) Maybe; (4) Special handling or corrections; (5) No answer, or never called.

- *Each following morning.* Immediately mail-merge and send thank-you letters with return envelopes.

If the organization has never conducted a phone-a-thon, conduct a trial of seven volunteers per night calling for two or three nights. Monday, Tuesday, and Wednesday work well from approximately 6:30 to 9:00 P.M. These few nights will enable fundraisers to find out if supporters are phone responsive and if volunteer calling makes sense for their organization.

Volunteer Recruitment

Grassroots organizations often call on board members to serve as phone-a-thon volunteers. Larger, well-established not-for-profits tend to involve board members more in major gifts programs. Therefore, these organizations need to recruit other volunteers for phone-a-thons.

So, who might be a volunteer for a phone-a-thon?

If an organization has a volunteer auxiliary, some auxiliary members might take responsibility for an annual volunteer phone-a-thon. If it has a relationship with a civic club, one of the club's leaders may be in a position to take on the whole project or help you recruit a number of volunteers. Friends of board members and staff can be recruited to serve as phone-a-thon volunteers. Stock brokers and real estate agents are comfortable phoning and frequently volunteer when asked. An organization's constituents and others familiar with the cause also can be recruited.

When recruiting, don't overwhelm the potential volunteer. Recruit people for only one or two nights. Show potential recruits a volunteer scheduling form (see Exhibit 10-1). Have them sign up for one or two nights that work best for them. Recruit a few more than may be needed. Cancellations are a fact of life when dealing with volunteer phone-a-thons.

Let the volunteers know that there will be a brief orientation each evening, during which time snacks will be available. Pizza helps gets most volunteers to come on time. Of course, fundraisers know their volunteers and their tastes best. Finally, let the volunteers know that easy-to-use scripts for the phoning will be provided.

EXHIBIT 10-1   VOLUNTEER PHONE-A-THON SCHEDULING FORM

Evenings 6:30 P.M. to 9:00 P.M.

Monday May 10	Tuesday May 11	Wednesday May 12	Thursday May 13
_____	_____	_____	_____
_____	_____	_____	_____
_____	_____	_____	_____
_____	_____	_____	_____
_____	_____	_____	_____
_____	_____	_____	_____
_____	_____	_____	_____
_____	_____	_____	_____

Monday May 17	Tuesday May 18	Wednesday May 19	Thursday May 20
_____	_____	_____	_____
_____	_____	_____	_____
_____	_____	_____	_____
_____	_____	_____	_____
_____	_____	_____	_____
_____	_____	_____	_____

NOTE: If volunteers are not already on the not-for-profit's database, ask them to provide addresses and phone numbers.

Be clear about the responsibilities, and let everyone know that a phone-a-thon is a fun and effective way to raise significant funds.

Approximately two weeks prior to the phone-a-thon, send a letter to each volunteer confirming the time and location (see Exhibit 10-2).

Orientation

On each evening of the phone-a-thon, provide orientation for new phoners. Needed for this orientation are:

- Tips and scripts
- Sample calling forms
- A simple instruction sheet

EXHIBIT 10-2   SAMPLE LETTER OF CONFIRMATION TO
PHONE-A-THON VOLUNTEERS

April 26, 2003

Jennifer Goodheart
1234 Volunteer Lane
Anycity, TX 78000

Dear Jennifer,

Thanks so much for agreeing to serve as a volunteer caller for the XYZ Not-for-Profit May Phone-a-thon. The calling will take place at _____ (location).

To confirm, I see that you signed up for the evening of Monday, May 12, 2003. There will be a brief orientation that evening beginning at 6:30. Calling will begin immediately after the orientation and will continue until 9:00 P.M.

Volunteers who have participated in our phone-a-thons frequently have remarked that they enjoyed the experience and were surprised at how much could be raised using this simple approach.

I believe you will enjoy the experience also. Besides, we will have pizza and light refreshments for the volunteer callers.

Again, let me express my appreciation for all you do for the XYZ Not-for-Profit Organization.

With Best Regards,

Jan Enright
Director of Development

The tips (see Exhibit 10-3) should encourage each volunteer phoner to make his or her own contribution. They also provide general advice and remind people to smile and dial.

The script (see Exhibit 10-4) begins by identifying the caller as a volunteer. Early on it states the purpose of the call and confirms the donor's address. A two-sentence case for support and a closing is recommended. The script also includes a number of closing options depending on how the donor responds to the request. A good script provides listening opportunities as well as the simple case for support. Most of all, a good script is easy to use and is effective at encouraging meaningful contributions.

EXHIBIT 10-3   SAMPLE TIPS FOR PHONERS

The following tips can be useful in a group setting or can be used by the solo caller.

- **Invest in your organization.**
  Your personal contribution is a tangible sign that you believe in our organization and its mission. If you have not done so already, please make your contribution or fill in your pledge on the appropriate call report form. Your calls to others will be more successful when you have made your early contribution.

- **Plan each call.**
  Review the giving or membership history. Decide on an appropriate request amount (always more than last year). Take a second to review any sample scripts or think through what you're going to say.

- **Smile and dial.**
  People can hear the smile in your voice. Smile before you dial. Smile when speaking.

- **Know your organization's case for support.**
  Your reasons for supporting the organization are most persuasive. Your sincere and convincing understanding will translate into financial support from the prospective donors you call. Let the prospect know why you support the organization. And tell the prospect why it needs financial support.

- **Always ask for or suggest a specific giving amount. (Again, please remember to suggest more than the donor gave last year.)**
  EXAMPLE: If the donor gave $75 last year: "With your support, your organization has been able to accomplish so very much . . . and I hope you're in a position to consider a donation of $100 or more to help us carry on this work."

- **Don't accept the first NO. Negotiate.**
  Use let-me phrases. Suggest alternatives. Maybe the no is only *no* to the request amount you suggested. Ask: "With what amount would you be comfortable?"

- **Strive to reach agreement on a specific donation amount.**
  If the donor doesn't pledge a specific contribution amount, it's the same as a refusal. Prospects who say "I'll send something in" rarely do. Try a let-me phrase. Example, "Let me enter that as a pledge of $25. You can send that in when we send the reminder—or if you want to, you can always add to that amount."

- **Always repeat the amount pledged.**

- **Always repeat any special payment schedules or information.**

(continued)

EXHIBIT 10-3   (CONTINUED)

- **Be warm and polite to everyone.**
  If the prospect made a pledge, say "Thank you." If the prospect gives you a firm refusal, say "Thank you for your time. I hope you'll consider supporting (organization name) in the future."

- **Record the results of the call.**
  ✔ The specific dollar amount of the pledge
  ✔ Instructions for reminder statements (any special information about when the pledge will be paid)
  ✔ Check the spelling of the donor's name—how does the donor wish to be acknowledged?
  ✔ Your name as the volunteer caller
  ✔ If refusal—clearly write refusal

- **Turn in all appropriate paperwork.**

Most dedicated fundraising software packages can generate the phoning forms (see Exhibit 10-5). The forms show the donor's name, address, phone number, and giving history. Flags, sort codes, and comments also can be included to give the caller a more complete sense of the donor or prospect's relationship to the organization. If flags or sort codes are printed out, provide a key for volunteers so they understand what the codes stand for.

In addition, the phoning form will have a place for volunteers to record the following key information:

- Pledge amount
- Expected payment dates or other special instructions dealing with reminder statements
- Donor listing information (for the annual report or for donor acknowledgment in a newsletter or other publication)
- Comments or corrections to the record
- The volunteer's signature

A simple instruction sheet tells volunteers how to fill out the form and asks them to place the finished forms in five stacks: (1) "Yes" forms with firm pledges; (2) refusals; (3) special handling or corrections to the record;

EXHIBIT 10-4   SAMPLE PHONE-A-THON SCRIPT

The Opening

"Hello Mr./Mrs. _____. I'm_____(volunteer name)_____, a volunteer with (organization name). I'm calling tonight for our annual membership drive. But first I'd like to thank you for your continued support of (organization name). By the way, are you still living on _____ Street/Blvd./etc. (If no, correct the address.) Thanks . . . so that's _____. [Repeat the address with the street number].

NOTE: We ask the address to be sure our records are correct. Perhaps more important, this gives the prospect a chance to say "YES," early in the conversation. It also prevents the run-on monologue that too many phone solicitors use.

The Two-Paragraph Case for Support

"I don't know if you're aware of how much (organization name) has been able to do with our membership contributions."

PAUSE: Wait for the prospect to say something. LISTEN and RESPOND. (Often prospects will state the case for support in their own words.)

"A lot of people seem to know something about our XXXXXXX program. (Mention your most popular program). But not everyone seems to know about our YYYYYY services. (Mention important outreach efforts, youth programs or other lesser known valuable services)."

NOTE: Mention some of the popular programs or some of the specific reasons you have become a volunteer for the organization.

The Close

"Of course, to continue our programs, we need your participation each year. So I hope you're in a position to consider a membership contribution of $100 or more."

SILENCE . . . Wait for an answer. Don't speak first!

NOTE: Remember to ask for more than last year's contribution. Please also remember to wait for the prospect's response.

- IF YES . . .

  "Thank you. Let me make sure I have the right information. How would you like to be listed in our [records or acknowledgments]. Do you prefer Mr. and Mrs. or first names?"

  "Thank you for your pledge of $___(repeat amount)___. I'll have (organization name) send you a thank-you letter with a return envelope to make it easy to send in your contribution. (Or repeat any special pledge reminder instructions.) Thank you."

- IF OBJECTION . . .

  NEGOTIATE: Use LET-ME phrases . . . **Examples:**

  Volunteer: "I understand that may be a bit much for you right now. Well, let me enter your pledge for $25. You can contribute that now, or in several months, if that would be more convenient."

  OR

  Volunteer: "Even $15 or $25 means a lot. Would you prefer to make a contribution like that or perhaps make a pledge that you can pay at a later date?"

- IF NO GIFT . . .

  "Thank you for your time. I hope you'll consider (organization name) in the future."

EXHIBIT 10-5   SAMPLE PHONING FORM

XYZ NOT-FOR-PROFIT
PHONE-A-THON FORM

Volunteer Name: _____

Donor Name:	Dr. & Mrs. Thomas Kelly
Address:	1234 Persimmon Court
City, St, Zip:	Little Rock, AR 72219
Phone (H):	(501) 374-2983
Phone (W):	

Spouse:

Flags: AB5,AL5

Amount Pledged: _____Date Pledged: _____

Payment Date: Now ❑ Other, Please specify: _____

_____

Listing as donor would like it to appear in
Annual Report and other printed materials:
Or Anonymous ❑

_____

COMMENTS:

_____
_____
_____

GIVING HISTORY:

Grand Total:	0.00
Largest Amount:	0.00
Last Amount	0.00
Last Date:	

Most Recent In-Kind Donation:

Desc:
Date: Value:

Reprinted with permission from DonorPerfect-Starkland Systems.

(4) will send something in (a commitment to donate but a reluctance to state a dollar amount). No-answers and forms that were never called are placed in a fifth pile that can be called later or the next night.

Managing the Process

A key volunteer or staff member remains with the callers throughout the evening. This person's first job is to motivate the volunteers, beginning with an upbeat orientation. Throughout the evening that person reminds callers to keep the finished forms in five stacks. Periodically he or she can collect the "yes" forms with the firm pledges. Adding up the totals as the evening progresses tends to keep volunteers motivated. Announcing totals that are close to impressive round numbers is especially effective. Announcements such as "The next $50 pledge will get us to $5,000" and "If

someone can encourage a $100 pledge, we will reach $10,000" never fail to get volunteers excited about the challenge.

In some systems, volunteers fill out the card or letter that goes to the pledger immediately following the call. In other cases, the staff member or key volunteer collects the "yes" firm pledge forms. The staff mail-merges and sends a thank-you letter confirming the pledge. This pledge confirmation letter (see Exhibit 10-6) always contains a postage-paid return envelope. It is imperative that this letter be sent immediately. Any hesitation can greatly reduce the response rate.

In addition to the highest-priority letters to people who made firm pledges with specific amounts, write a special letter to the people who said they would send something in but were reluctant to state the contribution amount. Thank them for pledging their support; also be sure to suggest a

---

EXHIBIT 10-6   SAMPLE THANK YOU AND PHONE-A-THON REMINDER

May 12, 2003

Mr. and Mrs. Samuel Betts
7521 Phone Responsive Road
Anytown, TX 78304

Dear Sam and Mildred,

Thank you so much for your pledge of $125 to the XYZ Not-for-Profit Organization's 2003 fund drive. When our volunteer called last night, you were kind enough to respond generously to our May phone-a-thon. Please know that your contribution will help us feed the hungry, cure the sick, enrich lives through arts and cultural events, and promote spiritual growth for the thousands of people who use our services each year.

I have enclosed a postage-free envelope for your convenience in making your pledge contribution. I have also enclosed a receipt for your records.

You can feel confident that you have made an important investment in the economic, cultural, health care, educational, and spiritual life of our city and state. When you use our services, please enjoy them with the knowledge that you have done so much to make the work of the XYZ Not-for-Profit Organization possible.

Again, thanks and best wishes to you and yours,

Arthur G. Whizz
Executive Director

gift range in the letter. As always, be sure to include a postage-paid return envelope.

Following the phone-a-thon, the staff can enter a "no-call" code in the database for the few people who may have complained or requested that no calls be made in the future. Also, carefully go through the special handling pile. Correct telephone numbers or remove phone numbers that are no longer valid. Make corrections to addresses. If a volunteer recorded useful information about the donor's interests or concerns, enter these thoughts in the comments field. If the volunteer has been told that one of the spouses is deceased, correct the salutation and title information. It is rude to continue writing to Mr. and Mrs. Smith years after Mr. Smith died.

There is no need to do anything special with the forms from people who do not pledge. These refusals have little meaning. The next time a spouse may answer and make a pledge. And many people who are not phone responsive will during the next mail appeal.

Phone and Mail Campaign Coordination

Many people called request written material or an appeal letter. Every fundraiser has heard "I don't give in response to telephone calls, send me something." Other people on the list are not home when the phone-a-thon is scheduled. Still others might be strong prospects but have unlisted phone numbers. Some people simply refuse to donate in response to a call but never tell us why. For these reasons and so many more, it makes sense to schedule mass mail appeals immediately following each phone-a-thon. When the mail lists are segmented, be sure to exclude the people who made firm pledges during the week. They will get the phone-a-thon pledge confirmation letter. All other prospects on the mail list can receive a mail appeal.

Ad Hoc Volunteer Phoning

Some not-for-profit organizations rely heavily on telephone fundraising but don't organize formal phone-a-thons. The simplest method of doing this involves printing out cards with prospect names, addresses, and phone numbers. If possible, include the giving history and comments. Volunteers look through the cards and take the names of prospects they wish to call. Volunteers also are given pledge cards on which to record the results of

each call. In most systems, the volunteers are responsible for getting the pledge information to the not-for-profit's office. The staff of the not-for-profit then sends a return envelope and thank-you letter confirming the pledge.

Organizations that use systems like this must be sure to record the names given to each volunteer. They need to know who is responsible for each call and who was most effective with each prospect. It helps to stay in touch with the volunteers to encourage them to complete their calls.

The advantage of such a system is its simplicity. A phoning site isn't needed. Staff members and key volunteers need not attend phone-a-thon evenings. And the volunteer phoners can call at their convenience. The method works well in that it allows a strong volunteer to visit some of his or her major gift prospects in person and call many additional prospects for more routine contributions.

On the other hand, these more ad hoc phoning techniques have several disadvantages over a more structured phone campaign. Phone-a-thons build on group dynamics. Individual callers often lack the motivation provided in a team setting. With organized phone-a-thons, staff members know precisely who was called and what each response was. Often this information isn't available with individual callers. Organized phone-a-thons ensure that the entire list is called within a tightly defined time period. With individual callers, the task appears to take longer—if it's completed at all.

Fundraisers who do decide that individual calling is the appropriate strategy should be sure to provide orientation, scripts, and tips at the gathering where the cards are selected. A strong support system—that includes follow-up calls to volunteer phoners—can help ensure the success of this fundraising strategy.

PROFESSIONAL TELEPHONE SOLICITATION CAMPAIGNS

When an organization has more donor names than the volunteers can call, a professional telephone solicitation campaign may be considered. Paid callers can be highly effective in renewing support and in encouraging donors to contribute at higher levels. A well-run professional telephone campaign can be effective for renewing lapsed donors and for prospecting.

As mentioned, it is difficult to motivate volunteers to make cold calls; however, paid phoners have an economic incentive to keep dialing.

The operational needs for a professional phone campaign are similar to the requirements for a volunteer phone-a-thon: scripts, tips, training, and approximately 40 names per caller-hour. This latter requirement can be the determining factor in whether a professional phone campaign is an appropriate strategy for an organization. Assume that an organization wants to conduct a one-month phone campaign. Further assume that 10 phoners will be employed per evening, 6:00 to 9:00 P.M., 5 evenings per week or approximately 20 evenings per month. With these assumptions, how many prospect names will be need? To answer this question, multiply the number of callers times the number of hours per evening times the number of evenings times 40 names per volunteer-hour. With this formula we get $10 \times 3 \times 20 \times 40 = 24,000$ prospect names needed for the month. A two-week intensive effort would require 12,000 prospects to call.

Once an organization decides to use a professional phone campaign, a number of choices exist regarding how to implement the strategy. Some service providers offer turn-key operations, with phoners and phone banks. They are skilled at writing effective telephone scripts. And if an organization has a potential for broad-based support, they can even furnish qualified prospect lists.

Another alternative would be to hire an experienced phone campaign manager who would help write scripts, hire and train the phoners, design the control and reporting system, and manage the day-to-day phone campaign operation.

One main difference between a volunteer effort and a professional phone campaign is the level of detail in the reporting system. Volunteers like to know how much they raised individually and as a group. Paid phoners need the same information; however, reporting is much more detailed. In a professional system each caller's productivity is monitored. How many hours each phoner called, the number of phone numbers dialed each hour, the number reached each hour, the percentage that made a firm contribution, the total dollars pledged per hour, and the average pledge attained by each phoner are all maintained and summarized on a nightly and weekly Phone Campaign Summary Form (see Exhibit 10-7).

The information on this form is used in calculating compensation. It is also a powerful motivational tool. Perhaps its greatest use is in determining

EXHIBIT 10-7   CALL SUMMARY FORM

Caller Evaluation Form   Date _____

Caller Name	# Hrs. Calling	Total #'s Dialed	# Dialed per Hr.	# Reached	# Reached per Hr.	# Pledges	$ Pledged per Hr.	Total $ Pledged

which phoners should be retained and which should be let go. While not-for-profits are reluctant to fire a volunteer, it makes no economic sense to retain the services of a paid phoner who is not productive or who cannot produce with good prospects to call.

Most compensation methods for paid phoners rely on a combination of a base rate plus commissions. This phone industry norm appears to conflict with several professional codes of ethics that bar percentage fundraising. Still, many universities hire student phoners and compensate them based on the amount they raise. Indeed, many not-for-profit organizations that uphold the highest ethical standards pay commissions to their phoners. The AFP Code of Ethical Principles states "Members shall work for a salary or fee, not percentage based compensation or a commission." Clearly AFP members—and by extension, senior development officers—should not be compensated based on how much they raise. However, development professionals and the organization must decide whether it is appropriate or ethical to employ percentage compensated phoners. An alternative to

consider is to pay a favorable flat rate per hour and be doubly sure that only the most productive callers are retained.

No matter how callers are compensated, costs and performance must be monitored. Paid phoning can require a major investment. The cost to raise a dollar can range from $.30 to $.50 when calling current, past, and lapsed donors. The cost to raise a dollar can be considerably more when calling prospects who have never donated before, reaching $.75 or more per dollar raised. The phone prospecting effort might even cost a bit more than is taken in. As with mail-prospecting programs, the aim of the phone-prospecting program is donor acquisition. By investing in attaining new donors and aggressively renewing their support, creating a phone donor acquisition program may well be as cost-effective as—or even more so than—a mail donor acquisition program.

The direct response nature of telephone solicitations allows professionals responsible for fundraising to test, analyze results, make incremental improvements, and implement a cost-effective strategy that can serve as an important component of the comprehensive resource development program.

Special Event Fundraisers

Moderation is a fatal thing. Nothing succeeds like excess.

—Oscar Wilde, *A Woman of No Importance*

Special events for fundraising purposes, such as testimonial dinners, celebrity waiter dinners, charity golf tournaments, art auctions, outdoor fiestas, garage sales, decorator showcases, Las Vegas nights, bike tours, runs, and raffles, enable not-for-profit agencies to increase the public's awareness of their mission and programs. Special events also create numerous opportunities for volunteer participation. As fundraising vehicles, these events tend to be costly, both in terms of efforts and dollars expended in relation to the net dollars contributed.

Even simple events require at least six months' lead time for planning, volunteer recruitment, site selection, preparation, implementation, and ticket sales. Larger events—especially banquets that require facilities to be booked far in advance—may take a year or more to plan. Fundraising special events should be well planned with careful attention to budget projections. The event should net at least 50 percent of the gross income, preferably more. Sponsorships significantly increase the net income of special events. Moreover, tributes or guests of honor tend to increase each event's fundraising potential.

The best special events are fun. Each year's success can help ensure the next year's positive outcome. Any event undertaken should be consistent with an organization's image, purpose, and mission.

In many organizations, a guild, auxiliary, or other support group takes responsibility for special events. These auxiliaries take pride in their autonomy. They determine the degree of staff support they need. This support almost always includes access to the in-house mailing list. Additionally, staff involvement can range from an advisory capacity to full-blown active support of the event.

The recruitment of a dynamic chairperson will help ensure the success of the special event. Ideal chairpeople have control of their time, are enthusiastic, have a wide circle of acquaintances, have organizing skills, and are fun to work with.

CHOOSING A SPECIAL EVENT

Auxiliary and volunteer support groups devote considerable effort to choosing, then staging their fundraising special events. Perhaps the most crucial step is deciding which events to do. Here is a step-by-step approach that can help fundraisers make the right decisions.

1. List as many special event fundraising ideas as possible.
2. Evaluate the potential to generate significant net revenue. Sketch in preliminary budgets using best estimates of the following:

   Income

   a. Ticket price multiplied by an estimate of the number of ticket purchasers (or table price multiplied by the number of tables); plus
   b. The amount expected to be raised through event sponsorships; plus
   c. Journal or program book ad sales; plus
   d. The amount expected to be raised from a silent auction, if any; plus
   e. The amount expected to be raised from a raffle, if any; plus
   f. The amount expected to be raised from shirt sales, if any; plus
   g. The amount expected from other sources of income unique to the event.

   This is the projected gross income. Now subtract the total dollars the organization expects to spend on the following:

Expenses

a. Meals, drinks, and other food expenses

b. Printing of event program books

c. Advance notification card or letter, if any

d. Invitation printing (don't try to save money on this expense)

e. Postage for the advance card and invitation

f. Ticket printing, if any

g. Staging and audio/video, if any

h. Music and entertainment, if any

i. Flowers and table decorations, if any

j. Awards

k. Photographer

l. Miscellaneous and other expenses unique to the event

Total the projected expenses and subtract them from the projected income; this is the estimated net income. In most modest-size cities, many fundraising professionals suggest that not-for-profit organizations should not undertake a major special event unless the organization foresees a realistic possibility of netting $40,000 or more. Please note this is a minimal standard. Too many smaller-scale efforts drain the organization's resources.

Now that the net potential of the events being studied has been determined, it is time to look at some other criteria.

- The event should be fun.
- The event should be consistent with the organization's image, purpose, and mission.
- The event should appeal to the organization's constituency and to others.
- The event should appeal to potential sponsors—especially high-end sponsors.

IMPLEMENTING THE EVENT

Gerald M. Plessner, an expert in special event fundraising, used to refer to his "Approximately Ten Commandments of Special Event Fundraising" (see Exhibit 11-1). These tongue-in-cheek suggestions remind

EXHIBIT 11-1   **APPROXIMATELY TEN COMMANDMENTS OF SPECIAL EVENT FUNDRAISING**

Gerald M. Plessner's Approximately Ten Commandments of Special Event Fundraising

1. The response card must fit inside the response envelope.
2. The entertainment must be auditioned.
3. There shall be an honoree for every special event—even a garage sale.
4. Thou shall count the tables and chairs before the first guest arrives.
5. The price of the ticket must provide net income to the causes.
6. Publicity will not be expected to sell one ticket, for only people sell tickets.
7. The honoree must genuinely deserve the tribute, and the chair must be a person of stature.
8. The honoree and chair must know about the cause—even if they learn about it only when they are recruited.
9. The event must be of the quality expected for the ticket price. Thou shall not take your donors for granted!
10. A lousy program will not hurt this year's participation, but as surely as night follows day, it will kill you next year.
11. Promises count for nothing, but cash (and sometimes written pledges) do.

development planners to devote sufficient attention to detailed planning and to effective marketing. Set the right tone for the event by designing an eye-catching invitation. Help the event by generating a great deal of publicity. But the tickets must be sold. The board and volunteers must take responsibility for this vital function.

When organizing the event, remember that sponsorships produce a large portion of net income. So seek larger-level sponsorships. Reread Chapter 8. Apply the principles related to major gift fundraising. And periodically raise the price of sponsorships.

For success in the future, volunteer workers and staff should maintain detailed records and notes concerning each special event fundraiser. Also remember to plan and allow what appears to be *more* than sufficient time for each phase of the event. Work backward in building time lines (see Exhibit 11-2).

Structure each event to have several donation levels. Create gift opportunities that require much more than the simple ticket price. Sponsorships, various size ads in a program book, table purchases, and other creative approaches can significantly increase net income.

EXHIBIT 11-2   SAMPLE SPECIAL EVENT TIME LINE

TASK	WHO	BY WHEN
Study all your options. Sketch in budgets for various special events. Outline a preliminary marketing plan for each of your options. Determine the most profitable, fun event possible.	Special Event Committee	6 or 7 months prior to expected event date
Make firm recommendation as to nature of event, estimated number of attendees, timing of event, ticket price, marketing plan, and budget.	Special Event Committee report to Board	Preferably 6 months prior to event
Secure board approval of plan. Then confirm site and date. Negotiate prices within budget limits.	Board approval; Special Event Committee follow-up	Preferably 6 months prior to event
Confirm guest of honor. Begin seeking sponsorships. If you are seeking ads for a journal or program book, begin these sales now also.	Special Event Committee recruits guest of honor; Sponsorship Committee seeks sponsorship	5 1/2 months prior to event
Secure sponsorship(s) . . . coordinate solicitation with fund drive. (Choose prospects most likely to respond generously to special events.) Staff prepares personalized solicitation materials. Continue to seek ad sales if needed.	Special Event Committee with help from other board members or staff, if needed	Wrap up solicitations 3 months prior to event (Allows sponsors to be acknowledged in pre-event publicity and printed materials)
Conclude journal or program book ad sales.	Appropriate Subcommittee	Not later than 2 months prior to event (Design the program and send to the printer about now)
Secure door prizes, auction items, raffle items, etc., if any. Also secure in-kind contributions of other goods and services that will help reduce the cash expense.	Special Event Committee or appropriate Subcommittee	Begin 5 months prior to event; complete as much as possible 3 months before event
Implement marketing plan. Budget more than expected for the invitation. Remember that tickets must be sold. Urge board members and other volunteers to buy and sell tickets.	Board and Special Event Committee	Presales at least 2 months prior to event
Write a simple letter or design a pre-invitation advance notice card and mail to prime constituents.	Appropriate Subcommittee	In mail 2 months prior to event

(continued)

EXHIBIT 11-2   (CONTINUED)

TASK	WHO	BY WHEN
Design, print, and mail attractive invitations. (The invitations alone could be expected to produce a 1 to 2 percent response rate with a good list. Again, the tickets must be sold. An attractive invitation will help sales.)	Special Event Committee	Work backward from event. Invitations should arrive at prospects' homes not later than 3 weeks prior to event. Allow 2 weeks for printing and mail handling. Allow 1 week for typesetting and layout. Therefore, you should have a complete mockup of the invitation and envelopes *at least* 6 weeks prior to the event.
Plan details such as record keeping, event check-in (eliminate bottlenecks), entertainment, scripts and run-sheets, decorations, color schemes, etc.	Special Event Committee	Well in advance of event
Stage a memorable event. Net sufficient income. HAVE A GOOD TIME!	EVERYBODY	Date of event
Consider special event opportunities where an outside sponsor runs the event and donates a portion of the proceeds to the organization. Make case-by-case decisions.	Board	As opportunities arise

Monitor the productivity ratio—the event's net income divided by the total number of volunteer and staff hours. This figure should *far exceed* minimum wages.

Example:

The Hokey Annual Celebrity Cook-a-Thon collects income totaling $7,500 from ticket sales. The publicity, food, rental, and other expenses totaled $5,000. Thus the event netted $2,500.

However, volunteers and staff spent a total of 6 months organizing the event, and 1,000 hours were devoted to making the event a reality. Thus the event produced only $2.50 per hour.

This would be a good event to restructure or cancel. Many events can be salvaged by seeking larger sponsorships and by layering them with additional income-producing opportunities, such as silent auctions, raffles, and/or event commemorative ad book sales. Again, if the volunteers and

staff work hard over a period of time, the organization should realize a significant return for the effort.

Cause-Related Marketing

Cause-related marketing is somewhat similar to corporate sponsorships. However, cause-related marketing goes a bit further. Two essential agreements are made between the organization and a corporation: The not-for-profit organization lends its name and good reputation to the corporation, while the corporation uses this tie to encourage sales of its goods and services and donates a portion of the increased sales to the not-for-profit.

In nationwide campaigns, large not-for-profit organizations may receive substantial public relations and financial benefits from the cause-related marketing program. During such campaigns, the corporations advertise extensively and promote the link to the not-for-profit organization. The national campaigns net anywhere from $250,000 to millions of dollars for the not-for-profit organization.

Even grassroots organizations can benefit from similar arrangements. For example, a bookstore might donate 10 percent of a day's proceeds to a not-for-profit organization. A restaurant chain may donate a percentage of a week's sales to the agency.

To conclude, not-for-profit organizations of every size can benefit from such arrangements. However, a few cautionary notes are in order:

- Before allowing anyone to use an organization's logo and name, be sure to state the terms and conditions in a written agreement.
- The agreement should describe the nature of the promotion and give a clear description of the product or service being promoted.
- The agreement should have a start and stop date.
- The agreement should describe the placement of advertising and the geographic area covered.
- The agreement should contain the percentage or fixed amount per sale of the product or service to be donated.
- The agreement may contain a minimum donation amount.

Of course, the goods and services must be of a quality and nature consistent with the image and good reputation of the not-for-profit organization. Exhibit 11-3 presents a sample cause-related marketing agreement.

EXHIBIT 11-3   SAMPLE CAUSE-RELATED
MARKETING AGREEMENT

1. This agreement is made by and between ABC Charity, a charitable, nonprofit corporation, having its principal office at 1234 Giving Lane, Pledge, NM 56789, and (*Full Name of Sponsoring Corporation*), and contains the conditions related to the Cause Related Marketing Project designed to raise funds for the ABC Charity.

2. The term of this Agreement will be from (*Beginning Date*) to (*End Date*). The term of this Agreement may be extended, prior to its expiration, if both parties mutually agree in writing to such an extension.

3. The name and/or logo of ABC Charity may not be imprinted on or used in association with any products, goods or services offered by (*Full name of sponsoring corporation*) without prior written approval from ABC Charity. Such permission will not be unreasonably withheld and will be granted for promotional purposes in a manner consistent with the ABC Charity proposal to (*Full name of sponsoring corporation*) dated (*date of original or amended proposal*).

4. ABC Charity must review and approve all promotional materials, including, but not limited to print and electronic media advertisements, letters, news releases, and promotional packaging that use the name and/or logo of the ABC Charity, prior to production, printing, and publication of such materials. Such approval will not be unreasonably withheld. ABC Charity must be allowed reasonable turnaround time for such approval.

5. In all printed and electronically produced materials, (*Full name of sponsoring corporation*) will use ABC Charity's name and logo in a manner consistent with ABC Charity's graphic standards. ABC Charity will furnish (*Full name of sponsoring corporation*) with a copy of the graphic standards together with ABC Charity's logo and name on hard copy and computer disk suitable for production.

6. All promotional materials must fully and truthfully state the percentage of net proceeds that will be contributed to ABC Charity and/or the portion of the product price or the fixed amount, amount per sale/transaction that is to benefit the ABC Charity.

7. After approval has been granted, both ABC Charity and the (*Full name of sponsoring corporation*) will certify in writing the final text of all materials to be used in the Promotion. Such certification will state as follows: "We, (*Name and Title of ABC Charity Representative and Representative of Sponsoring Corporation*) certify that the attached advertising and/or promotional materials represents the final, agreed upon language to be used in the promotion."

8. Any additional or new corporate sponsors of this Cause Related Marketing Project need to be approved in advance by ABC Charity. Sponsorship will not imply any product endorsement.

9. At its discretion, ABC Charity may require (*Full name of sponsoring corporation*) and/or any additional corporate sponsors to print or otherwise contain a disclaimer in all of the promotional materials which shall read as follows: "The ABC Charity name and logo are used with its permission which in no way constitutes an endorsement, express or implied, of this product or service."

10. ABC Charity will receive (*number*) percent of the net proceeds (defined as gross proceeds minus the cost of manufacturing and promoting the service and/or product) generated by this promotion or state fixed dollar amount per sale/transaction or otherwise describe the amount ABC Charity will receive in relationship to the Cause Related Marketing Project. Such funds will be forwarded on a monthly basis by the 15th day of the month following receipt by the (*Full name of sponsoring corporation*) to the following address: (*1234 Giving Lane, Pledge, NM 56789*). Checks will be made payable to the ABC Charity.

EXHIBIT 11-3   (CONTINUED)

11. (Optional) (*Full name of sponsoring corporation*) guarantees that ABC Charity will receive not less than (*fixed dollar amount*) in connection with this promotion. Such minimal amount shall be contributed in full not later than (*reasonable specific date following the close of the promotion*).

12. Three weeks after the close of the promotion, or three weeks following the expiration of this Agreement, on or about (*date Agreement will end*), or, if earlier, its termination, whichever comes first, ABC Charity will receive a full and final accounting of all funds collected and expended from the (*Full name of sponsoring corporation*).

13. The ABC Charity will incur no financial liability for this Cause Related Marketing Project. All financial liabilities will be assumed by the (*Full name of sponsoring corporation*).

14. The ABC Charity may be the recipient of funds from other similar promotions. Therefore, it is understood and agreed that this Agreement creates no exclusive rights for (*Full name of sponsoring corporation*) for such Cause Related Marketing Projects.

15. The ABC Charity reserves the right to inspect the financial records of the (*Full name of sponsoring corporation*) regarding the funds collected as a result of this promotion.

16. The (*Full name of sponsoring corporation*) agrees that it will comply with all state and/or municipal charitable solicitation statutes and/or ordinances which purport to affect or apply to this promotion. The (*Full name of sponsoring corporation*) agrees that it will not use the ABC Charity tax exemption in any manner as a part of this promotion, nor will the (*Full name of sponsoring corporation*) represent to the public that it enjoys any tax exempt rights or privileges as a result of its participation in this promotion, nor will (*Full name of sponsoring corporation*) state that any portion of the purchase price for any of the (*Full name of sponsoring corporation's*) goods or services is tax deductible for charitable purposes.

17. All ABC Charity approvals and authorizations are to be secured through (*full names and titles of ABC Charity representatives authorized to make decisions concerning this Cause Related Marketing Agreement*).

18. The ABC Charity reserves the right at its sole discretion to terminate this Agreement at any time by giving 15 days written notice to the (*Full name of sponsoring corporation*). Any default in, or breach of, the terms and conditions of this Agreement by the (*Full name of sponsoring corporation*) will result in its immediate termination, upon written notification to that effect from ABC Charity to the (*Full name of sponsoring corporation*).

19. This Agreement constitutes the sole agreement between the parties hereto and no amendment, modification, or waiver of any of the terms and conditions hereof shall be valid unless in writing.

20. This Agreement is made in and shall be governed by the laws of the state of (*Name of State*).

_____   _____

(Name & Title of Authorized Sponsoring Organization)   Date

_____   _____

(Name & Title of Authorized ABC Charity Representative)   Date

(NOTE:)

This is not offered as legal advice. Rather, this sample Agreement can serve as a point of departure for creating a Contract that is specific to each organization's unique circumstances. The not-for-profit organization and the sponsoring corporation will want to consult with their own attorneys.

The Philanthropic Advisory Service of the Council of Better Business Bureaus, Inc., has developed a statement of standards concerning joint charitable/corporate marketing ventures, which is included here as Exhibit 11–4.

EXHIBIT 11-4   COUNCIL OF BETTER BUSINESS BUREAUS,INC

Application of the CBBB Standards for Charitable Solicitations
to
Cause-Related Marketing

The Philanthropic Advisory Service (PAS) is the division of the Council of Better Business Bureaus (CBBB) that monitors and reports on nationally soliciting charitable organizations.

PAS reviews these organizations in relation to the 23 voluntary CBBB Standards for Charitable Solicitations. The Standards cover five basic areas: Public Accountability, Use of Funds, Solicitations and Informational Materials, Fund-Raising Practices, and Governance.

Established donors and potential contributors are increasingly interested in the accountability of publicly soliciting charities. New modes of fund raising and accelerated competition for the charitable dollar have underscored the importance of voluntary standards for charities.

An extremely popular, but comparatively new, method of fund raising involves promoting charity programs as part of marketing commercial products or services. This practice, often referred to as *cause-related marketing,* is being used to promote a wide range of local and national charitable programs together with specific consumer goods and services. These fund-raising/marketing campaigns feature everything from affinity credit cards and household products to fast foods.

These campaigns can be significant revenue sources for many nonprofit organizations and popular public relations and marketing vehicles for many businesses.

The voluntary CBBB Standards for Charitable Solicitations neither recommend nor prohibit such joint ventures. The choice of fund-raising methods is the decision of each organization. The voluntary CBBB Standards call for certain disclosures to be made at the point of solicitation and for certain controls to be in place even for cause-related marketing. Since you are a possible participant in such a campaign, we encourage your cooperation in ensuring that these disclosures and controls are in place as you plan and execute these programs. These basic procedures can help assure the participating charity's compliance with the applicable voluntary CBBB Standards and provide full accountability to the donor/consumer about how this purchase of a product or service will benefit the stated cause. While many campaigns have included the recommended information, others have been vague, unclear, or contradictory about how participation helps the named cause.

Recommendations

Participants in cause-related marketing should include the following elements in their campaigns if they wish to ensure the charitable organization's compliance with the voluntary CBBB Standards calling for charities (1) to establish and exercise controls over fund-raising activities conducted for their benefit and (2) to include certain information in solicitations made in conjunction with the sale of goods or services:

EXHIBIT 11-4   (CONTINUED)

1. A written agreement that gives (a) the corporation formal permission to use the charity's name and logo and (b) the charity prior review and approval of all joint-venture solicitations that use the charity's name and

2. Cause-related advertisements that specify (a) the portion of the product or service price or the fixed amount per sale/transaction to benefit the charity and, if applicable, the maximum or minimum amount the charity will receive, (b) the full name of the charity, (c) an address or phone number to contact for additional information about the charity or the campaign, and (d) the term of the campaign.

The additional suggestions listed below are not required to meet the CBBB Standards. However, in the interest of full disclosure and public accountability, PAS recommends that corporations consider the following questions:

- Some states now have specific guidelines for sales made in conjunction with charities. Does the promotion follow these regulations?
- Does the written agreement (a) indicate how long the campaign will last, (b) specify how and when charitable funds will be distributed, and (c) explain any steps that will be taken in case of a disagreement or unforeseen result with the promotion?
- Does the corporation have financial controls in place to process and record the monies received to benefit the charity?
- Will the corporation issue a financial report at the end of the campaign (or annually, if the campaign lasts more than a year), which identifies: (a) the total amount collected for the charity, (b) any campaign expenses, and (c) how much the charity received?

The Philanthropic Advisory Service welcomes your questions and comments about the issues outlined in this letter and stands ready to provide assistance to corporations and charities interested in following the above recommendations.

—Philanthropic Advisory Service
Memo to Charity and Corporate
Community Initially Issued
9/2/88.

NOTE: A complete copy of the 23 voluntary CBBB Standards for Charitable Solicitations is available free with a self-addressed, stamped, business-size envelope by writing to: Philanthropic Advisory Service, Council of Better Business Bureaus, Inc., 4200 Wilson Blvd., Suite 800, Arlington, VA 22203. These standards are also available by visiting the Web Site at *www.bbb.org*.

Grantsmanship

*The desire to understand the world and the desire to reform it are
the two great engines of progress.*

—Bertrand Russell, *Marriage and Morals*

Grants are the lifeblood of many not-for-profit organizations—especially those with long-term relationships with their major funders. The size of grants varies greatly from modest sums for grassroots organizations to multimillion-dollar grants for well-established institutions. Yet, as important as they are, grants are still surrounded by some common myths.

The most common myth is that writing grants is difficult. Actually, anyone who can follow directions and write clear, simple sentences can write a successful grant proposal.

The other widespread myth about grants is that they are the most important part of any not-for-profit organization's funding pattern. This is simply not true. Remember that 82 percent of all contributions comes from individuals. Bequests account for another 6 percent. Corporate philanthropy accounts for approximately 5 percent of annual contributions. Thus foundation support approximates only 7 percent of private sector annual contributions.

WHAT IS A GRANT?

Grants come from three main sources: government, foundations, and corporations. Each grant is an implicit or explicit agreement or contract. The grantor provides funds. The recipient, or grantee, commits to plan and implement some special project, or agrees to provide the community with a

needed service. Even grants for operating support carry with them an obligation to use the funder's resources wisely to help continue the work of the not-for-profit agency.

Grants are voluntary contributions. No matter how well a project fits the grantor's guidelines, an organization has no inherent right to that grant. In almost all cases the number of applications the grantor receives far exceeds the grant funds available. Moreover, the grantor has every right to assess the merits of a proposal based on any criteria the grantor chooses to adopt.

GOVERNMENT GRANTS AND CONTRACTS

The federal government of the United States of America is the largest source of grant funds in the world. Universities, national laboratories, colleges, and other institutions conduct research funded by the federal government. Agencies such as the National Institutes of Health fund biomedical research. The Department of Energy funds a broad spectrum of research in nuclear physics, alternative energy sources, and issues related to the safety and reliability of the nation's nuclear stockpile.

In addition to research, the federal government funds a wide array of programs—ranging from art exhibits, to after-school programs for children at risk, to job placement programs, to programs that benefit zoos.

Information about grant programs is most frequently published as a request for proposals (RFP). The RFP usually includes: a description of the work required, the time frame or schedule contemplated, detailed application instructions and requirements, and the criteria by which the proposal will be evaluated. RFPs always contain a submission deadline.

Not-for-profit agencies that have been awarded past grants from the government agency often receive RFPs directly from the agency. Similarly, not-for-profit organizations can request to be placed on the government agency's list of RFP recipients. Information about federal government grants also can be found by exploring the *Catalog of Federal Domestic Assistance*. This invaluable resource can be explored on the Internet at *www.gsa.gov/fdac*.

Many federal programs are administered through state and local government agencies or departments. Development professionals can ensure that they are notified of all relevant grant opportunities by maintaining strong relationships with local officials and program administrators. One highly

successful not-for-profit organization receives at least three notices or RFPs for each grant possibility. It obtains timely information by reviewing the literature regularly. It also receives phone calls and notices directly from friends working in the government agencies. Finally it has created a network of supporters familiar with government grant opportunities who keep the organization current on grant programs that fit its mission.

Government applications are frequently voluminous. Applicants should follow instructions with great care. Prior to submitting the proposal, applicants should double check the instructions and be sure that the proposal is complete. As with all grant applications, it is helpful to have someone not familiar with the project read the proposal. Often program developers or grant writers understand what they meant to say. However, an objective reader can help find places where the proposal is not clear.

FOUNDATIONS

There are nine major types of foundations: community, family, corporate, general-purpose, operating, philanthropic, private, and special-purpose foundations and public charities.

Community Foundation. Most often a community foundation is a publicly supported organization that makes grants for social, educational, religious, or other charitable purposes in a specific community or region.

- Funds are derived from many donor sources.
- Retention of donations as endowment usually is encouraged.
- Income from endowment/corpus is used to make grants.

Family Foundation. In a family foundation, funds are derived from members of a single family. Family members generally serve as officers or board members and play an influential role in grant-making decisions.

Corporate Foundation. Corporate foundations are established to coordinate the philanthropic interests of the founding corporation. These foundations are very explicit as to their fields of interest, often limiting grants to causes related to corporate profits and interests, such as the communities where they are headquartered or in which they have branches.

General-Purpose Foundation. General-purpose foundations are independent private foundations that award grants in many different fields of interest.

Operating Foundation. Operating foundations are funds or endowments designated by the Internal Revenue Service as private foundations; however, they differ from typical private foundations in that their primary purpose is to conduct research, promote social welfare, or engage in other programs determined by their governing body or establishment charter. These foundations may make some grants, but the sum is generally small relative to the funds used for their own programs.

Philanthropic Foundation. Philanthropic foundations are corporations or trusts that have been created with contributed funds, whether by an individual, family, corporation, or community, for support of 501(c)(3) organizations.

Private Foundation. While there is a technical definition of "private foundation" in the federal income tax law, the generic definition of the term is as follows: A private foundation is a 501(c)(3) organization that is originally funded from one source, that derives revenue from earnings on its investments, and that makes grants to other charitable organizations rather than administering its own programs. Gifts to private foundations are not normally as advantageous to the donor as gifts to a public charity.

Public Charity. A public charity is a 501(c)(3) organization that is not a private foundation, either because it is "publicly supported" (i.e., it normally derives at least one-third of its support from gifts and other qualified sources) or it functions as a "supporting organization" to other public charities. Some public charities engage in grant-making activities but most engage in direct service activities. Public charities are eligible for maximum tax-deductible contributions from the public and are not subject to the same rules and restrictions as private foundations. They are also referred to as public foundations.

Special-Purpose Foundation. Special-purpose foundations are public foundations that focus their grant-making activities on one or a few special areas of interest, such as a foundation that makes grants only in the area of cancer research or child development.

FOUNDATION RESEARCH

Information about foundations—guidelines, application instructions, gift information, contacts, and foundation priorities—can be obtained easily from the Foundation Center and its cooperating collections in each state.

The Foundation Center's Web site (*www.fndcenter.org*) contains up-to-date information about the location of the closest Foundation Center cooperating collection. Many universities also have foundation research libraries or materials. Also consider participating in the Foundation Center Associates Program—a fee-based research service of the Foundation Center. Alternatively, a number of fee-based foundation databases are available. These service providers can furnish not-for-profit organizations lists and application information concerning likely sources of foundation grants.

Stay plugged in. Maintain a network of foundation program officers and contacts. Also, schedule foundation research on a regular basis.

When beginning research, focus on grantors whose interests match the organization's mission and programs. Researchers using CD-ROM information at Foundation Center cooperating collections begin by searching on the Grants Database—looking most attentively at recipient states that match their own and for key words that most closely match their projects. Fundraisers using books as their primary reference materials should start their research with the subject index found within the *Grants Index*. Using this index, users can quickly find numbers that refer to specific grants for projects similar to the one being considered. The Grant Listings section of the *Grants Index* indicates which foundation made the grant, the amount funded, and information about the project. Armed with this information, turn to another reference source—the *Foundation Directory*. This very valuable book contains detailed information about thousands of foundations. Entries include the foundation's address and phone number, financial data, the foundation's purpose, types of support, limitations, publications, and application information (see Exhibit 12-1).

Summarize the information about each foundation on a form similar to that in Exhibit 12-2.

Some researchers enjoy working with books. They say that, when their eyes are free to scan the pages, they can uncover more subject key words that match their organization's programs and interests. These researchers report that they get good leads and ideas by conducting their research using the traditional foundation print resources.

Others find using print materials tedious and prefer computer searches of foundation databases. By searching on key words and geographic locations, they can quickly retrieve a listing of foundations that may be interested in funding their organization's projects.

EXHIBIT 12-1   SAMPLE ENTRY

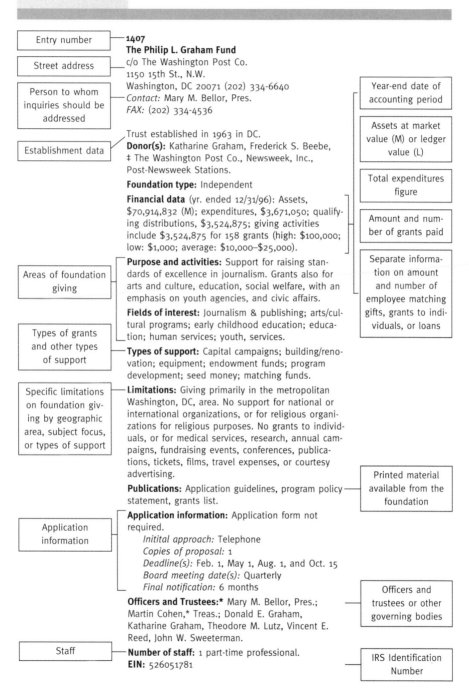

Entry number —1407
The Philip L. Graham Fund

Street address — c/o The Washington Post Co.
1150 15th St., N.W.

Person to whom inquiries should be addressed — Washington, DC 20071 (202) 334-6640
Contact: Mary M. Bellor, Pres.
FAX: (202) 334-4536

Establishment data — Trust established in 1963 in DC.
Donor(s): Katharine Graham, Frederick S. Beebe,
‡ The Washington Post Co., Newsweek, Inc.,
Post-Newsweek Stations.

Foundation type: Independent

Financial data (yr. ended 12/31/96): Assets,
$70,914,832 (M); expenditures, $3,671,050; qualifying distributions, $3,524,875; giving activities include $3,524,875 for 158 grants (high: $100,000; low: $1,000; average: $10,000–$25,000).

Areas of foundation giving — Purpose and activities: Support for raising standards of excellence in journalism. Grants also for arts and culture, education, social welfare, with an emphasis on youth agencies, and civic affairs.

Types of grants and other types of support — Fields of interest: Journalism & publishing; arts/cultural programs; early childhood education; education; human services; youth, services.

Types of support: Capital campaigns; building/renovation; equipment; endowment funds; program development; seed money; matching funds.

Specific limitations on foundation giving by geographic area, subject focus, or types of support — Limitations: Giving primarily in the metropolitan Washington, DC, area. No support for national or international organizations, or for religious organizations for religious purposes. No grants to individuals, or for medical services, research, annual campaigns, fundraising events, conferences, publications, tickets, films, travel expenses, or courtesy advertising.

Publications: Application guidelines, program policy statement, grants list.

Application information — Application information: Application form not required.
    Initital approach: Telephone
    Copies of proposal: 1
    Deadline(s): Feb. 1, May 1, Aug. 1, and Oct. 15
    Board meeting date(s): Quarterly
    Final notification: 6 months

Officers and Trustees:* Mary M. Bellor, Pres.;
Martin Cohen,* Treas.; Donald E. Graham,
Katharine Graham, Theodore M. Lutz, Vincent E.
Reed, John W. Sweeterman.

Staff — Number of staff: 1 part-time professional.
EIN: 526051781

Year-end date of accounting period

Assets at market value (M) or ledger value (L)

Total expenditures figure

Amount and number of grants paid

Separate information on amount and number of employee matching gifts, grants to individuals, or loans

Printed material available from the foundation

Officers and trustees or other governing bodies

IRS Identification Number

EXHIBIT 12-1   (CONTINUED)

Selected grants —— **Selected grants:** The following grants were reported in
1995.

$100,000 to District of Columbia School of Law, DC.
Toward campaign to establish Joseph L. Rauh, Jr., Chair of
Public Interest Law

$100,000 to YMCA, Down East Family Center, Ellsworth,
ME. For capital campaign.

$75,000 to Shakespeare Theater at the Folger, DC. 2
grants: $50,000 (For Shakespeare Free For All at Carter
Barron Amphitheatre), $25,000 (Toward Shakespeare Free
For All at Carter Barron Amphitheatre).

$75,000 to Strathmore Hall Arts Center, North Bethesda,
MD. For capital campaign for renovation and expansion.

$50,000 to Carnegie Institution of Washington, DC. For
Carnegie Academy for Science Education (CASE), program
that trains elementary school teachers in DC public
schools in interactive science and mathematics.

$40,000 to Best Friends Foundation, DC. To continue and
expand program in DC elementary schools to help prepare girls for successful adulthood.

$35,000 to Catholic Charities, DC. For continued support
of Teen Life Choices Center, helping youngsters make
positive decisions about their futures.

$30,000 to John F. Kennedy Center for the Performing
Arts, DC. For final payment of grant for activities and programs aimed at better serving people with disabilities.

$30,000 to Sasha Bruce Youthworks, DC. For full-time
instructor at Learning Center, providing academic remedia-
tion, GED preparation and other educational services to
vulnerable youth.

Whatever method was used to uncover the information, the next step is
to get the most up-to-date information directly from the foundation. Research already has indicated what each foundation publishes. Now write a
letter requesting foundation publications and general information (see Exhibit 12-3).

Be especially careful to record and monitor deadlines. If the foundation
accepts grant applications at any time, create an artificial deadline. Look to
see if there is any information concerning scheduled foundation board
meetings. If so, schedule the deadline one and one-half to two months
prior to the board meeting. Then summarize your plan of action by creating a chronological summary of grants due (see Exhibit 12-4).

Foundation Name: _____

Address: _____

Address: _____

City, State, Zip: _____   Phone: _____

Contact: _____   Title: _____

Areas of Interest: _____

Average Gift Range: _____   High: _____   Low: _____

Sample Project: _____   Sample Amount: _____

Deadline(s): _____

Board Meeting Dates: _____

Relevant Limitations: _____

Application Procedure: _____

Comments & Language from Mission or Priority Statement: _____

_____

_____

_____

Other Relevant Info: _____

_____

Source(s): _____

Date Research Information Gathered: _____

Use the following lines to summarize dates of telephone and mail contacts, subject matter and results: _____

_____

_____

_____

At all stages of research, remember that the aim is to uncover foundations that are most likely to fund the organization's projects. Remain focused on the appropriate amount to request and the foundation's philanthropic interests. When conducting research, carefully note all instructions pertaining to application procedures.

PROJECT DEVELOPMENT

Government, foundation, and corporate grantors tend to favor innovative programs that are responsive to pressing societal needs. Some grantors pro-

EXHIBIT I2-3   LETTER REQUESTING GRANTS INFORMATION

Date

Mr. Jonathan Grantsofficer
Director of Foundation Communications
Goliath Foundation
P.O. Box 1234
Hartford, CT 07483-1234

Dear Mr. Grantsofficer:

The XYZ Not-for-Profit Organization is considering a number of initiatives and capital projects that we believe match the philanthropic interests of the Goliath Foundation.

I would appreciate any grant guidelines, application forms, or other information you might have concerning proposals to Goliath Foundation.

Please send such information to:

    Harvey Teller
    XYZ Not-for-Profit Organization
    PO Box 1234
    Philadelphia, PA 19116

Thank you.
Sincerely,

Harvey Teller
XYZ Not-for-Profit Organization

---

vide general operating support for not-for-profit organizations. Many do not. Some grantors provide grants for capital or building projects. Many do not. Most grantors favor special projects.

Maintain detailed information about the need your organization serves. For example, if the organization serves homeless people, maintain information concerning the numbers of such people in the region and the root causes of their homelessness. Also maintain statistics concerning the number of people served and how they have benefited from the programs.

| EXHIBIT 12-4 | FOUNDATION DEADLINES SUMMARY FORM (IN CHRONOLOGICAL ORDER OF DEADLINE) |

Foundation	Deadline	Project	Request Amount	Comments

Review the literature. Ask "What programs have worked elsewhere? What pressing needs do the people we serve face? What services are most likely to provide long-term solutions? What projects or programs might serve as a model for the rest of the nation?"

Whenever possible, communicate directly with foundation program officers. What projects or programs are of greatest interest to the foundation? Has the foundation contemplated any initiatives in which your organization might play a role? Do your foundation contacts know of any other foundations that may be interested in your program or project?

Foundations respond most favorably to well-planned projects that are innovative yet feasible. High-sounding projects that claim to end poverty or assure world peace are simply unbelievable. Similarly, proposals that sound very vague are less likely to be funded than projects that have a tangible quality to them. A vague proposal for support of a farm that promotes sustainable agriculture may be less attractive than a specific proposal that requests funds for seeds and a model irrigation system.

When designing a program, think ahead to the goals and interests of the grant reviewers. Does the program truly match the priorities of the foundation that is being applied to? Does the staff have the expertise to carry out the program? Is minority participation in the program assured? Are the plans gender sensitive? Be specific. I recall one successful grant application for a computer lab at a children's museum. The RFP required information about the software that would be made available to the youngsters. The successful application provided detailed plans to include software suitable for young girls as well as young boys.

Set realistic goals. With a well-planned program—one that has clear and achievable objectives—it is possible to design a strong evaluation component into a project plan. Successful applications often have measurable goals or objectives, such as the following: to provide shelter for 200 homeless people each evening during the winter months; to perform concerts for 2,000 elementary school children in five rural communities; to test the efficacy of a new behavior modification therapeutic technique for children with severe dissociative disorders by conducting a longitudinal study of 25 patients at an institution; to purchase specialized Braille computer equipment to be used for client training; or to develop a job placement program for teens at risk and place not fewer than 1,500 teens in summer jobs.

THE APPLICATION

When preparing the grant application, be sure to follow all instructions meticulously. Answer all questions—but be sure to observe any space limitations. If the foundation guidelines call for a proposal of not more than five pages, don't submit a six-page proposal. Also, observe the spirit of the guidelines. Don't set the font to the smallest size print and margins to the narrowest setting. Grant reviewers don't want to have to use magnifying glasses to review a proposal.

Some foundations provide a form to be submitted. Many do not. However, many do issue guidelines that say something similar to the following:

> Our foundation does not require a form, but your proposal should include the following information: a brief history of your organization; your organization's mission; the need you serve; your approach to the problem; a project description including goals and plans; what population does your project or organization serve; how our grant funds are to be used; how you will evaluate the project; who else is working on this problem. Also describe any collaborative efforts with others and other information you feel might be helpful to the grant evaluators. Please limit your proposal to 10 pages.

With instructions such as these, it may be helpful to create a form. In other words, make each of the subjects mentioned a *section title* in your proposal outline. Then write a proposal that addresses the primary concerns of the foundation.

When writing each section, stick to the subject, do not stray from the main points. Every grant reviewer has seen pages upon pages of irrelevant and nonresponsive writing. For some reason, many grant writers view every question as an occasion to convey more information about their organization. When responding to the question "What need or problem does your project address?" they begin by writing: "Founded in 1956, our organization has a long history of innovative responses to pressing needs in our community. Our reputation for fiscal responsibility and inclusiveness place us in a unique position to address a broad range of social issues." In fact, some people never get around to answering the question at all. A more appropriate response might begin. "In Peoria, approximately 1,500 people sleep on the streets each night. A recent survey of the homeless population conducted by Peoria's human services department indicates

that 37.4 percent of these homeless people are suffering from treatable mental illnesses." The grant reviewer now knows that there is a need to serve the homeless population and that the program will deal specifically with the mental health needs of the homeless. As important, the grant reviewer knows that the writer is familiar with research dealing with the organization's area of concern.

To help clarify their thinking, grant writers may wish to use a form that limits responses to a very few lines (see Exhibit 12-5). These short responses

---

EXHIBIT 12-5   GRANT APPLICATION PREPARATION FORM

Use this form to help clarify your thinking and to help prepare lead paragraphs that can guide you through the proposal preparation.

<u>Use only the space provided!</u>

Project Title: _____

Amount of Request: $ _____

Specific Purpose for Which Funds Are Being Sought: _____
_____
_____

Need Addressed by Proposal: _____
_____

Measurable Objective Desired: _____
_____

Method of Achieving Objective: _____
_____
_____

Describe Agency and Its Qualifications to Meet This Need: _____
_____
_____

Timing (Status, date, and/or time frame of project): _____
_____
_____

How Will the Organization Evaluate Success? _____
_____
_____

Use reverse side to sketch in a project budget.

can serve as the lead sentences in the first paragraph of each section. The discipline involved in writing a short, relevant response will help writers stay focused. These strong lead sentences also will make the grant reviewer's job easier—and help ensure the success of the proposal.

The proposal should be succinct and readable. However, in pursuit of brevity, do not assume that because a question was answered elsewhere in the proposal, similar information need not be provided in another section of the application. For example, early in the application, the writer may have stated that the program is established in a poor, rural area with a high percentage of Hispanic and Native American people. Later the proposal may ask about the population served. Even though the population was mentioned earlier, be absolutely sure to give the most complete answer in this section. Don't be vague. Mention every minority or special population served. Be sensitive to the interest of people with disabilities. If the program has made special accommodations, cite these in the appropriate section of the proposal. But in the section dealing with the population served, be sure to reiterate that people with disabilities are included in the program. Similarly, be thorough in describing the demographics of the people benefiting from the program. Be specific concerning gender, nationality, socioeconomic characteristics, ethnicity, creed, and religion. If people are served without regard to race, religion, or creed, say so. If statistics are available that describe the people participating in the program, cite them. Language such as the following is most helpful:

> In a trial period last summer, 53 percent of program participants were women, 47 percent were male. Of these men and women, 42 percent were Hispanic, 39 percent were Anglo, 11 percent were Native American, 4 percent were Asian, and 4 percent were African American. In the region we serve, 78 percent of the entire population live below the poverty line. We anticipate that program participants will reflect the socioeconomic demographics of our region. Our program will directly benefit not less than 3,500 people. With the addition of the new Special Needs Program Coordinator, we anticipate that we will accommodate the needs of approximately 75 people with moderate to severe physical and developmental disabilities. All services are offered without regard to race, religion, creed, or nationality.

Be thorough in each section—even to the point of redundancy—because grant reviewers often skim through proposals. When looking for

their particular concerns, they may focus on one section only. Some want to know that an organization has measurable objectives. Some might be most concerned about the quality of the evaluation program. An occasional grant reviewer might be interested in the inclusion of a specific, under-served population. Most take a broader view but still can have a special interest in some aspect of a proposal. So answer each question in a manner that allows each grant reviewer to find the information he or she is looking for in the section that addresses the reviewer's particular concern.

Be sure that the proposal is complete and timely. Have a colleague help double check the grant submission package. Were all questions answered in the proposal? Have all attachments been included? Were all instructions followed? Is the grant amount requested clearly indicated? Is it clear how the foundation's funds will be used? Has the deadline been met? If the answer to all these questions is yes—and a project that matches the funder's priorities has been described—then submit the proposal. Funding is not assured; but the probability of getting the funds needed has increased.

Here are some more ideas that can help save time with grant applications—and also help increase your grant success rate.

- *Never* submit mass applications. Always personalize approaches and let the funder know how the project fits the foundation's interests.
- Duplicate batches of commonly used attachments: the list of board members and their affiliations, the 501(c)(3) tax exemption letter, the most recent audit, and recent financial statements. Keep a good supply of all these common attachments on hand.
- Maintain the annual operating budget and project budgets in the word processor. This will make it easier to format the budget information in a way that strengthens the grant application.
- Work smart! Spend time working on potential large gifts from qualified foundation prospects.

Some final advice. Anyone who ever has an opportunity to serve as a grant reviewer should do so. The time spent will be well worth the effort. Consider serving on a Rotary Club grants review committee. Or volunteer to review a local arts council's grant applications. Many organizations have grant review panels. Once a person has served as a grant reviewer, he or she will be far less likely to submit a vague, nonresponsive proposal.

ACKNOWLEDGMENT AND REPORTING REQUIREMENTS

After being notified that the application has been approved, be sure to send a thank-you letter to the foundation. Grant writers with personal contact with any representatives of the foundation should also call or visit them to express appreciation. Some not-for-profit administrators view foundations as impersonal monoliths. They forget that foundations are made up of living and breathing human beings. Personal contact and expressions of appreciation are not only polite but also help cement relationships and may influence future funding requests.

In addition to gracious acknowledgment of the contribution, the organization must ensure that it meets all reporting requirements. Many foundations don't require a formal report on the project, but fundraisers would do well to send at least a final report upon project completion or toward the end of the fiscal year if general operating funds were received. Foundation officers frequently tell resource development professionals horror stories of large grants that were never acknowledged. To make matters even worse, a number of not-for-profits fail to meet their reporting requirements and deadlines. Of course, these organizations find themselves ineligible for future funding.

Manage programs in a manner consistent with the grant application. If any major changes in a program have to be made, communicate with foundation representatives and let them know the reasons for the changes. Be mindful of evaluation tools. Maintain reliable records dealing with all measurable objectives. Monitor all reporting deadlines and requirements. Fulfill the organization's obligations and enhance your reputation for successful project management.

CHAPTER **13**

Planned Giving

*The generations of living things pass in a short time, and like
runners hand on the torch of life.*

—Lucretius, *De Rerum Natura*

DEFINING PLANNED GIVING

Planned giving, charitable gift planning, and the older term, "deferred giving," all refer to charitable contributions made with some level of professional guidance. Most planned gifts help reduce the donor's estate taxes, income taxes, and/or capital gains taxes. Charitable gift planning perpetuates the donor's values. At the same time, gift planning helps donors better provide for their families and loved ones. Some planned gifts provide donors with income for life.

Many planned gifts, such as bequests, are deferred contributions. The not-for-profit organization receives the bequest upon the death of the donor. Other planned gifts, such as donations of appreciated stock, produce current contributions for the charity.

THE IMPORTANCE OF PLANNED GIVING

In one recent year bequests from individuals to charities accounted for nearly $8 billion. Each year the amount donated through bequests is greater than all corporate donations in the United States. (Once this author stated this fact during a seminar. Someone in the audience said that there is a

simpler way to make the point. When asked, "How?" she replied, "Dead people give more than businesses.") No matter how it is stated, planned gifts produce significant resources for not-for-profit institutions nationwide. Charitable gift planning strengthens the organization's long-term strategic position. Moreover, planned gifts are essential to building the organization's endowment funds.

Charitable gift planning will become even more important in the years to come. Demographers estimate that between now and the year 2020, more than $12 trillion will be transferred to the baby boomers from their parents. This intergenerational transfer of wealth to people born between 1946 and 1964 represents an extraordinary opportunity for not-for-profit organizations. Members of the older generation have a strong desire to help their children. The older generation, people with strong values, also want to help the organizations that have been important to them—their church or synagogue, their university, and their other favored not-for-profit institutions. Yet less than 3 percent of adult Americans have made provisions for a not-for-profit institution in their wills.

Charitable Gift Instruments— Ways of Giving

Current Gifts

The simplest way for supporters to contribute to an organization is to write a check. However, for donors to maximize their income, capital gains, and estate tax savings, they may wish to examine all of their assets and design the most effective donation.

Outright gifts make funds available for the not-for-profit organization's immediate use and provide donors the advantage of income tax deductibility. Some current gifts also may help donors avoid capital gains taxes. Current donations may take many forms, including:

- Cash and checks
- Securities
- Real estate
- Life insurance policies
- Personal property

Look at how planning can affect the donor's taxes. Assume Mr. Smith wants to donate $10,000 to a Community College Foundation. If he writes a check for $10,000, most likely he will be able to take an income tax deduction for this amount. Assuming a 38.5 percent tax rate, the $10,000 donation will have, in reality, cost $6,150.

Assume Mr. Smith wants to donate $10,000 and has long-term appreciated stock. If the stock cost $4,000 but has a current fair market value of $10,000, Mr. Smith can donate the stock and take the full $10,000 income tax deduction, reducing income tax by $3,850. Additionally, he will have avoided capital gains taxes of $1,200 (20 percent capital gains tax × $6,000 capital gains). In this example, the $10,000 donation will have cost Mr. Smith only $4,950.

If, on the other hand, Mr. Smith has stock that has depreciated in value, he is better off selling the stock, realizing the loss, and donating the proceeds. Assume in this example that the donor has stock that cost $20,000 but has a current market value of only $10,000. If Mr. Smith sells the stock, he may be able to deduct the $10,000 capital loss and the $10,000 charitable donation.

Thus donors will want to consider contributions of appreciated assets. On the other hand, generally donors are better off selling capital assets that have declined in value and contributing the proceeds after the sale.

Other advantages are associated with this type of planning. Charitable donations reduce the donor's taxable estate. With current giving, the charity may use the funds immediately.

Wills and Bequests

Wills and trust agreements enable people to provide long-term financial security for their families and loved ones. Such bequests also help donors perpetuate their values and support the vital work of the charities that are important to them.

Wills and trusts can specify that the remainder of the estate can go to the not-for-profit organization after family and friends have been taken care of. Or the will can specify that the not-for-profit organization receives a predetermined, fixed gift, whether in cash, securities, property, or valuables.

Donors who already have executed their wills or estate plans can amend them easily through a simple legal device known as a codicil, a clearly

worded paragraph that can be added to a will. The codicil must be executed, signed, and witnessed in accordance with state law. It provides an easy vehicle for attorneys to include the donor's favorite not-for-profit organizations as beneficiaries in his or her estate. A codicil can be stated simply.

Not-for-profit organizations should publish sample codicil language, such as the following, frequently:

> I give, devise, and bequeath to _____ (legal name of not-for-profit organization) for its general purposes (or specify endowment, special uses, or restrictions) all (or state fraction or percentage) of the rest, residue, and remainder of my estate, both real or personal.
>
> OR
>
> I give, devise, and bequeath to _____ (legal name of charity) the sum of $_____ to be used for the general purposes (or specify endowment, special uses, or restrictions) of _____ (legal name of charity).

Bequests to not-for-profit organizations are not subject to estate or inheritance taxes. Furthermore, the value of the bequest is deductible from the donor's taxable estate, thereby lowering estate taxes. There is no limit on the amount of deduction.

Gifts by will may be designated for specific purposes or can be left unrestricted, thereby providing maximum flexibility in helping the not-for-profit organization enhance its services.

Whatever type of bequest donors wish to make, a will is essential. Not-for-profit organizations should encourage donors to seek the counsel of a competent attorney and other trained professionals when updating their estate plans. Representatives of the not-for-profit organization may make themselves available to discuss the donor's objectives with donors and their advisors.

Gift planners, weighing the merits of current contributions relative to gifts through wills, may wish to consider that assets left in the will produce no income tax deductions. Such gifts also do not avoid probate.

However, from the philanthropic individual's point of view, gifts through wills and estate plans produce three main benefits. The donor's legacy makes it possible for the charitable institution to carry on its work after the donor's demise. The will can be changed during the donor's life-

time. And charitable gifts in the will or estate plan reduces the donor's taxable estate.

Charitable Gift Annuities

A gift annuity agreement is a legal contract between a donor and the not-for-profit organization. In return for a contribution (usually $5,000 or more), the not-for-profit organization will pay the donor and/or designated beneficiaries a fixed amount every year for life.

The rate to be paid each year is determined by the ages of the person or people named in the agreement. The older the annuitant, the higher the fixed annuity payment rate. Agreements can be written to provide income for one or two lives.

Charitable gift annuities produce a number of significant benefits. Donors cannot outlive this source of income. These annuities offer attractive guaranteed rates of return. Donors receive an immediate income tax deduction equal to the present value of the future gift—that is, an income tax deduction for the value of the remainder. Donors also receive the satisfaction of knowing that their gift will be a legacy that will continue on for the benefit of their not-for-profit organization; upon death of a donor, the remaining principal passes to the charity. The charitable gift annuity reduces donors' taxable estate and avoids probate.

Charitable gift annuities are backed by the assets of the not-for-profit organization. In recent years some insurance commissioners throughout the United States have stated that charitable gift annuities are similar to insurance agreements and should be regulated as such. Thus far the laws vary greatly in each state. Moreover, insurance commissioners are in the process of drafting model legislation to be promulgated throughout the nation. Additionally, some states in which there have been no losses or reported abuses related to charitable gift annuities now are contemplating potentially burdensome legislation. Not-for-profit organizations will need to monitor this situation, become familiar with the laws in the states in which they operate, and work to influence legislation. The goal is to encourage full disclosure of the not-for-profit organization's financial status and ability to meet its charitable gift annuity obligations. Another goal is to avoid unnecessary or burdensome regulation.

Charitable Remainder Trusts

With a charitable remainder trust, the donor can transfer cash or other assets to the trust and receive income for life. The trust can sell valuable assets tax free. In many cases the trust can sell these assets and replace them with higher-income producing assets. In this way the donor avoids capital gains taxes and can increase his or her income dramatically. The income stream can be retained for the donor's life or in combination with a spouse or third party. Alternatively, the trust can be established for a specific number of years—not to exceed 20 years. Later, when the trust terminates, the trust assets will benefit the important activities of the not-for-profit organization.

Generally, the sale of assets through a charitable remainder trust will avoid the capital gains tax on any appreciation, reduce or avoid estate taxes, and eliminate the need to probate the assets placed in the trust. The transfer of an asset to the trust is deductible, in part, for income tax purposes. Distributions from the trust are taxable income to the donor.

The remainder interest (the value of the transferred property less the value of the retained income stream) is irrevocably donated to a charity. Even though actual receipt of the remainder interest by the charity is deferred until the income stream ends, the donor will receive an immediate income tax deduction for the value of the charity's remainder interest.

Charitable Remainder Unitrusts

The charitable remainder unitrust (see Exhibit 13-1) allows the donor and the donor's spouse to receive income for life while making a major contribution to the nonprofit organization. This gift vehicle is ideal for donors who wish to assure themselves growing income during inflationary times. As the trust assets increase, the donor's annual income also increases. Charitable remainder unitrusts ensure future support of the organization. They may be the best solution for donors who would like to make a gift of cash, securities, or real estate but wish to retain income for life (or the life of a designated beneficiary). Donors select a fixed percentage (not less than 5 percent) of the net fair market value of the contributed property. The amount paid will be this fixed percentage times the fair market value of the trust assets revalued annually.

EXHIBIT 13-1   CHARITABLE REMAINDER UNITRUSTS

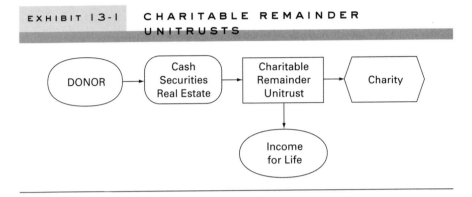

When considering establishing a charitable remainder unitrust, estate-planning professionals frequently advise donors—and most not-for-profit organizations require—that a $50,000 or $100,000 minimum donation is needed to establish the trust. Donors also must consider the setup costs and annual trustee fees when establishing the trust.

The benefits of the charitable remainder unitrust are as follows: Donors receive variable income for life, which may provide a valuable hedge against inflation; they receive an income tax deduction for the value of the remainder portion of the contribution; they pay no capital gains tax on appreciated securities or real estate; the contribution reduces donors' taxable estate; upon the death of the income beneficiaries, the principal passes to the charity; donors can contribute additional assets to a charitable remainder unitrust; if desired, the charitable remainder unitrust may be established to distribute deferred income; and assets in these unitrusts avoid probate.

Charitable Remainder Annuity Trusts

With annuity trusts (see Exhibit 13-2), the amount paid to the donor each year from the annuity trust is fixed. The annuity amount must be at least 5 percent of the initial value of the transferred assets. This income may be tax free if tax-exempt securities are used to fund the trust. At the death of the donor or designated beneficiary, the trust's principal becomes the property of the not-for-profit organization.

As with unitrusts, charitable remainder annuity trusts, whether in the form of real estate, securities, or cash, usually require a minimum $50,000 or $100,000 donation. Donors also must consider the setup and annual trustee fees. Unlike unitrusts, donors may not add to an annuity trust.

EXHIBIT 13-2   CHARITABLE REMAINDER ANNUITY TRUSTS

However, the donor who establishes a charitable remainder annuity trust receives a number of benefits, including an immediate income tax deduction for a portion of the gift in the year the trust is created. Because donated assets avoid capital gains taxes, appreciated securities are particularly well suited for annuity trusts. In addition, the trust pays no capital gains tax if the securities are sold. And finally, transfer of assets to an annuity trust removes the assets from the donor's estate, thereby avoiding estate taxes and probate.

Wealth Replacement Trusts

The wealth replacement trust (see Exhibit 13-3), also called the asset value replacement trust, is an insurance trust established to benefit the donor's heirs. The wealth replacement trust is funded with money saved through tax deductions and the increased cash flow that is associated with a charitable remainder unitrust or annuity trust.

Here is an example of how charitable giving combined with estate planning can produce substantial benefits for the donor, the donor's heirs, and the not-for-profit organization.

Mary Goodinvestor, age 57, purchased stock for $20,000 many years ago. Today the stock is worth $100,000. Unfortunately, the stock only pays $2,000 per year in dividends.

If Mary wishes to sell the stock and reinvest the proceeds in an asset that generates more income, she will have to pay capital gains tax of approximately $16,000, leaving only $84,000 to reinvest.

Instead, she establishes a charitable remainder unitrust funded by the $100,000 stock. The tax-exempt trust sells the stock. No capital gains taxes

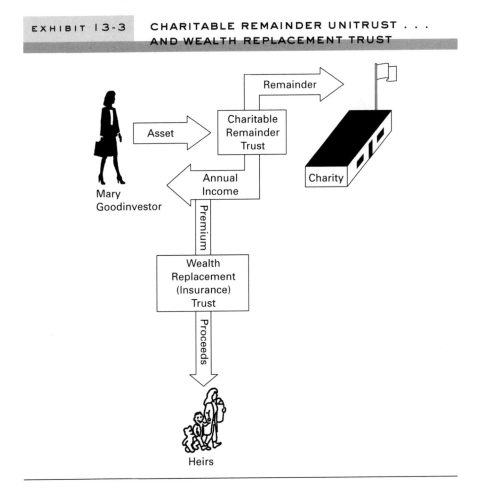

are due. The trustee invests the entire $100,000 in higher-yielding invest-
ments and growth opportunities. If Mary elects a 7.5 percent rate of return,
the trust will pay her 7.5 percent of the value of the trust each year. If the
trust remains valued at $100,000, Mary receives $7,500 each year for the
rest of her life, increasing her annual income by $5,500. If the trust declines
in value, Mary will receive less. However, if the trust, as expected, grows
in value, she will receive even more.

When Mary dies, the trust principal, which may now be greater than
$100,000, goes to the charity. But what about Mary's heirs? Mary got a tax
deduction when she established the charitable remainder unitrust. She can
invest the immediate income tax savings plus $3,500 each year from her in-
creased income. (Mary still has doubled her income from this asset from

$2,000 to $4,000 annually.) With these funds she can establish a wealth replacement trust that can grow to a $150,000 tax-free inheritance for her heirs.

Gifts of Real Estate

Many not-for-profit organizations are experienced in accepting gifts of real estate. In all cases, organizations need some time to review the property title, the appraisal, and perhaps most important the property's environmental condition. Not-for-profits must be careful not to accept property that carries with it any significant environmental liabilities.

Donors can make current or deferred gifts of real estate. A current gift, whether commercial, residential, or agricultural, provides immediate tax savings and relieves the donor of the expense and burden associated with property management. Generally, the tax deduction equals the fair market value of the property. The deduction will be reduced somewhat if the property qualified for depreciation write-offs in prior years.

Donors can contribute a personal residence or farm to the not-for-profit organization and continue to occupy the property throughout their lifetime. The property need not be the donors' primary residence; it also can be a second home or a vacation home. To be classified as a farm, the land must meet specific legal criteria. Gifts of residences or farms allow donors to: (1) make an irrevocable commitment to the not-for-profit organization; (2) continue to enjoy use of the property as usual; and (3) receive a current income tax deduction for the property's discounted value. The income tax deduction can be substantial. As expected, the donated property reduces estate taxes and avoids probate.

DONOR EDUCATION AND THE PLANNED GIVING PROGRAM

Many donors know about the importance of charitable gift planning. Therefore, well-respected not-for-profit organizations, even those that have not established a planned-giving program, receive contributions through wills or bequests. However, to encourage gift planning, increase the number of gifts through estate plans, and help donors maximize their gift potential, not-for-profit organizations proactively work to educate donors and prospective supporters.

The Board's Role and "Buy-In"

The first task involved with establishing a planned-giving program is to ensure that the board of directors supports the program. The board is responsible for the organization's strategic direction for setting policy. Therefore, board members are actively involved in a number of key decisions, including:

- What gifts will the organization accept? The board must adopt a gift acceptance policy.
- Should all undesignated bequests be used for operations? Or should the board place contributions over a certain amount in a board-designated endowment fund?
- How should the organization manage its endowment funds? Who acts as trustee? Does the organization establish a separate foundation? Should the organization consider placing all endowment funds in a community foundation?
- How should the organization invest endowment funds?
- How should the organization acknowledge planned or deferred gifts?
- How should planned or deferred gifts be counted toward campaign goals?

These and many other questions require serious deliberations. By encouraging board participation in these discussions, the development professional can help ensure support for a planned-giving program.

Board member "buy-in" also is essential to the success of a donor education program. Board members often facilitate introductions to estate planning professionals, top donors, and community leaders. Board members can be the most effective advocates for a planned-giving program, especially when they make provisions for the organization in their wills or estate plans.

The Planned-Giving Committee

Many not-for-profit organizations find it helpful to form a committee that focuses on charitable gift planning. This planned-giving committee usually is composed of estate-planning professionals who share the organization's values and support its mission. They can help develop or refine gift

acceptance policies. The committee can review materials for clarity and accuracy. Those members who are gifted at public speaking may speak at seminars. Almost every planned-giving committee serves in an advisory capacity. Individual committee members vary greatly in how much pro bono work they will perform for the nonprofit organization or for planned gift donors. Many will help donors with simple codicil language. Some might offer general advice on estate planning. However, to avoid conflicts of interest, not-for-profit organizations and estate-planning professionals serving as volunteers for those institutions must remind donors to work with their own estate-planning professionals.

Whether the organization decides to establish a planned-giving committee or not, its executive director, development director, and key board members should network with estate-planning professionals: attorneys, certified public accountants, trust officers, insurance professionals, financial planners, and planned-giving advisors. These professionals should be told about the important work the organization does and informed as to which types of planned gifts the charity accepts. Seek their advice and help.

Estate-planning professionals are among an organization's most important allies. Frequently they directly or subtly influence philanthropic individuals when they are making their estate plans. At a minimum, estate-planning professionals might ask if clients have any interest in remembering any charitable organizations in a will or estate plan. At times, professionals might suggest that charitable gift planning could help clients better provide for family and loved ones. At a critical point in the estate-planning process, estate-planning professionals might even mention the valuable work of a specific not-for-profit organization.

Seminars

Mature not-for-profit organizations might conduct a number of planned-giving seminars each year. The simplest way would be to conduct one seminar annually for supporters and prospective supporters. Many organizations prefer to conduct two planned-giving seminars each year, one for prospects and one for estate-planning professionals.

The seminars for prospects might focus on the general need for estate planning. People need to be reminded that without planning, the government can receive a disproportionate portion of their assets and estate. One

main message of each seminar is to encourage all people to make wills and estate plans. Another message is that it is possible for donors to perpetuate their values by remembering the not-for-profit organization in their wills.

Some seminars focus on wills and estate plans. Others provide a broad overview of gift-planning vehicles, such as charitable gift annuities, charitable remainder trusts, life insurance donations, gifts of residences, and wealth replacement trusts. Organizations with many supporters may try several formats with differing emphases. In any case, be sure that the seminars take place in a comfortable setting. Breakfast and late-afternoon gatherings work well. The invitation and presentation should focus on benefits to the donor. Be sure to give each attendee valuable information to take home, including sample codicil language.

The presenter should use helpful examples of gift-planning strategies. The examples used should refer to people in the same age group and socioeconomic circumstances as the seminar attendees. The situations and assets referred to also should be relevant. The presenter should use as many participatory techniques as possible. The objective is to engage the audience, not lecture. Above all, trust documents should *not* be read to the audience. It is very difficult to influence people who are asleep.

Make follow-up visits to attendees who indicate interest in the gift-planning strategies that were covered. Offer to share computer-generated illustrations of benefits. These printouts, generated by programs such as Crescendo and PG Calc, take basic information provided by prospective supporters and calculate income tax savings, estate tax benefits, and cash flows generated by life income gifts.

If the not-for-profit organization does not have planned-giving software, work with a consultant or find a colleague who can furnish presentation materials related to tax calculations and cash-flow projections. Also, development professionals who are not experienced in charitable gift planning should be sure to work closely with an experienced planned-giving professional.

Planned-giving seminars for estate-planning professionals generally take one of two approaches: a general overview of the organization and planned-giving strategies or a more in-depth technical presentation focusing on one or two estate-planning strategies. Often the general overview is presented as a social and informative gathering; the invitation might even mention that this gathering is an opportunity for networking. The more technical

seminars are especially attractive to estate-planning professionals when they can receive continuing educational units (CEUs) for attendance.

In all cases, spend at least a few moments in each seminar pointing out the good works of the organization. Also, furnish copies of the case statement and other promotional materials in the presentation folder each attendee receives.

Other points to be made at each seminar include:

- Planned-giving strategies allow the donor to better provide for family and loved ones while also making a significant investment in the charity.

- The organization will always approach planned giving from the donor's perspective.

- Many planned-giving vehicles provide the donor with income for life.

- Planned-giving strategies often increase the donor's current income.

- When considering charitable contributions, donors can use many different types of assets—and many gift-planning vehicles.

- The organization encourages donors to consult their own planning professionals; organization representatives are available to explain a number of charitable gift options.

- To sustain and enhance the valuable work of the organization, the institution needs current and long-term contributed income.

Print Materials and Publications

The simplest way to begin a planned-giving program for an organization is to publish the phrase "Please remember our organization in your will or estate plan" in each newsletter and in other publications. Of course, use the legal name of your organization.

If desired, the message may be varied. At times, a phrase such as "If you have remembered our organization in your will, please let us know so that we may acknowledge your thoughtfulness with membership in our Legacy League" may be appropriate. You may also include simple planned-giving articles in the organization's newsletter. A sample article is included on the CD-ROM that accompanies this book.

Some organizations print the "Please remember . . ." phrase on the bottom of their stationery. Others print the message on the back of the stationery used for acknowledgement letters.

An alternative inexpensive idea is to print simple gift-planning reminder messages on slips of paper that can be placed inside the envelope with the thank-you letter (see Exhibits 13-4 and 13-5). These reminder slips can be

EXHIBIT 13-4   **PLANNED GIVING REMINDER SLIPS**

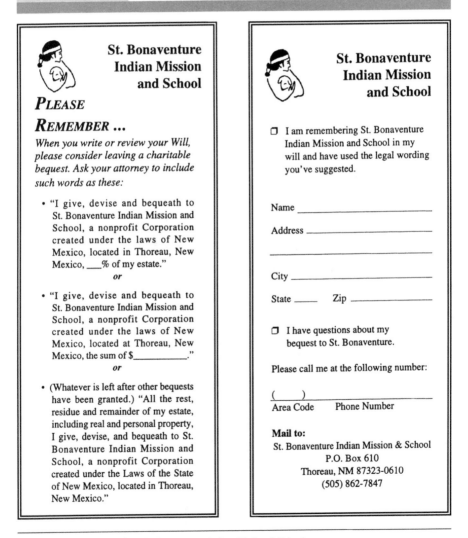

St. Bonaventure Indian Mission and School

PLEASE REMEMBER ...

When you write or review your Will, please consider leaving a charitable bequest. Ask your attorney to include such words as these:

- "I give, devise and bequeath to St. Bonaventure Indian Mission and School, a nonprofit Corporation created under the laws of New Mexico, located in Thoreau, New Mexico, ___% of my estate."
  or
- "I give, devise and bequeath to St. Bonaventure Indian Mission and School, a nonprofit Corporation created under the laws of New Mexico, located at Thoreau, New Mexico, the sum of $_____."
  or
- (Whatever is left after other bequests have been granted.) "All the rest, residue and remainder of my estate, including real and personal property, I give, devise, and bequeath to St. Bonaventure Indian Mission and School, a nonprofit Corporation created under the Laws of the State of New Mexico, located in Thoreau, New Mexico."

St. Bonaventure Indian Mission and School

❏ I am remembering St. Bonaventure Indian Mission and School in my will and have used the legal wording you've suggested.

Name _____

Address _____

_____

City _____

State _____   Zip _____

❏ I have questions about my bequest to St. Bonaventure.

Please call me at the following number:

( ) _____
Area Code   Phone Number

Mail to:
St. Bonaventure Indian Mission & School
P.O. Box 610
Thoreau, NM 87323-0610
(505) 862-7847

Reprinted with permission from St. Bonaventure Indian Mission & School.

EXHIBIT 13-5   PLANNED GIVING RESPONSE
CARD: EXAMPLE

Remember St. Bonaventure Indian Mission and School in Your Will

St Bonaventure depends on donations and bequests so that we can provide education, transportation, food, water and clothing for Navajo children, adults and community elders. Individuals and families who have provided for St. Bonaventure in their estate plans are eligible for membership in our Shepherd's Staff Society.

For information about how to remember St. Bonaventure in your will, or for information about membership in our Shepherd's Staff Society, please return this card in the enclosed envelope or call Bob O'Connell; Mission Director, at (505) 862-7847.

Name _____

Address _____

City _____ State _____ Zip _____

Phone (_____)
    Area Code

Over

St. Bonaventure Indian Mission and School Charitable Gift Annuities

If you are interested in learning how you can receive income for life, save taxes, and make a meaningful gift to St. Bonaventure, please complete the information on this card and return it in the enclosed envelope or call Bob O'Connell, Mission Director at (505) 862-7847. Charitable Gift Annuities help St. Bonaventure continue its spiritual work, social services and education programs for the Navajo people.

Name _____

Address _____

City _____ State _____ Zip _____

Phone (___)_____ Possible Gift Amount (Min. $1,000) $_____
    Area Code

Date of Birth _____ Second Beneficiary's Birthdate _____
    Day   Month   Year   Day   Month   Year

Reprinted with permission from St. Bonaventure Indian Mission & School.

printed three or four to a page; thus, the cost is extremely minimal. Even more important, by placing the slips in the thank-you letters, the message is being targeted to the best prospects, current donors.

Be creative. Vary planned-giving messages. Using the organization's newsletters, annual reports, program books, thank-you stationery and other internal print materials, consistently educate supporters about the importance of bequests and estate planning.

Besides sending internal publications, fundraisers may wish to purchase and mail gift-planning materials from organizations such as Robert F. Sharpe & Co., The Stelter Company, R&R Newkirk, and others. These gift-planning consultants and publishers offer a wide variety of brochures, pamphlets, and newsletters. Some provide a broad overview of planned-giving strategies; others cover specific topics, such as wills and bequests, charitable gift annuities, year-end tax planning, and charitable remainder trusts.

Often these materials are designed in a way that allows for the imprint of the not-for-profit organization's name, logo, and address on the pre-designed piece. Because the publisher enjoys an economy of scale, the price for each brochure is often less than the cost for the not-for-profit organization to print its own materials.

Every organization faces budget constraints. However, planned-giving professionals advise their organizations and clients to communicate with as many constituents as possible. The not-for-profit organization's newsletter should contain valuable gift-planning information and most probably is mailed to the entire mail list. The reminder slips placed in thank-you letters are targeted to current donors.

So, who receives the more expensive planned-giving brochures? Certainly those people who have requested the information receive them. Beyond that the answer becomes a bit more complex and usually is some compromise based on the demographics of the donor base and budget constraints. The best prospects for planned gifts are the most loyal supporters. There are three indicators of such loyalty: the donor's cumulative giving, the size of the donor's largest gift, and the number of donations the donor made. A donor whose total multiyear giving exceeds $10,000 has clearly indicated support for an organization. A donor who has given a single gift of $1,000 or more might very well share the organization's aspirations. And a donor who has made 10 or more contributions, no matter how small, has indicated a marked degree of loyalty to the organization.

The important point here is not so much the specific numbers used. Each organization has a different view of what a large gift is, which cumulative amounts are significant, and how many gifts indicate shared values. An organization will want to segment its mail list and send as many planned-giving brochures as are cost effective based on three criteria: cumulative giving, largest gift, and number of contributions. In this way the

organization will be sure to communicate with each of its very best planned-giving prospects.

A word of caution here. Many of the preprinted materials are designed with no response card. Others encourage the supporter to request more information. Too often, not-for-profit organizations mail a brochure . . . and respond to the supporter's request for more information by sending another brochure. To make matters worse, the second brochure frequently has no response card.

To avoid this seemingly never-ending cycle of responding to printed material with more printed material, choose brochures that have response cards. Especially look for or design planned-giving materials with response devices that invite further contact (see Exhibit 13-6).

If the materials ordered do not have a response card, design one and place it in the brochure. Or send the brochure with a cover letter that states: "I hope you find the enclosed information helpful. I'll give you a call early next week to answer any questions you may have."

Now that response devices are provided in the planned-giving materials, be sure to stagger mailings so that staff can respond in a timely fashion to those who call or send in the response cards. The aim is to keep the dialogue open and personal.

The Importance of Personal Contact

People who respond to planned-giving materials should be visited personally whenever possible. At a minimum, they should be contacted by telephone. After all, these people so believe in the organization's mission that they are considering a bequest or other planned gift. Make no mistake. This represents a unique level of commitment. People with resource development responsibilities absolutely must follow through in the most personal and empathetic manner possible.

It is also important to create opportunities to meet supporters to discuss gift planning, even those who have not yet indicated an interest in planned gifts. Some organizations make it a habit to proactively seek appointments with their top donors. Often the development director and a member of the board arrange a meeting to discuss a range of issues. The meeting, frequently a lunch or breakfast, is used to thank the donor personally. The representatives of the not-for-profit also might ask donors' opinions of

EXHIBIT 13-6   THE GIFT ANNUITY

THE GIFT ANNUITY

▶ Income for Life for You . . . Benefit for Future Generations

A charitable gift annuity is an extraordinary way to make a gift, increase your income and slice your tax bill—all in one transaction! Our charitable gift annuity program was created as a service to our many friends who have expressed a desire to make a gift of significance, while still retaining income from the gift property during their lives.

A charitable gift annuity is a contract in which you exchange a gift of cash or securities for a guaranteed, fixed income each year for the rest of your life. Your gift annuity offers five distinct advantages:

- **Income for Life**—at attractive payout rates for one or two lives;
- **Tax Deduction Savings**—a large part of what you transfer is a deductible charitable gift;
- **Tax-Free Income**—a large part of your annual payments are tax-free return of principal;
- **Capital Gains Tax Savings**—when you contribute securities for a gift annuity, you minimize any taxes on your "paper profit";
- **Personal Satisfaction**—from making a gift of lasting significance.

You can choose . . .

How frequently payments will be made quarterly, semi-annually, annually; one-life or two-life annuities; cash or securities to fund your gift. Cash gifts allow maximum tax-free income; gifts of securities allow you to minimize gains taxes.

▶ For More Information About Gift Annuities

We can provide you a free gift annuity analysis that answers all your questions. Just fill out and return the form below. Or simply call our office.

✂- -

❑ Please send me a gift annuity proposal with complete information on income and tax benefits. I am considering placing $_____ cash in a charitable gift annuity that will make payments to a person born _____ (or, a person born on _____ and a person born _____).

Please provide information based on

❑ quarterly   ❑ semi-annual

❑ annual payments.

❑ I am considering funding my gift annuity with appreciated securities.

❑ I originally purchased these securities at a cost of $_____.

I estimate that the current market value now is $_____.

Name _____

Address _____

City _____ State _____ Zip _____

Telephone _____

Benefits of a Charitable Gift Annuity for $10,000*

Age	Guaranteed Annual Income	Tax-Free Income	Taxable Income	Charitable Deduction	Effective Rate of Return**
90	$ 1,200	$ 831	$ 369	$ 5,929	19.3%
85	$ 1,050	$ 662	$ 388	$ 5,499	16.2%
80	$ 940	$ 532	$ 408	$ 4,996	14.0%
75	$ 840	$ 435	$ 405	$ 4,612	12.1%
70	$ 770	$ 360	$ 410	$ 4,277	10.7%
65	$ 720	$ 303	$ 417	$ 3,969	9.8%
60	$ 690	$ 264	$ 426	$ 3,640	9.1%

* The $10,000 figure is merely a convenient multiple. We will be glad to provide you with tax and financial results for any size gift.

** The "effective" rate takes into account the donor's charitable deduction tax savings and the benefits of the tax-free income in a 31% federal income bracket. Deductions vary according to current interest rates.

how well the organization is carrying out its stated aims. Donors appreciate the opportunity to offer advice. During these meetings the not-for-profit representatives might ask if the donor is familiar with gift-planning strategies. The discussion might also include the importance of bequests.

If the response is favorable, the representatives of the not-for-profit organization might ask the supporter to consider membership in the legacy league or whatever name the organization uses for its planned gift society. Thoughtful donors can be acknowledged generously and graciously when they indicate that they have remembered the organization in their estate plans.

ENDOWMENT FUND

With permanent endowment funds, only the earnings are distributed; the principal remains untouched and is invested in perpetuity. In recent years most endowment funds have adopted a total-return policy in which dividends and portfolio appreciation are counted as earnings.

Endowment funds are important to the not-for-profit organization's long-term viability and financial health. Contributions to endowment funds allow donors to make major investments in an organization and enable them to perpetuate their values.

If an organization was founded more than 10 years ago—and still does not have an endowment fund established—its creation should be a high priority. Remember the Kevin Costner movie, *Field of Dreams*. In the movie Costner's character, Ray Kinsella, heard a voice saying "If you build it, they will come." It is much the same with endowment funds. If you establish the endowment fund, they will donate. People rarely think of donating to an endowment fund that has not been established. On the other hand, by establishing the fund and referring to it in public statements and in the organization's publications, the endowment seems to take on a life of its own. Over time, donations and bequests will increase and the endowment will grow.

Organizations wishing to establish endowment funds have a number of options. They may create a separate 501(c)(3) foundation to manage the endowment funds for the benefit of the existing not-for-profit organization. Or the endowment funds might be placed or established in the city's community foundation. Some organizations hire trust companies or financial advisors to manage their endowment funds. Alternatively, if the funds

are still relatively small, the organization's board, staff, and volunteers might establish, invest, and monitor the funds.

In any case, the board will need to adopt appropriate gift acceptance and investment policies. Beyond establishing the endowment fund, the most effective way to ensure healthy growth of the endowment is to publicize the bequests program.

This chapter has devoted a fair amount of space to various gift-planning strategies. Now it is time to focus attention on the simplest, most common, and easiest-to-understand planned gift, the bequest. Mention wills and bequests in the organization's written materials and existing publications. Write short articles reminding donors of the importance of drawing up a will or establishing an estate plan. Publish the sample codicil language mentioned earlier. Be consistent in the reminders. These few simple steps will help ensure that the organization will have the endowment funds needed to sustain its work well into the 21st century.

SAMPLE MARKETING PLAN FOR CHARITABLE GIFT ANNUITIES

To see how these donor education strategies might fit together, consider the following easy-to-administer plan to promote charitable gift annuities. Follow this step-by-step approach.

Initial Activities

- Develop a charitable gift annuity brochure for the organization. The brochure should contain a "request for an illustration of benefits." Or use one purchased from one of the planned-giving service providers.

- Develop a standard ad format for the organization's newsletters with a clip-out coupon for more information, including birth date (see Exhibit 13-7).

- Develop a standard letter to respond to those asking for additional information (see Exhibit 13-8). Call the respondents prior to sending out this information.

- Develop planned-giving reminder slips to include with selected thank-you letters (see Exhibits 13-4 and 13-5).

- Consider using preprinted, purchased brochures.

EXHIBIT 13-7 CHARITABLE GIFT ANNUITIES: RESPONSE CARD

Please send me an Illustration of Benefits

To learn more about St. Bonaventure's charitable gift annuities, complete this form and return it to the address below. You are under no obligation and all information you provide will be held in confidence.

Name _____

Address _____

City _____

State, Zip _____

Phone ( ) _____

Birthdate: ____/____/____ __Male __Female

First Beneficiary: (Name) _____

Birthdate: ____/____/____ __Male __Female

Second Beneficiary: (Name) _____

Birthdate: ____/____/____ __Male __Female

Possible gift date: ____/____/____

Payments to start: __ now __ in the year _____

Possible gift amount (min. $5,000): $_____

Annuity income payment schedule:

__ semiannually __ annually __ quarterly

Original cost of gift if other than cash: $_____

Mail or Fax to:

Bob O'Connell, Director
St. Bonaventure Indian Mission & School
P.O. Box 610, Thoreau, NM 87323-0610
Ph: (505) 862-7847 Fax (505) 862-7029

Reprinted with permission from St. Bonaventure Indian Mission & School.

February 26, 2002

Mr. and Mrs. Generous Donor
1234 Main Street
Chicago, IL 00000

Dear Mr. and Mrs. Donor:

Thank you for this opportunity to provide an illustration of the benefits you will receive as a donor to our XYZ Not-for-Profit Annuity Fund. We appreciate your interest.

To summarize the attached illustration, your ages at the time you propose to send your gift (75 years for you and 77 years for Mrs. Donor) result in an annuity rate of 7.00%. Your gift of $10,000 will produce annual payments of $700.00. Until the year 2012, $362.69 of your annual payment will be tax-free and $337.31 will be taxable as ordinary income. On your 2002 tax return you may itemize $4,450.80 of your gift as a charitable deduction. A gift to the XYZ Not-for-Profit Organization Annuity Fund is irrevocable, and the lifetime annual income for you and Mrs. Donor is guaranteed by the full faith and credit of the XYZ Not-for-Profit Organization.

If you are ready at this time to make your gift, please complete the attached Charitable Gift Annuity Application form and return it with your check made payable to *"XYZ Not-for-Profit Organization Annuity Fund."* Also, provide a copy of each of your driver's licenses, passports, or birth certificates as verification of your ages.

Upon receipt we will complete a Gift Annuity Agreement for you to sign. You might wish to discuss this gift with your financial planner or attorney. If you or they have any questions, please call me at (505) 123-4567.

Thank you, Mr. and Mrs. Donor, for your kindness and generosity. Your continued support of XYZ Not-for-Profit Organization is truly appreciated.

Sincerely,

Michael Kroth
Director of Planned Giving

attachments

- Discuss potential segmentation. All current and former givers are prospects for planned gifts. The "best prospects" have given frequently. Of course, "best prospects" also include those whose cumulative giving is in the top 20 percent of the in-house list. Also include individuals who have made major gifts to the organization.

- Mail a charitable gift annuity brochure at least once a year. Include a postage-paid business return envelope with the mailing.

Response to Inquiry

Once a reply has been received from a charitable gift annuity prospect, follow this step-by-step approach:

- If the inquiry is in response to a piece that states "Send me information about charitable gift annuities," call and thank the prospect for his or her continuing support and interest. Send a response letter with a form that the supporter can fill out requesting an illustration of benefits. Or include a brochure and ask the prospective donor to complete the form in it. If the inquiry includes the charitable gift annuity response form, go directly to the next bulleted item.

- When the not-for-profit organization receives the response form, a knowledgeable representative of the organization should call and thank the prospect. Review the information on the application and say a personalized illustration of benefits will be put together. The conversation might include something like the following: "I'll be in your area Thursday. Could I stop by with the information?" If the prospect replies affirmatively, make an appointment. Take the illustration of benefits (see Exhibit 13-9). Help the prospect make a mutually beneficial decision. If an organization representative cannot meet personally with the prospect, send the illustration of benefits by mail with a letter indicating that someone will call "in case you have any questions."

Completion of Gift

When the charitable gift annuity document (see Exhibit 13-10) is prepared, call and mail it to the contributor. Or call and ask to visit. Once the supporter and the not-for-profit have signed the charitable gift annuity agree-

EXHIBIT 13-9   CHARITABLE GIFT ANNUITY RECORD CARD: EXAMPLE

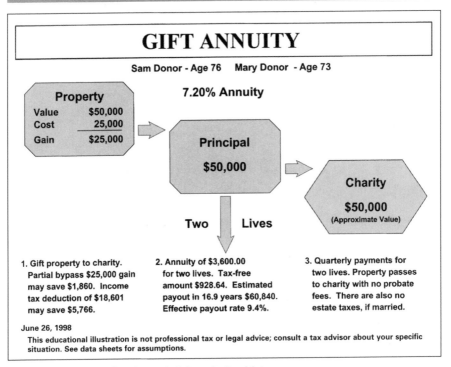

GIFT ANNUITY

Sam Donor - Age 76   Mary Donor - Age 73

Property

Value	$50,000
Cost	25,000
Gain	$25,000

7.20% Annuity

Principal

$50,000

Two   Lives

Charity

$50,000

(Approximate Value)

1. Gift property to charity. Partial bypass $25,000 gain may save $1,860. Income tax deduction of $18,601 may save $5,766.

2. Annuity of $3,600.00 for two lives. Tax-free amount $928.64. Estimated payout in 16.9 years $60,840. Effective payout rate 9.4%.

3. Quarterly payments for two lives. Property passes to charity with no probate fees. There are also no estate taxes, if married.

June 26, 1998

This educational illustration is not professional tax or legal advice; consult a tax advisor about your specific situation. See data sheets for assumptions.

Reprinted with permission from Crescendo Software by Comdel, Inc.

ment, send a thank-you letter indicating standard tax information about the nature of the gift and repeat the main benefits of the annuity. Also indicate when the supporter may expect the first annuity payment.

Follow-up

To maintain strong relationships with charitable gift annuitants, the not-for-profit organization can take a number of steps. For example, a key person with the organization may send Christmas cards, birthday cards, and periodic personal notes. Of course polite thank-you letters must be sent with the annuity payments. At the annual anniversary of the original gift, arrange for a visit, "to see how things are going."

Current annuitants are the not-for-profit organization's best prospects for additional charitable gift annuities. Some donors start with a modest

EXHIBIT 13-10   CHARITABLE GIFT ANNUITY
DOCUMENT

Sample Charitable Gift Annuity Agreement—Two Life

THIS AGREEMENT made and entered into this Twenty-seventh day of November 2002, by and between Frank and Judy Donor of Chicago, IL, and the XYZ Not-for-Profit Organization, a nonprofit corporation, incorporated under the laws of the State of Illinois and located at Chicago, IL.

WITNESSETH:

THAT WHEREAS the said Frank and Judy Donor have paid and delivered to the XYZ Not-for-Profit Organization the sum of $50,000 lawful money of the United States of America or its equivalent, the receipt whereof is hereby acknowledged:

NOW THEREFORE the XYZ Not-for-Profit Organization hereby agrees to pay Frank and Judy Donor jointly, and after the first of them to die to the survivor of them, during the natural lifetime of such survivor the sum of $2,950.00 in each year from and after the date hereof, payable in equal quarterly payments, the first payment being $737.50 on the Twenty-ninth day of February 2003, and subsequent payments of $737.50 on the Thirty-first day of May 2003, and quarterly thereafter on the last day of the month, as long as the said Frank and Judy Donor shall live.

IT IS FURTHER AGREED that all obligations under this agreement shall terminate with the payment made prior to the death of the annuitant and the remainder shall be the property of the XYZ Not-for-Profit Organization without any further claim or change thereon, to be used for the purpose of the corporation.

This annuity is non-assignable.

XYZ Not-for-Profit Organization

By: _____
              Executive Director

NOTE: *We are not offering legal advice. When drawing legal documents, each not-for-profit organization should consult with its attorney.*

contribution. Upon experiencing the benefits and favorable interest rates with the smaller gift annuity, they gain confidence and make arrangements for larger charitable gift annuities.

To expand an organization's charitable gift annuity program, send a special letter thanking current annuitants. In the letter indicate that "many of our friends who currently have annuities find it a good idea to consider another." Include a brochure and a postage-paid business return envelope. As always, the brochure should come with a response form.

PLANNED-GIVING SOCIETIES

One of the most effective ways of encouraging planned gifts is to create a gift club for people who have remembered the organization in their wills or estate plans. Membership should be open to all who have indicated that they have provided for the organization or who have otherwise made planned gifts.

Names for such groups include Legacy League, Heritage Society, Omega Club, Angels, or some other name more closely tied to the organization. Perhaps the most effective strategy is to name the planned gift society after a well-respected philanthropist in the community.

Using the organization's newsletter, announce the formation of the "Heritage Society." Also promote the society in all internal publications. Consider special mailings to planned gift prospects. Create a plaque or wall of honor acknowledging members of the planned gift club.

Invite planned gift club members to an annual lunch or dinner. At the dinner, introduce new members. Keep the program lively. Use the occasion for a "State of the Charity" talk or inspirational message.

In summary, people who make planned gifts are without doubt an organization's best friends. Treat them with the love and respect they deserve.

Capital and Endowment Campaigns

Make no little plans; they have no magic to stir men's blood. . . .
Make big plans, aim high in hope and work.

—Daniel H. Burnham, as quoted in *The Raising of May*

REQUIREMENTS FOR A SUCCESSFUL CAMPAIGN

To conduct a successful capital and/or endowment campaign, an organization must convince its constituents that the project deserves support. The plan must be visionary. The plan must make sense. And the project has to be consistent with the organization's mission and strategic long-range plan.

Each of the chapters in this book—especially Chapters 4 through 8—is integral to the planning and implementation of a successful capital campaign. The planned-giving information in Chapter 13 is essential to the success of any endowment-building program. Armed with the information from the earlier chapters, readers can focus attention on the critical success factors described in this chapter.

Resource development professionals who have had years of capital and endowment campaign experience have come to recognize seven fundamental prerequisites for successful campaigns:

1. Based on its record of service, the organization must be worthy of support. Potential supporters must have *confidence* in the organization.

2. The *case for support* for the proposed capital and/or endowment campaign must be *understood and accepted*.

3. The constituents must have the *capability* to support the campaign at the necessary giving levels (see Exhibits 14-1 to 14-6). The funds must be available and attainable. Remember the "rule of thirds": One-third to one-half of the total will come from the top 10 gifts; one-third will come from the next 100 donations; the remainder comes from all other prospects.

4. Attract *strong volunteer leadership*. The campaign organization will require enthusiastic and generous leaders and volunteers.

5. The philanthropic *environment and timing* must be right.

6. The campaign must be well organized and staffed with individuals *capable of supporting* a major project initiative and fundraising campaign.

7. The board of directors must have a sufficient number of members who are influential within the community. Moreover, all advisory and governing boards close to the proposed capital/endowment campaign must be totally committed to the project's success.

EXHIBIT 14-1   SMALL CONSTITUENCY $1 MILLION CAMPAIGN STANDARDS OF INVESTMENT

Standard of Investments Necessary to Achieve $1,000,000 Goal

Number of Gifts Required	Investment Level 3-year pledge period	Annual Amount	Value
1	$150,000	$50,000	$150,000
2	75,000	25,000	150,000
3	50,000	16,667	150,000
4	30,000	10,000	120,000
8	15,000	5,000	120,000
14	7,500	2,500	105,000
17	5,000	1,667	85,000
25	3,000	1,000	75,000
30	1,500	500	45,000
104			$1,000,000

EXHIBIT 14-2 SMALL CONSTITUENCY $2 MILLION CAMPAIGN STANDARDS OF INVESTMENT

Standard of Investments Necessary to Achieve $2,000,000 Goal

Number of Gifts Required	Investment Level 3-year pledge period	Annual Amount	Value
1	$300,000	$100,000	$300,000
2	150,000	50,000	300,000
3	75,000	25,000	225,000
5	50,000	16,667	250,000
9	30,000	10,000	270,000
15	15,000	5,000	225,000
20	7,500	2,500	150,000
26	5,000	1,667	130,000
30	3,000	1,000	90,000
40	1,500	500	60,000
151			$2,000,000

EXHIBIT 14-3 SMALL CONSTITUENCY $3 MILLION CAMPAIGN STANDARDS OF INVESTMENT

Standard of Investments Necessary to Achieve $3,000,000 Goal

Number of Gifts Required	Investment Level 3-year pledge period	Annual Amount	Value
1	$500,000	$166,667	$500,000
1	300,000	100,000	300,000
2	150,000	50,000	300,000
3	75,000	25,000	225,000
6	50,000	16,667	300,000
10	30,000	10,000	300,000
20	15,000	5,000	300,000
30	7,500	2,500	225,000
50	5,000	1,667	250,000
60	3,000	1,000	180,000
80	1,500	500	120,000
263			$3,000,000

EXHIBIT 14-4 # MODEST CONSTITUENCY $2.5 MILLION CAMPAIGN

Standard of Investments Necessary to Achieve $2,500,000 Goal

Number of Gifts Required	Investment Level 3-year pledge period	Annual Amount	Value
1	$300,000	$100,000	$300,000
2	150,000	50,000	300,000
3	75,000	25,000	225,000
3	50,000	16,667	150,000
5	30,000	10,000	150,000
20	15,000	5,000	300,000
30	7,500	2,500	225,000
50	5,000	1,667	250,000
100	3,000	1,000	300,000
200	1,500	500	300,000
414			$2,500,000

EXHIBIT 14-5 # LARGE CONSTITUENCY $5 MILLION CAMPAIGN

Standard of Investments Necessary to Achieve $5,000,000 Goal

Number of Gifts Required	Investment Level 3-year pledge period	Annual Amount	Value
1	$1,000,000	$333,334	$1,000,000
1	500,000	166,667	500,000
1	300,000	100,000	300,000
2	150,000	50,000	300,000
3	75,000	25,000	225,000
4	50,000	16,667	200,000
10	30,000	10,000	300,000
25	15,000	5,000	375,000
40	7,500	2,500	300,000
60	5,000	1,667	300,000
200	3,000	1,000	600,000
400	1,500	500	600,000
747			$5,000,000

EXHIBIT 14-6   SMALL CONSTITUENCY, STRONG LEADERSHIP $15 MILLION CAMPAIGN

Standard of Investments Necessary to Achieve $15,000,000 Goal

Number of Gifts Required	Investment Level 3-year pledge period	Annual Amount	Value
1	$3,000,000	$1,000,000	$3,000,000
1	1,500,000	500,000	1,500,000
3	1,000,000	333,333	3,000,000
3	500,000	166,666	1,500,000
6	300,000	100,000	1,800,000
9	150,000	50,000	1,350,000
11	75,000	25,000	825,000
15	50,000	16,666	750,000
25	30,000	10,000	750,000
35	15,000	5,000	525,000
109			$15,000,000

When all these factors are in place, the results are often spectacular. Universities raise hundreds of millions of dollars—even a billion dollars or more. Large health care institutions garner tens or hundreds of millions of dollars for buildings, endowment, and equipment. Arts institutions, independent schools, YWCAs, YMCAs, churches, synagogues, and not-for-profit institutions of every ilk have the potential to raise millions. In many cases organizations with little fundraising experience have been helped to organize successful multimillion-dollar campaigns.

Still, many organizations get it wrong. Some of the most common mistakes come from a lack of understanding of the true nature of capital campaigns. Many volunteers or less experienced staff come to the capital campaign with an annual fund drive focus or with a point of view shaped by the public phase of some other capital campaign. These misguided perspectives rely on direct mail and special events and a focus on a broad base of support. While such strategies may be helpful during the public phase of a capital campaign, they generally are incompatible with the success of a capital campaign.

Capital campaigns are built around leadership giving. As mentioned, one-third to one-half of the funds raised will come from the top 10 donors. In church campaigns, an old rule holds that 50 percent of the funds will

come from 15 percent of the congregation. To be sure, there are exceptions to these rules. Surprisingly, however, most exceptions lead to an *even greater* reliance on leadership gifts.

Because the leadership gifts are so important to the success of the campaign, the primary strategy used in capital campaigns is person-to-person contact. Preparation, research, and relationship-building activities take time. The institution must ensure that all constituencies support the visionary plan. Leaders of the not-for-profit organization also must know their current and prospective pace-setting donors very well. And supporters who are expected to play leadership roles must have an opportunity to shape the organization's plans.

Organizations get into trouble with their capital campaigns when they announce the goal prior to securing leadership contributions. Organizations should not announce or broadly promote their capital campaigns until 40, 50, or 60 percent of the pledges are secured during the "quiet" or "advancement" phase of the drive.

CHRONOLOGICAL STEPS FOR SUCCESS

Capital campaigns are characterized by visionary projects and large financial goals. The funds are to be attained during a multiyear pledge period. The project must be well accepted by the organization's supporters. And the funds are raised through an intense effort based on face-to-face contacts. The solicitations are sequential in nature. Leadership contributions are secured first from those closest to the organization who are capable of making pace-setting investments. Prospects and supporters close to the organization with more modest means are approached after the leadership gifts have been secured. Finally, there is a public phase when the larger base of supporters is approached for capital contributions.

But even before the advancement or quiet phase of the campaign, a number of important tasks must be accomplished. Exhibit 14-7 illustrates a comprehensive time line for a capital campaign.

Prestudy Phase

The first stage in preparation for a capital campaign is designed to ensure the institution's readiness to engage in such a significant undertaking. The following is a list of tasks to accomplish:

EXHIBIT 14-7   CAPITAL CAMPAIGN TIME LINE

ACTIVITY	2000 May	June	July	Aug	Sept	Oct	Nov	Dec	2001 Jan	Feb	Mar	Apr	May	June	July	Aug	Sept	Oct	Nov	Dec	2002 Jan	Feb	Mar	Apr	May	June
Define Need, Establish Costs, Develop Preliminary Statement of Need	XXX	XX																								
Pre-Study Counseling Visit		XX																								
Miniature Study		-XX																								
Develop Comprehensive Case Statement			XXX	XXX																						
Develop Awareness/Education Plan & Agenda					XXX																					
Develop Audio/Visual Presentation for Awareness Program					XXX	XXX																				
Identify Potential Invitees to Awareness Meetings							XXX	XXX	XXX																	
Identify & Recruit Hosts for Awareness Meetings							XXX	XXX																		
Conduct Pilot Awareness Meetings								XXX	XXX																	
Implement Awareness Program									XXX	XXX	XXX															
Conduct Planning Study Interviews												XXX														
Report Study Results													-XX													
Revise Case Statement, Recruit Campaign Leadership & Begin Advancement Phase														XXX	XXX	XXX										
Develop Plan of Campaign, Time Schedule, Brochure, etc.																-XX	XXX	XXX	XXX							
Intensify Prospect Research & Evaluation																-XX	XXX	XXX	XXX	XXX	XXX					
Advance Gift Solicitation																			-XX	XXX	XXX					
Intermediate Gift Solicitation																				XXX	XXX	XXX				
Public Phase Solicitation																					XXX	XXX	XXX	XXX		
Victory Celebration																							XXX	XXX	XXX	
Post Campaign Clean-up																										XXX

253

- Review all issues related to board development. Strengthen nominating criteria and processes. Seek people with affluence and influence. Seek diversity. Strengthen, expand, and activate the board's committees.

- Intensify the project planning. At every step involve as many board members, volunteers, and potential large supporters as possible.

- Prepare preliminary written materials describing the project, its history, rationale, and case for support. Stress the project's benefits to the community.

- Prepare a number of project budgets. Examine the total contributed income necessary to operate the organization and accommodate the capital/endowment requirements. Use a spreadsheet program to examine a number of what-if scenarios.

- Refine the preliminary materials based on discoveries during the preliminary budget formulation process.

- Prepare the following draft materials:

  —a case for support

  —a project plan and time line—consider obtaining architects' sketches or preliminary elevations and floor plans, if applicable

  —spreadsheets or draft budgets illustrating various options

  —the tentative income requirements—including the first estimate of the campaign goal

  —a description of your needs on a prioritized basis

  —a statement of how the project fits into the institution's over-all long-range plan

  —a preliminary gift pyramid also called Standards of Investments

Often the capital campaign counsel facilitates the process by which these tasks are accomplished. Development staff and/or campaign counsel also can help create the preliminary campaign materials.

Throughout this process, the organization must work to ensure that it is well positioned in the philanthropic community. Be sure that volunteers, advisory committees, governing bodies, and potential supporters stay actively involved in the planning process. If any key people or con-

stituencies have been neglected, brief them and make every effort to get them involved.

Provide numerous opportunities for key decision makers to learn more about resource development principles and practices. If it has not been done already, form a resource development committee that will help shape the organization's comprehensive fundraising strategy. This committee may seek advice and work with counsel to formulate the overall fundraising strategy. Most important, develop a core of knowledgeable people who will help the organization avoid the common mistakes in preparing for a capital campaign. These people will remind other board members and volunteers to focus on leadership gifts. This committee will remind others to seek support from individuals as well as from foundations and corporations. It will remind other volunteers that the appropriate strategy for a capital campaign is personal contact—not mail, phone, or special events. This is the group that will stress the importance of a multiyear pledge period.

As early as possible, the organization must make every effort to improve its record-keeping ability. Strengthen the fundraising information system. If it is not available, purchase dedicated fundraising software. The system must accommodate detailed information about each current and potential supporter. It must also enable you to segment lists based on the prospects' ability to donate at various levels, as well as other criteria. The system also will allow for the tracking of all volunteer solicitor assignments; will generate reports and record pledges; and will track pledge balances and payments.

Prospect research was discussed in Chapter 6. If you have not yet followed the advice in that Chapter, now is the time to reread it and get to work. While implementing the prospect research program, focus on the four key points:

1. The prospective donor's interests—especially as they may relate to the capital campaign

2. The prospective donor's relationship to the organization and to the capital project

3. The prospective donor's capacity to give—consider assets as well as annual income

4. The prospective donor's network of associates

Be sure to keep written records of this information. This is the time to begin to arrive at specific request amounts from specific donors.

If the services of fundraising counsel have not yet been engaged, now would be a good time to do so. Even organizations with a large experienced resource development staff find it helpful to work with a consulting firm experienced in capital campaigns. Such outside objective counsel helps reduce risk and helps ensure that the staff and volunteers stay on a path that maximizes the organization's fundraising potential. The services provided during the planning phase—including a feasibility study, philanthropic planning study, or market survey—are essential to the future success of the campaign. The services provided during the campaign help maintain momentum and also include guidance if unforeseen circumstances arise.

The Planning Study

A feasibility study, philanthropic planning study, or market survey is a study conducted by an independent and objective person or study team— almost always a fundraising consulting firm. A number of confidential interviews—usually 30 to 50—with selected individuals representing key prospective donors and volunteers of affluence and influence conducted by representatives of the consulting firm lie at the heart of the study. The confidential nature of the interviews allows the interviewees to speak candidly and have maximum input into the planning process. The study participants are sent a summary of the case statement prior to the interview.

There are two essential purposes of the planning study. It helps an organization determine its fundraising potential, and it is important to the relationship-nurturing process.

To understand how these two main purposes are achieved, consider the planning study process. To begin with, a planning study committee (a job description for such a committee is included on the CD-ROM that accompanies this book), task force, or other appropriate committee works to prepare and refine a preliminary case for support. This committee may also help refine the list of people to be interviewed. These initial activities are important steps in the process and can help strengthen an organization's bonds with those serving on this most important committee.

But consider the entire process from interviewees' perspectives. At first, potential study participants receive a letter similar to Exhibit 14-8 requesting

EXHIBIT 14-8   LETTER REQUESTING INTERVIEW

(Draft of Prescheduling Call Letter)
(XYZ Not-for-Profit Organization or Prominent Person's Letterhead)

DATE

Joseph Samplename
1234 Interview Lane
Anytown, TX 78000

Dear Mr. Samplename:

This is not a funding request. Rather, I am writing to ask for your insight and advice.

XYZ Not-for-Profit Organization provides compassionate services for children who are victims of physical, emotional, and sexual abuse as well as neglect. Today XYZ Not-for-Profit is a comprehensive child abuse intervention, prevention, and treatment agency serving more than 1,000 children and 400 parents each year.

As XYZ prepares for the future, our most pressing challenge is to provide safe and pleasant facilities for our children. Our Children's Shelter must be renovated. The counseling offices must be housed together with the other service programs. And our plan must offer the greatest flexibility to enable XYZ to respond to increasing demands for services.

In response to these needs, XYZ is embarking on a process designed to help us refine our plans and integrate the best advice from friends and community leaders. To help us with this process, Stanley Weinstein of Hartsook and Associates will conduct a number of confidential leadership interviews.

Your advice and perspective mean a great deal to us. I would be most appreciative if you could meet with Mr. Weinstein for a confidential interview to hear your frank opinions. The interview will take no more than 30 to 45 minutes. We will contact you in the next few days to arrange a time that is convenient for you.

Enclosed is a summary of XYZ's current situation and our vision for the future. I hope you have an opportunity to look this over prior to your interview. Thanks for your time and help.

With appreciation for all you have done for Albuquerque,

Richard Schuler, Executive Director
(or board president, other prominent signer, or individual who knows the interviewee)

the interview as well as a summary case for support. Next, they receive a gracious phone call to establish the time for the interview. During this phone call a representative of the organization or consulting firm—a person with good people skills—responds to any concerns potential interviewees may have concerning the reason for the study. Often participants need to be assured that the study is *not* a solicitation. Following the phone call, interviewees receive a letter confirming the appointment.

The next step is the interview. During the interview the consultant asks a number of open-ended questions (see Exhibit 14-9), introduces the campaign's Standard of Investments page and seeks advice concerning potential campaign donors and potential campaign leaders. The consultant also provides interviewees an opportunity to indicate their own potential range of support. Interviewees understand that they are not being solicited during the interview. The consultant explains that the support information is needed to estimate campaign potential.

Following the interview, study participants are sent a thank-you letter. Once the study is complete, representatives of the organization arrange a meeting to discuss the findings and report with each interviewee. This briefing often evolves into the first explicit solicitation. The conversation might include words like these: "Given these findings and your commitment to the project, we hope that you might be in a position to play an important role in the campaign and consider one of these leadership gift opportunities."

In summary, the planning study process engages prospective supporters through six steps taking place in a brief period of time: the invitation letter, the appointment phone call, the confirmation letter, the interview, the thank-you letter, and the poststudy briefing. These six steps bring people closer to the organization. Moreover, the information gathered during the interviews helps establish the campaign fundraising goal.

Immediately following the interview period, the consultant will review the findings and prepare specific recommendations regarding the campaign goal, strategies, and campaign timing; volunteer leadership; case for support; and other recommendations unique to an organization's particular circumstances. The consultant will furnish the organization with a number of bound copies of the report and also will meet with the board and key decision-making committees to discuss the findings, conclusions, and recommendations.

EXHIBIT 14-9 INTERVIEW QUESTIONS

XYZ Not-for-Profit Organization Confidential Pre-campaign Interview

Name of Interviewee: _____

1. Are you familiar with or have you been associated with XYZ Not-for-Profit Organization?

2. How would you characterize your relationship with XYZ Not-for-Profit Organization?

3. What, in your opinion, is XYZ Not-for-Profit Organization's image with people in this region? How well accepted do you think XYZ Not-for-Profit Organization is?

   Excellent _____   Good _____   Fair _____   Poor _____

4. What is your judgment of XYZ Not-for-Profit Organization?

5. With which XYZ Not-for-Profit Organization are you familiar? Which are strong? Are any weak?

6. Are there any proposed activities of which you disapprove?

   Why?

7. Are there specific projects or facilities you specifically would like to be put in place at XYZ Not-for-Profit Organization?

8. What is your opinion of the organization's administration?

9. What do you think of XYZ Not-for-Profit Organization's case for support?

10. Does any part of the case for support have greater appeal for you (personally, your company or foundation) than any other?

11. What factors would you point to that would *HELP* ensure a successful fundraising campaign at this time?

12. What factors would you point to that could *HARM* a fundraising campaign at this time?

13. Do you believe a $5.3 million capital campaign payable over a three-year period will be successful?

Present Gift Chart

14. Gifts by individuals account for most of our nation's philanthropic support. Could you, confidentially, identify the best prospects here in Anytown for XYZ Not-for-Profit Organization to approach who might give in these ranges?
    NAME   BEST CONTACT

    What organizations, corporations, or foundations might be approached?
    NAME   BEST CONTACT

15. We are not soliciting a gift at this time, but what would be an appropriate range—low to high—for you to consider as a gift to XYZ Not-for-Profit Organization's campaign by virtue of a pledge payable over a three-year period?
    (PERSONAL GIFT)   LOW   HIGH   PLEDGE PERIOD

(continued)

EXHIBIT 14-9 (CONTINUED)

16. Would you consider a gift based on noncash assets such as stocks, bonds, land, or as a result of estate planning?

     <u>YES</u>   <u>NO</u>

17. Can you recommend a few names of people who would ensure the success of the campaign if they assumed a volunteer leadership position?

18. Would you act as an intermediary to reach them?

     <u>YES</u>   <u>NO</u>

     Which ones?

19. Would you be willing to participate in such a campaign by making three to five introductions for fundraising purposes?

20. Again in confidence, are there any questions I should have asked but didn't? Or do you have any additional advice you care to give the XYZ Not-for-Profit Organization?

Name of Interviewer: _____ Date: _____

Well over 90 percent of all successful capital campaigns are preceded by a feasibility or planning study. Small wonder. Such studies position an organization to succeed and produce the following benefits:

- An organization's plans can be established within a context of rational financial goals. The study tests the reality of the project's contributed income requirements.

- The study uncovers valuable insights into community perceptions of the organization.

- Interviewees help identify potential volunteer leaders with the peer relationships needed for success of the campaign.

- Interviewees also help identify potential major gift donors—new prospects with whom the organization might not be familiar.

- Potential leaders and major gift donors will become more familiar with the organization's programs, aspirations, and need for the capital project.

- The study includes recommendations that enable the organization to strengthen, position, and organize its internal and external resources to meet the challenge of a major fundraising campaign.

- If the organization is not yet ready for a capital or endowment campaign, the report will contain specific recommendations concerning the steps needed to strengthen its position within the philanthropic community.

The Advancement or "Quiet" Phase

Successful campaigns begin with what some call the quiet or advancement phase of the campaign. During this period early generous and pace-setting supporters are identified, cultivated, and graciously solicited. A small core group of volunteers is recruited. This core group, in turn, intensifies the organization's other cultivation and leadership awareness activities.

Note that at this stage, the not-for-profit organization has not yet recruited the entire capital campaign leadership and volunteer team. Many volunteers are not needed until the intermediate and public phases of the campaign. If the organization recruits too many volunteers too early, enthusiasm dissipates because each group of volunteers must wait until the previous phase is completed.

Again, capital campaigns are sequential in nature. During the advancement phase, the organization can approach potential pace-setting contributors. The people who should make these approaches include the organization's president or executive director, the board chair, several of the most generous and influential members of the board, the chair of the capital campaign (if recruited shortly after the planning study), or one or two key volunteers who are very respected in the community. The organization's director of development and the campaign consultant also may participate as team members working with key volunteers.

Note that approximately seven key volunteers are required—not a large formal campaign cabinet and structure. These seven people might be responsible for nurturing relationships and involving approximately five prospective leadership donors each. Thus the small group of volunteers and key staff can manage a solicitation process for approximately 35 top prospects. From these 35 prospects, the organization might expect to secure the 10 lead gifts that will account for 33 to 50 percent of the goal. Not

until the organization is close to securing the lead gifts should the key volunteers begin to recruit the entire campaign team for the intermediate and public phases.

The main problem with recruiting volunteers too soon is that promoting second-tier gifts prior to securing the leadership investments should be avoided. During the advancement phase, all the focus and conversation should be about multimillion-dollar, million-dollar, and high six-figure gift opportunities (or the appropriate gift range for the top 10 investments in your campaign). Real and psychological momentum is lost when top prospects become distracted by attention given to modest-level gifts.

Another issue related to early volunteer recruitment is that organizations must be sure to take advantage of the advice offered by study participants. These interviewees are the organization's best prospects. Their advice is valuable. When study participants offer suggestions about who should and should not be considered for a campaign leadership position, this advice should be heeded.

Suffice to say, the advancement phase is the time to *begin* expanding and forming the volunteer structure. Focus on early solicitations and relationship-building activities. Breakfast briefings for businesspeople, focus groups, social/informative gatherings, and personal visits bring potential pace-setting donors closer to the not-for-profit organization and its capital/endowment campaign.

During the advancement phase, the core group makes its initial approaches—most commonly several in-person visits—to potential pace-setting donors. The early visits are informative. Frequently, volunteers might suggest gift levels. Later visits are devoted to more detailed discussions of gift opportunities, pledge requests, pledge payment schedules, and other circumstances unique to the donor.

During the quiet phase, the not-for-profit organization should secure pledges from 100 percent of the board of directors. Pledges from key administrative staff also should be sought. If the organization is a hospital, great care should be given to the staff solicitations. As much as 15 to 20 percent of the goal may be secured from the physicians and staff of the hospital.

Not until 100 percent participation from the board of directors and sufficient pace-setting pledges from key supporters have been secured should

the campaign and the goal be spoken about publicly. To repeat: Do not go public until at least 50 percent of the established goal has been secured. This allows the campaign goal to be adjusted based on the organization's ability to attract pace-setting gifts. Perhaps more important, public announcements following the 50 percent rule inspire confidence. Momentum is established and built on. Anything less, and prospective donors are left wondering if their gifts would even make a difference.

Some of the critical tasks that take place during the advancement phase include:

- Intensifying prospect research and capacity ratings. Determining request amounts and gift opportunities for specific donors. (This is an extension of work begun prior to the interviews.)
- Recruiting campaign leaders.
- Reconciling project plans to financial projections as determined by the feasibility study. Reaching agreement on the project budget, project phases, and fundraising goals.
- Revising the case statement based on suggestions from interviewees.
- Developing and refining campaign strategies, organization, plans, and time lines. Stressing the importance of "sequential campaigns." Those closest to the project and those capable of lead gifts are solicited first.
- Adopting campaign policies and procedures.
- Refining the gift pyramid and ensuring that a sufficient number of gift opportunities correspond to the various gift levels.
- Planning public relations activities and acknowledgment events that support the sequential nature of the solicitation process.
- Producing brochures and other visual materials. (Don't go overboard too soon. Early on, attractive word-processed materials are sufficient, although a well-produced video can serve an organization well at this stage.)

To reiterate, the advancement phase is the time to seek 100 percent participation from the board of directors, recruit campaign leaders, intensify cultivation activities, revisit study participants, and quietly solicit the lead gifts.

The Intermediate Phase

Following the solicitation of the board of directors and the prospective pace-setting leadership contributors, volunteers (who now include generous supporters recruited during the advancement phase) may approach the organization's second tier of contributors. These current and prospective supporters should have been invited to participate in cultivation activities during the advancement phase, so they know something about the capital and endowment campaign. In all probability, they are expecting a visit.

During this intermediate phase, the organization may develop more elaborate printed campaign materials, recruit a broader base of volunteers, and go public. Consider a public "kick-off" extravaganza any time after 50 percent of the established goal is achieved. Continue cultivation activities. And solicit contributions from the second tier of supporters.

Be sure that the volunteers are well oriented and have received enough role-playing and training opportunities. But do remember the advice offered in Chapter 8. Don't overtrain. The volunteers need to feel comfortable, not overwhelmed.

Public Phase

Conclude the capital/endowment campaign with a broad-based appeal. Give every potential supporter an opportunity to participate.

Expand the volunteer base to the maximum possible. Continue and intensify the number of social/informative cultivation gatherings. Early in this phase stage a public "kick-off" extravaganza if one has not been held already. Also, have a party to rally all volunteers to complete their assignments. The training sessions can have a party atmosphere. Maintain enthusiasm. Have fun. Keep everyone focused on face-to-face contact.

When the organization's ability to expand its person-to-person contacts seems exhausted, conduct a broad-based public phase such as a brick or tile campaign . . . or conclude with direct appeals through telephone and mail. This very late public phase is the *only* time during the campaign that *might* include mail or phone solicitations. Never abandon the face-to-face contacts. Keep track of all assignments. Urge volunteers and staff members to complete the follow-up visits generated by earlier contacts.

Be sure to stage a victory celebration when the goal has been reached. The celebration may be as elaborate or modest as you wish. But do

take care to acknowledge all volunteers and supporters as generously as possible.

Follow-up

Capital campaigns are built around multiyear pledges. So follow-up activities are needed to continue fostering positive relationships with donors and to help ensure pledge fulfillment. Occasionally people who sign pledge cards renege on their commitments. Resource development professionals estimate that, on average, not more than 2 or 2.5 percent of the capital campaign pledge total is lost due to donor's failure to make the pledged contributions.

Some attrition is unavoidable. Circumstances change. Supporters move or lose interest. People lose their jobs. Backers become infirmed. Donors die.

Still, business sense and good manners dictate that the organization stay in touch with pledgers and continue to make them feel important and appreciated. To begin with, all supporters should be invited to acknowledgment events celebrating the capital campaign victory. If there is a building opening or dedication of new facilities, capital campaign donors should be invited to the celebration.

The development office also should keep track of all pledge payment schedules. Some donors prefer to contribute annually. Others prefer to make their pledge payments monthly or quarterly. In many church campaigns, some members of the congregation contribute weekly. The important consideration from a systems point of view is that delinquent pledge payments must not be overlooked. Nor should it take too long for the organization to respond to the missed payments. It should not take months to respond to missed payments from a weekly pledger. The missed quarterly payment should be addressed early in the next quarter. If representatives of the organization wait too long to send a gracious reminder letter, make a follow-up phone call or visit, the pledger might get farther behind and find it difficult to adjust the pledge payment plan.

In every case, development professionals want to be concerned for donors' well-being. When professionals look at everything from donors' points of view, they help the organization's reputation. Such an attitude also is consistent with the organization's long-term best interests. There

will be other campaigns. And besides, it feels good to respond to each situation with compassion and understanding.

During the pledge payment period, organizations can increase their pledge total. The formal campaign shouldn't continue ad infinitum. Campaigns must have a beginning, middle, and conclusion. But small ways can be found to invite additional participation from new prospects or from previous donors. Almost every capital campaign project has some unforeseen or unanticipated expenses.

An old adage holds that no donor's arm and wrist ever got so sore writing the first contribution check that he or she could not write a second check. Organizations can approach their very best and closest donors for additional contributions to the capital campaign. Done selectively and with poise, such requests frequently are successful.

Another strategy that works well for many organizations is to print out a list of all donors who made a single gift or a single-year commitment to the capital campaign. Review this list and decide which donors to approach for additional capital campaign contributions. Often these people are reluctant to make multiyear pledges. However, many respond positively to a gracious solicitation in the second and third years of the pledge payment period. Of course, the organization already has declared victory. So the appeal should stress the importance of capital campaign contributions for unanticipated expenses or for refinements to the plan.

During capital campaigns new donors become involved with the organization. Some of these supporters are not in the organization's regular loop or sphere of influence. At times they are neglected. Development professionals must work to overcome this tendency. All donors to the capital campaign should be invited to the organization's relationship-nurturing activities. At the very minimum, capital campaign donors should receive timely news about the project, the building progress, programs, and the people whom the campaign has helped. Personal contact will help cement the relationship. The goal is to make these donors feel good about their contributions and to convert many of these new friends into long-term supporters of the institution.

BUILDING ENDOWMENTS

There are four main ways to increase an organization's endowment funds: (1) establish an endowment and promote planned gifts for the fund; (2) so-

licit current gifts on an ongoing basis for the endowment fund; (3) include endowment fundraising as part of the capital campaign; and (4) conduct a strictly endowment campaign following the same principles and organization as used in a capital campaign. Naturally, any combination of the four techniques is possible.

The board also may designate any part of the organization's surplus to serve as a "quasi" endowment fund. However, such board-designated funds are not true endowments. What the board can do, the board can undo. And generally accepted accounting principles require that all unrestricted funds be accounted for as unrestricted.

The first strategy—promoting planned gifts for the endowment fund—can be as simple as consistently reminding supporters to remember the organization in their wills and estate plans. Well-respected organizations that take this one modest step can achieve exceptionally positive results over time. Organizations that go further and implement many of the planned-giving suggestions in Chapter 13 can achieve even more extraordinary results.

The second strategy—soliciting current gifts for the endowment fund—can be implemented easily. Just ask. Face-to-face meetings are best. But the organization also might consider a once-a-year special mailing requesting contributions for the endowment fund.

During face-to-face get-togethers, donors might be thanked for their generous support; then the subject of endowment might be broached. Many donors are surprised to realize that a contribution equaling 20 times the amount of their annual contribution can perpetuate their annual support. A donor who contributes $1,000 annually can donate $20,000 to the endowment fund. Assuming a modest 5 percent yield, the endowment would produce $1,000 annually—an amount equal to the donor's annual support. If the yield is, as expected, somewhat greater, the endowment will grow and help respond to inflation. Some donors find the thought of current giving to the endowment simpler to deal with than making provisions in their wills or estate plans. Of course, donors should always be offered choices, and the many ways people can support the organization should be discussed.

The third strategy—the combined capital and endowment drive—is very popular. Donors to large building projects want to know that the not-for-profit institution can maintain the facilities. As important, capital and

endowment campaign contributors view their support as an investment. They want to know that the programs contemplated by the institution can be sustained. Endowment funds provide the long-term stability the institution needs to maintain the facilities and to support its visionary programs. In some institutions endowment funds also serve other important purposes. Some endowments provide scholarships. Some subsidize services for low-income people. And many endowment funds augment the organization's general operating funds. All of these needs are easy to wrap into a comprehensive capital and endowment campaign.

The fourth strategy—the pure endowment campaign—is somewhat less common. At times, foundations established to support a specific not-for-profit institution conduct endowment campaigns. By augmenting their endowment funds, these support foundations can help their mother institutions thrive and flourish. University and hospital foundations, foundations in support of a specific religious denomination, and other support foundations often conduct ongoing, comprehensive fundraising activities. However, sometimes the need for endowment funds dominates the organization's thinking. At such times the organization's closest supporters may respond favorably to an intensive endowment campaign.

The one way in which endowment campaigns differ somewhat from capital campaigns is the mix of current and deferred giving. In a pure capital campaign, the funds are needed within the three- to five-year pledge period to pay for construction, renovations, facilities, equipment, and furnishings. So the emphasis is on current multiyear pledges. In a capital and endowment campaign, the organization first must secure the funds needed for the capital aspects of the campaign. The endowment funds can be acquired in a mix of current and deferred giving.

In a pure endowment campaign, the organization must be prepared to show some immediate tangible benefits to the drive. At the same time, the emphasis can be on the long-term financial security of the institution. So endowment drives often create two goals: current and deferred contributions to the endowment fund. For example, the Foundation for the Support of the XYZ Not-for-Profit Institution may establish a $20 million endowment goal, $5 million to be contributed during a three-year pledge period and $15 million to be secured in new planned gifts.

In another twist on the endowment drive, several years back many arts organizations became involved in various versions of "arts stabilization funds." The idea was to eliminate deficits, establish a cash reserve, and es-

tablish or build endowment funds. In addition, the arts organizations were called on to produce balanced annual budgets or, more preferably, annual budgets that include a modest surplus. If organizations wished to establish an endowment that produced 10 percent of the annual budget, the endowment would need to be two times the size of the annual budget. For example, an institution with a $4 million annual budget would require an endowment of $8 million. Again, assuming a modest 5 percent rate of return, the endowment would produce $400,000 annually, or 10 percent of the operating budget. If the rate of return is greater, the difference can remain in the endowment fund, to help the organization cope with inflation.

The "stabilization fund" is made up mostly of endowment funds. Thus the campaign to establish the stabilization fund is organized using the same intensive techniques used for capital or endowment campaigns.

INSTITUTIONAL DIFFERENCES

All capital and endowment campaigns have some things in common: the importance of visionary plans; the multiyear pledge period; the sequential nature of the campaign; and the importance of the leadership gifts. However, not-for-profit institutions—hospitals, universities, colleges, community colleges, private schools, arts institutions, churches and synagogues, social service agencies, youth groups, preservation and conservation organizations, and professional associations—all have unique qualities that they bring to capital and endowment campaigns.

Indeed, no two campaigns are alike. However, it is helpful to be familiar with some of the expected characteristics of each type of campaign. Some are obvious. For example, symphony subscribers may be very fine prospects for the orchestra's capital and endowment campaign. On the other hand, the service recipients of a social welfare agency's poverty program are not in a position to make significant contributions to a capital campaign.

The following are some basic characteristics of various types of campaigns.

Churches and Synagogues

Church and synagogue capital campaigns generally are much shorter than other campaigns. A significant amount of time may be devoted to project planning. And members of the congregation need ample time to buy in to

the planning process. But the actual campaign can be accomplished in a two-, three-, or four-month period.

In church and synagogue campaigns, the distribution of gifts tends to be flatter than in other capital campaigns—but not necessarily. If the congregation has several very affluent members, they can be encouraged to make large leadership gifts during the advancement phase. In such a case, 50 percent of the contributions may come from 7 to 10 percent of the participating households. More commonly, as mentioned, approximately 15 percent of the households can be expected to contribute 50 percent of the campaign total.

Note that in church campaigns, 10 or 15 *percent* of the donors contribute 50 percent of the contributions. Thus in a church with 500 households, 50 to 75 donations will account for half of the donations. In other campaigns, the *top 10 donors* contribute one-third to one-half of the campaign.

Churches and synagogues are essentially closed constituencies. Contributions come from congregation members, their relatives, friends of the pastor or rabbi, former congregants, and a very few other people with some connection to the congregation. There is no possible broad base of support other than the congregation. The campaign leaders are already members or leaders of the congregation. Those who have been generous in the past may very well be expected to be generous in the future.

The most successful congregational campaigns are based on prayer and stewardship. Campaigns are structured so that each member of the congregation is offered an opportunity to give prayerful consideration to his or her commitment.

Hospitals

With a rapidly changing health care environment, hospitals and other health care institutions must build flexibility into their plans. The case for support must be relevant to the community, patients, the board, and all stakeholders, especially the staff. Above all, the plan must make economic sense.

In hospital campaigns, approximately 15 percent of the donations come from the board of directors. Another 15 percent may be obtained from the staff. Of course, this percentage is higher than in campaigns for other types of not-for-profit institutions where the staff is not composed largely of radiologists, neurologists, cardiologists, pathologists, surgeons, and other

physicians—that is, people who earn, on average, substantially more than the general population.

Universities

The trustee campaign is especially important in universities. Approximately 20 percent of the goal can be expected to be achieved from the trustees. Alumni might be expected to contribute at least another 20 percent of the campaign. In younger institutions, this may not be possible; however, in older established universities with numerous affluent alums, the percentage donated might be much higher.

Foundation funding can be expected to play a larger role in university campaigns. After all, university campaigns often encompass a broader array of projects and grant opportunities than any other type of institution might be in a position to offer.

Universities have a greater likelihood of recruiting large numbers of capital campaign volunteers than any other type of institution.

Community Colleges

Community colleges have not traditionally invested in alumni relations. Development professionals at these colleges point out that many alums go on to get a four-year degree at a state or private university. Invariably, the former community college student forms a stronger relationship with the university.

But this lament may be avoidable. Too few community colleges have made a concerted and consistent effort to create a sense of pride in their graduates and former students. Even the terms "alumnus" and "graduate" may miss the mark. Many students attend community colleges to acquire an education they can use immediately. Some get associate degrees. Some take courses in subjects that interest them. Some take practical courses such as accounting, drafting, or culinary arts. Some get an affordable liberal arts education. Others receive technical or vocational training that leads to immediate employment.

Suffice to say that community colleges must begin to strengthen their relationships with former students.

Community colleges differ greatly from each other. Some are in rural settings; others are in large cities. Some are funded by the state; others are

not. Some have established private support foundations; others have not. Some have a focus on liberal arts. Some have a focus on technical and vocational training. Some seek a balance. For these and many other reasons, each community college campaign is unique. Most often the campaigns succeed when corporate or financial institutions in the region form partnerships with the college. Corporations need well-trained employees. Community colleges have the capability to custom-tailor training programs to the needs of the corporate partner.

People in the region who are responsible for economic development often view the community college as the key to economic growth. Again, each institution must find its natural constituencies and mold the case for support to respond to the aspirations of those who might be expected to support the campaign.

Private Schools

If the school is old enough, alums might play a significant role in the campaign. Otherwise, the board of directors, founders, current parents, and grandparents form the heart of the campaign. Occasionally support can be garnered from local corporations and financial institutions. Some view strong private schools as important to their ability to attract and retain top management. And other decision makers view private schools as important to our nation's mix of educational opportunities.

Arts Institutions

Great cities have strong arts and cultural institutions. Season subscribers, museum members, and arts constituents form the heart of each organization's support. Arts organizations frequently also can attract "movers and shakers" to serve on their boards of directors.

In any capital or endowment campaign, at least 15 percent of the funds can be expected to come from the board. A more challenging yet achievable goal might be 20 percent of the campaign. The board of directors probably is composed of people who can solicit the vast majority of the funds needed for a successful campaign. They can approach affluent individuals and corporations that might be expected to support the endeavor.

A charismatic conductor and music director can play a role. A suave museum director can work miracles. Development staff might form strong re-

lationships with community leaders. But, when it's all said and done, for the campaign to succeed, the movers and shakers have to move and shake.

Social Service and Youth Groups

As with most campaigns, the board of directors might be expected to contribute 15 percent of the goal. Of course, the staff may be encouraged to participate, but the salaries paid to employees of such agencies are generally fairly modest. Similarly, the constituents cannot be expected to play a significant role. Therefore, the funds must come from affluent individuals living in the community, church groups, corporations with local headquarters and/or with significant operations in the area, financial institutions, foundations, and others.

If the organization has a long history of service in the area and a well-developed list of supporters, those who have been generous in the past may be expected to play a leadership role in the capital campaign.

As with all capital campaigns, the case for support should avoid "institutional needs" and focus on the people being served. When framing the case for support, also be aware of "compassion fatigue." Some donors are burned out when they hear of chronic social problems. Homelessness, poverty, hunger, the challenges faced by immigrants, and so many other social ills don't always resonate with donors. These supporters and former supporters view the problems as intractable.

The job of development planners is to demonstrate that the organizations they serve are addressing the root causes of these problems, not just the symptoms. The organizations are giving people a hand up, not a handout. The metaphor of teaching a person to fish rather than giving the person a fish is well received by donors. Invest in the time needed to refine the institution's plans. Also invest in the time needed to develop a well-crafted case for support.

CAMPAIGN ORGANIZATION AND STRUCTURE

Very large capital campaigns with numerous advance and major gift prospects require many volunteers and resource development professionals to ensure that as many of the potential supporters are visited as possible. One rule of thumb holds that the not-for-profit organization needs one

volunteer for every five prospects. Some volunteers can handle more; but five appears to be the ideal number. Volunteers who take more prospect assignments may develop a psychological block to doing any at all. The task just appears to be too onerous.

To pursue this analysis, another rule of thumb holds that at least three prospects are needed for every gift the organization will secure. So if a campaign's standard of investments gift pyramid indicates that 120 gifts are required to reach goal, the organization must approach 360 prospective donors. Then, dividing 360 by 5, it is clear that at least 72 volunteers are needed to complete the assignments. In a larger campaign requiring 1,000 capital campaign contributions, for example, the organization would need to identify 3,000 major gift prospects; in theory, it also would need to recruit and organize 600 volunteers. (Remember, we are talking here about conventional wisdom, not necessarily reality.)

To accomplish this Herculean task, the classic organization calls for a campaign chair, a capital campaign cabinet, an advance gift committee, a major gift committee, division chairs, team captains, and numerous volunteer solicitors. (See Exhibit 14-10.)

Campaigns may be organized by regions, around major departments of the institution, or by donor type—affluent individuals, major corporate prospects, banking and financial institutions, and foundations. Alternatively, aspects of the campaign can be organized around the prospect's relationship to the institution—trustees, administration, staff, faculty, alumni, vendors. In every case, the campaign structure reflects the sequential nature of the solicitations. The organization's closest prospects with the greatest resources are solicited first. An effective campaign is structured so that each subsequent gift level is solicited at the appropriate time by people with peer relationships to the prospects at each gift level.

The recruitment of key volunteers is a sensitive issue. The same care that goes into the solicitation of a major gift is required for a key recruitment. The approach must be gracious. It is best to have a volunteer with a peer relationship make the approach. Often relationship-nurturing activities precede the recruitment. And because volunteers are expected to donate before they solicit others, volunteer responsibilities must be explained during the recruitment—including the expectation of a generous campaign contribution.

EXHIBIT 14-10 CAPTIAL CAMPAIGN ORGANIZATION CHART

Campaign Chairperson

Executive Director
Consultant & Dev. Staff

Treasurer, Support & Records

Campaign Cabinet: Advance Gift & Division Chairs
& Other Key Liaisons

Division 1	Division 2 Major Corporations	Division 3	Division 4 Major Individuals	Division 5	Division 6 Other Special Constituents
Advance		Pace-setters		Business	
Team Captains 1 2 3 4	Team Captains 1 2 3 4	Team Captains 1 2 3 4	Team Captains 1 2 3 4	Team Captains 1 2 3 4	Team Captains 1 2 3 4
Vols × 4	Vols × 4	Vols × 4	Vols × 4	Vols	Vols
1__	1__	1__	1__	1__	1__
2__	2__	2__	2__	2__	2__
3__	3__	3__	3__	3__	3__
4__	4__	4__	4__	4__	4__
5__	5__	5__	5__	5__	5__
6__	6__	6__	6__	6__	6__
7__	7__	7__	7__	7__	7__

The organization also may be expanded regionally.
Have each division chair help recruit and solicit 4–5 team captains.
Assign 7–10 volunteers to each team captain. (The team captain should help recruit and solicit
    at least 5 of these volunteers.)
Have each volunteer select 4–5 prospective donors. The volunteers should be comfortable
    approaching their prospects.

Many organizations become discouraged after considering all this information about the projected number of volunteers needed. Either they get overly caught up in organizational and recruitment issues, or they conclude that they cannot possibly have a successful campaign. After all, 600 volunteers may very well represent a number greater than the total number of supporters for an organization—let alone the number of major gift solicitors and donors that can be recruited.

So much for textbook organization.

Although it is true that as many volunteers as possible should be recruited, things must be kept in perspective. The simple truth is that most of the capital and endowment funds will come from the leadership gifts. If the top 10 gifts account for one-third, one-half, or even more of the campaign total, as expected, then it makes abundant sense to concentrate efforts on recruiting and organizing the top leadership of the campaign.

A number of factors ameliorate the need to recruit numerous volunteers at the intermediate and public phases. Some of the gifts acquired will be from the foundation and the development staff that is responsible for writing the grant applications. In many cases, the executive director or chief executive officer of a prestigious institution has the peer relationships needed to call on many of the prospects. During the public phase of the campaign, it is possible to solicit 10, 15, 20 prospective supporters or more at group gatherings. For this to work, development professionals must invite prospects rated at the same capacity levels to the gathering. In this way, when a representative of the organization says, "I hope many of you here tonight will be in a position to consider a pledge of $1,000, $2,500, $5,000, or even more, per year for three years to help XYZ Not-for-profit Organization achieve its visionary aims . . ." the audience will not include donors who may be expected to donate $50,000 a year or more.

This is not to say that an organization should not make every effort to recruit and organize the maximum number of volunteers possible. The point is that, in many campaigns, a few key volunteers and staff raise the vast majority of the dollars pledged. So be sure to recruit the 7 to 10 key people who will make introductions and help solicit the organization's very best prospects. Also realize that in some special situations a very limited number of donors contribute nearly all the funds raised. If a prospective donor cares for the institution and has the capacity to contribute half of the capital campaign goal, by all means explain to him or her why such a commitment is needed and request such a contribution. If the organization cannot mount a classic campaign with numerous volunteers and hundreds or thousands of prospects but can identify 50 to 100 leadership prospects capable of making six- and seven-figure contributions, by all means organize the campaign around thoughtful approaches to these few angels.

In fact, all campaigns should be prospect driven. The campaign structure and time line are, in fact, driven by specific prospects and the organization's relationship to them. If the best hopes are pinned to people who have not

yet formed close relationships to an organization, sufficient time must be allowed for intensive cultivation activities prior to implementing the study and quiet campaign. If, on the other hand, the organization has nurtured strong relationships with 10 to 30 very generous supporters, a campaign can be built around the extraordinary leadership gifts donated by this core group.

Saying that a campaign is prospect driven reminds development professionals that a series of questions lies at the heart of every resource development effort: Who are the best prospects? How much might be requested from each of these prospects? What steps can be taken to get them even more excited about the campaign? Who on the team has the best chemistry with Mr. and Mrs. Specific Prospect? What are their interests? What gift opportunity might be offered to them? Is now the best time to approach them? Who is going to offer Mr. and Mrs. Specific Prospect an opportunity to make a significant investment in the campaign?

When a campaign is organized in such a way that these basic questions are asked, it is well on its way to success. When all these questions have been answered and the flow of appointments, requests, and follow-up action steps have been monitored, the organization is poised for victory.

Human Resources

When you cease to make a contribution, you begin to die.

—Eleanor Roosevelt, letter to Mr. Horne (February 19, 1960)

Not-for-profit organizations recognize that their most important assets are their people—the board, staff, and volunteers whose expertise and hard work make the organization succeed. Strong managers have strong staffs. Effective boards nominate and recruit strong leaders to serve. People committed to their mission surround themselves with competent people who share their vision.

In short, organizations are made up of people. The quality of the people and how well they work together determine the effectiveness of the institution. This chapter discusses the board of directors, staff, volunteers, and consultants—with a particular focus on their role in resource development.

THE BOARD OF DIRECTORS

The board of directors is the not-for-profit organization's governing body. When an organization is first formed, or when it is in its grassroots phase, board members frequently perform staff functions. This is true particularly during the formative years when the organization has little or no staff.

As the organization evolves, there is a transition period when board members cease to carry out the day-to-day operations and turn these duties over to paid staff. Often this is a stressful period for many institutions. People resist change. And, at times, dedicated founding board members

find it difficult to give up control. At such times lines of responsibility are less clear than they ought to be. Staff members complain that board members are "operating." And some board members find the new staff members unresponsive to the demands placed on them by the governing board.

Once the organization has weathered these early storms, it settles into a more mature state in which board and staff roles are very well understood. The board of directors generally is recognized to have seven main roles:

1. It is responsible for the organization's mission and strategic direction.
2. It is responsible for the organization's fiscal health; the board approves and monitors the organization's budget.
3. It hires and evaluates the organization's executive director.
4. It serves as an advocate for the organization and promotes positive public relations.
5. It makes and monitors organization policies.
6. It participates in the resource development process by contributing and by helping garner financial resources for the organization.
7. It assures the future of the organization by attracting and retaining volunteers for leadership positions.

The staff implements policy and carries out the organization's day-to-day operations. It also supports the board of directors, its committees, and members in the conduct of their duties.

Board sizes vary greatly. A board of 7 to 12 people may be adequate for a small not-for-profit organization with adequate resources and a highly focused mission. Many administrators and consultants find that 17- to 24-person boards are manageable, diverse, and of an ideal size to perform the needed functions. Some resource development professionals prefer to have somewhat larger boards—with up to 30 to 35 members—in order to encourage more leadership giving and to ensure an adequate number of dedicated people to serve as volunteer solicitors at the leadership levels. Of course, organizations with larger boards also must have a somewhat larger staff to support the board committees and members in their work.

Ideal Characteristics

From a fundraising perspective, it is essential to have a board composed of people of affluence and influence. Some board members serve because of

their particular knowledge of or experience with an organization's mission. Others serve because they represent a constituency or significant population of importance to the institution. But the majority serve because they represent the community-at-large and because they have the ability to ensure the organization's future.

Two old adages used to dominate the board recruitment process: The first is the adage about the three Ws, wealth, work, and wisdom. The three Gs are Give, Get, or Get off. If ever a board candidate is found with two of the three Ws, the organization has identified a viable candidate. Over time, leaders of not-for-profit organizations realized that one of the attributes had better be wisdom. It doesn't matter how hard a person might work or how much money he or she might have. If a board member attains a leadership position and does not have wisdom, the poor decisions can prove disastrous for the not-for-profit organization.

The second adage deals with the three Gs, give, get, or get off. These words form a crude view of the board's role. Still, most resource development professionals stress the importance of board giving and the board's role in resource development.

Bruce Flessner, of Bentz Whaley Flessner, once had a large lapel pin that read "Give, Get, or At Least Set Up the Meeting." GGOALSUTM may not be as catchy as the Three Ws or the Three Gs, but that pin captured the essential hope of all resource development professionals. We want board members to be generous. We want board members to help secure contributions. And, if board members are uncomfortable in the solicitation process, we hope that they will make introductions and help facilitate the solicitation.

In addition to affluence and influence an organization will want to recruit people with a mix of attributes. These include: skill and specialized knowledge, clout, program knowledge and experience, desirable personal qualities, and willingness to get involved.

Skill and Specialized Knowledge   Every not-for-profit organization can benefit by having an attorney serve on the board of directors. An attorney with expertise in estate planning can serve as a key advisor in the organization's planned-giving program. Attorneys with other areas of expertise can prove helpful at key stages in the organization's development.

Similarly, every not-for-profit organization can benefit from having someone with a strong financial background serve on the board of directors.

Certified public accountants (CPAs) frequently serve as treasurers of the not-for-profit organization or chairs of finance committees. The most effective CPAs to recruit have an entrepreneurial talent. They are as gifted at helping form financial projections as they are at reporting past results.

Not-for-profit organizations also find it helpful to recruit people with marketing and public relations expertise. These invaluable board members can help secure media sponsors for the organization's events. They help get free publicity. And at times they help the organization develop long-term strategic marketing and public relations plans.

Experience with banking and finance rounds off the list of skills and specialized knowledge. As with all business entities, not-for-profit organizations need to maintain strong relationships with their community's financial institutions. All organizations should form a strong relationship with at least one bank. They should foster relationships with the many financial institutions that might be expected to donate to the cause. Every not-for-profit organization can benefit by having a banker or representative of a financial institution serve as a board member.

Clout   Boards of directors are strengthened when prominent community leaders serve. They have contacts in the business community. They know and associate with decision makers. Because of their prestige, it becomes easier to recruit additional people of affluence and influence to serve on the board of directors.

Program Knowledge and Experience   Early in the organization's history, service volunteers often are recruited to serve on the board. Some of these dedicated people serve on and off the board for years. Some boards also recruit prestigious experts in the organization's field. A symphony orchestra might ask the dean of the local university's School of Music to serve on the board. A social service agency may ask the university's dean of the School of Social Work to serve. A museum might invite a published expert on the arts to be a board member. Such people can add perspective to the board's deliberations. Almost every board can benefit by having one or two such people as members.

Desirable Personal Qualities   When recruiting board members, not-for-profit organizations look for people with moral suasion. Their integrity and reputations are such that they can influence the behavior of others.

They are believable. They are principle-centered. Obviously, such people avoid even the appearance of a conflict of interest. But more than that, they inspire confidence and enhance the reputations of the organizations they serve.

Willingness to Get Involved   Ideal board members are team players. They may offer a broad range of advice but, once a decision is made, they support the decision with enthusiasm.

Ideal board members have good attendance records. They go to meetings and they stay involved. If their schedules keep them away for a period of time, they let the other team members know of the conflict. They also find ways to stay involved or to see that their responsibilities are covered during the interim period.

The Nominating Process

The nominating process begins with selection of a nominating committee. Frequently the past president of the organization is asked to serve as chair of the nominating committee. This often works well. After all, the president usually has a good sense of history and also knows who has performed well in the past.

However, it is also true that many past presidents are exhausted. Some have had to deal with many stressful issues during their presidencies. Some are burned out. Some simply want a break. So an organization might want to avoid making a hard-and-fast policy that the immediate past president chair the nominating committee. An effective approach might be to remain flexible. Perhaps the organization will name the past president to this post many times—but also will consider other people when the past president seems less than enthusiastic about the assignment.

The ideal members of a nominating committee are people who think strategically. It is also of utmost importance that generous people be asked to serve. Parsimonious people seem to nominate others with a similar outlook. On the other hand, generous people tend to identify other cheerful givers.

The next consideration is the order in which the nominating committee's work should be accomplished. Too frequently, nominating committees get together immediately prior to the annual board meeting and begin bringing up names for consideration. Even committees that do schedule

EXHIBIT 15-1   SAMPLE AGENDA FOR NOMINATING COMMITTEE

XYZ NOT-FOR-PROFIT ORGANIZATION
Nominations Committee Meeting
February 9, 2003 — 7:30 a.m.

AGENDA

I.   Attributes and the Board Grid
   • Board size
   • Minimum numbers of members filling each attribute
   • Current makeup of board
   • Discussion of "ideal board" prior to discussion of specific names

II.   Responsibilities and Profile of Ideal Board Members

III.   Names of People Meeting the Profile

IV.   Recruitment Techniques

V.   Other Business and Issues
   • Orientation and Involvement

VI.   Next Steps

---

several meetings fall into a similar trap. They begin discussing names prior to examining board membership from a strategic point of view. Exhibit 15-1 is a sample agenda for a nominating committee meeting. Notice that the ideal makeup of the board is discussed early in the meeting. After that conversation takes place it is possible to move into an analysis of the current board makeup. A nominating grid such as the one in Exhibit 15-2 is a helpful tool. But please note that in the sample agenda the minimum numbers needed for each attribute were decided first. Also note that in Exhibit 15-2 one of the attributes is personal affluence. Most not-for-profit administrators have seen board nominating grids before. However, often such grids do not list the affluence category. Most people were brought up to believe that discussions about other people's money is rude. Polite people don't do that. However, to attract $1,000, $2,500, $5,000, or $10,000 annual contributions, people who serve on the board must be able to afford donations at such levels.

EXHIBIT 15-2   BLANK BOARD NOMINATIONS GRID

NAME	SEX		AGE			ETHNICITY					PROFESSION									RELATIONSHIPS				
	M	F	20-35	36-55	56 –	Anglo	Hispanic	Native American	Black	Asian	Other	Accountant	Lawyer	Media	Banking	Medical	Public relations	Artist	Arts administration	Other	Volunteer organizer	Personal fund raising	Access to people w/ money	Personal affluence	Political influence

Actual Number

Minimum Desired

EXHIBIT 15-3 BOARD NOMINATIONS GRID

NAME	Political influence	Personal affluence	Access to people w/ money	Personal fund raising	Volunteer organizer	Other	Retail	Manufacturing	Public relations	Medical	Banking	Media	Lawyer	Accountant	Other	Asian	Black	Native American	Hispanic	Anglo	56+	36-55	20-35	SEX F	SEX M
A. ADAMS					X		X							X											X
C. Murphy	X			X																					X
R. Mustard																									X
Q. Pester					X																			X	
P. Nimrod																								X	
B. Opara		X	X	X			X			X						X			X						X
C. Peters		X	X	X							X													X	
D. Pluto		X	X	X				X										X							X
S. Quincy		X	X	X				X																	X
S. Richards		X	X	X	X																			X	
V. Roberts		X	X	X			X																	X	
G. Stevens						X																		X	
G. Thomas						X																		X	
A. Ulrich	X	X	X	X				X									X								X
R. Victor		X	X	X				X																	X
Actual Number	2	6	8	7	3	2	3	3	0	1	1	0	0	1	1	2	2	3	3	3	5	18	1	10/14	8
Minimum Desired	2	6	8	3	3	3	3	3	1	1	1	1	1	1	1	1	2	1	3		5	8	1	8	8

The first step is to decide on the minimum numbers required for each of the board categories. Then the organization can produce a board grid that highlights the actual numbers serving vis-à-vis the minimum requirements. Exhibit 15-3 depicts an organization that has too few affluent people. That organization also does not have an attorney or a media expert serving on the board. In response to this deficiency, this organization might very well look for several affluent people, most likely attorneys, heads of advertising agencies, or corporate decision makers with strong marketing backgrounds.

Again, the important thing is that the strategic decisions were made before the names of potential board members were suggested. This approach keeps the nominating committee focused on the organization's future and helps stimulate thinking about people whose names otherwise might not have surfaced.

Once the discussion about the ideal board mix has taken place, and the critical needs have been identified, the nominating committee can turn its attention to specific names for consideration. It is most helpful if the development staff helps with this process. To begin with, the development staff can prepare a list of potential board members, focusing on active volunteers and generous donors. The staff also can help identify community leaders who have a relationship to the organization.

Each board member and other staff members might be encouraged to suggest names of potential board members. Again, it is helpful to remind people that the nominating committee is especially interested in people of affluence and influence or those who have the other specific attributes needed for a well-balanced board of directors.

Other sources of names might include board members of local corporations or financial institutions. Chief executive officers of successful local or regional businesses also are excellent candidates for board membership. Of course, if an organization is national in scope, people in leadership positions nationwide should be sought.

Recruitment

The recruitment of board members and other key volunteers requires the same care as a major gift solicitation. Ideally the recruitment should take place at a face-to-face meeting. The person responsible for the recruitment

should have a peer relationship to the potential board member and act with poise. At the time of recruitment, the potential board member should gain a clear understanding of the time commitment and responsibilities of board membership.

When explaining the fundraising responsibilities, it is best to let the potential board member know that board members help in a broad range of ways. Some host cultivation events. Many provide information about potential supporters. Many make introductions for fundraising purposes. Some help arrange fundraising events. Some participate directly in the solicitation process.

Let the potential board member know that participation in the resource development process is expected and that the organization is dedicated to finding and helping expand each board member's comfort zone.

Such recruitments work. On the other hand, when potential board members are told that they are expected to make five or more solicitations, they almost always refuse.

Another sensitive issue that must be discussed with every potential board member is the board giving policy. Many boards adopt policies such as "Each member of the board will make a self-satisfying annual financial contribution to the XYZ Not-for-Profit Organization." Often potential board members will ask what is expected. Most resource development professionals have come to realize that suggested minimum giving standards tend to evolve into an expected amount. The floor becomes the ceiling. When it is suggested that each member of the board gives not less than $500, for example, most board members tend to give precisely that amount.

A better approach would be to say that the goal is 100 percent participation from the board. When explaining the expectation to potential board members, something like this might be said: "Our primary objective is to have 100 percent participation from our board members. We also hope that each member will make a gift that is generous in relationship to the member's means. A few of our board members give approximately $500 a year. Several give $5,000 and $10,000 annually. One board member makes a $50,000 a year contribution. Most contribute something in between. Again, each decides what is generous for his or her means."

If an organization finds it difficult to recruit chief executive officers and community leaders of the first rank, one of two recruitment strategies may be attempted.

The first is to "ratchet up" from the current level of board membership. If the board currently attracts bank tellers, perhaps it can successfully recruit branch managers. If the equivalent of branch managers are on the board, the next recruitment might be a senior vice president. At times spouses of community leaders may be recruited. The ratchet-up strategy stresses the importance of leveraging the current level of clout and taking a stepwise approach to advancing the organization's influence in the community.

The second strategy can be considered the adopt-us approach. Many boards find that they do not have any obvious links with their community's top leaders. Perhaps the nominating committee feels strongly that the organization needs people of that caliber to accomplish its visionary aims. In such a situation, direct approach might be tried. Identify one or two of the organization's most committed and articulate spokespeople to call the community leader who might respond best to the cause. Be bold. Ask for an appointment. Go and explain the case for support. Tell the community leader how important the not-for-profit organization's work is. Also, let the person know that the not-for-profit needs people of his or her caliber to help the organization evolve and achieve its greatest potential. Be frank. Ask the person to consider "adopting" the organization. The aim is to convince the community leader that his or her involvement will make a huge difference. He or she also should recognize that involvement in the board of directors will be a rewarding and enjoyable experience.

Motivation and Involvement

Many board members lose their enthusiasm even before they begin to serve. This happens when an organization has a recruitment process that takes place months before the annual meeting when new members begin their service. One obvious remedy is to allow new members to come on board at various times throughout the year by filling expiring terms or taking unfilled positions. If the bylaws allow 24 members, and a board only has 21 current members, it seems appropriate to allow a new board member to take a seat at any time during the year. The organization can draft bylaws to accommodate such situations. Most important, every effort should be made to shorten the time between recruitment and actual board service.

Another rule is to ensure that every new board member is offered a meaningful orientation experience within one or two months of recruitment. Also, discover on which committees the new board member may wish to serve. A Committee Preference form is on the CD-ROM that accompanies this book.

Get new board members involved early. Moreover, be sure to involve them in the board's social life. Plan evenings when board members and their spouses can attend enjoyable events or gatherings.

A recent and positive trend in many not-for-profit organizations is to broaden the range of responsibilities of the nominating committee. This committee is sometimes called the Committee for Board Development. In addition to the nominating responsibilities, members also examine how the board conducts its business. The committee is charged with the responsibility for building a strong board, developing the organization's leadership, strengthening board committees, and making recommendations on ways to strengthen board processes and how to enhance the experience of serving on the board.

Such committees are extremely helpful. However, no one has to wait for their reports to institute some commonsense ideas now. Consider the following:

- Board meetings should be lively and meaningful.
- The meetings should start and end on time.
- Committees should be assigned a great deal of the work. However, the whole board should discuss significant issues prior to sending the issues to the committees.
- Even after a committee reports, board members have a right to ask questions and suggest improvements to the committee's recommendations.
- Backbiting, second-guessing, and parking-lot discussions do nothing to advance the organization. Candid discussions at board meetings do.
- All discussions should be conducted in a respectful and appropriate manner. Board members can be encouraged to find agreeable ways in which to disagree.
- Discussions and debates must end eventually. Decisions must be made. Once a decision has been made, all board members can be expected to back the plan.

- Have fun. Schedule lots of social occasions. Some can be for the board as a whole; some can be for committees. Some are formal. Many are informal.

Board and Staff Retreats

Board and staff retreats are invaluable. When done well, they help develop a shared vision for the organization's future. Board and staff retreats also are essential to the strategic planning process to team building, and to help gain consensus concerning a wide range of organizational development issues.

Retreats can concentrate on mission and vision, strategic planning, resource and/or board development, finance, human resources, facilities planning, marketing and public relations, or any pressing issue unique to the organization. For the purposes of this book, the focus is on strategic planning and resource development.

Prior to any retreat, it may be useful to take the pulse of the board. Interviews help, as do surveys. Most often informal talks with board members will uncover the dominant attitudes and questions that will shape the retreat.

While planning the retreat, be sure to give early attention to the steps needed to stimulate attendance:

- Schedule the retreat at a convenient time. Saturdays seem to work well for many organizations.
- Give ample advance notice. An early postcard with an upbeat "Mark your calendar" message can be sent several months prior to the retreat. Board notices also can contain repeated reminders.
- Develop an "inviting" invitation. A standard meeting notice on 8½-by-11-inch copy paper just won't do. Be clever. Be creative. And make the invitation look like fun.
- Follow up the invitation with warm, encouraging phone calls from a respected board member.

When planning the retreat, recognize participants' various needs. Some board members serve primarily for social interaction. Some serve because they are very close to the organization's mission and programs. Still others serve because they feel that they have a civic responsibility to help create strong not-for-profit institutions.

For those whose primary motivation for serving is social interaction, icebreakers and socialization exercises are a must. Opportunities for mingling—meals, get-togethers, and free time—are appreciated. During the retreat it also helps to keep an eye on the human element. Share poignant stories about the people the organization serves. This latter point is meaningful for all board members.

For those whose primary motivation is their closeness to the organization's mission and programs, reports from program officers, the executive director, and leaders in the field have a great impact. The parts of the retreat that are devoted to the organization's mission, vision, and programs keep these people involved. Again, people stories, testimonials, and motivational accounts of the services lend life to the reports about organizational benchmarks and statistics.

For those whose primary motivation is civic responsibility, governance issues, strategic planning, finance and budget, bylaws, and a host of organizational issues have the greatest meaning. Many CPAs, attorneys, and community leaders serve because they want to help create strong institutions. As they become more involved in an organization, they begin to share the values of those board members most closely identified with the not-for-profit's mission and programs.

A well-structured retreat seeks a balance of subjects covered. It also employs a number of presentation and participation techniques. When these board members' needs are accommodated and care is given to physical comfort, a successful retreat is practically unavoidable.

On the physical side of the equation, be sure that the location chosen is away from the hubbub of everyday life. The room layout should be attractive, practical, and conducive to interaction. Check out the temperature. Be sure that all the audio-visual equipment works and is in focus before the participants arrive. Schedule convenient breaks. And provide ample food and beverage.

A sample board retreat agenda is illustrated in Exhibit 15-4. Exhibits 15-5A and B are simple icebreakers. These icebreakers are a bit time-consuming, as each member of the board and staff answers each of the questions. Some people tend to speak longer than others. However, the time usually is well spent because board members find out things about each other that they might otherwise not have known. Moreover, the final question usually elicits some poignant stories of why people have

EXHIBIT 15-4   MOCK NONPROFIT ORGANIZATION
BOARD RETREAT

AGENDA June 20, 2003

I. RETREAT GOALS

- To assure a unified approach toward the organization's mission and vision for the future.
- To build a sense of teamwork among the organization's leadership.
- To evaluate board and staff roles, responsibilities and work processes . . . and identify opportunities for improvement.
- To identify feasible goals that will enhance the organization's effectiveness and strengthen the organization's governance and administrative practices.
- To explore resource development principles and practices and discuss the board's role in fundraising.
- To have fun!!!

II. RETREAT AGENDA

9:00 a.m.   Board gathers—retreat convenes
- Preliminary introductions
- Review goals for the retreat

9:15 a.m.   Icebreaking and socialization exercise (includes an opportunity for everyone to tell what brought them to the organization)

9:55 a.m.   Facilitated process to reexamine the organization's mission and explore shared values
- A lot of people know something of the history and roots of this organization. Given *today's* environment, if this mock nonprofit organization didn't exist, why would anybody bother to create the organization?
- What is our organization actually doing? Brief discussion: Compare expectation, actual practice, and mission statement.

10:30 ish   BREAK

10:45 a.m.   A new way of looking at the organization's strengths and weaknesses: Each participant writes their best and worst three memories of their association with the organization. Capture ideas, discuss, and summarize.

11:15 a.m.   Affirm, tweak, or rewrite mission statement. (Four groups work independently. Compare the four versions. Refer all four versions to the strategic planning committee for refinement of the organization's mission statement.)

12:00 p.m.   LUNCH

1:00 p.m.   Goals and Strategies—a facilitated process. (Remind board members that these exercises will provide *general* guidance to the strategic long-range planning committee. The committee will use this information for guidance and will develop a comprehensive strategic plan.)
- Brainstorm wishes and dreams
- Priority dot exercise

(continued)

EXHIBIT 15-4 (CONTINUED)

2:00 p.m.	Summarize priorities and form preliminary "vision statement"
2:15 p.m.	Break
2:25 p.m.	Goals and Roles—a facilitated process designed to examine board and staff roles, responsibilities, and work processes and identify opportunities for improvement.

- What is the board's role?
- What is the staff's role?
- What can the board do to make the staff more effective?
- What can the staff do to make the board more effective?

3:25 p.m.	Resource development: informal talk and participation activities

- Fundraising principles and practices
- The board's role in fundraising
- Three bags of money; three questions

3:50 p.m.	A call to action—an opportunity to reaffirm decisions and action steps. Each retreat participant can quietly or overtly commit himself or herself to a course of action and level of support to achieve the aspirations of the organization.
4:00 p.m.	Adjourn

EXHIBIT 15-5A MOCK NONPROFIT ORGANIZATION

BOARD AND STAFF RETREAT

June 20, 2003

ICEBREAKER

A. My name is: _____

B. Before I head off to that Last Round-up in the Sky, I would like to do or accomplish the following: _____

_____

_____

_____

C. Something most people don't know about me is: _____

_____

_____

_____

D. The circumstances that brought me to this Mock Nonprofit organization were:

_____

EXHIBIT 15-5B   MOCK NONPROFIT ORGANIZATION

MISSION STATEMENT

The mission of the Mock Nonprofit Organization is to help left-handed trombonists and other unusual people feel more at home in polite society. Through advocacy, funding, and outreach programs, the Mock Nonprofit Organization helps unusual individuals and communities protect and preserve their uniqueness and resources.

Group alternatives:
- Affirm
- "Tweak"
- Substantially rewrite

---

chosen to serve the organization. Naturally, many involvement techniques and some more active icebreaking exercises might be used; however, these seem to get a lot of retreats off the ground with humor and warmth. The Mock Not-for-Profit Organization Mission Statement (Exhibit 15-5B) exercise is meant to be done in group breakouts. It gets people up and around during the retreat. Besides, if instructions are kept to a minimum, new potential board leaders might be uncovered. Often board members take charge of the subgroup discussions. These natural leaders understand mission. During this exercise, people who might not have been viewed as leaders show remarkable resources as they bring their group to consensus in a very short amount of time.

Presentation techniques were mentioned in Chapter 4. Since many board retreats include a resource development component, it might be helpful to describe several participation ideas that can help motivate volunteers to participate in the fundraising process.

The first is one of the oldest in the business. The facilitator stands before the group and asks board and staff members to take out their wallets. At this point there are usually giggles and murmurs in the room. In fact, this simple act is so energizing that it helps to do it soon after the lunch hour, when everyone otherwise might be lethargic. Once all the wallets and purses are out, the facilitator asks to find out who has the largest denomination of currency. In some gatherings, someone might have a $100 bill. In others, a board member or staffer might have a $50 bill. In almost any gathering, quite a few people have $20 bills. The facilitator asks the person with the

largest bill to please pass it forward or to directly hand it to the facilitator. If the person seems reluctant, the facilitator might say, "It's okay, you can trust me."

Now the facilitator asks, "Why did Sally give me her $50 bill?"

It doesn't take long before someone on the board says, "Because you asked." Others might say, "Because she trusted you."

This simple exercise makes the most important points in any resource development training environment. People give because they are asked. And they give to people they trust.

A second exercise was developed to help participants remember two other important points: Different people can afford to donate different amounts; and fundraisers must decide how much to ask of each prospect prior to the visit.

To make these points, props that look like three stuffed bank money bags are prepared. One is tagged $25 million. The second is tagged $600,000. And the third has a large "?" printed on its tag. The facilitator asks for volunteers to come take one of the bags and sit in front of the board. This creates an opportunity for levity, as some board member will invariably make a strong effort to hold the $25 million bag. The facilitator now asks a series of questions and engages the board members in a conversation about prospect ratings. One typical summarized discussion might go as follows. The facilitator explains to the group that each of the people before them has an established relationship to the organization. The bags represent their net worth. The person with the $25 million bag inherited wealth but has also helped strengthen the family-owned businesses. The person with the $600,000 bag is a mature professional who has made approximately $80,000 to $100,000 a year, and has saved and invested. The $600,000 represents the organization's estimate of the prospect's assets exclusive of the person's home. The person with the "?" appears to be affluent. Several key volunteers suggested that the "?" prospect may have resources; however, prospect research to date has been unable to establish an estimate of net worth.

The facilitator now says, "We will discuss a capital campaign later. For now let's assume that we are serving on a board of an organization with a $750,000 annual campaign. Our volunteers are going to visit these three prospects. When they go to Sam here who has $25 million, how much

might they request? When they go to Mirna with her $600,000, how much should they request? And finally, when they go to Fred with his unknown amount, how much should they request?"

Conversations flow freely. The facilitator is careful not to judge any suggestions. Rather, participants are encouraged to discuss each suggestion thoroughly. Typically, opinions range widely regarding how much the wealthiest prospect should be asked to donate. Frequently board members settle on a gift range of $25,000 to $50,000 as appropriate suggested amounts for annual campaigns. However, some board members point out that the prospect might be approached for larger amounts for special projects. The $600,000 person might be asked to consider annual contributions in the $1,000 to $2,500 range. Of course, conversations and suggestions might vary greatly. Some board members will suggest more research regarding the person with unknown wealth. Others might boldly suggest a request amount. Some might suggest that it doesn't make economic sense to request less than $1,000 on a person-to-person visit. Still others might suggest that a list of gift opportunities begin at the $500 or $1,000 level—but also go much higher. In such an instance, the volunteers might say, "We need gifts at all of these leadership levels on an annual basis. Where do you see yourself participating?"

The facilitator next turns attention to capital campaigns. The lead question might be "The XYZ Not-for-Profit Organization is contemplating a $5 million capital campaign with a three-year pledge period. What might we ask of each of our three prospects sitting before you today?" Often a bold board member suggests that the person with $25 million be asked for the entire amount. Some members may point out that if the prospect is very committed to the organization, such a request would not be out of the question. Frequently the board agrees that a $1 million request might be ideal. The facilitator might point out that a person with a $25 million net worth generally can afford to donate $1 million without changing his or her lifestyle. The $600,000-net-worth person who is close to the organization may consider a pledge of $10,000 to $20,000 for a visionary capital campaign. Such a person also might consider a larger planned gift for the organization's endowment fund. Invariably, with capital campaigns at stake, board members ask that more research and cultivation take place prior to soliciting the "?" person.

The important consideration with all these discussions is not so much the specific request amounts. Rather board members need to remember that these choices must be made prior to visiting the best prospects.

A third presentation technique that is very powerful in motivating board members to increase their contributions has come to be called Weinstein's Three Questions. The first question is: "What is the largest cumulative amount you donated to a single charity in a single year?" This question is stated on a small slip of paper that reads: "The largest amount I donated to a single charity in a single year is $_____." Board members fill in the dollar amount, fold their unsigned slips of paper, and pass the folded slips to the facilitator's assistant, who totals the amounts. While this is taking place, the facilitator asks the second question: "What do you believe is the largest amount you could part with, without changing your lifestyle or sense of security?" Usually there is not much discussion, but the facilitator may observe. "I imagine many of you wrote or thought of an amount at least three to five times greater than the largest cumulative amount you donated in a single year." Upon making this observation, a large percentage of the participants will look the facilitator in the eye and nod their heads yes. The facilitator may say: "Well, that doesn't surprise me. Statistics indicate that, on average, Americans give one-fifth of what they can afford to donate without changing their lifestyles."

After these observations, the facilitator asks the concluding third question: "If you could make one donation that would end poverty, cure cancer, or guarantee world peace, how much would you be willing to donate?" (As with the second question, board members think of the answer or write it on a slip of paper, but they do not pass anything forward. The only slips that are passed forward are for the first question.)

A brief period of quiet falls over the room as board members contemplate the third question. After a brief pause, the facilitator might say: "I suppose many if not most of you in this room today would consider giving up all you have if you could end poverty, cure cancer, or guarantee world peace. Of course, there is no one gift that could accomplish any of those aims. But your contribution to XYZ Not-for-Profit Organization will help ensure that 60,000 meals will be served this year. You can donate knowing that your gift will help save the lives of homeless people during the bitter winter months. . . ." In each case, the facilitator states the case for support in the most direct and dramatic terms. The aim is to remind each

board member how the organization makes a significant difference in the lives of the people it serves.

To conclude this exercise, the facilitator or trainer might say. "Many people ask how much board members should donate. There is no one right answer to this question. Each board member should make a decision based on his or her means. However, some guidelines might help. Some say that if you are serving on the board, the institution for which you are serving should be one of your top three not-for-profits each year that you serve. So, we might conclude that it would be reasonable to consider a contribution equal to that given to your favorite not-for-profits in the past: an amount equal to what you donate to your university or to your church or synagogue, for example. If you are very close to some other not-for-profit, perhaps the amount you donate to this institution would be at least half of what you donate to your favorite not-for-profit. When this organization considers a capital campaign, you might want to consider a standard established by Harvard University. They ask their supporters to recall the largest donation they ever made to a not-for-profit organization in a single year. Then they ask their supporters to double this amount and pledge it for three years. Let's see how these differing standards might work for this not-for-profit organization."

The assistant, who has totaled the board slips turned in after the first question, also has divided that amount in half, multiplied it by three, and multiplied it by six. So the assistant already has calculated the four figures including the total. For example, if the board slips totaled $70,000, the assistant would have four numbers: the $70,000 total; $35,000 half total; $210,000 figure representing three times the total; and $420,000 figure representing six times the total.

Now, what do these figures mean? The facilitator explains, "If each board member were to donate exactly the same amount they have given to their other favorite charities each year, we would begin each fund drive with $70,000. If everyone gave just half of what they donate to their universities, churches, or other favored not-for-profits, we would begin each year with $35,000 for our annual drive." (Note that in almost all cases, these amounts are considerably higher than the organization is receiving from its board members on an annual basis. Too frequently, board members don't donate or only make token gifts to the organizations they serve.) The facilitator continues: "When this organization contemplates a capital

or endowment drive, we might expect each board member to pledge an amount equal to the most the member has donated to a charity in a single year—but pledge that amount for three years. If this were the case, we would begin our capital campaign with $210,000. If all board members followed the Harvard standard, we would double that amount and we could begin the campaign with $420,000."

The facilitator or trainer might conclude by bringing the conversation back to the importance of the organization's work. However, this exercise accomplishes a number of objectives. Board members are encouraged to think about the most they have given. They are encouraged to give similar or greater amounts to this not-for-profit organization. They uncover for themselves that there are circumstances under which they would donate vastly greater sums. Board members also are encouraged to consider an amount double their greatest gift. And they are encouraged to consider multiyear pledges of that amount. Please note that the board members themselves supplied the key information. Because they played the critical role in this discovery process, the three questions are a powerful motivator in stimulating dramatically enhanced board giving.

THE RESOURCE DEVELOPMENT STAFF

Effective resource development staff form close working partnerships with board members and volunteers. The relationship works best when expectations are crystal clear. It may be helpful to write a mission statement and job description for the development office. (Two sample job descriptions for the Director of Development are included on the CD-ROM that accompanies this book.)

For the organization to succeed, it is imperative that the performance of development staff—especially newly hired staffers—be monitored closely. The organization should provide as much training as possible early on. The evaluation should include "means" and "ends." Means include tasks such as writing and refining the case for support, making enhancements to database management, creating and interpreting meaningful fundraising reports, increasing and enhancing the mailings, increasing the number of personal solicitations and grant applications, and enhancing research. The first concern regarding ends is net contributed income. Other goals include

an increased number of donors, total dollars raised, grants funded, and income from a broader range of fundraising strategies.

Be realistic and seek advice from experts when setting goals. And, as is stressed in the evaluation material in Chapter 16, seek incremental improvement over a broad range of goals. Also recognize that the development staff cannot achieve these goals without board and volunteer support.

One final word about goals. Don't be misled. Many people will say that fundraising is really friend raising. This is true. However, one of the main purposes for nurturing relationships is to help bring prospective donors closer to the organization so that they can be asked to consider making significant contributions to the not-for-profit institution.

Some very smooth people take responsible development positions. They attend civic clubs. They work with the public relations department to develop attractive materials. They make speeches. They are engaged in all sorts of activities. They are also quick to remind anyone who will listen that it takes a long time to nurture relationships. Besides, they complain that board members don't make their calls.

Upon examining their development offices, few, if any, tangible signs of meaningful resource development work are visible. There is no case for support. Many database management issues have not even been addressed. Few grants have been applied for. The number of mailings is the same as it always has been, and the sponsorship levels for special events have been the same for years. No one really feels comfortable visiting major donors. In sum, the development officer may have a commanding presence and may stay quite busy. But the amount of money being raised is relatively flat or declining.

The answer, of course, is to clarify expectations. It also helps to hire people with experience and an obvious record of achievement. After all, the organization has every right to expect tangible results in three to six months. Visits should be increasing, grant applications should have increased, and, if appropriate, the mail campaign should be more aggressive. And as a result, contributions should begin to increase.

Naturally, people and their skills should be matched to the job requirements. Yet mismatches are frequent in development positions. If interviewers cannot imagine a candidate for director of development sitting down with a bank president and dealing with him or her as a colleague,

then the candidate should not be considered for the job. If a person has strong people skills but doesn't appear to be detail oriented, that person should not be assigned data management responsibilities. A person with a public relations background but no fundraising experience should not be assigned resource development responsibilities without intense training . . . if at all.

The ideal director of development must use both sides of his or her brain. To succeed, this person must be a planner, persuader, writer, analyst, operations manager, cheerleader, and expert in organization development. In today's environment, he or she also should be computer literate. Above all, the ideal director of development is a good listener—someone who listens empathetically.

The database manager and development office support staff must be meticulous and detail oriented. And every development office needs a strong writer. Graphic skills and desktop publishing experience, while not a necessity, are also of great benefit to the development office.

The people responsible for implementing each of the fundraising strategies should be experts in their fields. The person responsible for special events should be experienced, detail oriented, and knowledgeable. He or she also should work well with volunteers. The direct mail specialist should understand response rates and segmentation strategies, and should often attend seminars on copyrighting, mail management, and direct marketing techniques. Similarly, the grants writer, planned giving officer, and major gift personnel should be experts in their fields. In smaller organizations, the director of development must understand the basics of all resource development strategies and, to the extent possible, become an expert in those strategies most important to the not-for-profit organization served.

Organization and Growth

Development offices often grow following a pattern that traces the evolution of the not-for-profit agency. During an organization's earliest years, volunteers do everything. In these grassroots organizations, the volunteers serve as board members and also perform all of the staff functions. After a period of time the organization grows to the point that it can hire an executive director. The executive director, often supported by an administrative assistant, performs all key staff functions, including grant writing and

perhaps mail campaigns. Volunteers continue to run the special events. Fundraising activities are somewhat limited due to the lack of staff.

After another growth period the not-for-profit organization hires a person with fundraising, marketing, and public relations responsibilities. Because it is so difficult to balance these responsibilities, this solution rarely works as well as the organization may have hoped.

At some auspicious moment in the organization's history, the agency hires its first full-time development director. If this person is experienced and has a quality assistant with whom to work, miracles begin to happen. Given board support, the development director can initiate a major gifts program, increase the number of mailings, improve the grantsmanship program, provide assistance to the volunteers running the special events, increase sponsorship levels, and begin a simple-to-administer planned-giving program that focuses on wills and bequests.

Once the organization has a full-time development director and it experiences continued growth in net contributed income, the development staff continues to grow in response to new opportunities. To be sure, the first hire is a gifted assistant who provides valuable support services for the development director. As the gift volume increases, the organization will need to hire a data entry specialist. Depending on which fundraising strategies are most important to the organization, the not-for-profit may then hire a special events person, an annual giving/mail/phone specialist, a grants officer, a major gifts officer, and finally, a planned-giving specialist. The reason that the planned-giving officer is one of the last hires is that an organization must be at least 10 years old before donors feel confident in making planned gifts to it.

Often universities follow a somewhat different pattern in the evolution of their resource development functions. Typically one finds a development director at each school of the university. Over this large structure is a person who serves as vice president for institutional advancement. This person, who has overall development responsibilities, may have a broad array of job titles. Many serve as chief executive officers of the university's support foundation. At the senior levels there might also be major gift and planned gift officers. The university development organization also recognizes the importance of alumni relations. So large development operations result. One key to success is to organize the efforts around prospects. For example, if a major donor attended the school of engineering, the devel-

opment director of that school may be assigned primary responsibility for nurturing the relationship. However, if the major donor is the president of a large corporation, the university's corporate giving officer—or even the university president—may be assigned prime responsibility. Again, the important issues are peer relationships, chemistry, and the donor's interests. In the best of worlds, intelligent decisions are made regarding these matters. In the worst of worlds, internecine battles over prospects prevail and gracious contact becomes impossible. In such a scenario, the development director for the school of engineering may struggle to gain an appointment before the university president calls. Oops!

Obviously, the larger the institution, the more important prospect management becomes. It has been said before, but it should be repeated: No prime prospect is assigned to more than one development officer.

The Search Process

When hiring a director of development or any other key person, follow these steps:

- *Form a search team.* The team should develop a job description and search strategy. The team also should study compensation plans and determine a salary range for the position. Also, consider the dynamics of the organization. What skills and experiences are needed? What kind of management style fits the institution? What values and beliefs should the ideal applicant possess? What special issues of "chemistry" must be considered? What type of people have worked well with the executive director and board leaders in the past?

- *Review resumes.* What is the overall impression? Is the experience relevant? Did the applicant personalize the materials in response to the organization's needs? The vast number of applicants can be eliminated at this stage.

- *Preinterview the applicant.* A brief telephone conversation prior to any formal interview process is helpful. Use this call to be sure that the applicant would consider a position in the salary range that can be offered. Also find out when the applicant might be available, should a position be offered.

- *Interview three to five finalists.* Whenever possible, schedule the interviews somewhat close together. Ideally, the same interview team in-

terviews each of the applicants. Group wisdom is very difficult when interviewers come and go throughout the process.

Allow sufficient time for a thorough yet structured interview. Be gracious and relaxed. Help interviewees feel comfortable. After introductions and a brief review of the job requirements, allow interviewees 10 to 15 minutes to tell a bit about themselves and how they can serve the organization.

When asking about experience, form inquiries using involvement questions. In other words, rather than asking "Have you ever written a successful grant application?" say "Please tell us about any grants you have written . . . and especially let us know how you went about the entire grant process beginning with your research and ending with how you went about preparing the grant application." Other useful involvement questions include: Describe a situation where you disagreed with a volunteer. What was the situation and how did you handle it? Describe a time when you had multiple priorities and competing deadlines. What were the circumstances? How did you organize your work flow? Think back to the best boss or supervisor you ever had and the worst boss or supervisor you had to deal with. Describe both sets of circumstances and focus especially on how you dealt with the situation where you had the less than desirable supervisor. What is the largest charitable contribution you were involved with? What was your role . . . and what did you do to help secure the contribution?

When the interview team focuses on involvement questions— rather than merely encouraging a skills inventory—the organization ends up with a more complete understanding of how the candidate works and functions in a broad array of real-life situations.

- *Reach group consensus.* Don't let a lot of time elapse. Conduct a comprehensive review of the candidates immediately or soon after the last interview. To discourage "group think," have everyone write down their first choice on a piece of paper. See if there is already preliminary consensus on the search outcome. However, encourage everyone to keep an open mind throughout the entire search process. Encourage everyone to listen to each other carefully. Even brilliant managers and board chairs can err if they make unilateral decisions. Group wisdom is valuable under many circumstances, especially when hiring key people.

Make a decision based on experience and results. In previous positions, did the applicant really play a major role in increasing contributions? Does the applicant have experience helping obtain contributions at the levels the organization needs?

Make a decision based on chemistry and values. Will the person really fit into the organization? Was the candidate clearly a good listener? Will he or she relate well to top donors and supporters?

Finally, make a decision based on management style. Again, is the candidate results oriented? Does he or she have a demonstrable record of motivating volunteers and staff? Does the candidate sound sincere when speaking about openness and team building? Can he or she bring about change without causing a major eruption within the organization?

- *Check references.* No decision is final until references have been checked. Reference letters are always positive. Otherwise, the applicant would not have furnished them.

Unfortunately, many employers are reluctant to give full information about previous employees. However, the organization's financial statements are often a matter of public record. Therefore, it is easy to confirm the range of charitable contributions received during a particular development director's tenure.

Reference checks should focus on work behavior, job performance, chemistry with other colleagues, and the reasons for leaving previous positions. It is often helpful to ask "Would Ms. Job Candidate be eligible for rehire?"

Most important of all, make every effort to find out if the job candidate really helped motivate and obtain large or increased contributions for the previous institution. Prior to hiring a resource development professional, the financial results he or she helped produce must be known.

Retention and Maturation

Volumes have been written about job satisfaction. A great deal of the literature focuses on compensation. However, faced with the vast number of volunteers who work hours upon hours without compensation, it is obvious that motivation encompasses a great deal more than salary. Responsible

people working in the not-for-profit sector have an obligation to ensure that the organization pays adequate and competitive wages. But job enrichment may play an even larger role in job satisfaction. Educational opportunities are important and appreciated. Perhaps every organization should set a policy that each employee is offered not less than one major education experience each year. Above all, organizations should ensure that each employee is treated with respect. Openness in communications is a big plus. So is attention to physical comfort. For example, allowing each employee to choose his or her own chair is a relatively inexpensive investment.

Too often performance appraisals and job evaluations are matters of stress in an organization. Make every effort to reduce the stress related to the formal appraisal process. But also adopt an informal and more human approach. When something goes well, thank the person who did it. When a situation needs improvement, simply say so. "Next time let's . . ." works well. Communications experts also tell us that "I" statements work better than "you" statements. Example: "I am concerned that donors who see typos in our materials may form a negative impression of the XYZ Charity" is a lot softer than "You keep giving me unproofed materials. Can't you produce a letter without typos?" Mean people don't belong in leadership positions—especially in not-for-profit institutions whose mission is to make the world a better place to live.

Lots of positive feedback accompanied by courteous reminders or suggestions for improvements helps create a productive and pleasant work environment. Most important, these feedback statements should be intermittent but frequent. They should never be mechanical, but always sincere and timely. Compelling legal considerations force institutions to adhere to the performance appraisal practice. However, to truly motivate employees, immediate feedback is the key to success.

VOLUNTEERS

Volunteers play a central role in the life of not-for-profit organizations. Because of their dedication, these organizations can keep the cost of providing vital services lower than they might have been. When these volunteers are treated with respect, shown appreciation, and assigned meaningful work to do, they become an invaluable resource. Because of their involvement, many also become financial supporters of the organization.

Volunteer identification, recruitment, and training are time-consuming. Too frequently, not-for-profit staff find it easier just to do the job themselves than to recruit a volunteer to complete the task. This is a very short-sighted point of view. Once a volunteer has been recruited, there is a good chance that he or she will be available on a regular basis. Therefore, remember that many responsibilities related to volunteer recruitment and orientation are time-consuming only the first time. The more the organization engages volunteers, the more cost effective are their services.

Roles

Volunteers can fill every conceivable role in the not-for-profit organization. One retired community leader on several occasions served as interim executive director of a not-for-profit while the organization conducted a search for a permanent executive director.

Volunteers can be called upon to perform clerical duties for the organization. For example, some modest-size not-for-profits use volunteers to prepare their mass mailings.

Volunteers can be called upon to deliver vital services. Doctors and health care providers frequently volunteer to provide services to the poorest of the poor.

Volunteers can be called upon to provide expertise. Real estate agents, graphic artists, professional writers, finance experts, attorneys, CPAs, printers, and a host of other professionals have been known to donate services to not-for-profit organizations. The line between voluntarism, in-kind services, and pro bono services is a bit muddled. However, there is no doubt that people who share the organization's values can be asked to donate their personal and professional time to the cause.

From a fundraising perspective, an organization will want to surround itself with people of affluence and influence. Many can be recruited for the major gift program. Some may serve on the board. Some may be asked to serve on an advisory board. Some may be recruited to serve on a campaign cabinet. The key here is to find each person's comfort level in the fundraising process. Not everyone feels comfortable directly soliciting contributions. Professionals and experienced volunteer leaders can help others become more comfortable in a fundraising environment.

Encourage the institution to use volunteers in as many capacities as pos-

sible. Identify and recruit as many volunteer leaders, organizers, and "worker bees" as possible. Some of these folks will never solicit personal gifts but can prove invaluable in organizing large-scale special event fundraisers. Some may help in the ways just described.

By the way, many volunteers who would be unlikely to help in a one-to-one or team solicitation will help with group solicitations. Here are the few steps that can be taken to encourage these group solicitations.

- Find volunteers who are willing to open their homes.
- Encourage them to invite their friends.
- Augment the invitation list with supporters from the volunteer's geographic area.
- Prepare attractive invitations.
- Prepare and conduct the group solicitation. State the case for support. Keep the presentation short. Share testimonials. Use attractive visuals when possible. When soliciting the gifts, refer to a gift range that reflects the capability of the people in attendance.
- Distribute and collect pledge cards and contributions at the gathering. Ask for what is expected.

Other volunteers will open their houses only for cultivation events. Some people are very uncomfortable with the thought of soliciting friends and neighbors. However, some of these very same people—especially those with attractive homes—feel comfortable in inviting people to a gathering where the friends, neighbors, and other prospects can learn more about the not-for-profit institution.

Another way volunteers can help is by providing information concerning prospective donors. People who are knowledgeable about the community can help with prospect ratings and research. Naturally gatherings of such volunteers should be small and confidential.

Recruitment and Retention

Volunteer recruitment should become a key element in every not-for-profit organization's corporate culture. All board members, staffers, and volunteers can be reminded that volunteer recruitment is the institution's number-1 priority. Staff members should be ever vigilant for volunteer

opportunities. Volunteers should be made to feel welcome at the agency. Everything possible must be done to avoid a we-and-they mind-set. The coffee room should be open to staff and volunteers alike. Volunteers can be engaged in key organizational decisions. Break down as many barriers as possible. Create as many volunteer job slots as possible. And maintain lists of things that can be done on a when-a-volunteer-is-available basis.

By establishing and maintaining relations with an auxiliary group, the organization can develop a reliable cadre of volunteers. It may be useful to establish a young professionals support organization. Yuppies have boundless energy, great ideas, and close relationships to community leaders.

When the organization needs more volunteers than it can recruit by itself, consider approaching a civic club to adopt the cause or project. Civitans, Rotarians, Lions, and Kiwanians often can be motivated to move en masse on behalf of a not-for-profit organization with a compelling case for support.

The number-1 way to retain volunteers is to show appreciation for their work and dedication consistently. Take steps to avoid burnout. Provide snacks and food for volunteer get-togethers. Say thank you. Say thank you. Say thank you. Smile. Be warm and genuine.

WORKING WITH CONSULTANTS

Every consultancy takes on a life of its own. However, the conceptual framework, the consulting cycle, illustrated in Exhibit 15-6, is fundamental to most consulting relationships.

Not-for-profit organizations find consultants helpful at key points in the organization's history. Consultants help grassroots organizations transition to more mature institutions. Organizations beginning strategic planning processes often find it helpful to work with consultants. Organizations contemplating capital campaigns find consultants indispensable. Many organizations turn to consultants when beginning a search for a key employee.

Perhaps a consultant's main role is to provide an objective perspective to key decisions and processes. At times, the decision to work with a consultant is greeted with misgivings or skepticism. However, the consultant/client relationship is strengthened when the key decision makers understand the gravity of the challenge being addressed. It is also helpful if board

EXHIBIT 15-6 THE CONSULTING CYCLE

1. Needs Assessment/Situation Analysis
   a. Interviews
   b. Document review
   c. System analysis
   d. Direct observation of work processes

2. Development of Alternatives
   a. Suggestions from in-house team
   b. Suggestions generated by the consultant
   c. Brainstorming sessions
   d. Review of literature
   e. Surveys and suggestions from peers
   f. Surveys of industry practice

3. Decision
   a. Pros and cons
   b. Quantify expectations
   c. Stakeholder analysis
   d. Reach consensus prior to written report

4. Implementation
   a. Who does what by when?
   b. What financial and human resources are allocated to the project?
   c. What are the critical success factors?
   d. Who's in charge?
   e. Inspect what you expect
   f. Project management tools
      • Gantt chart
      • PERT and CPM diagrams
      • Simple tables indicating a and b above

5. Evaluation

members have had an opportunity to meet with the consultant and have gained an understanding of his or her track record in dealing with similar situations.

In the resource development arena, consultants are called on to provide the following services:

• Development audits—assessments of fundraising offices and recommendations to enhance resource development programs

- Precampaign studies—feasibility studies, market surveys, and campaign assessments designed to assess fundraising potential, refine plans, and nurture relationships with potential major donors
- Capital and endowment campaigns—campaign support, advice and counsel, and/or resident campaign management
- Prospect research—intensive research concerning specific prospects, electronic screening of databases, and/or facilitating the ratings and evaluation process
- Annual giving—direct mail and phone campaign consultation, special event support, and comprehensive resource development planning
- Major gift initiatives—prospect research, volunteer recruitment, materials development, cultivation, and solicitation training and support services
- Planned giving—materials development, board orientation, planned-giving seminars and marketing, individual gift planning, and general advice and counsel
- Strategic planning—board retreats and gatherings facilitation; analysis of the organization's strengths, weaknesses, opportunities, and threats (SWOT analysis); strategic planning committee meeting facilitation; preparation of notes and draft versions of the strategic long-range plan; plan refinement based on board suggestions; preparation of final version for board approval
- Executive search—job analysis, preparation of job description, analysis of salary and benefit packages, proactive recruitment, screening of applicant résumés, interview process participation, reference checks, recommendations to the decision-making body
- Fundraising software—needs assessment, situation analysis, dedicated fundraising software options reviews, examination of institutional interfaces, customization of system, data transfer, annual system support, and/or delivery of turn-key system
- Grantsmanship—grants research, project development, writing and editing, monitoring deadlines, and fulfilling report requirements
- Board development—board/staff relations, the nominating process, potential board member identification, recruitment, and orientation; also, committee structure, bylaws, and work processes

- Retreats, seminars, workshops, and process facilitation—training, orientation, role playing, involvement activities, and a broad spectrum of planning processes

The scope of work is described in a contract between the not-for-profit organization and the consulting firm. Some firms define a very narrow scope of work. A few create contracts that allow greater flexibility and a broader range of services in response to changing circumstances. Some firms provide advice. Others take a more hands-on approach.

The best consultants realize the importance of people, not just facts and situations. They ask: "What is the situation as it now exists? . . . What would the ideal future be like? . . . What steps are needed to get to the ideal future? . . . What person or persons can help bring about the changes needed? . . . How can we motivate them to help? . . . Do any stakeholders oppose the change? . . . How can we neutralize them or bring them around to our point of view?"

Ultimately, *people* make decisions. In any consulting or planning process, the motivations of the stakeholders must be understood.

Selection and Contracting

Once a decision has been made to engage the services of a consultant, the organization can follow 10 steps in choosing the consultant to perform the work:

Form Selection Committee   The consultant selection committee should be composed of three to seven people, usually five. Look to recruit visionary people, wise people, generous people, and decision makers.

Clarify Expectations   Prior to developing a request for proposal, the committee members should thoroughly discuss and understand the consultant's role in the proposed project. The committee's first task, therefore, is to develop realistic expectations of what deliverables are expected. The committee also should have a firm understanding of the desired outcome. After interviewing potential consultants, this understanding may be refined and modified. But the team must begin with a common understanding.

Develop a Request for Proposals   RFPs need not be complex. A simple one- or two-page letter will suffice for most situations. The RFP

should state expectations as clearly as possible. Describe the situation. If the services are for a campaign, include the initial estimate of the goal. State any concerns that are unique to the not-for-profit organization.

The RFP should contain specific questions about the consultant's experience. At a minimum, the consultant should be asked to provide relevant background information concerning the firm's experience with projects such as the organization's.

The RFP should ask the prospective consultant to state how he or she will accomplish the work described in it. If the consulting firm has a unique approach to the problem, this approach should be highlighted or described as clearly as possible.

Every RFP should have a due date for the proposal. It also should request the name and background of the consultant who will be assigned to the project and request references.

Finding Prospective Consultants   Not-for-profit organizations have a number of ways of finding prospective consultants to approach. Avoid sending 25 to 50 RFPs to consulting firms across the nation. It is far better to identify not more than 7 firms to approach. The initial list should include names of realistic candidates for the contract—respected people or firms with the background needed. Here are some suggestions:

- *Consulting firms the not-for-profit organization has dealt with in the past*
  A full formal search may not have to be conducted if the organization already had a strong relationship with a successful consulting firm. In such a case, the consultant or firm may know the situation very well and perhaps can give the project a jump start.

- *Referrals from colleagues*
  Call colleagues working with other not-for-profit organizations. Ask them which consultants have been helpful in conducting projects or campaigns similar to yours.

- *AFP referrals*
  The Association of Fundraising Professionals can furnish a list of member consultants in your region.

Screening of RFPs   Even when dealing with a small group of qualified consultants, several RFPs may appear nonresponsive to a particular organi-

zation's needs or circumstances. Therefore the first step is to eliminate the obviously unqualified or nonresponsive RFPs.

If the organization wrote to numerous consulting firms, staff may make this initial cut. However, to ensure board buy-in, the rejected applications still can be made available to committee members for their review and possible reconsideration.

After the initial screening, the committee can reach a consensus on two to five finalists.

Checking References   Checking references prior to final selection can help eliminate a wasted interview. Ask:

- What was the nature of the project the consultant worked on?
- How long was the consultancy?
- Did the project succeed? If not, why not?
- Did the consultant ever have an occasion where he or she had to convey advice that not all board members agreed with? How well was the situation handled?
- Was the consultant always objective?
- How would you rate the consultant's flexibility?
- Was the consultant a good listener?
- How well did the consultant relate to the board, staff, and volunteers?
- How well did the consultant develop solutions to the problems you faced?
- Would you hire the consultant again?

The Interview   Have the entire committee present for all interviews. As with interviews of key hires described earlier, ask "involvement" questions. Examples:

- When you last did a needs assessment, what organizational issues did you cover and how did you uncover the information needed for the findings?
- Some of our board members believe that they need not make a financial contribution to the organization because they donate so much time. How have you handled this attitude when you have encountered it in the past?

- Have you worked in a fundraising campaign where the volunteers were simply not making their calls? What steps did you take to ensure that the campaign reached its goal despite this obstacle?
- When you are conducting a feasibility study, and the interviewee appears reluctant to answer your question about a giving range that he or she might consider, how do you respond?

Request that the consultant bring sample materials to the interview, such as past development audits, feasibility studies, other precampaign studies, and development plans. Be sensitive to the need for confidentiality, however. Here the consultant has a number of options:

- He or she may be willing to share briefly an older study performed for a client in a faraway location.
- He or she may be willing to share a strategic long-range plan, comprehensive resource development plan, feasibility study, or development audit that has been word-processed so that the client's identity would not be revealed.
- Consultants are free to show campaign brochures and promotional materials produced for other clients. (These, of course, are freely available to the public.)
- The consultant may get permission from a previous client to share the work for the purpose of allowing potential clients to assess the consultant's experience.

Structure the interview so that the prospective consultant has an opportunity to ask questions. The questions asked will reveal a lot about the nature of the consultant's thought processes. Additionally, these questions will reveal what homework the consultant did prior to the interview.

Decision   When decisions are made, most committees tend to focus on the Four Cs: competence, confidence, chemistry, and cost. The consultant must have the competence, experience, and knowledge needed to accomplish the work, and he or she must inspire confidence. The chemistry must be right; the consultant must be a person who relates well with the board, staff, and volunteers. And finally, the consultant's proposal must be cost-effective.

In all probability the consultant selection committee adopted a set of selection criteria early in the process. Such criteria might include the following:

- Will the candidate inspire the board and staff to make the changes needed?
- Does the candidate have the knowledge and experience needed?
- Did the candidate receive good references?
- Will the candidate work well with the board, staff, and volunteers?
- Will the candidate "tell it like it is"?
- Does the candidate have a demonstrable record of helping similar organizations dramatically increase their contributed income?

Contract The consultant's response to your organization's RFP forms the basis of the contract. The final contract should be clear as to start and stop dates and should define the scope of work to be accomplished. Build in some flexibility, but ensure that the final contract is as specific as possible as to deliverables and due dates. It should specify what services the consulting firm will perform and include a description of the not-for-profit organization's responsibilities. The contract should include a dispute resolution clause and may include a mutual right-of-termination clause. The contract should be clear as to compensation.

Notify Consulting Firms As a courtesy to the consulting firms who responded to the RFP but were not chosen to perform the work, send a gracious letter acknowledging the proposal and stating the outcome of your search. Good manners are not reserved for prospective donors only.

Implementing Recommendations

This is where the rubber meets the road. Too many reports gather dust on shelves. Don't let that happen.

The first step in the implementation process is to refine the plan and gain board approval. If the consultant's recommendations are richly detailed, refining the time line and agreeing on responsible parties for tasks and subtasks becomes a simple matter. Board and staff members should be made aware of the study, plan, or audit's recommendations. Everyone involved should understand the major tasks to be accomplished, the time commitments required to complete these tasks, and other circumstances unique to each consultancy.

Board approval or "agreement in principle" is imperative. It is not enough simply to acknowledge receipt of the report.

Now that the work has been planned, the plan must be worked. Remain focused on the need to build a solid case for support. Improve the information system. Use a thoughtful nominating and relationship-building process to recruit board members of affluence and influence. Identify, cultivate, and solicit major gift supporters. If a project involves a campaign, assiduously follow the advice contained in the precampaign study. Stay on track. Monitor deadlines. Refer back to the report frequently. Make corrections and refinements throughout.

While working, keep the lines of communication open and clear. If a contract with the consultant includes a continuing relationship, expect the consultant to remain proactive. Periodically let the consultant know how he or she is doing. Foster strong relationships and communications among the staff, board members, volunteers, and the consultant. Listen to everyone. Let common sense prevail. Stay focused on the primary objectives of the campaign or project. At every stage of the process, remain sensitive to the wants and needs of current and prospective donors.

Evaluation

The cure for admiring the House of Lords is to go and look at it.

—Walter Bogehut

One central theme dominates this book: Not-for-profit organizations can increase their contributed income dramatically by monitoring and making improvements across a broad range of critical success factors.

Fundraising involves many measurable objectives and outcomes. Many of these are the keys to the organization's success. Earlier chapters indicated that some of the factors measured are means—ways to achieve the organization's fundraising goals. These include the number of mailings, personal contacts, and grants applied for, and a host of other technical factors. Previous chapters also explored how to measure the ends—the desired outcomes. These ends included the total dollars contributed, the total number of contributors participating in programs, and how the contributed income met the not-for-profit organization's programmatic goals. Above all, the importance of focusing on net contributed income was stressed.

The Complete Guide to Fundraising Management also has explored the importance of building positive relationships with donors and prospective supporters. It is not possible to create an evaluation tool that accurately reflects how well an organization relates to its volunteers, board members, donors, and prospects on a personal level. No form accurately can capture the warmth experienced when dealing with another person. However, the outcome of such encounters can be measured. People who are kind and

gracious in their dealings with their constituents garner more support for their organizations than those who never learn how to relate well to other people.

Periodic evaluation is needed to ensure success over time. Any not-for-profit organization can benefit by conducting the self-assessment contained in this chapter. To conduct a more intensive review with an outside perspective, the organization also may consider a peer review conducted by an experienced resource development professional from a similar organization. Another alternative would be to engage the services of a consultant to conduct a development audit. This latter step might be most helpful the first time an intensive evaluation is done. By working with a consultant, the organization will gain a fresh insight into its resource development program. In future years, the annual self-assessment will be more productive because of this earlier investment.

The following pages contain a quick self-assessment (see Exhibit 16-1) followed by a three-part comprehensive self-assessment (see Exhibit 16-2). Part 1 is the scorekeeping portion; it deals with results and "ends." Part 2 contains an evaluation of a wide range of fundraising strategies and techniques. Part 3 covers a broad spectrum of organizational issues and measures that can lead an organization to dramatically increased contributed income. How wisely these increased financial resources are used may very well determine how well an organization continues to receive the funds needed to carry out its mission.

Please carefully monitor all of these critical success factors. It is my hope that your organization will thrive and flourish. It is also my hope that you will continue to have the resources you require to accomplish its aims and to better serve our communities, nation, and world.

EXHIBIT 16-1 QUICK SELF-TEST

Questions	Scoring	Points Earned
1. Percentage gain in true net contributed income. (Most recent fiscal year over previous fiscal year.)	2 points per each percentage gain; 0 points if declining net contributed income	
2. Did 100% of your board members make a financial contribution this fiscal year?	7 points if yes 0 points if no	
3. Did you "drop" at least 16 times the number of prospect mailing pieces as the number of donors who contributed in the last 12 months?	10 points if yes 5 points if 10× the # of donors 0 points if less than 10×	
4. Organization regularly generates and files fundraising reports that indicate net contributed income from *each* appeal?	10 points if yes 0 points if no	
5. Development officer or executive director participates in personal major gift solicitations or event sponsorship solicitations?	1 point for each *personal visit* during the most recent fiscal year	
6. Which of the following fundraising strategies does your organization employ: mail; return envelopes with thanks; phone; grants; tributes; special events; major gifts?	2 points for each strategy employed during most recent fiscal year	
7. Which of the following planned gift strategies does your organization employ: newsletter articles; personal contact; seminars; brochure mailings; computer-generated benefit illustrations; reminder slips in thanks; check box on return envelope?	2 points for each strategy employed during most recent fiscal year	
8. Does the organization promptly thank each contribution?	5 points for 2-day turnaround or less; 3 points if 7 days or less; 0 points if longer or if each gift is not thanked	
9. Has the organization adopted a formalized acknowledgment program?	5 points if yes 0 points if no	
10. Has the organization adopted a prospect identification, rating, and cultivation system?	5 points if 75 or more prime prospects identified; 5 points if request amounts assigned to 50 or more prime prospects; 5 points if the prime prospects have been invited to an event within 6 months	
TOTAL POINTS		

90 and above = Excellent. Keep up the good work! Consider improving in the areas where you scored a bit less.

80–89 = Very Good You're doing as well as or better than most. But there's still lots of room for growth.

70–79 = Average Focus on high-payoff activities and dramatically increase your contributed income.

0–69 = Poor to Fair Please review the longer evaluation and look for opportunities for improvement.

EXHIBIT 16-2 FINANCIAL DEVELOPMENT SELF-ASSESSMENT

PART 1—RESULTS

I. SCOREKEEPING MEASURES

    A. SUMMARY OF FUNDRAISING RESULTS—Arranged by Fundraising Strategy

       Advice: Focus on Net Contributed Income and Trends.

            (Many not-for-profit evaluation forms focus on gross contributed income and "snapshots" in time or single-year results. Try filling out the following tables; see if something new about the financial development program is learned.)

        1. Mail Results

           The following table can be used to summarize the results of the not-for-profit organization's Mail Campaigns for fiscal year 2000 through fiscal year 2003. Try to fill in two or three past fiscal years and the current year's projected results. Expense figures represent direct expenses only. Salaries and other overhead are not to be included.

MAIL CAMPAIGNS				
	FY-00	FY-01	FY-02	FY-03

In-House List: membership, donations, tribute gifts and return envelopes sent with thank-yous
  Income
  Expense
  Net				

Prospect Mail
  Income
  Expense
  Net				

Unsolicited Mail Income				
MAIL TOTAL NET				

EXHIBIT 16-2 (CONTINUED)

2. Special Events Results (Including Sponsorships)

The following table can be used to summarize the results of the not-for-profit's special events fundraisers for fiscal year 2000 through fiscal year 2003. Expense figures represent direct expenses only. Salaries and other overhead are not to be included.

SPECIAL EVENTS				
	FY-00	**FY-01**	**FY-02**	**FY-03**
Special Event 1 Ticket sales and other revenues Sponsorships Income total Expense Net				
Special Event 2 Ticket sales and other revenues Sponsorships Income total Expense Net				
Special Event 3 Ticket sales and other revenues Sponsorships Income total Expense Net				
SPECIAL EVENTS TOTAL NET				

Note: We do not recommend conducting multiple special events; one or two highly successful special events per year may be desirable. Of course, actual events conducted in the last several years should be listed.

(continued)

EXHIBIT 16-2 (CONTINUED)

3. Major Gifts Results
The following table can be used to summarize the results of the not-for-profit's major gift program for fiscal year 2000 through fiscal year 2003. Expense figures represent direct expenses only. Salaries and other overhead are not to be included.
NOTE: Do not double-count major gifts. List only those major gifts that are **not** included in the mail campaigns or special events sponsorship information.

MAJOR GIFTS				
	FY-00	FY-01	FY-02	FY-03
Major gift club income Other major gift income (Not included in mail or special events)				
Subtotal Major gift income				
Major gift direct expense				
MAJOR GIFTS TOTAL NET				

4. Grants

GRANTS				
	FY-00	FY-01	FY-02	FY-03
Total Grant Income				

5. Telephone Solicitations / Telemarketing / Phone-a-Thons

TELEPHONE SOLICITATIONS				
	FY-00	FY-01	FY-02	FY-03
Phone-a-Thons or Telemarketing Income Expense				
Net				

EXHIBIT 16-2 (CONTINUED)

B. SUMMARY OF FUNDRAISING RESULTS—Arranged by Gift Level
Advice: Focus on **modes** rather than mean averages.
(The "average gift" can be a very misleading number. The aim is to have a broad range of contributions and gift opportunities. When filling in the next table, consider:

- Are contributions increasing at each gift level?
- Is the gift range narrow or broad? (Are there gifts at each of the levels listed, including the highest levels or greater?)
- Are there any gaps in the gift range table? (Is the distribution curve smooth—many small gifts, slightly fewer at the next range, a bit less in the next range, and so on?)

GIFT RANGE	FY-00		FY-01		FY-02		FY-03	
$ Amount	# Gifts	Total Value	# Gifts	Total Value	# Gifts	Total Value	# Gifts	Total Value
1–99								
100–249								
250–499								
500–999								
1,000–2,499								
2,500–4,999								
5,000–9,999								
10,000–24,999								
25,000–49,999								
50,000–99,999								
100,000 & above								
TOTAL								

(continued)

EXHIBIT 16-2 (CONTINUED)

C. OVERALL TRENDS
Use this table to summarize the *net* direct income from fundraising strategies.

NET INCOME TRENDS				
	FY-00	FY-01	FY-02	FY-03
Mail (net)				
Special events (net)				
Major gifts (net)				
Grants (net)				
Telephone solicitations (net)				
Unsolicited and miscellaneous (net)				
Bequests and other realized planned gifts (net)				
United Way				
Other contributed income (net)				
Subtotal direct net contributed income				
Indirect expenses, salaries and identifiable overhead				
TRUE NET CONTRIBUTED INCOME				

EXHIBIT 16-2 (CONTINUED)

PART 2—METHODS AND MEANS

I. MAIL
   A. IN-HOUSE LIST—RENEWALS AND UPGRADES
      1. How many mailings (include all in-house mail appeals) were dropped last
          year? _____#

      2. How many mailings are scheduled for this year? _____#

      3. Approximate or historical numbers: How many receive each specific
          mailing?   FY1 _____,
          FY2 _____,   FY3 _____,   FY4 _____,
          FY5 _____,   FY6 _____,   FY7 _____,
          FY8 _____,   FY9 _____,   FY10_____

      4. What is the response rate for each?   FY1 _____,
          FY2 _____,   FY3 _____,   FY4 _____,
          FY5 _____,   FY6 _____,   FY7 _____,
          FY8 _____,   FY9 _____,   FY10_____

      5. What is the average gift for each mailing?   FY1 _____,
          FY2 _____,   FY3 _____,   FY4 _____,
          FY5 _____,   FY6 _____,   FY7 _____,
          FY8 _____,   FY9 _____,   FY10_____

      6. How many people have donated through mail in the last
          12 months? _____ 18 months? _____

      7. How many lapsed donors (18 months or greater) are on the in-house list?
          _____#

      8. Is an envelope included with thank-you letters to give donors the
          opportunity to send additional contributions?   ❏ Yes   ❏ No

      9. Is the organization working with a mail house, mail vendor, or mail
          consultant concerning the in-house list?   ❏ Yes   ❏ No

   B. PROSPECTING—DONOR ACQUISITION
      1. Total prospect mailings dropped each year? _____#
          (Total # of packages mailed)

      2. What is the ratio of the number of prospect mailings dropped vis à vis
          the number of donors who contributed in the last 12 months? (Annual
          number of prospect packages ÷ number of 12-month active donors.)
          _____/____

(continued)

EXHIBIT 16-2 (CONTINUED)

3. What are the response rates for each of the following?
FY Prospect Mailing 1 _____%
FY Prospect Mailing 2 _____%
FY Prospect Mailing 3 _____%
FY Prospect Mailing 4 _____%

4. What is the average gift for each of the following?
FY Prospect Mailing 1 $_____
FY Prospect Mailing 2 $_____
FY Prospect Mailing 3 $_____
FY Prospect Mailing 4 $_____

5. What is the cost to raise a dollar for each of the following?
FY Prospect Mailing 1 $_____
FY Prospect Mailing 2 $_____
FY Prospect Mailing 3 $_____
FY Prospect Mailing 4 $_____

6. What is the cost to acquire each new donor for each of the following?
FY Prospect Mailing 1 $_____
FY Prospect Mailing 2 $_____
FY Prospect Mailing 3 $_____
FY Prospect Mailing 4 $_____

7. Is the organization working with a mail house, mail vendor, or mail consultant for the prospect mailing? ❏ Yes ❏ No

II. SPECIAL EVENTS
   A. SPONSORSHIPS
      1. What is the largest sponsorship level sought on an annual basis? $_____

      2. When is the last time the top sponsorship level was raised? (date) _____

      3. Have multiple sponsorship levels been created? ❏ Yes ❏ No

      4. What is the total dollar value of *all* sponsorships from all special events? $_____

      5. Has this amount been growing each year? ❏ Yes ❏ No

   B. OTHER EVENT INCOME AND MEASURABLE RESULTS
      1. How many people attend special events each year? _____#

      2. What is the average ticket or participation price? $_____

EXHIBIT 16-2 (CONTINUED)

3. How many events are conducted?   _____#

4. List each event, record net income from each, estimate the total number
   of volunteer and staff hours involved, divide the net income by the
   number of volunteer and staff hours—this is the dollars raised per hour.
   Event 1 dollars raised per hour $_____
   Event 2 dollars raised per hour $_____
   Event 3 dollars raised per hour $_____

III. MAJOR GIFTS AND PERSONAL SOLICITATIONS
   A. PERSONAL SOLICITATIONS
   1. Has a list of at least 50 to 100 prime prospective major
      donors been assembled?   ❑ Yes   ❑ No

   2. Have attractive solicitation materials that can be person-
      alized for each in-person presentation been assembled? ❑ Yes   ❑ No

   3. Has training or major gift orientation been provided
      for your key volunteers?   ❑ Yes   ❑ No

   4. Has the prospect pool been rated? (i.e., has a specific
      request amount for each prospective major gift donor
      been determined)?   ❑ Yes   ❑ No

   5. Has the presentation material been personalized to
      reflect the specific request amount?   ❑ Yes   ❑ No

   6. How many "eyeball-to-eyeball" solicitations did the
      organization (volunteer and staff) conduct during the
      most recent fiscal year?   _____#

   7. In how many "in-person" solicitations did a member of
      the staff (executive director, development director, other)
      participate during the most recent fiscal year?   _____#

   8. Percentage of all visits (volunteer and/or staff) that
      resulted in a contribution to the organization?   _____%

   9. Total funds raised from personal solicitations? $_____

IV. GRANTS
   A. RESEARCH AND GRANTS TOOLBOX
   1. Has anyone from the nonprofit conducted grants
      research during the most recent fiscal year?   ❑ Yes   ❑ No
      Describe the nature of the research. _____

(continued)

EXHIBIT 16-2 (CONTINUED)

2. Has a list of intended applications and deadlines for this fiscal year been prepared? ❏ Yes ❏ No

3. Have frequently used attachments been duplicated? ❏ Yes ❏ No

4. Has standard language been written for most frequently asked questions? ❏ Yes ❏ No

5. Have planners networked and checked with other similar organizations to garner ideas for fundable projects? ❏ Yes ❏ No

B. OTHER MEASURES AND TRENDS
   1. How many grants were applied for during the most recent fiscal year? _____#

   2. In the most recent fiscal year, what was the total dollar value of all applications submitted? $_____

   3. What percentage of the proposals was funded? _____%

   4. In the most recent fiscal year, what was the total dollar amount funded through grants? $_____

V. TELEPHONE SOLICITATIONS
   A. OVERVIEW
      1. Does the organization conduct any telephone solicitations? ❏ Yes ❏ No

      2. What overall strategies are employed?
         Volunteer phone-a-thon only ❏ Yes ❏ No
         Professional telemarketing ❏ Yes ❏ No
         Some volunteer calling combined with professional telemarketing ❏ Yes ❏ No

   B. SEGMENTATION
      1. Who is called?
         Prospects (donor acquisition) ❏ Yes ❏ No
         Lapsed donors ❏ Yes ❏ No
         Major donor upgrades ❏ Yes ❏ No
         Members and regular contributors (often in combination with mail campaigns) ❏ Yes ❏ No
         Other ❏ Yes ❏ No
         Please describe: _____

      2. If any of the above segmentations are being used, have the results of each been tracked carefully? ❏ Yes ❏ No

EXHIBIT 16-2 (CONTINUED)

VI. PLANNED GIVING
   A. OVERVIEW
      1. Does the organization promote planned gifts in any way? ❑ Yes   ❑ No

      2. Who has assumed prime responsibility for the organization's
         planned giving activities? (Check all that apply.)
         A major gift and/or planned gift specialist   _____
         Director of development   _____
         Executive director   _____
         A board or community volunteer   _____
         Some combination of the above   _____

   B. STRATEGIES AND PLANNED-GIVING PROMOTION
      1. Which, if any, of the following planned giving promotional
         techniques does the organization employ? (Check all that apply.)
         Seminars and informative gatherings   _____
         (If checked, also check below indicating segmentations.)
            Estate planning professionals   _____
            Prospects   _____
            Board members   _____
            A combined invitation   _____
         Planned-giving articles in newsletters   _____
         Simple reminders in newsletters (Example: A boxed
         reminder stating "Please remember the XYZ Nonprofit
         Organization in your will or estate plan.")   _____
         Slips with planned-giving reminders enclosed with
         thank-yous? (Alternative: Bequest language on reverse side
         of receipts.)   _____
         Annual or periodic mailing(s) of planned giving brochures
         (If checked, also check below indicating segmentations.) _____
            Wills brochure?   _____
            Charitable gift annuity brochure   _____
            Planned giving generic brochure   _____
         Personal contact with planned-giving prospects ... especially
         those who request planned-giving information   _____
         Personalized illustration of benefits for charitable gift
         annuities or other gift vehicles?   _____

(continued)

EXHIBIT 16-2 (CONTINUED)

PART 3—OTHER FINANCIAL DEVELOPMENT ISSUES

I. BOARD INDICATORS
   A. OVERVIEW
   1. Has a job description been adopted for board members? ❑ Yes   ❑ No

   2. Does the job description clearly describe the board members' fundraising responsibilities? ❑ Yes   ❑ No

   3. Does the job description clearly state new board members' responsibility to donate annually? (financial contribution) ❑ Yes   ❑ No

   4. Does the nominating committee consider affluence and influence among the key success factors for Board membership? ❑ Yes   ❑ No

   5. Do the people responsible for recruiting board members graciously discuss fundraising and giving policies with potential board members during the recruitment process? ❑ Yes   ❑ No

   6. Is a board campaign conducted each year? ❑ Yes   ❑ No

   B. MEASURABLE RESULTS
   1. Is there 100% participation in board giving each year? ❑ Yes   ❑ No

   2. How much is raised from the board campaign? $_____

   3. Has this amount been growing each year? ❑ Yes   ❑ No

   4. How many members of the organization's major gift club are there on the board of directors? _____#

   5. Has the number of board members been growing each year? ❑ Yes   ❑ No

   6. Number and percentage of board members who are active with personal or major gift solicitations? _____#_____%

   7. Number and percentage of board members who are actively involved in any aspect of fund raising? _____#_____%

II. ACKNOWLEDGMENT
   A. GENERAL ACKNOWLEDGMENT ACTIVITIES
   1. Is every gift thanked by mail? ❑ Yes   ❑ No

EXHIBIT 16-2 (CONTINUED)

2. What is the average turnaround time in days between receipt of a gift and mailing acknowledgment? (One, 2, or 3 days turnaround time is highly desirable.)   _____

3. Is *every* gift thanked within 7 days of receipt?   ❏ Yes   ❏ No

B. FORMALIZED DONOR RECOGNITION PROGRAM
   1. Is there a formal donor recognition program?   ❏ Yes   ❏ No

   2. What are the elements of the formal donor recognition program? (Check all that apply.)
   • Permanent recognition
     Donor walls   _____
     Other named gift opportunities   _____

   • Donor recognition (tokens of appreciation)
     Plaques   _____
     Certificates   _____
     Pins   _____
     Other specialty gifts   _____

   • Donor benefits
     Membership "perks"   _____
     Gift clubs   _____
     Acknowledgment listings in newsletters
     and/or annual reports   _____
     Sponsorship benefits   _____
     Recognition receptions   _____

   • Involvement opportunities
     Founders' Circles or advisory councils   _____
     Gift club social/informative gatherings   _____
     Legacy league, codicil club
     luncheons, etc.   _____
     Recruitment to serve   _____

III. CULTIVATION
   A. OVERVIEW
      1. Has the organization developed a formal or informal cultivation strategy?   ❏ Yes   ❏ No

      2. Has a list of prime prospects for cultivation been developed?   ❏ Yes   ❏ No

(continued)

EXHIBIT 16-2 (CONTINUED)

B. CULTIVATION STRATEGIES
   1. Which of the following relationship-nurturing strategies does the organization employ? (Check all that apply)
   Social/informative gatherings _____
   Surveys _____
   Personal interviews _____
   Recruitment to serve _____
   Focus groups _____
   Invitations to tour the organization _____
   Luncheons with the organization executive director or
   board chair _____
   Informative mailings (annual reports, personalized
   friend-raising letters, newsletters, etc.) _____
   Annual recognition receptions _____
   Other _____ _____

   2. Does the organization track who and how many people
   participate in each of the cultivation activities?   ❏ Yes   ❏ No

IV. RECORD KEEPING AND DATABASE MANAGEMENT
A. RECORD MAINTENANCE
   1. Is the name, address, phone number, and all usual and
   common information of each donor and prospect recorded
   in an integrated, segmentable database?   ❏ Yes   ❏ No

   2. Is the database dedicated fundraising software?   ❏ Yes   ❏ No

   3. Is each gift, contribution date, solicitation method/appeal,
   and use/restriction/ purpose of each contribution
   recorded?   ❏ Yes   ❏ No
   Is this faithfully recorded in a relational database or
   dedicated fundraising software?   ❏ Yes   ❏ No

   4. Is the database used to record other information?
   Type (individual, business, foundation, church,
   government, etc.)   ❏ Yes   ❏ No
   Sort codes or flags (former board member,
   volunteer, etc.)   ❏ Yes   ❏ No
   Profession   ❏ Yes   ❏ No
   Ratings or request amounts   ❏ Yes   ❏ No
   Volunteer assignments   ❏ Yes   ❏ No
   Division, etc.   ❏ Yes   ❏ No
   Other _____   ❏ Yes   ❏ No

EXHIBIT 16-2 (CONTINUED)

B. AUTOMATION
  1. Is the acknowledgment process automated?   ❏ Yes   ❏ No

  2. Are segmented lists generated in label format?   ❏ Yes   ❏ No
     In list format?   ❏ Yes   ❏ No

  3. Are highly targeted communications regularly
     mail-merged?   ❏ Yes   ❏ No

C. REPORTS
  1. Scorekeeping Reports
     Is some version of the following "scorekeeping" report
     regularly generated, examined, and filed?
     Summary of fiscal year-to-date giving?   ❏ Yes   ❏ No
     (Should indicate number of gifts, number of donors,
     pledges, pledge balance, etc. Often arranged by gift level.
     Alternatively may be arranged by solicitation method,
     fund/use of contribution, division, or type of donor. Often
     in a format that compares this year to last year.)

  2. Attention-Directing Reports
     Are any of the following reports regularly generated and
     examined?
     • Prime prospects who have not yet been assigned a
       volunteer solicitor   ❏ Yes   ❏ No
     • Pledge receivables   ❏ Yes   ❏ No
     • Solicitor reports that indicate which volunteers have
       performed their assignments successfully and which
       ones must be urged to complete their tasks   ❏ Yes   ❏ No
     • Other attention-directing reports   ❏ Yes   ❏ No

  3. Problem-Solving Reports and Analysis
     (These reports help us make better decisions.)
     Are any of the following analytical reports regularly generated and
     examined?
     • Solicitation analysis: number of donors, dollars received,
       related expenses, numbers mailed or contacted,
       response rates, average gift, and so on. for *each*
       fundraising appeal and event   ❏ Yes   ❏ No
       This information is crucial to the evaluation of any
       fundraising program. Such analysis encourages the
       elimination of poor performers and the focus on
       high-payoff activities.

(continued)

EXHIBIT 16-2 (CONTINUED)

V. ORGANIZATION ISSUES
   A. INSTITUTIONAL INDICATORS

1. Is the board and staff relatively stable?   ❏ Yes   ❏ No
   Has there been any remarkable turnover on the board
   or staff?   ❏ Yes   ❏ No

2. Has the organization adopted a strategic long-range
   plan?   ❏ Yes   ❏ No

3. Does the board have an active committee structure?   ❏ Yes   ❏ No

4. Is the organization's financial posture strong?   ❏ Yes   ❏ No

5. Does the organization have a cash reserve equal to
   90 days operating expense?   ❏ Yes   ❏ No

   B. DEVELOPMENT STAFF

1. How many full-time professional, paid development
   staff are employed by the organization?   _____#

2. How many full-time paid development support staff
   are employed by the organization?   _____#

3. Are the job descriptions clear?   ❏ Yes   ❏ No

4. Have the development professionals been given clear
   responsibility and authority with a focus on net
   contributed income goals?   ❏ Yes   ❏ No

   C. EXTERNAL RELATIONSHIPS

1. How would the reader rate public awareness of his or her organization's
   services? _____

   _____

2. How would the reader describe the organization's relationship with major
   community funders? _____

   _____

3. Does someone in the organization maintain an "opinion
   leaders" list of "movers and shakers" and regularly
   communicate with these people?   ❏ Yes   ❏ No

About the CD-ROM

INTRODUCTION

The forms on the enclosed CD-ROM are saved in Microsoft Word for Windows version 7.0. In order to use the forms, you will need to have word processing software capable of reading Microsoft Word for Windows version 7.0 files.

SYSTEM REQUIREMENTS

- IBM PC or compatible computer
- CD-ROM drive
- Windows 95 or later
- Microsoft Word for Windows version 7.0 (including the Microsoft converter★) or later or other word processing software capable of reading Microsoft Word for Windows 7.0 files.

  ★Word 7.0 needs the Microsoft converter file installed in order to view and edit all enclosed files. If you have trouble viewing the files, download the free converter from the Microsoft web site. The URL for the converter is:

  http://office.microsoft.com/downloads/2000/wrd97cnv.aspx

  Microsoft also has a viewer that can be downloaded, which allows you to view, but not edit documents. This viewer can be downloaded at:

  http://office.microsoft.com/downloads/9798/wd97vwr32.aspx

  NOTE: Many popular word processing programs are capable of reading Microsoft Word for Windows 7.0 files. However, users should be aware that a slight amount of formatting might be lost when using a program other than Microsoft Word.

How to Install the Files onto Your Computer

To install the files follow these instructions:

1. Insert the enclosed CD-ROM into the CD-ROM drive of your computer.

2. From the Start Menu, choose **Run**.

3. Type **D:\SETUP** and press **OK**.

4. The opening screen of the installation program will appear. Press **OK** to continue.

5. The default destination directory is C:\FUND02. If you wish to change the default destination, you may do so now.

6. Press **OK** to continue. The installation program will copy all files to your hard drive in the C:\FUND02 or user-designated directory.

Using the Files

Loading Files

To use the word processing files, launch your word processing program. Select **File, Open** from the pull-down menu. Select the appropriate drive and directory. If you installed the files to the default directory, the files will be located in the C:\FUND02 directory. A list of files should appear. If you do not see a list of files in the directory, you need to select **WORD DOCUMENT (*.DOC)** under **Files of Type**. Double click on the file you want to open. Edit the file according to your needs.

Printing Files

If you want to print the files, select **File, Print** from the pull-down menu.

Saving Files

When you have finished editing a file, you should save it under a new file name by selecting **File, Save As** from the pull-down menu.

User Assistance

If you need assistance with installation or if you have a damaged CD-ROM, please contact Wiley Technical Support at:

Phone: (212) 850-6753
Fax: (212) 850-6800 (Attention: Wiley Technical Support)
Email: techhelp@wiley.com
URL: www.wiley.com/techsupport

To place additional orders or to request information about other Wiley products, please call (800) 225-5945.

Exhibits on CD-ROM

File Name	Exhibit Title
Exh0301.doc	Two Time Management Models
Exh0302.doc	Sample Not-for-Profit Agency Budget Process
Exh0304.doc	Summary of Old and New Gift Potential
Exh0305.doc	Priority Evaluation Form
Exh0311.doc	Prospect Assignments and Summary Information
Exh0502.doc	Cash-Flow Projection Report
Exh0505.doc	Solicitation Analysis
Exh0602.doc	Sample Prospect Rating Form
Exh0603.doc	Sample "Key" Page
Exh0604.doc	Compiled Prospect Rating Form
Exh0702.doc	Prime Prospect Tracking Form
Exh0801.doc	Summary of Prospect Assignments
Exh0803.doc	Board Pledge Card
Exh0804.doc	Regular Pledge Cards
Exh0805A.doc	Call Report Form, Short Version
Exh0805B.doc	Call Report Form, Longer Version
Exh0806.doc	Sample Request to Include as Section of Personalized Case Statement
Exh0808.doc	Advice to the Volunteer or Staff Solicitor

Exh0904.doc	Checklist for Effective Fundraising Letters
Exh1001.doc	Volunteer Phone-a-Thon Scheduling Form
Exh1003.doc	Sample Tips for Phoners
Exh1004.doc	Sample Phone-a-Thon Script
Exh1005.doc	Sample Phoning Form
Exh1006.doc	Sample Thank You and Phone-a-Thon Reminder
Exh1102.doc	Sample Special Event Time Line
Exh1202.doc	Foundation Research Summary Form
Exh1203.doc	Letter Requesting Grants Information
Exh1204.doc	Foundation Deadlines Summary Form (in chronological order of deadline)
Exh1205.doc	Grant Application Preparation Form
Exh1310.doc	Charitable Gift Annuity Document
Exh1409.doc	Interview Questions
Exh1501.doc	Sample Agenda for Nominating Committee
Exh1502.doc	Blank Board Nominations Grid
Exh1601.doc	Quick Self-Test
Exh1602.doc	Financial Development Self-Assessment

ADDITIONAL FORMS ON CD-ROM

File Name	Exhibit Title
Form 1.doc	Key Indicators of Organizational Strength and Capability
Form 2.doc	Community Relationships Survey
Form 3.doc	Sample Newsletter Article: Charitable Gift Planning
Form 4.doc	Philanthropic Planning Study
Form 5.doc	Charges to Committees and Committee Preference Form
Form 6.doc	Position Description: Director of Development
Form 7.doc	Position Description: Director of Marketing and Resource Development

Index

For information about the CD-ROM see the About the CD-ROM section on page 337.